THROWN FOR A CURVE

"Hot hero, interesting characters, and great love story!"
—*Fresh Fiction*

"Jamison's latest is a sexy read with another full-figured heroine at its center. The author's stellar writing and witty dialogue are the highlights of this story along with Cherri and Colin's passionate and endearing romance. Another sweet and heartfelt story in which Jamison's snarky, modern voice shines through." —*RT Book Reviews*

ALSO BY
SUGAR JAMISON

Dangerous Curves Ahead
Thrown for a Curve

Gentlemen Prefer Curves

SUGAR JAMISON

St. Martin's Paperbacks

This is a work of fiction. All of the characters, organizations, and events portrayed in this novel are either products of the author's imagination or are used fictitiously.

GENTLEMEN PREFER CURVES

Copyright © 2014 by Sugar Jamison.

For information address St. Martin's Press, 175 Fifth Avenue, New York, NY 10010.

ISBN: 978-1-250-03299-7

Printed in the United States of America

St. Martin's Paperbacks edition / October 2014

St. Martin's Paperbacks are published by St. Martin's Press, 175 Fifth Avenue, New York, NY 10010.

10 9 8 7 6 5 4 3 2 1

To my mother—
for always encouraging me to take risks

PROLOGUE

The art of not getting caught . . .

"Shh!"

Carter Lancaster leaned against his pantry door watching his five-year-old daughter as she hissed at the chair she was trying to drag across the kitchen floor.

What's she up to now?

Every five or six inches she would stop and look to the doorway to make sure she wasn't caught.

It was too bad she didn't look behind her, because she failed to see she had a witness to whatever crime she was about to commit.

He smiled to himself, truly amused for the first time in a long time. His little girl would have no life in crime. She was horrible at being sneaky. She was a bad liar and made more noise than a marching band at a football game as she scampered across the kitchen. But he didn't stop her.

He was more interested in seeing what she was going to do with that chair.

Obviously something she wasn't supposed to be doing.

He wasn't supposed to be in the kitchen, either. He was supposed to be on his way to dinner in one of San Francisco's finest restaurants with his boss and the potential clients they had been wooing for weeks.

His firm had put in a bid to design the brand new San Francisco opera house. If they got the job, it would be huge for his firm and for his career. It was the kind of job any architect would dream of. It was the kind of job that could put him down in the books, but right now all of that slipped out of his mind as he watched his baby girl scurry up the chair and onto the counter.

He should have made his presence known as soon as he walked into the kitchen, but he didn't. Maybe he remained silent because he realized that he had no idea what was going on with Ruby. He hadn't been home in time for dinner in weeks. He hadn't put her to bed in as long, or read her a story or watched her brush her teeth. He hadn't been there, too busy working. Their nanny, Mrs. Marsh, had taken his place.

It wasn't the first time the uncomfortable thought had entered his head, but he had justified it to himself. This career move could be huge for them. It would catapult him to the top of his field. It would mean more money, more security. More of everything life had to offer.

Bullshit, a little voice whispered to him. He was afraid it was his conscience.

"Ruby?" he called to her softly as her little fingers reached the top of the refrigerator. "What are you doing up there?"

She turned to look at him, her little arms crossing over her chest. "What are you doing home?" she countered. "You never come home early."

"You answer my question first," he said, trying to ignore the huge bubble of guilt that rose in his chest. He was the adult, after all.

"I was trying to get cookies," she said in her soft voice. "You shouldn't have called me when I was up here. I coulda got scared and fell and hit my head and you would have had to take me to the doctor. And then you would have said damn it and had to put money in the cuss jar because you don't like it when I get hurt."

He shook his head. Sometimes he felt like he was living with a forty-year-old. It was his fault. She was painfully shy. She spent her entire life with adults. She never had time to be a kid. He never had time to make sure she was being a kid. And as the days went on he saw his baby slipping away, replaced by this tiny adult. He didn't like it.

"Why are you trying to sneak cookies? Didn't you have some for snack when you came home from school?"

She frowned at him, reminding him so much of himself in that moment. "No. Mrs. Marsh told you I was porky and you told her that it was okay to give me raisins and dried fruit for snack so I would lose some weight. Remember?"

"Oh, no." He took a step toward her but stopped when he noticed the hurt look on her face. He vaguely remembered Mrs. Marsh saying something about Ruby's weight, but he'd barely listened. Yes, Ruby had round cheeks and chubby little hands and a bit of a belly. But she was perfect. His tiny little curly-haired elf. "You're not porky. She must have said pretty. You're very pretty."

She tapped her bare foot on the counter. "She calls me pork chop. And Porky Pig and she pinches my cheeks and calls me a fat little thing, *Dad*."

The way she said "Dad" made him cringe. Not Daddy like she usually did, but Dad. Like Dad equaled asshole. And in this case he truly felt like one.

"I'm so sorry, honey." He grabbed her off the countertop and sat in the chair she pulled across the room. "I'll talk to Mrs. Marsh about that. You aren't fat. You're perfect."

She nodded and cuddled into his chest. For all her big talk she was still just a little girl. He got so caught up in his work, in his own selfish stupid bullshit, that he had forgotten that. He squeezed her tighter, unable to remember the last time he just held her. That was unacceptable.

He had almost lost her once. He smoothed his thumb over the scar that covered half her arm, remembering that. After that dark time in his life he swore she would always come first. Somehow he had let that promise slip.

When he took over sole responsibility of raising her, he knew it was going to be hard, but he didn't expect it to be *this* hard—and as she got older he screwed up more and more. If she gave him heart palpitations at five, what the hell was going to happen when she was fourteen?

"Why did you come home early? Are you staying?"

She looked so damn hopeful.

"I'm sorry, Rube." He felt like an asshole just saying it. "I just came home to get a file and say hello. I have an important dinner meeting tonight."

"Oh." Her face fell. "Mrs. Marsh says all you do at those meetings is drink and talk about money. That doesn't sound very important. You could do that here and send Mrs. Marsh home and I could help you with your meeting. I know how to make peanut butter and jelly sandwiches and I can pour the milk without spilling it now."

"That sounds very nice." He ran his hand over her curls. "I wish I could, but we can't have little girls there. It's really important that Daddy goes out to dinner with his clients, and his boss."

"Why? So you can make more money? Mrs. Marsh says you're richer than God and don't need any more money. She said if you had your nose any farther up your boss's behind, it wasn't going to be the only thing that was brown."

He took a deep breath to prevent himself from cursing and then kissed his daughter's cheeks. He was going to have to get rid of Mrs. Marsh tomorrow. She talked entirely too much. "I'm sorry, honey, but I have to go. This is important."

"Okay." She got off his lap, and watching her turn away from him almost killed him. "I'm gonna go to my room now."

"Wait." He called her knowing there was little he could do to fix this short of buying her a pony. "I thought you wanted cookies. I'll get them for you. As many as you want."

"No, thank you. My tummy hurts."

He sat back in his chair, loosening his tie to try and relieve the suffocating feeling. Ruby wasn't happy. That thought had been sneaking around in the back of his mind for a couple of months now, but he'd ignored it. No parent wanted to accept that their child was unhappy. He had to change that. His actions now would shape her future. And the image of his baby, all grown up dating a guy with a face tattoo and a rap sheet longer than his arm, entered his head. He couldn't let that happen.

Pulling out his cell phone he called his boss, realizing he was about to commit career suicide and not really caring. He had to make a lifestyle change. He had to do it for her. "Mr. Allen, I'm afraid I can't make it tonight. My kid needs me."

He disconnected and went to the stairs. "Ruby! Put your shoes on. Daddy's taking you out tonight."

CHAPTER 1

Parents just don't understand . . .

Parents. Can't live with them. Can't toss them off the roof.

Belinda Gordon walked up her parents' driveway. She had moved out of their home practically on her eighteenth birthday but in the last five years she had probably spent more hours in her parents' home than her own. Her mother had called half an hour ago, for the third time that day, this time begging her to come over.

"*I need you, Pudge,*" she'd purred in her lispy Spanish accent. "*Please.*"

She found it hard to say no to her mother—to both her parents, actually. She could say no to men who had asked her for dates over the years. She could say no to donating to the countless fund-raisers the high school kids kept bringing her way. She could even say no to those cute little Girl Scouts who tried to tempt her with boxes and boxes of those damn delicious cookies. But she couldn't say no to her parents.

Ever.

How annoying.

She was their only child. After years of fertility problems they had only produced her.

You're all I have. Her mother never let her forget it.

Her mother was damn good at guilt. A master at it. But then again most mothers were. She wondered if that came naturally when one became a mother or if it was something one had to work at. Were there guilt drills? Little sayings mothers everywhere practiced every night to ensure their children turned into guilty balls of mush?

You never call me.

Why don't you want to spend time with me?

But Belinda had deserved being the recipient of such guilt. She had made some pretty big mistakes in her life.

Colossal mistakes.

Breathtakingly stupid mistakes.

Like moving across the country alone on a whim. And turning down a high-paying job at an insurance company because it would have stifled her creativity. She made the mistake of buying two pairs of harem pants because she thought they were coming back in style. And her biggest mistake, the one she could barely bring herself to think about: falling in love with a man who was totally wrong for her.

She had disappointed her parents with her choices and now she was still trying to make up for it.

So she was here, in her sexiest black dress and her newest pair of Spanx, prepared to spend the last remaining minutes before her second date with Brian Warren with her parents. She had to admit she was also there because she needed the distraction her parents would inevitably provide.

She was nervous about her date, and she was woman enough to admit it.

She was nervous about going out with Brian again because . . . well . . . everything had gone so freaking well on their first date. That was *not* the norm for her. Since she had started dating again, just after her thirtieth birthday in February, she hadn't had one good date.

But then there was Brian. Brian was the type of man—a sensible man—a thirty-year-old woman should date. He was cute, worked in finance, owned his own condo, smelled like he bathed regularly, and always paid for dinner.

Dreamy . . .

He wasn't too cheap or too touchy or too shy or too freaky or any of the things that sent her red flags flying. Brian was a far cry from the other men she had dated in the past few months. There was that guy her neighbor set her up with. The one who called himself a Green Scientist. She thought she was getting a nice bookish type, who worked to stop chemicals from being dumped into rivers and championed the rights of animals. What she got was a man who didn't wear deodorant and refused to eat anything he hadn't scavenged from the earth. On their first date he took her to look for edible wild mushrooms in the park.

Fungus you can eat! Yum.

Then there was Mr. Obsessive-Compulsive, who on the surface seemed to be very normal. That was until she watched him count every leaf of lettuce in his salad, cut his steak into sixteen equal pieces, and turn his plate counterclockwise five times before he would eat.

One two three four five. One two three four five. One two three four five.

And then there was Mr. Married with Three Kids. Who was married with three kids.

They showed up at their date. Begging him to come home.

Daddy, please. We miss you.

But still she trudged on, agreeing to be set up. Agreeing

to date after four years of seeing no one. She was thirty now.

Thirty.

The big Three-O.

It was the birthday that told the world that you were no longer a kid. Your twenties were like an extended childhood. A simpler time where you could get away with still getting drunk, or blowing rent money to see a concert or on a pair of really kickass shoes. At thirty, you really had to stop doing those things. Thirty was the birthday that meant it was time to stop screwing around. The birthday that meant no more excuses. That it was time to grow up and really know who you were.

Both her best friends seemed to have figured it out; Cherri and Ellis had gone off and gotten married. Cherri was a mother. Ellis designed beautiful wedding dresses for brides who were a little harder to fit. She opened the shop that both she and Belinda worked in. Cherri was an extraordinary painter, commanding thousands of dollars for her work. Their lives were moving forward when Belinda's life seemed to be staying still. They were leaving their mark on the world.

But what was Belinda's mark?

She thought she was fine with the way things were going. Happy even, but then she turned thirty. And yet another Valentine's Day had passed. And cashiers stopped checking her ID when she bought wine. And people started calling her ma'am everywhere she went. And her Facebook newsfeed was now littered with baby pictures and honeymoon photos. And she had marked off four years since her heart had been broken.

Belinda snapped herself from her thoughts as she walked up to her parents' house. She heard their heated voices from outside. They we're arguing. Again. But then again Bill and Carmina Gordon's fights were as normal as the setting sun. And so were their makeups.

"I think you're trying to kill me!" Belinda heard her father say as she entered through the kitchen door.

She stepped back to survey the scene. Her father was facing her mother, a dinner plate filled with fried confections in his hand. He was still in his work clothes. Sweatpants, a Durant University windbreaker, and his old Mets cap. He was six foot four, burly, mean looking at first glance. And then there was his wife with her elegant designer clothes, her long lean body, glossy black hair, and perfectly refined features. As opposite as they were, both her parents were tall and gorgeous. They looked like they belonged together.

And then there was Belinda, with her crazy shade of dark-red hair, her tawny skin, and her short, roundish body. She looked like neither of her parents, which often led her to wonder if she was adopted.

But she knew she wasn't. It might be easier if she were.

"Why would you say such a thing?" Her mother shouted the question. "I'm not trying to kill you. If I was, you would be dead by now!"

"Then why do you keep doing this?" He pushed the plate in her direction. "First it was your seven-cheese macaroni. Then it was your double-dipped chicken-fried steak. Served with deep-fried okra and cheesy corn bread. Then you made me go out with you at ten o'clock on a Sunday night so we could have bacon ice cream sundaes. And now you're deep-frying the shit out of Snickers bars. I thought I was a decent husband but I must not be because you're trying to kill me."

Carmina blinked at her husband. "But my food is good. No?"

"Carmina!"

"What? If you don't like what I cook, then you can cook for yourself!"

"The hell I will. I spent a damn fortune remodeling this damn kitchen. If I paid for it, the least you can do is cook me what I want. It's your job."

Belinda covered her eyes as the last of her father's words slipped from his mouth. Her father had just said probably the wrongest thing a man had ever said to a woman.

"*Bastardo!* My job? My job! You think I wanted . . ." Her rapid tirade switched to Spanish and Belinda took it all in quietly. Her parents weren't typical. Her mother used to be a model. Her father had played professional ball for the Mets until his knees gave out. They had moved from New York City to Durant when she was in seventh grade when her father had taken a job coaching the university's baseball team. They were an odd little family. And after a few years of separation they were a close-knit one.

"Damn, you look sexy when you get mad."

Carmina stopped her rant and smiled. "I have to admit, I like it when you get so angry, too. I can see the cords of your neck. It is very sexy. My mother hated when I married an American man, but there is something very sexy about American men from Texas."

"Come here," he ordered softly.

Carmina sauntered over to her husband and wrapped her long, slender arms around him. "I make these things for you, because I want to feed you. I want you to be happy."

"I am happy. Just keep being my wife." Bill leaned down to kiss his wife, and just like that their argument was over.

"I hope you two didn't call me over here to watch you make out," Belinda said, making her presence known. "I get it. You guys are still hot for each other, but seeing you make out makes me want to toss up my cookies."

"Bill Junior!"

"Pudge!"

They separated. Her father clapping her on the back. Yes, he called her Bill Junior. He'd always wanted a son. The fact that Belinda didn't have a penis didn't stop him from treating her like she was a boy.

Her mother called her Pudge. Short for "pudgy." She'd rather be called Bill.

"How are you, my love?" Her mother cupped her chin in her delicate hands as she smothered her cheeks with kisses. "I am so glad that you are here. Please explain the difference between a Mars Bar and a Milky Way to your father."

Her head spun. She thought back to the urgent call her mother had placed to her half an hour ago, not believing that this could be what that was about. "Did you seriously call me here from across town, half an hour before my date, to ask the difference in candy bars?"

"Yes." Her mother nodded. "You do love your chocolate."

Belinda took a deep breath. Not knowing why she was surprised that her parents had called her over for this. "You know, when you said you needed me—that it was urgent—I imagined the worst. Like you had chopped your finger off. Or the house was on fire. Or Daddy was having massive chest pains and needed to be taken to the hospital. I did not think you called me over here for something you could have looked up on the Internet!"

Her mother blinked at her. "We tried to look it up on the Internet, but we don't know how to work the computer."

"I didn't call you, Junior." Her father pointed to his wife. "That was your mother."

Carmina gasped. "You didn't try to talk me out it."

"I can't talk you out of anything! If I could I would be a lot happier!"

Carmina opened her mouth to retort, but Belinda stopped her.

"Enough! Unless you have a good reason for calling me over here I'm leaving."

"We thought it would be good to see you, Junior," her father said gruffly. "You didn't come over for dinner on Sunday."

"We only ask for one night a week, Pudge. It's now Friday. We missed you."

"I'm sorry but I really was busy on Sunday," she said, feeling that sneaky little bastard, guilt, rise up in her chest. "But calling me over to ask me about candy is not cool. I thought something was wrong!"

"I'm sorry, Pudge." Her mother nodded. "You said to call you over if there was an illness, fire, death and . . . home invasion."

"Yes, and that means no calling me over when you can't figure out how to work your cell phone, or when you can't decide what shoes you should wear with your dress." She looked at her father. "That also means no calling me over when the Mets go into extra innings or calling me away from work so I can test out the new gloves you got for your teams. We need to have some boundaries."

"But you're my only child. My precious." Her mother grabbed her hand and squeezed it. "We love you so much. Don't be mad."

They would never stop calling her over for little unimportant things, and she would never stop coming. "I'm not mad, *Mamá*."

"Good. Stay. I want to talk to you about your date." She led her to the kitchen table and sat beside her.

"Here, Junior." Her father slid a plate in front of her. "Eat this." And what a plate it was. All she could do was stare at the dough-encrusted, deep-fried, chocolate-syrup-and-whipped-cream-covered candy bar in front of her.

"Don't give her that!" Her mother pushed the plate

away from her. "That's the last thing she needs. All that sugar and fat."

"You were willing to give it to me two minutes ago!"

"That was different. Pudge needs to watch her weight. You know it's very hard for her."

"There is nothing wrong with her weight," her father said through clenched teeth, just as she was about to defend herself.

There wasn't.

She had long ago come to terms with the fact that she would never be like her mother. She would never be tall and willowy. She would never be elegant and graceful. She would always be too short, too curvy, too red. Too imperfect. And she was okay with that. She liked herself. She spent her days at Size Me Up telling women that it was okay to be comfortable in their skin, it was okay to love themselves, no matter what size they were. But her mother had always lamented over her appearance. Carmina sometimes looked at her as if she had wondered what had gone wrong.

"No." Carmina touched Belinda's cheek. "No. Of course, there isn't anything wrong with her weight. I just don't want her looking poochy before her date." She patted Belinda's stomach. "No woman wants a poochy belly before she goes on a date."

Belinda shook her head, trying to ignore her mother's little poke at her weight. "What did you want to know, *Mamá*?"

"Do you like Brian?" She smiled brightly. "When I first saw him I thought he would be perfect for you. He's got the nicest blue eyes, Pudge! Oh, he reminds me of Robert Redford. Do you know the first movie I saw Robert Redford in was *The Way We Were*? Oh, I cried at the end of that movie. But I cry at a lot of movies. Even movies that others don't think are very sad." She looked up at her husband. "Do you remember when you took me to see *Dumbo*, Bill? And how I cried and cried and how you sank down in your chair so that you would not be seen with me. I was quite put out with you, you know. Your father doesn't like to take me to movies anymore, but he did when we were dating because he wanted to spend time with me. Do you think Brian will take you to the movies, Pudge?" She went right on without waiting for an answer. "Some say that is a cheap date but I like cheap dates. That's why I fell for your father. He didn't try to impress me. He just wanted to be with me."

"We are going to *Tortola's* for dinner, *Mamá*," she said when her mother took a breath. "We had a very nice time last week. I like him."

"How wonderful!" She clapped her hands and hugged her. "He could be the one, Pudge," she said into her ear. "I want to have grandbabies and plan a wedding. Ellis will make your dress. And I will put together a big reception. It will be so exciting. You don't know how I've longed to actually see you get married."

Belinda pulled away from her mother, guilt, her familiar friend, eating at her once again. She had disappointed her parents with her last choice in a man. She had once again robbed them of their dream of seeing their only child married. "I've got to go, *Mamá*. I don't want to be late."

"Yes, of course. Go! And call me after your date, I want to hear everything. Maybe we can go to yoga tomorrow morning. It's really good for you, you know. And it would help you slim down. Ellis's mother and I really enjoy our six AM class."

She nodded noncommittally. As she got up, her father pulled her into a gruff hug. "Don't let her bother you, Junior. She means well." He ruffled her hair. "Let's go fishing next week. I got some new bait that's sure to get the big ones biting."

"Okay, Dad." She offered him a small smile before she walked out. It was time for her date.

Two hours later she and Brian had finished yet another nice dinner. A plate of tiramisu sat between them. Sometime over the course of the evening he had reached across the table and linked his fingers through hers. It startled her at first. It had been a long time since anybody had touched her so intimately.

It was sweet, but she was wondering why she didn't feel the butterflies she should have.

"I'm really glad I asked you out." Brian took her hand in both of his and stroked his thumbs down her palm. "When your mother introduced us at the historical society's gala, I wasn't sure that I should."

"Why?" She grinned at him. "Were you afraid that I would be no fun because I was hanging out in a room of people whose average age was a hundred and nine?"

He shook his head, his eyes twinkling in the process. They were nice eyes, reminding her a little of an old-school Paul Newman. "You're a lot of fun, Belinda. I knew you would be the moment I saw you doing the cha-cha with Dr. Petersen."

"Ah, you saw me cha-chaing with my date. Is that why you almost didn't ask me out? I only went with Dr. Petersen because he's my father's good friend and his wife was too sick to go. You didn't really think we were a couple, did you?"

"No." He shook his head. "You didn't strike me as the type of woman who dates men who could be her grandfather."

Her brows went up, curiosity starting to gnaw at her,

and she wished it would stop. She shouldn't care why he almost didn't ask her out. He had asked her out.

Still, she couldn't stop herself from asking, "You didn't like the color of my dress?"

He laughed. "No. If I recall, you look really good in green."

She flashed him a smile to thank him for the compliment. "Then what was it? Did I have food in my teeth? Toilet paper on my shoe? Did my breath stink? Come on, Brian. You can't tell a girl you almost didn't ask her out without telling her why."

He shrugged and leaned back in his chair. "I don't usually date girls like you."

"Like me? What kind of girls?" She kept her voice light. "Redheads?"

"I've got a thing for redheads." He winked. "Your size kind of put me off at first."

His words must have had some kind of powerful stun effect because it felt like the world slowed down for her in that moment. She studied his face carefully to see if he was serious.

"When I saw you—" He paused to study her. "—I thought, *If she were just thirty, thirty-five pounds thinner she would be perfect.*"

Oh.

Ouch.

Her size put him off.

Did you hear that, Belinda? If you were thirty-five pounds thinner, you'd be perfect. Perfect.

Perfect?

What a crock of shit.

"But then I realized that I was being an asshole. You're probably the sexiest woman in this town."

Thirty, thirty-five pounds. The size of a well-fed cocker spaniel.

Insecurity, her old and nearly forgotten friend, snuck up on her.

She had to shake that feeling off.

Her size would never be in the single digits, her legs would always rub together when she walked, she would always have more junk in her trunk than a '68 Caddy. And she was okay with that. Why wasn't everyone else?

Brian's words should have had no effect on her. But they did.

Let it go, she ordered herself. *His words are like water off a duck's ass.*

Inhale. Exhale. Inhale. Exhale.

She clenched her teeth instead.

"I like you a lot," he went on. "I'm attracted to you and I figured if we got you on a good regimen we could get that weight right off you."

"Regimen?"

"Yeah. Like an exercise routine. I know you don't have one. You wouldn't be so soft-looking if you did. I hit the gym five times a week. I spend an hour on cardio and an hour doing free weights. I can't stand to see jiggly. I try to keep my body as firm as possible."

She shut her eyes, trying desperately to hold on to her calm. "I wouldn't call it a routine but sometimes I take dance class at the community center. I've even been known to do yoga on occasion. It may not be the type of routine you are referring to, but I certainly do more than sit on the couch lifting the fork to my mouth."

"That's great." His eyes lit up, as if she had just given him a gift. "So you're not lazy. All we have to do is turn up the intensity. If we get you down to twelve hundred calories a day, and put you in the gym four times a week, you could have that weight gone in a couple of months. It'll be great. You'll see. We can go together and I can help transform you into a healthier, better version of yourself."

Lazy?

Twelve hundred calories?

Transform?

"Better version of myself?"

"Yeah, Belinda. You obviously have to know when you look in the mirror that you could look better. I think this is why we met, so I can help you get on the right path. You need me. I can see a future for us."

Her head spun. A whole bunch of thoughts collided and she felt like she was about to have one of those *Exorcist* moments. Pea soup spewing and all.

He didn't just—

He couldn't have said—

Did he just offer to put me on a diet?

Oh, fuck that!

She threw back her head and laughed. That kind of hysterical laughter that got people put in institutions. She was going to lose it. First the episode at her parents' house and now this. The bad Belinda was about to rear her bitchy head. The Belinda who'd once made a cop cry. The Belinda who just didn't give a shit anymore and there wasn't a damn thing anybody could do to stop it.

"Isn't that ironic? I almost didn't say yes when you asked me out."

"Oh?" His eyes widened with curiosity.

"Yeah. Judging by the way you walk and that big expensive sports car you drive, I figured you must have an extremely tiny penis." She leaned back in her chair, crossing arms nonchalantly. "But I told myself I was being a bitch. I can get over a man having a little weenie. It's not the size of the boat, right? It's the motion of the ocean. And if I can't get off, it's no big deal. That's what vibrators are for."

She took great joy when his dumb grin melted from his face. He had hit her where it hurt and now she was only out to return the favor.

"Belinda, I—"

"You what, honey? Can't get laid regularly? Sorry that you kiss as well as a cold dead fish? Have a hard time finding somebody who'll accept that you keep a large jar of toenail clippings on your nightstand?"

He looked around in a panic, noting that she was beginning to draw attention from the other patrons. "I do not have toenail clippings on my nightstand."

"And I do not need nutrition or exercise advice from you!"

"You're overreacting," he hissed.

"I'm overreacting? You're clueless!" She sat up straight. "And since you're obviously too stupid to know these things, I'll be nice and school you. There are three things a man should never talk about with a woman. Her hair. Her mother. And her weight. But you seemed to have skipped class the day God was handing out common sense. What kind of man in his right mind tells a woman that she needs to lose thirty-five pounds? Haven't you considered that I love myself just the way I am? Big ass and all, and I don't need some man with a God complex telling me different. I wouldn't lose a pound for you or any man. I am healthy and happy and if you can't accept me for who I am, then you can go to hell. You better wise up, buddy. You keep talking to women like that and the only thing that's going to be keeping you warm at night is your sports car. And that would suck because I hear metal chafes."

She stormed out, vowing never to date another jackass again. Vowing to join a convent. Vowing to do something, anything to change her luck. How? She had no clue, but she knew she was going to try like hell to figure it out.

CHAPTER 2

You've had a bad day . . .

It was the perfect day for sulking, Belinda thought as she sat beside Cherri on a bench in Elder Park. The sky was gray. The air was damp and nippy that early-March day. There was hardly anyone in the park, just a couple of kids tossing a baseball around. It was cold, quiet, and dreary. The only thing that kept her from sliding into a complete funk was the fact that she was holding Cherri's ten-month-old baby in her arms. She wasn't very fond of children, but Joey was okay. He was cute as hell and he smelled like heaven and he always smiled at her. He was more of a gentleman than most of the men she had dated. But unlike the others, Joey produced some very unexpected feelings inside her. He made her heart feel all achy and tuggy. She tried to chalk it up to the fact that he was Cherri's son and she loved him because she loved Cherri like a sister.

She didn't want to face the troubling notion that her body was telling her she was yearning to have one of her own.

"So . . . You going to tell me who pooped in your bran flakes this morning or are you just going to hog my baby and be all quiet and moody?"

Belinda looked over at Cherri, not willing to give the boy up. "He's warm and he looks especially handsome in this hat I bought him."

"He does. Now what's up with you?"

"I think I should get a cat."

"Oh, here we go again." Cherri rolled her eyes skyward. "We go through this about once a year. You want a cat or a dog, or a miniature pig. But you never follow through."

"I went to the shelter last year to pick out a pet, but when I walked in there, there were about four dogs and three cats I wanted to take home. They all looked so damn sad. And then I got this image of myself on *Hoarders*, wearing a fabulous silk muumuu and turban, feeding my forty-seven animals and lamenting over what went wrong in my life."

"You're nuts." Cherri shook her head. "You've gone nuts."

Belinda shrugged. "You're right. I was thinking about going back to school. I have my associate's degree in fashion merchandising management. Maybe I should get a bachelor's degree."

"I thought you didn't like school."

"I didn't."

"Then why go back? You've managed stores for years, now you own Size Me Up with Ellis. What more do you want to learn?"

"I don't know, maybe I could get a degree in chemistry."

"But you suck at science."

"Or archaeology."

"You're the last person I can picture digging in the dirt."

She looked down at Belinda's shoes, one of her favorite pairs: navy-blue patent-leather platform pumps with matching blue bows on top. "I don't think they let you wear five-inch heels in ancient ruins."

"You're not being supportive!"

"I'm sorry." She smothered a laugh. "But why don't you start out small. Take a cake decorating class, or photography. You're so creative. I've been asked to teach a beginners' painting class at the community center. I think I'm going to do it. You can be one of my students."

"You're going to teach me how to paint?"

"I taught elementary school art. I think I can manage to teach you a thing or two. What brought on this need to better yourself anyway?"

Suddenly the ball the kids had been tossing around flew in their direction. Without thinking, Belinda shoved Joey at Cherri and caught the ball right before it smacked her in the face.

"Hey, lady. Great catch," one of the boys said as he trotted up to her to retrieve the softball.

"Great catch? Great catch! How about saying *I'm sorry*, dingus? I was holding a baby, and you could have seriously hurt him. Or me. You've got to be careful around here."

Belinda stood up and winged the ball over the kid's head. It landed right in his friend's glove.

"Wow," the kid said. "You're good. You could coach our Little League team."

He couldn't have been more than eleven or twelve, and suddenly she felt shitty for losing her cool with him. If she couldn't keep her temper around tweens, then why the hell was her body telling her she wanted a kid of her own?

"I'll pass. I'm sorry I yelled at you. Go play. Just be careful."

"You know, you could coach Little League," Cherri said

when Belinda sat back down. "You have amazing reflexes. If that was me I would have been hit."

Belinda shrugged. "I'm not athletic, but I can catch a ball. I guess that comes with being a pro ballplayer's daughter." She looked down at Joey. "Is he okay? I didn't mean to scare him."

"He's a tough boy." Cherri stroked her son's cheek. "Now let's get back to you. What the hell is going on with you today?"

"My date last night. It didn't end well."

"Oh, no," Cherri groaned. "What happened?"

"He told me that if I lost thirty-five pounds, I would be perfect. And then he offered to put me on a diet-and-exercise program. So I lost it on him in one of the most expensive restaurants in Durant. I'm pretty sure I'm banned from there but that's okay. The food wasn't that good anyway."

"What's wrong with you?" Cherri asked in wonder.

"I've been trying to figure that shit out for years."

"I don't mean it that way. I'm just trying to figure out why you seem to attract every loser, jackass, and asshole in a twenty-mile radius. You're gorgeous, Belinda. And you're smart and you're funny. Why can't you find a man?"

"I don't know. I think going to take a break from dating for a little while. My mother is going to have a shit fit and lament over where she went wrong raising me, but I need a break. I think I need to shake things up a little. I'm feeling restless."

Cherri nodded. "Just as long as you don't give up on love. Your guy is out there."

Belinda said nothing, not so sure that that was true.

"I've got some old bread in here." Cherri pulled a loaf out of her diaper bag. "Let's go feed the ducks."

They made their way to the intersecting paths that led to the lake, finding them nearly deserted, like the rest of the park.

The lake was set about two or three feet down from the path. As kids she and Ellis used to take off their shoes and slide down the small incline and play in the water, screaming and splashing at the fish as they tried to nibble at their toes. There was a larger dock on the other side of the lake where her father liked to go fishing for bigger game. She spent so much time here as a kid. It was nice that Cherri took her son here weekly. Belinda thought that if she ever had children of her own, she would do the same thing. She would like to raise them right here in Durant. It was a funky little town, centered around a university. It was filled with coffee shops, hiking trails, and friendly quirky people. She'd spent half of her childhood and some of her adulthood in New York City, then passed some time in San Francisco and a bit in Chicago. But she kept coming back, because Durant was the only place that ever felt like home.

"I don't see any ducks," Cherri said, sounding a little disappointed. "I wanted Joey to see them."

"Maybe they're a little farther down. I think they like to hang out on the other side of the lake." They started walking again. "If we can't find the ducks, maybe we can take him to Moon Panda. They've got really good Peking duck, and their rice is to die for. We haven't been there for ages. Wanna go there for lunch?"

"I wanted to take my baby to feed the ducks. Not feed him duck," she grumbled. "But yeah, that place is delicious. Only I refuse to eat duck. Chicken, maybe some shrimp, but not duck."

They grinned at each other for a moment and moved to side of the path as two other park visitors made their way toward them down the path. "I was thinking about taking another trip abroad, but alone this time." Belinda said.

"Really?" Cherri looked at her. "Where would you go?"

"All over. But Spain mostly. I—"

"Bell?" A man's voice called. At first she thought she was imagining it.

Nobody had ever called her Bell. Nobody. Except for one man. And it couldn't be him.

But in the distance she could see a dark-haired man coming toward her.

"Bell, is that you?"

Not him. Not now.

No. No. No. No. No. Shit. No.

She left him three thousand miles away. She left him in a former life. No. Some other woman there must be called Bell.

"Belinda?"

The voice was familiar. Too familiar. It was one that she'd listened to every day for ten weeks in another lifetime.

She looked up to face her mistake, the demon from her past. Her biggest regret. The man she threw it all away for. And as soon as she did, she regretted her decision. The blood rushed out of her head. She felt nauseous and dizzy and confused all at the same time.

It is him.

HIM.

It had been four years since she had seen or spoken to or touched him. Four years, and now he seemed like a ghost.

"Haven't you received any of my calls?"

His words barely penetrated her ears because she was too busy processing his presence in her world. He was there. In her park. On her side of the world. After four years of silence and hurt and too many thoughts about him.

She forced her eyes upward and locked them on his. They were the same gray eyes that had caused her to melt four years ago. The same jet-black hair. The same patrician features.

The same look of disgust she saw on his face the last time she was with him.

It was him. Carter Lancaster. Her first and only love. But the sight of him proved to be too much, too painful. She tore her eyes away, but not before she caught a glimpse of the female he had with him. The dark-haired little creature whose appearance had marked the end of them. Seeing her more than anything sent her off the deep end.

She took a step back, feeling her heels sink into the soft earth.

"Bell. I . . ." He came toward her, his hands extended. She took another step back. Her heart was beating too fast. Too hard. She could feel herself shaking. She had to get away from him. She took yet another step back but it proved one too many. Her heel got caught in the dirt, all five inches of it sinking into the ground. She yanked it hard and her foot came flying from the shoe. She stumbled backward, expecting to hit the ground, but she didn't. She barely processed Cherri's scream before she hit the water. She went under but just for a moment; the water wasn't deep. She landed on her back, and immediately the icy water seeped into her clothes.

"Belinda!" Carter was there in front of her. In the water. In his dark suit. His strong arms lifting her out of the iciness. "Are you okay?"

She was in his arms and leaning against him, her chest pressed to his, and for a moment everything stopped. She looked up into his face. Their eyes met. It must have been for only a second or two, but they met and she could see so much in his. Looking into his eyes she saw hurt and surprise and regret and anger and something softer. It seemed impossible but in that same moment she felt him, too. Felt the strength of his arms as they held her close to him, and the warmth of his body as it penetrated her cold clothes.

She felt the pounding of his heart, beating so fast that for a moment she thought it might explode. Maybe that was her heart pounding; she just hadn't realized it before because she was smashed against him and not sure where he began and she ended.

She shivered and not from the cold.

Four damn years.

Four damn years apart, too many tears and a shitload of hurt and she still reacted to him. Still felt that funny feeling in her stomach and the heat rise in her cheeks, just from being near him.

And she hated herself for that.

She yanked herself away from him, pissed at herself, at her body for betraying her mind. "What the hell do you think you're doing?"

"You fell in. I thought you were hurt. I was coming after you."

"You were coming after me? Now?" She dragged her hand through her sodden hair, needing something to do, to distract herself from her shaking hands. "You thought I was hurt? I was hurt four years ago. Why the hell didn't you come after me then?"

He blinked at her. His face unreadable as it always was. He said nothing. She didn't know why she was expecting that he would. He never said anything. That was always the problem with them.

"Stay away from me. I don't ever want to see you again."

She trudged up the small incline, now completely shoeless. Cherri reached for her hand, helping her back to the path. Belinda took her hand and squeezed, glad her friend was there, glad she hadn't been alone when she faced him again.

"Are you okay, honey?" Cherri whispered.

"No. But I'll be fine. I always turn out fine." They

walked away in silence for a few moments, her bare feet feeling each rough piece of gravel as they made their way back to Cherri's SUV.

"Who is he?" Cherri said once they were in and she had cranked up the heat to warm Belinda. "Who was that man?"

"My husband."

"You were married?"

"No. Not past tense. He's still my husband. We're still married."

CHAPTER 3

What'll I do . . .

Carter lay on the couch with his eyes closed and a throw pillow over his face. His head and heart pounding.

Belinda. Belinda. Belinda.

Seeing her today was a shock to his system. It shouldn't be.

He knew he would see her again one day. He was planning to see her again. They had things to settle.

Like the fact that she was still his wife.

He just didn't expect her to be in Durant. She was supposed to be living in Manhattan. The last time he had checked, she was managing some upscale clothing store in the Village. But judging by his half dozen unreturned phone calls, her life wasn't there anymore.

He had figured she'd moved on to a new city. He'd figured she was halfway across the planet.

He never thought she would be here.

Or maybe, in the back of his mind, he did. Maybe he had hoped he would see her here. In this place that they both were so connected to.

He just wasn't prepared to see her. Or for the reaction she had when he did.

They had met and married within four weeks of laying eyes on each other. It was fast. The whole world told him it was too fast. That they were too wrong for each other. That they were going to fail. But he ignored them. Foolishly ignored them. Because when he was with her, he felt this rush, a kind of high that was not describable. She excited him. She made him want to do things that he'd never thought he was capable of. She distracted him from his otherwise painfully boring life. And when he was with her he began to feel those stirrings of happiness that had always eluded him.

Then she walked out on him, without a word, without giving them a chance. She proved the world right, proved his parents right. She showed them she was just another mistake that Carter Lancaster had made.

He kept telling himself that it was better they had crashed and burned so early in their marriage. If six short weeks with her could affect him so greatly, he could only imagine how he would be after a lifetime with her.

"Daddy?"

"Yes?" Ruby crawled on top of him, placing her knee right in the center of his gut. "Oomph. Watch that knee, Rube, you're going to kill Daddy."

"Sorry," she mumbled. Pulling the pillow off his face, she stared down at him.

She resembled a street urchin. Mrs. Marsh had helped him with Ruby's everyday care, but now that he was raising her without any help he let Ruby dress herself. Her hair was a tangled mess. Her clothes were stained from the ice cream he had bought her after lunch. She didn't have on a thing that matched, but he still got the indescribable ache in his chest every time he looked at her.

The love didn't happen immediately. At first he'd been so shocked to learn she existed that he could only see her as a crying, pooping, vomit machine. And frankly, she scared the shit out of him. Fatherhood, at that time in his life, seemed so far away. He thought he would have time to prepare. He thought he would have the chance to plan for it with the woman he loved, and when Ruby came along he was almost angry with her at first. Angry at a baby. Because when Ruby showed up Belinda went away. His life as he knew it disappeared. His plans for the future. His bright spot.

But all the anger, all the resentment, all of his extreme selfishness, melted away and the love came all at once when she was six months old. It happened when he walked into her room and her face lit up in recognition. And it grew tenfold the day he almost lost her.

"What can I do for you, babe?"

"You owe money to the cuss jar."

"Do I?"

"Yeah." She traced the pattern in his shirt with her chubby little finger. "You said a lot of bad words when we got into the car."

Cursing had been Carter's biggest bad habit. It was something only people without good breeding did, or so his mother always said. He had picked it up in boarding school, where those with good breeding sent their children, and he had been doing it ever since. But when Ruby came along he made an effort to stop. And that's how the cuss jar was formed. Ruby got to keep any money that was put in there. At this rate she'd be able to buy a new car before she hit ten. "How much money do you think I should put in there?"

"About twenty dollars," she said gravely. She reminded him of Bethany, her mother, in that moment.

Bethany was another one of Carter's mistakes, or so the world thought, but he couldn't regret the way things had gone for them. Bethany was his childhood friend. His first wife, if *wife* was the proper term for what she was to him. They had only been a married a total of sixty-four hours before their marriage was annulled. And in that sixty-four hours they had made Ruby. It was too bad a tragic accident had robbed her of the chance to see her baby grow up.

"Do you like living here?" he asked his daughter, trying to push his past to the back of his mind.

He had moved them to the beautiful, funky college town of Durant. Belinda's hometown. He had loved this place long before he loved her. His old friend Steven was from here. They had become friends in college and on breaks, instead of returning to his stuffy house in one of San Francisco's wealthiest areas, he came here. When he was fresh out of college and doing his externship in the city, he used to escape to Durant just so he could breathe. He had always felt connected to this place.

There was just something about it.

So when Steven called him out of the blue and told him he was looking for a partner in his architecture design firm, he jumped at the chance. He did it for Ruby, because he thought she would be happier here. He did it for himself because he needed to spend more time with his daughter.

But Belinda was here and even though he knew there was a slim possibility he could run into her again, actually seeing her knocked him on his ass.

He had their divorce all planned out. She would agree to a small but generous settlement. He would file no-fault papers with the court. There would be no long, drawn-out battle. No splitting of assets. Neither one of them would care enough to put up a fight over anything. She hadn't cared enough to even say good-bye.

Deep down he knew that wasn't true. She had been shocked to see him. He could see it on her face. The way the blood drained out. The way she stared at him as if he weren't real. The way she backed away. She was still hurt. He felt the pain, too. And that surprised him. But what surprised him most was his physical reaction to her. When she tumbled into that water she scared him, but when he pulled her out and he felt her cold, curvy body pressed against him, that rush of heady feelings returned, the attraction, the racing of his heart.

Damn.

He'd made it a point to put her out of his mind so many years ago. He'd thought, after so long, that he had—that he wouldn't feel a thing for her when he saw her again.

He was wrong.

"I like it here a lot," Ruby said, once again pulling him from his painful thoughts. "You stay with me more."

He had found a little three-bedroom bungalow in a quiet neighborhood near the center of town. It was very different from San Francisco. There was no opera house, no high society. None of the things he had grown up with. But there was green space everywhere, and a cool little downtown area with funky shops and kids who felt safe enough to ride their bikes around the neighborhood. It was perfect for Ruby. She seemed more content here than in San Francisco.

"That was the whole point." He pulled her closer so that her head rested on his chest. They used to take naps like this when she was a baby. She was getting bigger now, and it made him realize how much time he had missed with her while he was trying to advance his career. But that was over now. Everything he did from now on had to be for her.

He rubbed her back until her breathing was slow and even. He thought she had fallen asleep until she said, "Daddy? Who was that lady in the park?"

He should have known that question was coming.

"My wife."

She sat up and frowned at him.

Shit.

He always said the wrong thing. "I-I mean . . ." It was the truth. He didn't want to lie to her. "I married Belinda before your mommy brought you to me. But she had to go away and I haven't seen her in a very long time."

He watched her process that, her little forehead scrunched. "Don't married people live in the same house?"

"They're supposed to, but Belinda and I never did things the right way."

"Are you going to live with her now?"

"No, honey. She's not going to be my wife much longer."

"Oh." An almost sad look crossed Ruby's face. "She's very pretty."

"You think so?"

Pretty wasn't the right word for it. Belinda was suggestive and stimulating and sensual and a dozen other things. She was the stuff pinup girls were made of.

He wasn't sure if it was the dark-red hair that fell softly around her shoulders. Or her skin that was somewhere between bronze and tan. Or those brilliantly colored dark-green eyes or those brightly colored femme fatale clothes that did it to him, but once he'd locked eyes with her five years ago it was all over for him.

"Yeah. Why did she run away from you? Was she scared?"

He didn't know how to explain it to her. There had been terror on Belinda's face. She'd run from him today like she'd run from him five years ago. It seemed like running was what she was best at.

"I don't know, baby. I think she might have been surprised to see me."

"Oh." She looked away from him, seeming lost in thought for the moment. "Was she mean to you? Is that why you don't live with her?"

We don't live together because she didn't want anything to do with you. But he didn't say that. That was the hardest thing for him to accept. He thought she loved him. He thought that despite her wild energy, despite her restlessness, she would always stick by him. Because when he looked at Belinda he felt a certain sense of rightness. He felt at home with her. It wasn't like it was with Bethany. He never expected her to take off at the first sign of trouble.

"We just didn't like the same things."

She nodded as if she understood the complexity of adult relationships. "I won't like her for you, Daddy." She lay back on his chest and cuddled into him.

"Such a loyal kid," he said to her as he kissed her forehead. A few minutes later they were asleep.

Belinda sat at the small desk she kept in her bedroom blankly staring at her laptop screen that afternoon. She told herself that she was going to order stock for the fall collection for Size Me Up. She was going to do something productive to take her mind off the shitstorm that had just entered her life. But she was failing miserably. Instead she'd spent the past few hours replaying the incident over and over in her head.

Cherri had been so good to her. She walked her inside, put on a pot of coffee, and urged her to take a nice long hot bath. The only thing she didn't do was ask questions, and Belinda was grateful for that. Cherri should have asked questions. She should have demanded to know every detail. She should have been pissed at Belinda for keeping this secret for so long. They were best friends. She had the right to know, but she said nothing. She just kissed her cheek and told her to call her if she needed her. Belinda glanced at her phone, thinking about picking it up and calling her friend, but it was hard to talk about Carter. Just thinking about him caused the back of her throat to burn. But she wouldn't cry.

Big girls don't cry.

What bullshit.

She had cried for him enough those first few weeks after their marriage ended. She had cried for him until she was all cried out and she hated herself for it. She swore that she would never cry for a man again. She told herself the only person worth loving besides her friends and family was herself. And for so many years she had kept that promise. Until this year. When she turned thirty. When she watched both of her best friends get married. When she saw Cherri with her baby. When she saw Ellis and Mike so happy that they failed to realize that there was anybody else in the room.

She hated herself for feeling that little bit of jealousy. She hated herself for feeling left out. For thinking about Carter and what could have been, for feeling like there was something missing in her life. It was why she was dating again, but in the back of her mind she knew she could never really have what Ellis and Cherri had.

Not while she was still married to Carter.

She was still his wife.

That thought never left the back of her mind. So she spent the past four years in Durant staying still. Not looking back. Not moving forward. Secretly wishing that her mistake would just undo itself. Maybe it was a good thing that he'd showed up. It was time she put him in her past. It was way past time. It was time she came clean about him to everybody.

Carter had entered her life when she was in a weird

space. Ellis was so busy in law school that they went months without speaking. Belinda was on the other side of the country, away from her parents, her friends, and her hometown. In a new job. In a place where she didn't know anybody. She was having a hard time adjusting, and then Carter came along . . .

She knew he was all wrong for her when she met him. He was too put-together. Too quiet. Too handsome. Too aloof. Too-too everything.

Too *good* for her according to some's standards.

And she was too much for him, for his family. She never fit neatly into his life. His parents hated her. His friends laughed at her behind her back. But she married him anyway. She jumped into marriage with both feet because she loved him that much. And she had actually thought that love could conquer all.

What a big dumb-ass you were.

Now Carter was back. Back with the little girl who'd changed everything for them. She didn't know why she was so shocked by his presence but she was. It had been four years since they had spoken. Four years of silence. Four years of waiting for him to reappear in her life and finally put an end to a marriage he clearly didn't want.

But why now, she kept asking herself. He must be ready to remarry. Maybe he was ready to make it official with Bethany, his first wife, the mother of their child. It made sense. Bethany fit into his life. She was everything Belinda wasn't.

Instead of feeling sadness about the end of her marriage, she was feeling pissed at herself. She should have been the one to do it. She should have been the one to end the marriage. She should have taken the steps to end it years ago. But she couldn't bring herself to. The breakup of their marriage was not her fault. Or maybe it was. It was her fault she had married a stranger.

"Pudge?" Belinda turned away from her computer as she heard her mother's voice calling to her from downstairs.

"Bill Junior?" Her father's voice came from much closer. "You up here?"

Her parents were there? She wasn't sure she could survive a visit from them today. She loved them, but she just didn't know if she had it in her.

"I'm in here," she called back to them. She left her desk to open her bedroom door only to find that her father had beaten her there.

He stood there for a moment, seeming not to know what to say to her. "You all right, Junior?" he asked in his Texas twang. "Your friend Apple called me at work. Told me I should check on you."

"Apple?" She shook her head. "Her name is Cherri, Dad. And she called you?"

"Yes!" Her mother came bursting through the door. "She called and we came right over."

Belinda stood there a little stunned by the news. Cherri had called them? She wasn't sure if she wanted to thank her friend for her thoughtfulness or choke her for the same reason.

She blinked at her parents. They blinked back at her, twin expressions of concern on their faces.

All six feet of her mother came at her, cupping her face in her hands and peppering kisses all over her. "What's the matter with my baby?" Carmina purred at her. She placed her hand on Belinda's stomach and gave a rub. "Do you have a bellyache? You know you cannot eat ice cream and such things, Pudge. It always makes you bloated and gives you the toots. And when you get bloated you get cranky. No wonder why Cherri called."

"*Mamá!* I am not five!"

Carmina went right on as if she didn't hear her. "It runs on my side of the family, you know. My mother! She could never eat ice cream, or yogurt, or cheese. Fresh cheese was the worst. Sometimes she could handle Parmesan and for some reason she could have goat's milk with no problem. You know what I heard on the news, Pudge? There is actually such a thing as camel's milk. Can you believe that! Milk from a camel. I wonder how ice cream would taste from camel's milk, or goat's milk for that matter. I should try it sometime. I have that ice cream maker your Nana Mary gave me ten years ago. We could try it. You can come over and put on the apron I made in my embroidery class. And we could put fresh strawberries in it or chocolate or—"

"Carmina!" Bill barked. "Would you shut up about ice cream? We're here for Bill Junior."

"Don't tell me to shut up! You shut up. I know why we are here. I am talking to our daughter, who didn't call me after her date last night and kept me up all night with worry."

He took off his hat and twisted it in his hands, his frustration palpable. "Can't you just find out what's wrong with her? Her friend Celery doesn't call every day."

"Her name is Cherri, Dad! Short for Charlotte. You've known her for three years."

"Oh, Pudge!" her mother scolded. "Don't you raise your voice to your father." She left Belinda and looped her arms around her husband, smoothing kisses along his jaw. "He's been so worried about you. Your friend Cherri called him at work. She called me on my cell phone, too, but you know I can never remember to turn it on. Your father has to do it for me, but today he left for work early and forgot so I didn't know she had called me until we were on our way here."

"Carmina," Bill growled in his low voice.

She sighed. "I was having lunch with your father in his office. We do that sometimes. Did you know that? We have lunch together in his office. He likes for me to spend the afternoons with him and I like to go because I have to! If I don't go in there with those smelly plug-in things, your father's office will smell like sweaty socks. Those boys he coaches smell just horrible after practice. I don't know how he deals with them."

"Why did your friend call us?" Bill interrupted, finally tired of waiting for his wife to get to the point. "What's wrong with you? Your face is all pale and stuff. You don't ever get sick. You take after me that way."

"Yes. Tell *Mamá* what's wrong, Pudge? I had to ride all the way over here in your father's dirty pickup truck. I swear he finds every inch of mud in the city and drives through it. I got mud on my pants. These are linen pants. Do you know how hard it is going to be to get the dirt out of here? I—"

"If you don't stop complaining about your damn pants . . . I'll buy you a new pair if the mud doesn't come out."

"I don't want a new pair. You can't buy me another pair. These were custom-made in Italy."

Belinda plopped herself facedown on her bed as her parents argued.

She just wished they would shut up sometimes.

"I saw Carter in the park today," she lifted her head and blurted out when the argument started getting louder. "You know, Carter. The man I married after knowing him a month. I got so flustered I fell in the lake at Elder Park. That's why Cherri called you."

The room went silent, and for a split second it was bliss.

But then she came back to reality. Her parents just stood there staring at her. This was the one thing they never talked about. Her mistake with Carter. How she disappointed them as their only child when she ran off and got married without telling them. She knew she had hurt them. And she knew they silently said *I told you so* when she came running back to them after six weeks of marriage.

Neither one of them said much of anything to her about it. She knew why. She was their only child. They just wanted her to be happy. But sometimes she wished they had told her what a big ass she had been. It would have lessened her guilt.

"What does he want?" She watched as her father's jaw grew tight. His nostrils flared just a bit.

Carmina stared at her with an open mouth and looked back at Belinda. "Well, Pudge, what does he want?"

She was almost afraid to tell them. She thought they had known, but how could they? Once she came home to nurse her wounds she never said another word about the man she married. "He said he's being trying to contact me. I think he wants a divorce."

"A divorce!" Bill snapped. "You two aren't divorced? What the hell have you been doing these past four years?" He let out a long stream of curses.

"William," Carmina said in a hushed voice. "She doesn't need you barking at her right now. Go to the store and bring us back some cookie dough." She looked at Belinda and squeezed her cheek. "I know my Pudge. Cookies will make you feel better, won't they, beauty?" She looked at her husband. "And the drive will make you feel better. Now go."

But for once Belinda didn't want to avoid this confrontation with her parents. They never spoke of how they felt about what she did. Maybe it was time they did. Maybe it was time they cleared the air. For once she didn't want Carter being the elephant in the room. "But, *Mamá*—"

"Hush," she said firmly. "It's okay now. Everything is going to be okay."

Belinda looked at her mother wanting to believe that, but this time it wasn't true.

CHAPTER 4

I can't go for that . . .

"Daddy? My feet hurt," Ruby said as they walked up to his new firm.

"Did you step on something?" he asked her absently as he unlocked the door. They were there to pick up a file he had forgotten before he took her out to lunch. He had been distracted for the past few days. Absentminded. He was falling behind on his projects. He had misplaced his keys three times. He had even forgotten to give Ruby breakfast once.

And it was all Belinda's fault.

He thought about her constantly. About their short marriage, their breakup, how his life had changed so much in the past five years. Seeing her again reminded him how angry he was with her.

But anger wasn't going to get him anywhere. He had to make a fresh start for Ruby. He couldn't do that if he was still legally, emotionally, or mentally attached to Belinda.

"I didn't step on anything. My shoes squish my feet."

"Oh." He stopped in his tracks and for the first time that day focused fully on his daughter. She wore cute little red shoes, but for the life of him he couldn't remember the last time he'd bought her a new pair.

Guilt eased into his chest.

"Are all your shoes bothering you?" he asked, hoping she would say no.

"Yeah," she said quietly. "I think maybe you should buy me some new ones."

Ass. Can't even remember to get your kid new shoes.

"I'll do that today," he promised. "Right after we get this file. Okay?"

She nodded.

"I'm sorry, Ruby, but you need to tell Daddy these things sooner. Sometimes I forget that you're growing."

She nodded again and looked up at him with understanding. She was so serious, his little girl. Such a little adult. For once he just wanted her to act like a kid. To whine and complain. To be a brat. But she never was. She never giggled or was silly. She wasn't loud. She never bothered him, and it caused him to think he was screwing up this parenthood thing.

"Let's hurry up and grab the file so we can get you some shoes."

They entered the building. His new firm was tiny compared with where he had come from, just him and Steven. Before he moved here he hadn't seen his old friend in years, since after his first wedding to Bethany where Steven served as his best man. They had been so close in college, at times he felt much more at home with his friend's family than his own. But something changed between them when he moved back west. They lost touch, only exchanging a few brief emails a year. His old friend barely knew his daughter, or half the stuff that had gone in his life for the past few years. Carter felt guilty about losing touch with the man who had once felt like his brother.

He was grateful Steven asked him to join his firm. It was the change he needed. They weren't designing multimillion-dollar opera houses, but they did good solid work. Carter was currently making plans for a new restaurant while Steven was designing a motel that was going to be built on the outskirts of town. The work would always be steady here. People in Durant wanted to use local businesses, which initially surprised Carter. New York City was less than two hours away and world-class architects could be found by the dozens, but these people were loyal and a hell of a lot less fussy than his San Francisco clients. They also didn't require three-hour dinners and weeks of wooing before they made a decision or mind that he had to conduct all his meetings before Ruby got out of school.

He thought he would miss the huge jobs he was so used to working on for the past ten years, but he was surprisingly content with his new work. It allowed him to spend more time with Ruby. He refused to get a babysitter, determined to do it right this time. But it was hard to juggle things. She spent a lot of time in his office with him. Sometimes when he couldn't help it he had to put her in the afternoon program at her school, even though he knew she didn't like it. But he was raising her completely alone. He didn't have any other choice.

"Are we staying long?" she asked him. "I didn't bring anything to do. I could play on your computer but you got mad the last time."

"I didn't get mad," he sighed. "I was just wondering how you got to CNN when I left you playing Sesame Street."

"I just wanted to know what it was. The guy on the TV keeps saying this is CNN." She pitched her voice lower.

"This is CNN. I didn't know what it was so I looked it up. I don't know why you got so mad. There was nothing on there but a lot of words."

Those words happened to be about sex slave trafficking, which she had asked him about for half an hour. He didn't ever think he would be prepared to have "the talk" with his daughter, but he sure as hell didn't expect her throwing out sex trafficking questions at five years old.

"Well, I'd prefer it if you asked me questions instead of looking them up on the Internet."

"Okay," she said. "But you get mad when I ask you questions, too."

"I do not." He took her hand and led her to back of the small building where his office was located.

"You do. You got really mad when I asked you what a drunk hussy was. Your face got red and you left the room and never told me what it was."

He did get angry that time. Mrs. Marsh liked to talk to her sister on the phone in front of Ruby about the antics of their niece. It wasn't the first time, either. When he asked Ruby what she wanted to drink once and she said a tequila sunrise he had to ban all phone calls at his house.

"It's something you never want to be," he said hoping she would drop it.

But she was Ruby, after all, and she didn't. "Like an entomologist. We learned about that in school yesterday. They study bugs. Did you know that, Daddy? That's something I never want to be. I hate bugs. Is a drunk hussy a gross job?"

"Please stop saying that, Ruby. And yes. They study throw-up and get really bad headaches and that's the last thing you want."

"Oh." She blinked up at him.

"And we aren't staying very long. I just need to get a file. Remember?"

He saw the light on under Steven's door and was surprised to see him there. But they both had big client meetings on Monday, and he knew his new partner liked to be as prepared as possible.

"Hey, Steven. You studying for the big test?"

A head popped up but it wasn't Steven's; it belonged to his intern instead. Molly Flanders wasn't a typical intern. She was in her early thirties, a former teacher who wanted to change careers. He hadn't paid much attention to her, other than to note that she was attractive. Short blond hair. Big friendly eyes. In good shape and very eager to learn.

"Oh, I'm sorry, Mr. Lancaster! I didn't hear you come in." She stood up, dropping the plans she had been studying as if they were on fire.

"Does Steven have you working on something for him this weekend? That seems a little harsh."

"No. But I did ask for permission to be here." She picked up the phone. "You can check."

"Calm down." He raised his hands in defense. She always seemed a little nervous around him. "You aren't in trouble. I was just wondering why anybody would want to be hunched over plans on a Saturday afternoon."

"These are your plans," she said, blushing. "Of that department store you designed in Toronto. We talked about your former firm in class last week and I wanted to see what you did up close. You have done some amazing work."

"Oh." He had to admit he was a little flattered. "Well, you don't have to come in on a Saturday to do that. You can ask me about my work anytime during business hours."

She smiled prettily at him. "That's very nice of you to offer, Mr. Lancaster."

"Please call me Carter. You're making me feel like an old man."

Molly's gaze passed over his body. "There is nothing old about you, Carter."

She was looking at him with interest, and that took him by surprise. He had dated sporadically since Belinda left, but nothing that ever turned serious. He couldn't give a woman the attention she needed. It had always been work and Ruby. There was nothing else for him.

"Maybe I could pick your brain over dinner sometime. It would really help me to learn from a master."

She locked eyes with him, giving him a small smile that he could only classify as seductive. It was an odd feeling. When was the last time he had had sex? Too long ago. Maybe it was time he started dating again.

A small pair of arms wrapped around his legs, reminding him that his daughter was still with him. "You said you wasn't gonna take a long time," she whispered.

"I'm not, baby. You remember Molly, don't you?"

"Hi, Ruby!" Molly left her spot behind her desk and knelt before Ruby. "How are you?"

Ruby hid her face behind his legs.

A little pang of sadness touched him. Ruby was so shy. Too shy, uncomfortable, almost scared of new people and places. It was one of the things he'd worried about when he decided to move her here. He would like nothing more than to keep her content in a little bubble where he could control who came into her life and block out anything that made her unhappy, but the real world wasn't like that. She needed to come out of her shell. He just wished he knew how to make it happen.

Just as he was about to prompt her to answer, to remind her that it was rude not to return someone's greeting, she said, "I'm fine. Thank you."

He didn't realize how tight he was holding himself until he finally heard her speak. He rested his hand on her hair, silently telling her he was proud of her for answering.

Ruby got her shyness from him. Growing up with the social queen of San Francisco, he wasn't allowed to be shy, but he had always been a quiet person, someone who was uneasy with a lot of words. Ruby was so smart. He didn't want her to be like him.

"That's great." Molly looked up at him, seeming unsure for a moment, but then turned her attention back to Ruby. "I always want to come play with you when I see you, but you always look so busy."

"I am," she said in a voice barely above a whisper. "I'm working. Just like Daddy."

"Oh." Molly didn't seem to know what to say to that.

"We can go now, Ruby." He trailed the back of his fingers down her cheek, wanting to end her discomfort. "I just need to grab a file off my desk. Say good-bye to Molly."

"Bye."

"Bye-bye, cutie pie."

Ruby left the room to wait for him in front of his office door. "I guess I'll see you on Monday."

Molly nodded. "And if you want to have dinner, let me know. I can cook. All you need to do is show up with a bottle of wine."

He thought about it for a moment. A date. The last time he had been out socially was eight months ago. All his other time was spent working or with Ruby. It might be nice to have dinner at a restaurant that didn't serve chicken nuggets or come with paper place mats. He studied Molly for a moment. She was attractive. She loved architecture. They would have a lot in common. But for some reason he couldn't agree to the date. Maybe it was that she was an intern, and he couldn't see dating her while she worked there. Or maybe there was another reason he couldn't date her. The same reason he hadn't dated anyone for the past five years. "I'm pretty busy with Ruby, but thanks for the offer."

A few minutes later they left, his file retrieved. He buckled Ruby into the backseat of the car. "Ruby? Can I ask you a question?"

She studied him with eyes that were so eerily like his own. "You can ask me anything, Daddy."

He smiled at her adult answer. "You've known Molly for a little while now. Why are so still so quiet around her? Don't you like her?"

"No." She frowned. "She looks at your butt when you turn around."

"Really?" He grinned at her bluntness.

"Yeah."

He studied her for a moment. She wasn't a fan of Molly's and he had no intentions of dating her but he thought it might be the moment to get back out there. Single parenting could be a little lonely and it was past time he moved on.

"How would you feel if I started to spend time with ladies my own age?"

"You want to date?"

He blinked at her for a moment, not really sure where his five-year-old had learned about dating, but he was too afraid to ask so he pushed on. "Yes. I might want to start dating. Would you be okay with that?"

She stared at him for a moment, her little forehead scrunched. "I don't think married people is supposed to be dating."

"You're right," he said suppressing a sigh. He wished he hadn't come clean about Belinda. "But Belinda isn't going to be my wife anymore. So I can date other ladies after that. Would you be okay with that?"

Ruby shook her head. "I have to think about it."

He wanted to laugh at the absurdity of the moment. He never imagined he would be asking a five-year-old for permission to date. But he was. She had to be okay with it. He wanted to get married again one day. He wanted her to have a woman in her life that she could trust.

"Can we have hot dogs for lunch?"

"Sure," he said, climbing into his seat. He guessed the conversation was over.

"Belinda?" She turned around at the sound of her name to spot one of her favorite customers peeking into her office. "I know I'm not supposed to be back here, but I need your help."

"Of course." She smiled at Katherine. "I would love to help you."

Ever since Belinda had bought into Size Me Up, she hadn't spent as much time with the customers as she would like. She did the books. She managed the salesgirls. She ordered merchandise. That meant she didn't spend much time dressing women anymore. She missed it. She loved fashion and people and all things beautiful.

It was something she got from her mother, but while Carmina was slender and tall and could wear anything, Belinda and most of the other women in the world were not. It was hard to find clothes that didn't make her curvy body look like a stuffed sausage. It took years of trial and error to learn what looked good on her. That's why Size Me Up was so important to Belinda. It was a place where women who couldn't just walk into any store could come and find something that fit them well. It was also the first place Belinda felt like she belonged.

"What do you need, Katherine?" she asked as she led her back to the front.

"I have a date."

"Oh, really." Belinda grinned. "Tell me he's successful and charming and that you could bounce a quarter off his abs."

"He's a seventh-grade math teacher with a bit of a belly

and a love of comic books, but he's adorable and he treats me like a princess."

"Which you deserve. I met your last boyfriend. Asshole. Capital A."

"I know," she sighed. "It took me a long time to see that, but Rich is a good guy and he's taking me to Tortola's for our fourth date."

"And you need me to help you to find sex clothes."

Katherine's face turned red but she nodded. "You always look so . . . seductive. I want to look like you for just one night."

Seductive. Belinda smiled at the word. She didn't feel the least bit seductive. The only thing she had ever wanted to feel was pretty. Growing up with a father who treated her like a son and a mother who was the epitome of feminine grace, she sometimes had a hard time achieving that.

"Well, you can't look like me. Rich doesn't want me. He wants you. And you want to look sexy. We can make you sexy. We can make it so he's pawing you like a horny teenager before the night is over."

"Good. Thank you! Where do we start?"

Belinda took in Katherine. She was pleasantly plump with apple cheeks and an all-around wholesome look. "We need to start from the bottom up. How do you feel about black lace panties?"

"Black lace panties?"

"Yeah, I thought crotchless and garters were a little too much at this point, but if you want that I'll get my bag and we can head out to the lingerie store."

Katherine's eyes widened. "Black lace is fine. Black lace is more than fine."

"Good. Let's get started."

An hour later Belinda watched Katherine walk out of the store armed with an outfit that was sure to turn her math teacher beau into mush. It made Belinda smile knowing that she could help Katherine feel confident. Confidence was a precious thing. It was one of those things she'd struggled with all her life. Especially growing up with her set of parents. She couldn't count how many times people had said, "That's *your* mother?"

It made her feel like she was some sort of creature from the black lagoon. That's why being a part of Size Me Up was so important to her. She wanted to make women feel beautiful, even if the rest of the world kept telling them they weren't.

She headed toward her office in the back of the store when Mike, Ellis's husband, stopped her. Before she could speak he looped his arm across her shoulder and pulled her toward the storeroom. "I need to talk to you, Red."

"You know, Mike, if you wanted me to go to the storeroom all you had to do was ask. I would be glad to accompany you there."

He looked back at her but didn't say a word until they were in the storeroom and out of earshot of everybody else. "There's something wrong with you."

"There are a lot of things wrong with me, but you're not so perfect either, buster."

He shook his head. "Quit with the sassy mouth. Ellis has been too crazy to notice with all the dress orders she has, but I can tell. You've been weird for the last few days."

"Weird?" She laughed, and even to her own ears it sounded forced. "I'm fine."

"You've been quiet and you're never quiet unless you're sick. And I know you're not sick. You're hiding something."

"Damn." She was busted. Before Mike quit to help them run the shop he used to be a detective. He was more perceptive than any man should be. That's why he was so good for Ellis. He could read her like a book, but Belinda didn't need reading.

"It must be something big." He stared at her for a moment and shook his head. "Stay here."

He was gone for less than ten seconds until he returned, tugging his wife into the storeroom.

"Mikey, what are you doing? You know I have to finish this dress by tomorrow."

"The damn dress can wait. You need to talk to Red."

He left them alone. Belinda gaped after him for a moment. She wanted to talk to Ellis. She meant to. She really had. But there never seemed to be a good time. They had expanded Size Me Up by opening a bridal boutique next door. Ellis spent her days making gowns for hard-to-fit women and Belinda took over all the day-to-day duties of running Size Me Up. Their business was doing well, much better than anyone had expected, but they had been so busy lately that they barely had time to talk.

Liar, liar, pants on fire. You could have talked to her. You're afraid to.

It was true. She didn't want to tell Ellis. She didn't know how to tell Ellis. Ellis was her best friend. They had known each other since seventh grade, but there were some things they just couldn't talk about. Ellis was good at everything she ever tried. She was a super brainiac in school. She went to an Ivy League college and graduated early. She practiced law for a few years. And now she owned this store, which was a success. The girl never failed at anything, while Belinda had tried to find one thing she was really good at her whole life and never could find it. She had bounced from job to job, from state to state, from boyfriend to boyfriend; nothing stuck. And then there was Carter, the one thing she had hoped would stick. But she had failed at marriage, at being a wife, at finding her forever. She didn't want to tell Ellis that. Especially now that she was so happy with her new husband.

"What's wrong?" Ellis put the dress she was holding down on the counter and grasped Belinda's hands.

"I have something to tell you."

"What is it? Are you pregnant?"

"No, honey. Pregnancy would have to involve sex, and frankly it's been drier than the Sahara down there."

"Oh." She thought for a moment. "You have a gambling addiction? A drinking problem? You're a shoplifter? You owe money to the mob?"

"No to all of those." She frowned at Ellis. "What exactly do you think I do when I leave here?"

"You're sick?" Ellis shut her eyes. "Please don't tell me you're sick. I won't be able to take that."

"I'm not sick," she said before Ellis could go any farther. "Well, I might be a little sick in the head, but that's not what I have to tell you. I'm married."

"Married." Ellis opened her eyes and blinked at her. "As in married to the Lord? I'm cool with that. Just as long as you don't ask me to stop cussing in front of you."

"I'm not married to the Lord, Ellis. Although I do think about joining a convent from time to time. I'm married to a man. I have been for the past four years."

Ellis recoiled. "What do you mean you've been married for four years?"

"I got married while I was living in San Francisco."

"You fell in love with someone, you married someone, and you never bothered to tell me?"

"I—I." She was at a loss for words for a moment. "You were in Boston and we weren't really talking at the time . . . It only lasted six weeks before I left. We only knew each other for ten."

"I don't care if it lasted six hundred years." She reached out and pinched Belinda's arm. Hard.

"Ouch, damn it. That hurt!"

"It should hurt." She pinched her again. "I'm your best

friend. You know everything about me. When I fell for Mike you were the first to know!" She pinched her four times in a row all over her already sore arms. "How could you keep this from me?"

Ellis came after her with two hands, but Belinda was quicker, grabbing them both and twisting them to immobilize her.

"Calm down. Let me explain."

"Explain? Let me go right now, Belinda Jane Gordon!"

"Are you crazy? You think I'm going to stand here and let you try to kick my ass."

"Try? I'm going to succeed! I've got four inches on you, short stuff."

"Short stuff?" She twisted Ellis's wrist backward. "My father made me take four years of karate."

"Ow. Ow. Okay. Okay. I'll stop. Just let me go!"

Belinda released her and backed away. "Just stay on your side of the room and let me explain."

Ellis folded her arms beneath her chest and impatiently tapped her foot. "There is nothing you can say to make this better."

"I didn't purposely deceive you," she started.

"No excuses, just talk."

She opened her mouth to tell her everything, but the words weren't coming out. Ellis looked so . . . hurt. "I'm so sorry, Ellie." Her eyes watered. "I didn't mean to keep it from you. I just didn't know how to tell you."

It was then that Ellis did something that surprised her. Her face cleared and she came toward Belinda, her arms extended. "Tell me now. I'm here."

"His name is Carter and I met him when I was in San Francisco—"

"He's the guy who broke your heart, isn't he?" Ellis backed away from her a little and looked into her eyes. "He's the guy you can never talk about."

She nodded. Not knowing what else to say.

"He's the guy you've been so hung up on for the past four years that you haven't had a single relationship since."

"I'm not hung up on— Ouch!"

"Don't lie to me, and more important don't lie to yourself. I've known you more than half my life. You don't give your heart away. For you to marry him, you had to have loved him a lot."

"He's here, Ellis. He's in Durant and I don't know what to do."

"He's come back for you?"

"No." She shook her head. The possibility of that was so far-fetched, it had never crossed her mind. "I think he's here to divorce me."

"That's not a bad thing. Is it?"

"No." She nodded. "It's the best thing. I can finally move on with my life."

"What happened between you two?"

"Ellis?" Maggie, one of the salesgirls, popped her head into the storeroom. "Your one o'clock is waiting for you next door."

"Oh shit. Tell her I'll be right there." She looked at Belinda. "I can't keep this client waiting. But we need to talk. Really talk."

"Yeah. We haven't been doing much of that lately."

"We'll make time." Ellis hugged her tightly. "And if you ever keep anything like this from me again . . ." She pinched her one last time before she scampered out of the room.

Shopping always made a shitty day better. Or at least Belinda hoped it would. She left work soon after Ellis went to her appointment. She needed a break, a moment to clear her head. Some people did yoga, or meditated. Others went for long walks in the woods or hikes up mountains.

Belinda went to the mall. Shoes. A girl always needed new shoes. They were always there for her. No matter what stupid mistakes she made.

She mindlessly searched through the rows of them in a vain effort to distract herself from the mess that was her life. Ugly. Ugly. Too tall. Too strappy. Too flat. Too everything. Then she found her perfect pair. Two-and-a-half-inch wedges in rose gold with four crisscrossing straps. And they were on sale, which lifted her mood greatly. She picked up the box and turned for the register when she saw him.

Carter.

Again.

She'd sworn she wouldn't run away the next time but she wasn't mentally prepared to see him today. Not so soon after the spat with Ellis.

Shit.

She hit the floor, crouching behind the athletic shoes, praying he hadn't spotted her. Why of all the shoe joints in all the world did he have to walk into hers?

She would never forget the day Carter Lancaster had walked into her life. She was the assistant manager of a little boutique in San Francisco, the type of store that only people who made over six figures could afford to shop in. She spent most of her days helping women find dresses for the symphony or some black-tie affair. She also spent most of her days bored out of her skull. And then Carter walked in. Every eye in the shop went to him, not only because males usually never walked through their door, but because he was beautiful. Tall. Black hair. Rock-hard jaw. Patrician features.

As he walked farther into the store she noticed that there was nothing warm about his beauty. He didn't smile at the salesgirl who greeted him. He didn't even relax his face. There was a kind of cold efficiency that surrounded him.

He walked past all the salesgirls, who were clearly dying to get to him because he looked like old money and smelled like a big fat commission, and stopped directly in front of her. He towered over her, staring down at her with his dark gray eyes and stony face. She took an involuntary step backward, her heart suddenly racing. He made her nervous and she didn't know why.

But she mentally shook herself and smiled up at him. "Can I help you?"

He nodded once. "It's my mother's birthday and I would like a gift certificate." His deep, smooth voice distracted her from what he was saying for a moment. It was the type of voice she could listen to reading the tax code. It was the type of voice she wanted to listen to in bed.

"Of course." She had to shake herself from her inappropriate thought. She must have been hornier than she thought if a few words from one good-looking man could warm her up.

The quicker she helped him, the quicker he would be out of her store, but something made her stop short. Even though he made her slightly uncomfortable, he deserved the best from her. She turned around to face him, but he was following so closely behind her she ended up crashing into him. Their bodies made contact for just the smallest of moments, but she couldn't deny the jolt she felt when they connected, that little bit of heat that sizzled inside her, or ignore the way his large hands felt on her arms as he tried to steady her.

When was the last time she had been touched by hands so big?

Had there ever been a time? Thoughts of how they would feel on her bare skin crept into her mind and she was mortified. She wasn't sure why. She was a woman who liked sex. Who liked men and wasn't ashamed of it. But why this guy? A customer. With a stern face and sterner disposition.

"Oh! Excuse me." Her voice had taken on a nervous breathlessness, and she hated that she couldn't be cooler. She backed away, needing space from him to re-gather her thoughts. "This is probably none of my business, but don't you think your mother would prefer something you picked out yourself?"

He looked into her eyes, and for the first time since he walked into the store she saw emotion coming from him. Weariness mixed with a little bit of uncertainty. "You see . . ." He looked at her expectantly.

"Belinda."

"Carter. You see, Belinda, that's my problem. I never know what to get my mother. She has hated every gift I have given her since I was a child. I want to get her something she would enjoy but the truth is I have no idea what women enjoy."

"A good-quality vibrator is what most women enjoy, but you obviously can't get her that. It would just be plain weird."

As soon as she heard the words slip from her lips she slapped her hand over her mouth. She always said stupid things when she was nervous. Carter made her nervous. She expected him to be shocked or disgusted. She expected him to get angry and walk out but he didn't. His lips curled ever so slightly into a smile.

"I didn't think this was that kind of shop. Is there something else you could recommend?"

She simply nodded, afraid to speak in case she got another bout of verbal diarrhea.

"I know I look like a humorless bastard, but I'm not." He briefly touched her shoulder as his deep voice rumbled through her. "I would like it if you would relax."

She forced herself to and they spent the next twenty minutes looking for gifts. They settled on a set of crystal perfume bottles and a beautiful understated silver bangle. They weren't the most expensive things in the store and she probably could have gotten him to spend more on a gift certificate, but thoughtful gifts were always better than cash. At least they were in her book.

"Thank you for visiting us today. I hope we see you again," she said as she handed him his wrapped packages.

"What time do you get off work?"

"Huh?"

He frowned at her for a moment. "If we are going to be seeing each other again, I need to know what time to pick you up for dinner."

She turned around to see if there was somebody behind her. There wasn't. "You're asking me out?"

He nodded.

"Like on a date?"

"Well, asking you to be my sex servant crossed my mind, but I figured I should at least take you to dinner first."

She blinked at him. "Was that a joke?"

"It was an attempt at one."

"Oh." She couldn't believe this was happening. She couldn't believe that a man like him would ever want to date a girl like her. She wanted to say no. They would have nothing in common. Nothing to talk about. They were from two different worlds. "Eight o'clock. I'm done here at eight."

But he was so damn handsome. And there was something about him. Something a little naughty about him. Something that made her a little nervous and a little excited. And she'd rather spend a couple hours tonight with this coldly beautiful man than in her tiny apartment alone.

"Thank you, Belinda." He took her hand and squeezed softly. "I'll see you at eight."

They were married four weeks later.

"Why are you sitting on the floor hugging shoes?" she heard a quiet voice ask, and she snapped out of the past and opened her eyes.

A wild-haired little girl stood in front of her, her chubby face scrunched with curiosity.

Shit.

She got caught being crazy.

"Because I am trying them on," she lied.

The kid frowned at her. "You don't look like you're trying them on. You don't even have your shoes off."

She was right. Belinda couldn't argue with logic.

"Fine. You caught me. I have fallen so in love with these shoes that I had to hug them. I hug everything I really love. I once held a Michael Kors coat for an hour and a half."

"Oh." The child didn't seem to know what to say to that. Belinda hoped she would scamper off back to her mother, but she didn't—she stepped closer. "Can I see your shoes?"

"I guess." She opened the box and held them up for the little girl to see.

She stroked one of the straps, her eyes wide in wonder. "I like them very much."

"I do too, kid."

"I'm here to buy new shoes, too." She lifted her tiny chubby leg to show her a red patent-leather ballet flat. "These are too small. My daddy doesn't know that he's supposed to buy me new shoes. I have to tell him everything."

Belinda nodded, trying to ignore how cute the kid was and that annoying little pull she felt in her chest looking at her tiny feet. She didn't even like kids, she kept telling herself. They were always dirty and sticky, like they had maple syrup for blood or something. And they always needed something. Like shoes. She wanted no part of them. But this one was really frigging cute. "Daddies can be really kind of dumb sometimes."

The little girl nodded, and Belinda noticed the large angry-looking scar that covered the upper half of her arm.

"You're looking at my burn."

"I am. I'm sorry for staring but it looks like it hurt a lot." Belinda didn't know what made her do it but she lifted her hand and ran her fingers across the little girl's arm. But then she realized that she must seem like a crazy lady and that she shouldn't be touching or talking to other people's kids.

"Maybe you should go find your mommy now. Or do you need help finding her? I can help you."

"It don't hurt no more."

"What?"

"My scar. I got in an accident when I was a baby so it don't hurt no more."

"Oh, I'm glad to hear that." She started to rise to her feet. "Let's go find your mommy."

"I don't got a mommy," the little girl said softly. "She died."

"Oh." That stopped her in her tracks. "Oh, shit. I'm sorry, kid."

Nothing was going right for Belinda today. First her fight with Ellis, then spotting the husband she wished would go away, and now she was faced with a cute lost kid with a dead mother. She should have stayed in bed.

"It's okay. I don't remember her. She died when I was a baby." She shrugged. "You're not supposed to say the S word. You got to put money in the cuss jar if you do."

"You take credit cards?"

"Nope." She grinned again, showing off those damn cute missing teeth.

"Ruby! Ruby!" a man's voice called.

"I'm over here, Daddy."

Carter appeared.

Shit. Shit. Shit. The little girl couldn't be his. But she was. Belinda could tell by the way he looked at her. Relief and love and anger. It fascinated her to see Carter like that. That one look contained more emotion than she had seen from him their entire short marriage.

She was so wrapped up in staring at him that she didn't notice that he didn't notice her sitting on the floor. He was too focused on his daughter, and for a split second she wondered if she could get up and sneak away. But she couldn't force herself to move. She hadn't seen him for four years and more than she wanted to run away, she wanted to take him in.

He was thirty-five now. There were fine lines around his eyes. The jaw she used to spend hours kissing seemed a little more chiseled. He was still coldly beautiful. Still an enigma to her. Still a stranger. Looking at him even now, four years later, she still felt jittery, but she could see that he hadn't changed very much. Except that he was a father now and he was looking at his daughter with a mix of frustration and worry and love that made her ache all over.

She should have suspected that the kid was Carter's, but she'd honestly had no idea. The last time Belinda saw her she didn't look at her closely. She couldn't before. Even now looking at Ruby, knowing she was Carter's kid almost hurt. Sometimes she couldn't help but to think that if she hadn't come along they might still be married, but it seemed wholly unfair to blame a baby for the breakup of her marriage. It never had a shot in hell in the first place. There were just too many things against them.

"Ruby, what have I told you about walking away from me?"

"Not to do it," she said matter-of-factly. "But I didn't go far."

"I don't care," he said firmly. "You know the rules. Don't ever walk away from me. You could have gotten lost."

"But I wasn't lost, Daddy. I was with your wife."

"What?" His eyes hardened when they finally settled on her. His body grew tight. He hated her. There was no mistaking it. "Hello, Belinda."

"Hello, Carter." She willed her voice to stay steady as her heart raced. She didn't want him to know how much he affected her. "Long time, no see."

His hard gray eyes took her in. "I see you've met Ruby. Ruby, this is Belinda."

"I know," Ruby said softly. "I was talking to her."

Carter froze. "You were talking to her?"

She nodded. "Are you mad at me?"

"Of course he isn't." Belinda raised her hand to Ruby's face and touched her chubby cheek. "I'm very glad we met today, Ruby," she said, feeling the strange need to reassure the child. "You're probably one of the most hideously ugly kids I have ever seen."

"Belinda!" Carter snapped.

"She's just joking, Daddy," Ruby said softly.

Belinda *was* joking. Ruby looked just like her daddy. Curly jet-black hair and steel-colored eyes, strong brows. It might have been a lot on a little girl but Ruby had a small round button nose and a light dusting of freckles that made her look almost delicate.

"Yeah, Daddy. Take the stick out of your butt. I was joking." She winked at Ruby. "You're smarter than him already, aren't you, gorgeous?" She ran the backs of her fingers down the girl's soft cheek, unable to take them away, unable to stop studying the child who came from the man she had loved.

She nodded. "A little."

"Make him buy you at least three pairs of shoes," Belinda said, taking her hand away. "One pair of sneakers so you can play outside, one pair of sandals, and one pair of dressy shoes. Okay? And they need to be half a size bigger than what you need. And make him come back in September before school starts and buy you some more."

Ruby nodded as Belinda got to her feet. "And new clothes, too. I don't wear uniforms to school no more."

"Yeah, and new clothes, too. I have to go now. It was nice meeting you, Ruby."

She turned to go but Carter grabbed her wrist. Feeling his warm touch on her skin did something to her. It sent tingles along her already frayed nerves. Four years had gone by. Four long years, and his touch still had the power to affect her. "Bell."

"Yeah?" She knew that she wasn't going to be able to escape so easily this time.

"I've been trying to get in contact with you."

It was hard but she forced herself around to face him again. She even managed to look into his eyes. They heated for a moment. Anger. He was pissed at her but it only showed for a moment. The cool mask returned, that coldness that always lurked just beneath the surface. "I swear to you, Carter, I never got your calls."

He nodded stiffly. "I take it you don't live in the city anymore?"

"Not for three years now. Are you here just for a visit?" she asked hopefully.

"No." He shook his head. "I moved here. I'm a partner in Steven's firm."

"Oh." She lost the ability to form words. It was too much. Of course he'd moved to Durant. To her hometown.

When she left California he was supposed to stay behind along with all the memories of him. He wasn't supposed to leave and make a bigger mess of her life than it already was. "Why?"

"Why what?"

"You know damn well what I'm asking," she snapped. "Why here? Why did you have to move here?"

He looked down at his daughter. "I did it for her and honestly, it's the last place I thought you would be."

"How could you think—"

He held up his hand, cutting her off. "We will not have this discussion in front of my child. It's time we settled some things. We need to sit down and talk."

"I think you're right." It was past time. "Call me." She freed her wrist to pull a business card out of her wallet. "I promise I'll pick up when you do."

CHAPTER 5

Do that to me one more time . . .

For two days after his run-in with Belinda he stared at her business card.

Belinda Gordon. Manager of Size Me Up.

How many times had he and Ruby walked past that store in the near month they had been there? Durant wasn't a huge town. He was surprised he hadn't run into her sooner. He would probably run into her a thousand times now that they were both living in Durant, and the next time he did, he wanted things to be settled between them.

He wasn't sure that was possible. He wasn't sure he would ever be able to look at her and feel settled. He wasn't sure if he could ever look at her and feel nothing.

After two days of staring at her card, after two days of trying to think of what he would say to her, he picked up his phone and dialed her number. He held his breath as the phone rang and couldn't help but wonder how she had spent the last four years, if she dated, if she was seeing anybody now.

It didn't matter anyway. They were over.

Keep telling yourself that.

Part of the reason he hadn't sent the divorce papers before was because he was waiting for her to end it first. She had left him. She should be the one to take the steps to dissolve their marriage. If it was up to him they would still have been together. They would have still been happy.

His call went to voice mail, her slightly husky voice telling him to leave a message. For some reason he was relieved he didn't have to speak to her. It was ironic. He had always been a quiet man, a man who liked to keep to himself, but he always liked to hear Belinda speak. She could talk about everything and nothing. She could go on for hours, but instead of her chattiness annoying him, it used to make him feel not so empty.

Ruby filled up his life these days and he couldn't fathom his existence without her, but there was still that emptiness, that hole that never felt filled after Belinda had gone.

"Hello, Belinda." He paused for a moment, his voice not sounding as steady as he wanted. "It's Carter. I think it's time we talked. Please call me back at this number when you get the chance."

He disconnected and walked down the hallway to Ruby's room, needing a distraction from his thoughts. She was sound asleep, curled up on side, her chubby hand resting on her cheek. It was the same way she had slept when she was a baby. Unwillingly his mind flashed back to two days ago in the department store. He kept seeing Belinda reach up to touch Ruby's face. He kept seeing how Ruby leaned in to Belinda's hand, how she responded to a woman she barely knew, how Ruby had talked to Belinda, like she was comfortable, like she wasn't afraid. Nobody but him could understand how huge that was for his child. His child who barely spoke in school, who grew terribly embarrassed around strangers, had walked away from him to talk to Belinda. He would have expected Belinda to be cruel to her, to shoo her away to make her feel unwanted. But she was the opposite of that. She was kind to her.

Why the hell was Belinda kind to her? She was sweet. She reminded him of that woman he had fallen crazy in love with. *Crazy* was the right way to describe it, because he had never felt sane again after the moment he laid eyes on her.

He thought she'd walked out because she wanted nothing to do with Ruby, because she didn't want to be a part of her life. That made him hate her, that made him mistrust his judgment, his heart. If he could be so wrong about the woman he married, he must have been wrong about so many things in his life.

His cell phone rang, startling him from his thoughts. He quietly exited the room so that he wouldn't wake his daughter. He answered it, not bothering to look at the screen.

"Carter Lancaster."

"I know who you are, dummy. I called you."

"Belinda . . ." He almost wanted to smile. She still had that mouth. Some things never changed about her.

"Yeah . . . I'm sorry I missed your call. I was in the shower."

Immediately a thousand thoughts entered his mind when he heard that. The last time they had made love it was in the shower. He still remembered the way she looked, with the water running down her ultra-curvy body, and the way she smelled like shampoo and felt like heaven wrapped around him.

"Did you want to talk?" she asked interrupting his thoughts and the long moments of silence that came with them.

"Yes. Can you meet me tomorrow at Mina's at eleven thirty?"

"Mina's?"

"Yes. Is there something wrong with that place?"

"No," she paused. "No. I can meet you there."

"Good. I'll see you then."

He disconnected before she could say another word and went to go look at the documents he had his lawyer draw up before he left San Francisco.

Belinda walked into Mina's ten minutes late. She had arrived at the restaurant on time, but she had spent the last ten minutes pacing in front of it trying to suck up enough courage to go inside. Why out of all the cafés in Durant did Carter pick this one? Did he remember that it was her favorite place in the world to eat? Or that her parents had taken her here for every single one of her birthdays? Didn't he know that by choosing to end their marriage here, she would never be able to walk in this place without remembering what happened?

She spotted him sitting alone in a booth, a thick stack of papers in front of him. He was such an odd contrast with the setting. Mina's was a romantic little hole in the wall with red-checkered tablecloths and candles illuminating the room. It wasn't a place businesspeople met for lunch. It was far from the trendy cafés that littered the streets of Durant. It was a comfortable place. A cozy place, and Carter didn't fit in sitting there all buttoned up. She wanted to go over there and mess him up. Ruffle his hair. Dump the cup of coffee he was sipping into his lap. He shouldn't look so freaking calm when she was a mess.

Maybe that's why she'd been attracted to him in the first place. When she met him she had no idea where her life was going to take her, but Carter seemed to have all his shit together. He was stable and secure. He had plans.

He was the opposite of her. And for some reason she craved that. She never thought at the age of thirty she would still be in the same place she was all those years ago. She never thought she would still be on a search for what made her happy.

She took a deep breath before she approached him. "Hello, Carter."

He looked up at her and gave her a chilly nod, and it immediately rubbed her wrong. He was mad at her, but he had no right to be. She wasn't to blame for the end of their marriage. She wasn't the one who'd kept a large chunk of her past away from him.

"I don't want to take up much of your time." He motioned to the seat across from him before she cut him off.

She couldn't sit. She couldn't approach this as coldly as he was. She'd married him. He was her first love. Her only love. But it seemed he was so much more to her than she had ever been to him. "You never were one for idle chitchat, were you? No *How are you, Belinda?* No *You look great*? No *What have you been up to for the past four years?*"

He blinked at her for a moment. "You're beautiful," he said, his eyes gently roaming over her before returning to her face. "You're so much more beautiful than the last time I saw you. When we got married I didn't think it would be possible for that to happen, but I guess I was wrong. I guess I was wrong about a lot of things. I never thought that you would have walked out on me like that, either. How's that for your idle chitchat?"

She stood there frozen for a few moments, unable to react, because too many things smashed into her all at once.

"I had my lawyer draw up a settlement that I hope is agreeable to you," he continued as she was still trying to process his other words. "If not, have your lawyer contact him and we can negotiate."

"You bastard!" Of all the things she was feeling, of all the sadness and hurt, the regret and attraction to him, anger won out. How the hell could he treat her so cavalierly when all she had tried to do was be a good wife, all she had ever tried to do was love him? "You son of a—"

He grabbed her hand pulling her into the booth beside him, cutting off her words. She smashed into his side, her body once again unwillingly coming into contact with his. Her skin was hot because she was so damn angry with him, but it grew hotter because she was near him, and touching him. She could smell him. It hadn't dulled. The attraction never decreased. How the hell was that possible?

"You think you're the only one who's angry?" His cold gray eyes heated up as his fingers slid up to her throat. His thumb stroked her pulse as his lips settled on her ear. She shivered, her nipples tightening painfully, because his touch, his breath on her skin was seductive. "You think that you're the one who's hurt here? I married you because I thought we would be forever. I trusted you to stand by me, to listen to me, to be the wife I expected you to be, but you let me down. You let me down when you walked out. You let me down when you wouldn't listen. You wouldn't even give me a chance. You fucked me up, Belinda, and I'll never forgive you for that."

She looked into his eyes and all she could see was raw naked pain. That sent her reeling. She had hurt him.

She had hurt *him*?

He didn't come after her, he didn't call her or try to explain; he had just let her go. She thought it was because he hadn't cared, but there was apparently more to it than that. There was much more to him than she had given him credit for.

She touched his face, cupping his hard jaw in his hands before she kissed him. It wasn't something she meant to do, but her mind had lost control and her body had taken over.

Damn it.

His lips still felt the same, smooth and firm and hot to the touch. He still responded the same to her kiss, opening his mouth over hers, sliding his tongue inside, stroking her mouth. It all came back to her, the heat, the familiarity, the longing that he always set off inside her. His fingers tangled in her hair as his body pressed against her, and the fire that was always lit between them threatened to bloom into an explosion. But she pulled away before she forgot where she was and why. She had to pull away because there was so much more to them than this—so much that was left unsaid. Because she had come here to finally settle things between them.

"I loved you, Carter. Maybe I wasn't blameless, but I'm not the only one to blame. Your friends would say nasty things behind my back. They whispered about me, talked down to me. Your mother said I wasn't good enough for you, your father treated me like a prostitute and offered to set me up with one of his friends so that I would leave you alone. And when that didn't work, your parents tried to pay me to stay away from you. They humiliated me. Every single day I felt like I wasn't good enough for you, that I was dirt beneath your feet, but I didn't give up on us then because you never treated me that way. Because I believed in us. But then I found out that you were married to someone else—that you made a baby with her! You proved your parents right. You proved that I wasn't important to you, that I wasn't good enough for you to share that huge part of your life with me. You think I fucked you up? Marrying into the Lancaster family almost killed me."

Carter stared at her silently, his jaw clenching, redness starting to form under his collar. "My parents did what?"

"You had to know they hated me. You had to know your parents didn't want their son married to . . . What did your mother call me? A money-hungry tramp?"

His jaw ticked. She watched him clench and unclench his fist for a moment, and then a deadly calm settled over him. "You're lying. They couldn't have done that."

"Half a million dollars they offered me," she whispered. "You should be flattered. Your parents must really love you."

"This is not a joke." He slammed his fist on the table, causing the silverware to jump. "Shit. I need to go." He got up, forcing her to move out of his way.

He snatched his papers off the table and left without another word. She sat back down, her legs too shaky to support her. She was ridiculously close to tears, but she wouldn't allow herself to cry. She had cried enough over Carter Lancaster.

Her cell phone rang, and for a moment she was too wrapped up in what had just happened to hear it. But soon the familiar ring penetrated through her fog, and she blindly reached into her bag and pulled it out, not caring who it was. She would talk to a telemarketer for an hour if it helped to pull her out of her head. "Hello?"

"Pudge? What's wrong? Why does your voice sound so high?"

"*Mamá?*" Her mother may not always understand her, but sometimes she just knew when she needed her. "I'm fine," she said quickly. "I'm on Lafayette. Do you think you could meet me in town to go shopping?"

"Shopping? Of course. I'm just leaving my hair salon. I can be there in five minutes."

Her mother walked up four minutes later, her thick black hair shining as it brushed her shoulders. She looked elegant as always in black wide-leg trousers and a blush-colored long-sleeved fitted blouse, her sunglasses perched on her delicate nose. She was so beautiful that she looked out of place in their small town. People seemed to stare at her wherever she went, but it never bothered Carmina. She wore her beauty like a badge and was never above flaunting it.

"My Pudge." Carmina wrapped her arms Belinda and squeezed. "What's the matter?" She slid her hand down her back and patted Belinda's behind. "Oh! Your bottom looks quite round in this dress. I've always wanted a big fat bottom like this. It's why I could never do swimsuit work. The bikini bottoms would just droop on my butt, making me resemble an overgrown toddler with a dirty diaper. But you have a perfectly fat bottom. I think you could be in one of those magazines. You know. The ones where the girls wear thongs and lean over the cars. I'm not really sure why they make those magazines. Surely it's not to sell cars. Who could look at a car when they have a girl who is greased up like a pig hanging all over it? I hate being covered in oil. A photographer once had me covered in vegetable oil for a photo shoot because they didn't have baby oil—"

"*Mamá*," she said, cutting off her absentminded mother before her train of thought turned into a two-hour conversation. "Let's go buy some stuff."

If nothing else her mother was good for a distraction.

They were having a local artisans' fair on the town's green. It was one of Belinda's favorite places to go. It was the only place in the area to get handmade furniture and original artwork without paying a fortune. Her entire town house was decorated with things from here. One of her favorite pieces being the modern quilt she had picked up last year made by Two Crazy Grannies. It was made with bold red and white squares cut in an almost mind-bending pattern. This year she hoped to find something equally spectacular. This year she was planning on buying a whole bunch of crap she didn't need.

Retail therapy. A hell of a lot more fun than seeing a shrink.

"Aye, Pudge. I wish you would have told me that we were coming to the green. I wouldn't have worn these shoes. I'm sinking in the dirt, and look." She pointed at Belinda's heels. "So are you! How are you ever going to get the dirt out of that purple suede? You're not. You must come home with me so I can clean them. I learned a trick from a wardrobe stylist when I was modeling in Ibiza. Who knew it would come in handy when I had a little girl? The way your father always had you playing in the dirty, dirty mud. You two produced enough stains to keep the Tide people in business for the next fifty years! Oh, look! I smell Indian fry bread. Let Mommy buy you some before we go look at old dusty furniture."

Belinda wanted to say no, but she loved fry bread, especially when it was drizzled with honey and coated in powdered sugar. Plus after the meeting she'd just had with Carter, she deserved a little pick-me-up. "I think I can manage to choke some down."

"Good." Carmina wrapped her arm around Belinda and pressed a kiss to her forehead as they made their way to the stand. "I've been thinking about my Pudge all week. I wish you would have stayed with us like we wanted."

After she had told them about her run-in with Carter, her parents didn't leave her. They stayed all day and cooked her dinner—her father standing watch over her like some kind of guard dog, her mother fawning as if she were still a child. Belinda let them. She let them smother her because they took her mind off Carter and because she was their only child. And because they were still making up for her early childhood when both of them were so busy working that they missed out on much of her life. But all that had changed when they moved to Durant.

"I was fine. You don't have to worry."

"Don't have to worry! Of course I worry. I blame you for the end of my modeling career because all I do is worry about you. I worry if you are eating enough vegetables and I worry that you live across town by yourself and I worry that you will stop breathing in your sleep, just like I did when you were a baby. I worry so much that it has caused a nasty crease between my eyes. And you know I don't believe in that Botox stuff. Did you know that was poison, Pudge? They put poison right in your face. And speaking of poison, did you know that hamburger place that your father likes to go to got shut down because four people got food poisoning? What do you want to drink? I've heard this stand makes very good sweet tea."

It took a moment for Belinda to follow her mother's rapid changes in subject. "Is it too early for liquor?"

A few minutes later they headed to the picnic area, fry bread and coffees in hand. Belinda was half listening as her mother went on about her aunt Azuela, who was having man troubles again.

"I told Azuela that maybe she should try computer dating. My friend Martina, you remember her, don't you, Pudge? She just got engaged to a nice man that lives in Hoboken."

"That's nice," Belinda replied automatically as a group of children caught her eye. Schoolchildren out and about in Durant wasn't out of the ordinary. It was a kid-friendly place. But there was one child who caught her eye.

Ruby. First the father, now the daughter.

Crap.

She was sitting away from the other children, almost directly across from Belinda, her little legs far too short to reach the ground. Her hair was a mess. She was wearing a carrot-orange shirt and pink skirt and flat strappy gold sandals.

Shit, damn, and hell.

It was a warm day for early spring but it was barely sixty degrees out. Too cold for bare legs and sandals. She wasn't sure why she cared. Why did it bother her? The kid probably didn't even feel cold.

"I'll be back in a bit, *Mamá*."

She purchased a little handmade cardigan from a nearby booth and approached Ruby even as her brain was screaming at her to turn away. "Hey, kid."

"Oh, hello," she said softly.

"You've got great taste in shoes."

"Thank you." Her cheeks went pink. "They're like yours."

That stupid achy, tuggy feeling snuck up in her chest again.

She's Carter's kid. Stay away.

But she's Carter's kid. Carter's cute, motherless, burn-victim kid.

"So I saw this sweater over there and I thought you would look pretty stinking cute in it. Do you think you could put it on for me?"

Ruby nodded and Belinda helped her into the sweater, noting that her skin was cold. "I'm really surprised that your father let you out of the house without a sweater on."

"He lets me pick out my clothes now. I'm a big girl."

"I know, but you're going to be big frozen Popsicle. If you want to wear skirts, you should get some leggings or tights. Okay? And a couple of little funky cardigans."

She stopped herself from saying any more. She sounded like somebody's worrying mother.

Belinda looked into the little girl's small serious face and then at the classmates she was sitting away from and realized something was wrong. "Why aren't you eating junk food and being a loud giggly kid like everybody else? Not that's there's anything wrong with sitting quietly. I actually prefer my children that way. But what's wrong?"

"My dad forgot we had a field trip today, so he didn't give me money." She shrugged. "It's okay, though. I don't need to have a snack. I've got a lard butt."

Belinda stopped herself from swearing. "Who told you that you have a lard butt?"

"Elroy." She looked at a small blond child who was sitting at the head of the table with a group of very rowdy boys. She recognized the kid. She knew his father. They had gone to school together.

"Elroy? Don't you let that little pointy-eared dumbass make you feel bad about yourself. You do not have a lard butt!"

Ruby grinned at her, showing off her two missing front teeth. "I don't think grown-ups are supposed to talk about kids that way."

Belinda shrugged. "I'm not like most grown-ups, and don't ever let anybody make you feel like you aren't beautiful or less than wonderful. Because you are, and if they try, you let them have it."

Why the hell did she just say that? What business did she have giving advice to a five-year-old? None! But she couldn't help it.

She looked at Ruby, remembering what it was like to be her age, remembering what it was like to be teased unmercifully when she was a child. Ruby didn't look like most kids. She had a grown-up face and frizzy hair and a round little belly. But she was gorgeous, and if she didn't believe that about herself now she was going to have a hell of a time come adolescence. "I've got money." She took a ten-dollar bill out of her pocket and pressed it into Ruby's hand.

"Oh, no, thank you."

"I want you to have it. I want you to get something nice from here and I want you to try some of this fry bread. It's one of my favorite things."

"Excuse me, ma'am. I'm Ruby's teacher—"

"It's okay, Miss Milan," Ruby said so quietly her teacher had to lean in to hear her. "She's not a stranger. She's my daddy's wife."

"His wife?" Miss Milan asked tightly.

"Yup." Belinda tossed her hair over her shoulder and smiled. It was true at least for the time being. "We've been married for years. I hope it's okay that I share a little snack with Ruby."

"Sure. We're leaving in fifteen minutes. Ruby, please join us at the other table when you're finished." She smiled stiffly and walked away.

"Your teacher wouldn't happen to think your dad is hot, would she?"

"A lot of ladies do."

"Of course."

"Pudge?"

Belinda looked up to see her mother frowning at her in confusion. She had all but forgotten about her mother when she saw Ruby sitting alone. "I'm sorry. I saw my friend."

Ruby tugged on Belinda's dress. "Is that your mommy?" she whispered.

"Yeah. How did you know?"

"You're pretty like her."

"Oh, what a brilliant child!" Carmina sat on the other side of Ruby. "I keep telling my Belinda that she looks like me. She doesn't like her red hair, but it's beautiful, too, no?"

They spent the next few minutes talking and eating fry bread while Carmina heaped attention on Ruby. When it was time to go back to her class, Ruby was smiling. Belinda was sad to see her go and she wasn't sure why. Ruby is the last child on the planet she should be spending time with.

"Belinda, who was that delightful child? She's so smart. She reminds me of you as a little girl. I like her very much."

The funny thing was, Belinda kind of liked her, too—which was bad. "That's Carter's daughter."

"Oh?"

She looked at her mother, expecting her to say something, anything, but she didn't. Even if her mother had no thoughts about the little girl and the man who was her father, Belinda had plenty of them. She couldn't be around the kid anymore, just like she couldn't be around the kid's father. But it was going to be impossible to avoid them. The only way was to move out of Durant.

"I'm thinking about moving away for a year, *Mamá*. Maybe to Spain. I really loved it there when we visited last winter."

Carmina looked at her, raised one of her perfectly arched eyebrows, and said, "No. Absolutely not. Over my dead body."

CHAPTER 6

Stop in the name of love . . .

Carter watched his daughter as she bopped her head from side to side and swirled spaghetti around her fork. It was one of his few attempts at cooking, and while it was far from five-star, it was edible and it wasn't take-out or fast food. Now that he was home earlier he could cook for Ruby or at least try to. His last two tries hadn't gone so well. He burned the hell out of the instant rice he was cooking, and the pancakes he'd tried got so stuck to the pan they couldn't be salvaged. But the spaghetti came out okay. Ruby wasn't complaining about it, and for the first time in a long time she seemed . . . happy. And he was relieved. For so long he felt like he had no idea what to do when it came to her. He still didn't, but lately he hoped that he was making his way to the right track.

"Did you have a good day, Rube?"

"Yes, we saw a lady making baskets at the fair and a man let us paint on his big picture."

"Shit," he swore and then immediately shook his head. "Sorry. I know. I owe money to the cuss jar. But I was supposed to give you money for your field trip, wasn't I?"

"Yes." She stared down at her plate, unable to make eye contact. His stomach sank. "But it's okay. Your wife gave me some."

"Excuse me?"

"I saw your wife today," she said barely above a whisper. He knew his tone had been too sharp. "She gave me some money for the trip."

"Shit."

What were the chances that Ruby would run into Belinda the same day they had their own run-in? The same day she kissed the breath out of him. The same day he found out something no son wanted to hear about his parents.

They'd tried to pay her to leave him. His father had treated her like a prostitute when he offered her to his richer friends. It was the only way he could describe what they'd done to her. They hadn't treated her like his wife, like somebody who deserved respect. They'd treated her like a problem to be dealt with, like somebody unworthy of human kindness. And as much as he hated what they'd done to her, as much as it disgusted him, he couldn't stomach what they did to him. His parents didn't care for him enough to respect his decisions. They went behind his back, they manipulated things to go their way. And for what? To preserve their reputation? It sure as hell wasn't to preserve his happiness. He could never do that to Ruby. He could never pull her away from somebody who made her happy.

Belinda may have walked away from him, but his parents had driven a huge wedge between them long before she did.

He called his parents to confirm what Belinda had

thrown at him because at first he hadn't believed her. He didn't want to believe her, but he knew it was true. His mother wasn't home when he called, her cell phone going to voice mail when he tried calling there. His father was out of town on business, unreachable to him for the next few days. It was probably a good thing, he supposed. He was too worked up to think straight.

They had always tried to control his life. He thought it was over when he and Bethany broke up, but he was wrong. They still manipulated him at every turn.

"She gave me the sweater, too. But I didn't spend the money, Daddy," he heard Ruby say as one reached into her pocket and produced a crumpled ten-dollar bill. "I'm sorry. You said not to take things from strangers but I didn't think she was a stranger no more."

She looked close to tears, and he realized how he had been looking at her. He sighed. What kind of child did he have who blamed herself for his failures? "You don't need to be sorry, Ruby. I'm sorry. I'm the one who messed up. I'm not mad at you. I'm mad at myself. Please forgive me."

"It's okay." She left her side of the table and crawled into his lap. "I like my sweater." She stroked her arm down the soft white wool. "Do I gotta to give it back to her?"

"No. Of course not. I'm just wondering why she bought you a sweater."

"Because I was cold. She said I needed to wear sweaters and tights when I leave the house because it's not warm yet. She said she was surprised you let me leave the house without one."

"Did she?" He felt himself growing angry. She was giving his kid money, buying her a sweater, making him feel like he was an incompetent parent. Acting like . . . She was acting like a mother would. What the hell gave her the right? She could have stayed. They could have made things work, but she didn't stay, and he was raising Ruby alone. She'd lost her right to have an opinion about her the day she walked out on him.

"I don't like it when you're mad, Daddy. I'll give the sweater back."

"I'm not mad at you, baby. I promise. You can keep your sweater," he said even though he wanted it out of his house. Every time he looked at it he would know the source, but he wasn't a petty man. He would never dream of asking his daughter to give back something that made her happy. "Tell me about the rest of your day."

She looked up at him unsure for a moment. She could read his moods better than anybody. He was angry but he didn't want her to know that. He didn't want her to know how miserable his day had been.

"Talk to me." He pressed a kiss into her curls. She relaxed then.

"Your wife and her mommy shared some fry bread with me. Do you know what fry bread is, Daddy? It's like fried dough but puffy. The Native Americans invented it. I liked it. Belinda's had honey and powdered sugar on it and Mrs. Gordon's had apples and cinnamon on it."

Carter's head spun as he tried to keep up with her story. "Belinda ate with you?"

"We talked, Daddy. She shared her snack with me because you forgot to give me money and she told me I didn't have a lard butt and that I was beautiful and if anybody tried to make me feel bad to let them have it."

He inhaled, taking all of what she said in. The knot in his stomach was growing larger with every word she spoke.

"Daddy?"

"Yes, babe?"

She looked up at him shyly. "I know I said I wouldn't like her for you, but is it okay if I do?"

What could he say to that? How could he tell his daughter not to like her? What kind of man would he be if she said no? "Sure, you can like her. It's okay with me."

She smiled at him, a full bright smile that he hadn't seen in a very long time. "Can I go color now?"

"Yes, but make sure you read first."

He sat there for a long moment, knowing what he was going to have to do but not liking it. Belinda and he couldn't be friends. Their lives couldn't intersect. He had come to New York to divorce her and he would. After that he wanted no part of her. If they were going to live in the same town she was going to have to stay the hell away from his kid.

Belinda sat in her den staring at the monitor of her desktop. She had off from work that day but she still liked to get some work done at home. Mother's Day was less than two months away, and she was trying to stock the store with gift items. It never failed: Every year at Christmas, Valentine's Day, and Mother's Day, a bunch of hapless men would flock to Size Me Up looking for gifts for their wives and mothers. She was about to place an order for silk robes when she heard her doorbell. Glancing at her clock, she saw that it was almost lunchtime. And that meant it was probably her father. Sometimes he would stop by so he could take her out for burgers and beer. She had wanted to tell her father long ago that she hated beer, but she couldn't bring herself to. If she had to choke down a Bud once in a while to make her father happy, she would. Her father liked to spend time with her even though she knew he'd rather have a son. He was still a good dad.

She opened her front door and instead of seeing a man in sweatpants and a Durant U windbreaker she saw a man in dark trousers and a crisp white buttondown shirt. He was the last man she ever expected to see at her door. "Carter? How did you find out where I live?"

His jaw was tight. He looked no happier since the last time she saw him less than twenty-four hours ago. His hands were empty. She expected to see the heavy packet of divorce papers. It was the only reason he had for coming here. To finally put an end to their marriage.

"You're listed in the phone book. Can I come in?"

He didn't wait for her answer, instead just brushed by her to get in her house. She couldn't help but notice how rock-hard his body was as it briefly touched hers. He used to jog every morning when they were together. She could still see him in her mind. Shirtless and sweaty. His body more beautiful than any man she had ever seen. She wondered if that was a habit that he still kept up. She also wondered why instead of her attraction to him diminishing over the years, it was more intense than ever.

She shut the door behind her and turned to face him. He was staring at her, his hard eyes taking her in, his face nearly expressionless. Immediately she felt self-conscious. The way she always had around him. Her hair was too red, her skin too tawny, her body too thick to pass his inspection. But she wouldn't let him know that. She lifted her chin and met his gaze. "Why are you here, Carter?"

"I don't want you giving my kid money." He held out a crumpled ten-dollar bill. "She doesn't need anything from you."

She was bewildered for a moment, not expecting that from him. "You forgot to give her money, Carter. She was sitting by herself on her field trip while the kids around her were laughing and eating snacks. You may not remember being a five-year-old but it sucks to be the only kid without."

He stepped closer to her. "She doesn't go without. I give her what she needs. I don't need you interfering in her life."

"It's ten fucking dollars," she snapped, feeling her temper rise dangerously. "I didn't do anything wrong."

"It's not just the ten dollars. It's the sweater you bought her. It's that you told her what I should allow her to wear. I don't need you critiquing my parenting. I don't need you anywhere near my child. I don't want you to talk to her."

She laughed bitterly, not allowing the hurt to clog her chest. "You're just like them. You don't think I'm good enough to be around your kid. Just like I wasn't good enough for you."

"That's not true, damn it. I married you. I wanted you. I never thought you weren't good enough."

"Then why are you here, Carter? Why are you in my house demanding that I stay away from your kid? I'm not trying to corrupt her. All I—"

"You left me because you didn't want her."

"What?"

"You walked out on me—on our marriage—because you didn't want to be around my child. Because you were too selfish to even try to love her."

She hadn't realized that she had raised her hand to hit him until she heard the crack of her hand across his cheek. His comment was so cruel it took her breath away. She would have loved Ruby, because she loved him. But he didn't love her. If he did, he would have told her the truth. He would have noticed how his family and friends treated her. He would have realized how unhappy she was all along. "Is that what you think of me? You think I left because of Ruby? She was just a baby. She was the only innocent one in this. I left because you never told me about your first wife. I left because I realized I was married to a stranger who I was never going to be good enough for."

"Is that when you took my parents' money? Was that a good enough excuse to take it? Did it soothe your conscience? 'My husband left out one detail about his life.

That's the perfect reason to take half a million dollars and run'."

"You asshole." She went after him with both fists but he caught her this time. "I didn't take their money. I wouldn't take their money. I loved you. I love you." She struggled against his tight hold, but he just pulled her closer. "Get out of my house, Carter. Get out. I hate you."

"No," he barked at her. "No." He slammed his mouth on hers. It shocked her because it was nothing like their last kiss. This kiss was too hard. Too angry. Too consuming and she fought it. She fought him. Because when he kissed her it made her forget herself. It had the power to make her forget that their marriage had only really ever been about this. About kissing and touching and their extreme attraction for each other. It had been just about sex. For him at least. She was the stupid one. She's the one who didn't have sense enough not to fall in love.

He lifted his lips for a moment only to look into her eyes. She thought she almost saw regret cross his face for a moment, but it passed quickly and then his lips were on hers again. She bit down on his lower lip hard. He winced, lifted his head again, but he didn't move away. Instead he dug his fingers into her hips and pulled her closer. He was hard. She was surprised to find his erection prodding in between her legs and even more surprised at her reaction to it. Her nipples tightened painfully as the rest of her became aware. Every inch of her body was pressed against his. There was no space between them, no way she could escape him.

"Don't do it again," he warned. She had never heard his voice so raw. It scared her. It sent shivers through her entire body, and she involuntarily shuddered against him. He smiled. Cold. Brutal. Triumphant. And then he kissed her again. This time his tongue slid deep into her mouth. The kiss overwhelmed her. It was hotter, softer, wetter. It was more intense than before and for a moment she could do nothing but let him kiss her, let herself wonder at the sensation of being kissed by him, a man who at one time she thought she would never see again.

He curled one hand over her behind, under her dress, and pulled her even closer. She rubbed against his erection unable to stop herself from moving. He shoved one hand into her hair, pulling her face closer to his. He licked across her lips, squeezed her flesh, and then he looked into her eyes. "Kiss me," he ordered. "Kiss me back."

She did, and as soon as she slid her tongue into his mouth she knew what was going to happen. She knew she was powerless to stop it. And so was he. Their first date had been like this. A kiss that had too quickly turned to fire.

He was pulling down her underwear before she even had time to process it. His hands seemed to be everywhere on her body and yet not enough places at once. He cupped her behind, ran his hands over her hips, stroked her belly in some kind of too-sensual frenzied motion. It wasn't until his fingers gently probed between her legs that she understood what was happening and by then it was too late. The rough pads of his fingers caressed her too-sensitive clitoris, and it jolted her. She looked up at him. Her mouth opened to ask him to stop but her brain simply wouldn't allow her to.

"Undress me," he said, but it sounded more like begging.

She didn't know why she did it. Especially when she knew that this was wrong. That they were wrong, but her fingers went to his shirt and unbuttoned each button. The whole time he watched her. His expression never changing. She couldn't tell what he was thinking. Part of her didn't want to know. She revealed his hard chest. The tattoo was still there. A black dragon. She had been so surprised the first time she had seen it. It seemed so out of place on Carter Lancaster, a man she thought to be overly serious and too straitlaced, but there was a naughty side to him, a rebellious side, and she was reminded of that every time she saw his tattoos during their short marriage.

She simply touched the dragon at first. Then she nipped it with her teeth, eliciting a grunt from him. His fingers tightened in her hair but that didn't stop her. She nipped him again and then soothed the bite with the tip of her tongue. He groaned. She found his nipple, and licked across it while she loosened his pants. Her hands slid inside, not to free him, only to feel the heavy hard length in her hands.

"Enough," he barked. He pushed himself away from her, only to come at her and yank her dress off her shoulders. He pulled at the clasp on her bra. Her breasts came free in moments, and when she was bare to him he stood and stared at her. He looked so long she almost came to her senses. Her hands moved to cover her body. He was the only man she had ever made love to with the lights on. In the daylight with no covers or no shields. He never allowed her insecurities when they were together, and now was no different. He grabbed for her, pulling her so hard against him. Their bodies slapped when they met.

It felt good. Hard body. Hot skin. Spicy smell. Carter.

"I need you," he panted and half lifted her off the floor. Her couch was the closest place they could land, and before she felt her back hit the soft fabric he was pushing inside her. She was ready for him, more than ready for him, and he let out a deep guttural cry that she felt in her chest.

She almost came. She felt herself tighten around him, but he grabbed her hips and stopped moving. "Not yet, baby." He looked into her eyes. "Please not yet."

She didn't know if she could grant his wish even as she

nodded. It was too much. He was too much. The way his heavy body felt on top of her. The way his manhood felt inside her. His smell. His skin. Him. It was too much for one woman to take. Especially because there hadn't been another man since she'd walked out on him four years ago. Especially because she'd foolishly carried him around in her heart for so long.

He slid into her hard. His rhythm set to drive her out of her mind. She couldn't hold on any longer. Her body wouldn't let her and she came harder than she ever had before.

He cursed and looked down at her for a moment before his face twisted. It looked like extreme pain and pleasure all wrapped up in one moment. And then she felt it. The hotness that ran out of him and into her. She felt incredibly fragile then—breakable, raw, stupid—and when he lifted his head to look into her eyes the tears came. And before long a sob ripped from her throat.

He was horrified when he looked down at her and saw her tears. And he felt powerless. There were only three times in his life when he'd truly felt powerless. When his parents forced him to marry Bethany. When he sat beside a gravely injured Ruby in the hospital, and when he realized the depth of his feelings for Belinda. And now he was there again. He'd hurt her. Not physically. The sex between them was how it always was. Explosive. Exciting. Frenzied. Hot. He had hurt her heart and he had done it on purpose. He knew she hadn't taken his parents' money. She said she didn't leave because of Ruby and now he believed her. He had lashed out at her because even after all these years he felt bewildered by her abandonment. And even though he now understood the reasons behind it, he was still hurt by it. The first time he had ever taken a chance on a woman and she smashed his heart.

"Oh, Carter. Why did you do that?"

"Hush." He rolled them so that her weight was on him and stroked his hand down her back. It was a good question. He didn't know why he'd done it. Maybe because it had been four years since he'd had sex. Maybe it was that she looked so sexy when her temper sparked. Or maybe it was that she told him she loved him.

I loved you. I love you.

She had said it in the heat of the moment but it unfolded something inside him. For weeks after she had left he'd wondered if she had ever really loved him. He wondered if he had been too blinded by the way she made him feel to see her true feelings.

"Don't cry. Please, Bell." He kissed her forehead. "I'm sorry. I'm so sorry."

She pulled away from him and sat up, her breasts still exposed, her dress bunched at her waist. Immediately regret settled in his chest. He hadn't made love to her like she deserved to be made love to, like he wanted to.

"I think you should go."

And now he was being kicked out of her house. But he didn't want to go. He didn't want to walk away just yet.

"We need to talk, Bell." He reached over to touch her shoulder, but she pulled away. He didn't let that discourage him: He inched closer to her, pulling her dress into place, covering up her beautiful, nearly naked body. She let him this time, all the fight seeming to have left her. "We didn't use protection," he said quietly as he wiped the still-flowing tears from her face.

Her eyes sharpened on him. "You don't have to worry, Carter. I'm clean."

"It's not that. It's . . ."

"You're worried about me having your baby? Don't. I'm still on birth control and I know your family would hate it if I sullied your bloodlines with my dirty blood."

"Bell." He rested his forehead against hers, shutting his eyes to her hurt. "I wanted a family with you."

"And I wanted to be happy. Please go. I need you to go."

This time he couldn't deny her request. There was too much hurt between them to settle this in one day. His relationship with Belinda was far from over.

A few minutes later he walked back into his office, passing Molly in the hallway without even acknowledging her smile. He was too preoccupied with Belinda, with the enormity of what they had just done.

He sat at his desk feeling weary. He had to pick Ruby up from school in an hour. He would have to pull himself together. His little girl always knew when something wasn't right in his life, and he didn't want her to see it today. He didn't want her to know how fucked up he was.

"What the hell happened to you?" he heard Steven say, but he didn't bother to turn his head.

Belinda had happened to him.

Steven walked closer. He could feel his friend's eyes on his face. "If I didn't know any better, I would say that somebody beat the hell out of you. I know you got in your fair share of scrapes when we were in college but I thought you grew out of that shit. You're thirty-five, man. You don't have to prove yourself anymore."

He looked up at Steven then, remembering their shared past. Carter had been a fighter when he was a kid, but he was pissed off and powerless then. Under the weight of his parents' expectations and unable to express himself in any other way, he used his fists to communicate. First on the boys at his boarding school, and then on anybody who got in his way at college. But he wasn't like that anymore.

"Why the hell do you think I got into a fight? Last time I hit anybody I was twenty-two."

"Your clothes are wrinkled and your cheek is bruised."

He reached up to touch his face, gingerly feeling the place where Belinda's hand had landed.

"Belinda," he mumbled.

"Belinda did that?"

"Yeah."

Steven blinked at him. "You're telling me Belinda, the woman you secretly married and didn't bother to tell me about until two years after it happened, hit you?"

He nodded once. He hadn't told Steven about Belinda until long after she'd left. He had planned to. He had planned to introduce his friend to her when they came to Durant to visit her parents, but that trip never happened and he couldn't bring himself to tell his friend that he had failed at another marriage so soon after Bethany. So he kept Belinda a secret from Steven until his old friend told him about his own broken engagement.

"She hit you hard enough to leave a mark."

"I might have deserved it."

"You probably did, man." He came closer, studying him and shaking his head. "You never were very smooth with women. You should have paid closer attention to how I worked when we went out all those years ago."

"Oh, yes," he said drily. "How could I not have learned from the master of the shitty pickup line? Gems like, 'Are you a parking ticket? Because you've got fine written all over you.' And my favorite: 'If beauty were time, you would be eternity.' A lot of good those did you. You're still single."

"By choice and I'll have you know I do okay, but you would know that if you ever hung out with me."

Steven was right—he always did okay with women. He looked like a young Harry Belafonte. He was tall, good-looking, successful. It always surprised Carter that his friend had never settled down.

"Hey, I'm working with you now. We hang out every day."

"No we don't. We need to hang out at night with women and have drinks, and not talk about work or your kid."

"I thought you liked my kid."

"I do, cutest damn kid on the planet, but she's all you talk about or think about."

"No, she's not," he said, not even believing himself.

"Yeah, that's right. You think about Belinda now, too."

"Why didn't you tell me she was back in town?"

Steven shrugged. "It never came up and I thought you already knew she lived here. Besides we haven't talked much since Ruby came around. The last thing I wanted to do is talk about your ex-wife."

"She's not my ex. She's my current."

"What?" He shook his head. "Shit, man. Do you mean you're still married? Why haven't you divorced her yet?"

"I don't know," he said truthfully. She could have been gone from his life long ago, but he could never bring himself to end things.

"You slept with her today, didn't you?"

"Yeah, I did."

"She's beautiful"—Steven patted him on the shoulder—"and her ass is amazing. I understand why you slept with her. Hell, I applaud you for actually getting a woman that hot to sleep with you, but I never understood why you married her. She . . . She doesn't fit with you."

"What do you mean by that?"

"Belinda grew up here. She went to school with my sister. Her dad may have been a pro ballplayer and her mother a model, but they are decent folks with humble beginnings. They raised Belinda to be humble to work hard for what she's got."

"And you're saying my parents raised me to be a rich asshole?"

"Well . . . kind of. You aren't, but if they'd had their way you wouldn't be the man you are now. You would have still been married to Bethany, living in San Francisco, and working for your father. We would have never been friends." He shook his head as if trying to make sense of it all. "I've been to your parents' house, I visited you in San Francisco, and I know I couldn't hack it in your world. I knew this black kid from Durant, New York, with a bus driver father and a scholarship was never going to be good enough."

The hairs on the back of his neck stood up. "Were my parents unkind to you?"

"Not openly. But I knew if they had their choice they wouldn't have chosen me to be your best friend." He shook his head again. "Never mind. I didn't mean to get into this."

"No. I want to know. Belinda said they were nasty to her. I never knew. I guess I just didn't pay enough attention."

"I don't want to speak poorly about your parents, but I can believe they treated her like shit. She's the last girl they would have ever picked for you, especially after Bethany."

"Is that why you never came to visit me in San Francisco? Because of my parents?"

"It wasn't just your parents. It was you, too. You were different there. You were uptight and unhappy and I didn't want that shit rubbing off on me. I'm much better looking when I'm happy and relaxed."

"Thanks. Your support overwhelms me."

Steven grinned at him briefly. "I don't know what went down between you and Belinda exactly, but I'm on your side. Just think about what it was like for her to live in your world. Think about what it must've felt like for her to come face-to-face with a kid you had with another woman."

"I— Are you her lawyer or something?"

"No. But I can tell that you still got something for her. It's not like with Bethany. There's a reason you never divorced her."

"And that reason is that I'm stupid and was too preoccupied with my kid and my job to get it done."

Steven shrugged and began to walk away. "Keep telling yourself that but you should know that she's been single since she's been back," he said over his shoulder. "And you have been single since she left you. If you don't get her soon, some other man will, and instead of you getting to spend some more quality time with that amazing ass some other man will. Just saying."

He left then, and Carter sat there unable to form coherent thoughts for a moment. Get Belinda back? He wasn't sure that was possible. There was too much hurt between them.

CHAPTER 7

All I ever wanted . . .

Belinda sat on the couch in a daze. She couldn't make herself move. Her body wouldn't let her. She could still feel him. His mouth on hers. His body between her legs. His hands all over her. She should have stopped him. She should have kicked him out. She should have never let him in. But she didn't do any of that.

Her phone rang and she blindly reached over to her side table. "Hello?" She felt shaky. Her voice didn't sound like her own.

"Belinda?" It was Ellis. "Are you . . . I'm coming over right now. Don't go anywhere."

Ellis hung up and Belinda finally dragged herself off the couch and into her bathroom. She had to at least wash Carter off her before she faced her friend. But she was afraid there wasn't enough water in the world.

Ellis didn't even bother to knock before she came into her house ten minutes later. She had a key to use for emergencies, and for her this must have been one. "Belinda?" she called, but Belinda didn't have the energy to answer. She sat on the closed toilet seat, trying not to think about Carter but failing miserably.

It was Cherri who opened the door. Her eyes filled with tears when she saw her. "What happened?"

Ellis pushed past Cherri and knelt before Belinda. "You've been crying. Are you hurt?" Ellis asked calmly, but there was no denying the worry in her eyes.

She shook her head. "I had sex with him." She didn't mean to worry her friends, but she was shocked at her stupidity.

"Come on, Belinda. Let's get out of here and talk." She turned to Cherri. "I think we are going to need some reinforcements."

"I'll order pizza with the works. And double fudge brownies. Does that sound good?"

"That sounds perfect." Ellis tried to lead her to her couch but Belinda wouldn't let her. She couldn't sit there. Not where she'd had sex with him. Not so soon. Maybe not ever.

"Dining room, please."

"Oh. Oh! Mikey and I had sex for the first time on my couch, too. I couldn't look at it for weeks without blushing. Even now I get a little excited when we sit on it sometimes."

"Oh, Ellis! Gross."

"What?" Cherri appeared behind them, her phone still in her hand.

"Nothing. Ellis is just the queen of TMI."

"I may be the queen of TMI. But you're the queen of no information at all. I think it's past time that you spilled your guts to us."

She eased herself into a chair. Ellis and Cherri took seats on either side of her. It was past time she told them her story. She knew that. She just didn't know how to explain to them something she couldn't wrap her head around herself. "Carter came over. We got in an argument. I hit him. He kissed me and then we had sex on my couch."

"You actually hit him?" Cherri's eyes bulged a little.

"Bastard probably had it coming," Ellis huffed. "Start from the beginning, Belinda. How do you know this guy?"

"He came to my store looking for a gift for his mother and he asked me out. At first I didn't want to go out with him. Carter is . . ." She shook her head. "He's different from every other guy I have dated."

"He's gorgeous," Cherri said. "He reminds me of Cary Grant."

Ellis spun to face Cherri. "You've seen him?"

"Yeah, I was with Belinda when she bumped into him at the park."

"And you didn't tell me?"

"It wasn't my place to tell you."

Ellis made a little miffed sound before she turned back to Belinda. "Go on."

"He's a Lancaster," she said as if that explained everything. "His grandfather was a senator. And he's from old money. He's serious and super focused and really quiet and we had nothing in common, but there was something about him. I felt like there was a whole other man on the inside that was trying to get out. So I went out with him. He took me to this little hole-in-the-wall Mexican restaurant where we drank three-dollar margaritas and shared nachos."

"He sounds cheap," Ellis said, rolling her eyes.

Belinda shrugged. "Maybe he was but I was glad we went there. I would have felt out of place if he had taken me somewhere fancy. He made me nervous enough as it was, and I babbled on like an idiot that night. I talked for two hours straight and I was sure when he dropped me off that night I was never going to see him again. I wasn't sure why he'd asked me out in the first place."

"Because you're beautiful and sexy," Ellis said.

"Because you're smart and funny and you've got an ass that no man can keep his eyes off," Cherri added.

"He told me he liked me that night. He, who barely said two words all night, told me that if he didn't see me again he would regret it for the rest of his life."

"That sounds so sweet," Cherri gushed.

"It sounds like a line," Ellis said.

"It was sweet," she admitted. "And I reached up and kissed him and before I knew it I was inviting him to stay. I couldn't get rid of him after that. I didn't want to. I had this quiet, beautiful man who wanted to be with me all the time. I thought it was just for the sex, which was amazing, but a month into seeing each other he was watching me get dressed and he asked me to marry him."

"Had you just had sex?" Ellis asked. "Men always do crazy things after good sex. How do you think I get my husband to take me to the garment district?"

"No, that's the thing. We hadn't had sex that day. I was getting ready to meet his parents for the first time when he looked up at me and said, 'I'm glad you're meeting my parents today. I want them to meet the woman I'm going to marry.' I looked at him for a second and before I even got the chance to think, he asked me to marry him. I said yes and I knew as soon I did that it was a mistake. But I loved him, or I thought I did. And instead of meeting his parents for lunch we went to the courthouse."

"Oh, Belinda." Ellis reached across the table and squeezed her hand. "It took you three years to decide your college major. Four months to pick out a car. Two years to pick out this place. You never move so quickly."

"I know. I should have said no, but I thought I might never find a man who made me as happy as he did."

"What happened?" Cherri asked.

"A lot of things. His mother hated me on sight, told me that I wasn't good enough for her son, that the only thing I saw in him was dollar signs. She and her husband offered me half a million dollars to leave him."

Ellis shut her eyes. "I hope you let her have it. I hope you verbally tore her a new one."

"I didn't. I wanted to make things work. I didn't want to be the reason that Carter and his mother didn't get along. I simply told her she was wrong and that I had everything I ever wanted from Carter."

"What did Carter say when you told him?" Cherri asked.

"I never told him. Not even when she sent a check to my job. I mailed it back to her, which only seemed to make her hate me more. At first I didn't understand why Carter married me. It wasn't for love. He never once said he loved me. I think he did it to get back at his parents. Things were never easy between them, and I represented everything they hated. He's a little bit of a rebel in his own way. He didn't go into the family business. He's got tattoos. He almost doesn't fit with the life he was born into."

"He sounds like a regular badass," Ellis said drily. Belinda shot her a look. "I'm sorry. Go on."

"Suddenly I found myself thrust into Carter's world. I had to go to charity events with him and be his date for work functions and on Sundays we ate dinner with his family and the whole time I would hear whispers about me. I somehow became the tart who tricked Carter Lancaster into marrying her. People treated me like I was dirt but I stuck with him. I would have stuck with him forever because I wanted to prove them wrong, but then his ex showed up at our door one day. His ex-wife, a person I never knew existed, and she was holding a baby that looked exactly like my husband. I left him that day and I hadn't seen or heard from Carter since. But then he showed up here."

"What do you think he wants?" Cherri asked.

"He moved here. His best friend is Steven Oliver. They have their own architecture design firm downtown."

"I think he wants you back," Cherri said. "Why else would he move here?"

"I don't think he does. If he did, he wouldn't have waited four years to come after me."

"I want to believe that," Ellis said. "Trust me, I want to grab a knife, go to his house, and slice off his balls. But something is not meshing. What man picks up his life and moves to the hometown of a woman he has no feelings for?"

Carter opened his eyes when he felt a forty-pound weight settle on his chest. "Good morning, beautiful," he said to his daughter as he kissed her forehead. Her curly hair was a matted tangled mess and she had pillow lines on her cheeks, but the sight of her on his chest made him smile.

"Good morning, Daddy. Did you sleep good?"

"I did," he lied. He hadn't been sleeping much since he slept with Belinda. His nights were spent unwillingly reliving that afternoon. All he could think about was how she felt against him, and how she smelled and the husky sound of her voice when she moaned. But he also remembered her tears and how hurt she was. He never wanted that. He never wanted to be a witness to that kind of pain. He had been so set on divorcing her, on starting his life over without her, but these past few days he had been doubting his decision.

"You look real tired," Ruby said, touching his still-bruised cheek.

"That's because my daughter woke me up at six o'clock on Saturday morning."

"I wanted to talk to you," she said softly.

"About what?" he asked cautiously. He knew she was still curious about Belinda, but she hadn't said a word about her since the day of the trip. Belinda might be an uncomfortable subject for him, but he never wanted his daughter to be afraid to talk to him about anything. "You can talk to me about anything, you know."

"I know. I wanted to talk about what we was gonna do today."

He was behind at work and he knew he should spend the day catching up but the world wouldn't end if he forgot about work for a couple of days. He had been preoccupied this past week. He owed his daughter a day. "What would you like to do?"

"I want to go to the park with the lake and I want you to take me in a rowboat and I want to look at the sky."

"Really?" That was the last thing he'd expected to hear from her, but then again she wasn't the typical five-year-old. "You like looking at the sky?"

"Yeah. I like to see stuff in the clouds."

"Okay, beautiful. We'll go to the park and I'll take you in a rowboat and we'll look at the sky. How about we have some breakfast first? Maybe pancakes."

That earned him a frown. "I don't think you should make pancakes, Daddy."

"Why not?" He grinned at her. "Don't you like them?"

Her eyes went wide. She was an honest kid but a sweet one, and he could see her struggling not to hurt his feelings. "I think we should make cereal instead."

"How about I buy you breakfast? I know a place that makes pancakes that are way better than mine."

"Okay," she said, smiling. "That's a good idea."

CHAPTER 8

Gone fishing . . .

Belinda woke with a start. Her cell phone was ringing and someone was pounding on her front door. For a moment she was in a complete daze, unable to do anything but lie in her bed and process what she was hearing. Her phone went to voice mail but the door . . . Somebody was at her door. She looked at the clock on her nightstand. Just after six AM.

Who the hell could be at my door this damn early?

She made herself get up and shoved her arms into her bathrobe so she could get down the stairs to make the awful pounding stop. Her neighbors were probably ready to skin her alive, and she didn't blame them. Whoever was at her door was going to get it. She wished she had grabbed a baseball bat on the way down, but it was probably for the better. A girl like her couldn't do hard time in jail.

She finally reached the door and flung it open to see her father standing there in full fishing gear.

"Bill Junior!" He barged in and gave her a rough hug, causing her to wonder if he really thought she was a boy instead of a girl.

"Hi, Daddy." Her anger melted away. She couldn't really be mad at her father. Slightly annoyed, yes, but not angry.

"No time for chitchat, Junior. Go get into your gear. We need to get to the lake. The fish are biting today."

"I'm sorry, but did we have a father–daughter date I'm forgetting about?"

"Nope. I wanted to see my kid so here we are. I've been wondering about you since your friend Cucumber called."

She didn't even bother to correct him. "I'm fine, Daddy. I promise."

"Good. Now go get dressed. I got a special pole for you in my truck and a cooler full of beers. It's going to be a good day."

She was supposed to go into the store this afternoon, and she had planned to spend her morning doing absolutely nothing, but she couldn't tell her father no, even if fishing was the last possible thing she wanted to do.

Carter and Ruby arrived at the lake a little after eight that morning. The park surrounding it was mostly empty this brisk morning. Only a few joggers and a couple of guys fishing. Carter envied the joggers. He used to run in the park before he had Ruby, but since she'd come into his life he'd had to stop his daily morning runs in the park. He now had only a treadmill to look forward to each day. Maybe when she got older he could start running outdoors again. Or maybe she could ride her bike alongside him while he jogged. He wouldn't mind having her with him.

"Can I hold one of the paddles?"

He looked down at his daughter, who had blueberry syrup dripped all down her shirt, and handed one over. It was really too big for her to handle, but he let her try anyway—it was only a few feet to the docks and she looked kind of cute when she was so determined.

"You got something, Bill Junior?" he heard a deep booming voice say. He thought the voice sounded familiar; something about the slight Texas twang alerted his memory. He looked at the two fishermen at the dock. One was massive; even from a distance Carter could see the man's muscles bulging beneath his gear. The man he was with was much shorter, and soft looking, chubby almost. Carter guessed it was a father and son out for a day of fishing. They were dressed in identical dark-green waders, khaki vests, and floppy camouflage hats. If he ever had a son, he might like to do that. His grandfather had taken him fishing a few times. His father never had, but then again his father had spent most of his childhood at work.

"Come on, Rube." He took the oar away from her. "I think that boat in the middle has got our name on it."

"Reel it in, Junior," they heard as they got closer. "That's it. You've got a big one on there. Look at that! Your first fish of the year! That'll cook up nicely for dinner tomorrow." The man slapped his son on the back. "Now take it off the hook and toss it in the cooler."

"I don't want to take it off the hook. You do it."

"Oh, don't be such a girl!"

"I am a girl, Daddy!" Carter recognized that voice yet he couldn't stop himself from approaching them just as Belinda was ripping the hat from her head. "See? A girl with boobies and everything."

"Aw, Bill Junior! Don't say stuff like that to me."

"Why not? You seem to forget I'm a daughter and not a son."

"I don't. I just like my girls a little tougher is all."

"Really? You married *Mamá* and she is the girliest girl on the planet."

"Yeah, well, I just married her. I don't like to hang out with her. I like to hang out with you."

"Oh, Dad." She sighed, grabbed the fish, and pulled it off the hook. "This is the grossest thing I have ever done ever, but I'm a tough bitch and I don't want you forgetting that."

Belinda's father ruffled her hair. Now Carter recalled how he knew his voice. Bill Gordon was one of the best damn ballplayers in the history of the game. He remembered watching him as a kid—his grandfather had taken him to a game when they came to New York on a trip. It was funny that he ended up married to his daughter twenty years later.

"That's my girl."

She grinned at him and then proceeded to wipe her hand on his shirt. It was funny that he would meet Belinda here again. In the same park. At the same lake she'd fallen into. As hard as he tried, he couldn't get the image of her out of his head—the one with her clothes plastered to her soaking-wet body. He went to sleep with that image in his mind. He went to sleep remembering the passion that had overtaken them a few days ago. He went to bed missing it, missing the way his few minutes with her had taken the hollowness away.

"Belinda?" Ruby called softly as she walked ahead of him a bit. He didn't stop her, even though he knew it was a bad idea to approach Belinda. He couldn't make himself turn away.

Belinda turned and smiled genuinely at her. "Hey, baby doll!"

"I didn't know you was gonna be here today. My daddy is gonna take me in a boat."

"I'm here with my daddy, too. We're fishing." She looked over to Carter then, her smile quickly dropping from her face. For a moment he thought he saw hurt in her eyes, but she quickly covered it. "Hello, Carter."

"Carter?" Bill Gordon turned at the name. His big hulking frame moved quickly toward Carter, and for a moment Carter was sure a broken nose was in his future. But Belinda grabbed her father's massive hand and held it between her own, stopping him from doing any bodily harm.

"Dad, I want you to meet my friend Ruby." She gave her father a very pointed look and then smiled down at Ruby.

"Ruby?" Bill gently removed his hand from Belinda's and scooped Ruby up. Carter's instincts kicked in, and he stepped forward. He knew his child. He knew how uncomfortable she was around strangers, and Belinda's father was a giant.

But Belinda grabbed his hand this time, saying nothing—just watching her father with Ruby.

"Ruby? They should have called you Diamond, because you are just about the prettiest thing I've ever seen. Look at this girl, Bill Junior! Isn't she beautiful?"

"Gorgeous."

Ruby surprised him by giggling. Immediately Carter felt himself relax. She wasn't scared. Maybe she was growing out of her shyness, or maybe the Gordons just had a welcoming way about them.

"Oh, look at that. She's missing teeth! That's the damn cutest thing I've ever seen. I guess I should be introducing myself. I'm Mr. Gordon, Ruby. I'm glad to meet you."

"It's nice to meet you, Mr. Gordon. Can you show me how to fish?"

His face lit up. "You want to learn? Of course I'll teach you, but you have to touch worms. Are you ready for that?"

She nodded.

"Good. But we have to get off this dock and go where the water is a little more shallow so I can show you how to cast. I don't want you falling in so soon. Can you swim, girl?"

"Not very good. Daddy always has to go in with me."

"Well, you'll learn this summer." He set her on the ground and handed her the bag they kept the bait in. "We've just got to head down that way a little." He pointed to the shore to their left. "Are you ready?"

"Maybe we should check with her father first, Dad," Belinda stated.

Bill gave Carter a hard look. "Mr. Lancaster doesn't have any objections. I think it's best for all of us if me and Ruby go fish over there for a few minutes."

"That's fine with me, sir."

"Good. Come on, Ruby Red. We've got fishing to do."

Carter watched his little girl head off with Belinda's father. Normally he wouldn't have let her walk away without him, but this time he did.

"My father loves kids," Belinda said, reading his mind. "You don't have to be worried about her. He raised me and I came out pretty good." She smiled softly at him, and awareness of her trickled through his body. It was then he realized that their hands were linked. How long had it been since he held hands with anybody except Ruby?

She must have realized it, too. She pulled away from him and stared off at her father in the distance.

"She's shy," he told her. "She doesn't speak to anybody. I worry about her because I see her struggle to talk—but she talked to you. She went off with your father. This is very big for her."

"We're not bad people, Carter. Despite what you think of me, I would never do anything to hurt her."

"You only like to hurt me."

She looked up at him then, her mouth open. But no words came out.

"You don't hit like a girl." He pointed to the fading bruise on his cheek. "I take it you learned that skill from your father."

Her eyes flashed with regret. "I'm sorry I hit you. I shouldn't have done it."

"I probably deserved it. Given the way your father was coming at me, I'm guessing I would have had two black eyes if you hadn't stopped him."

"He's fifty-six years old, but he's a big son of a bitch and he would have killed you."

"What did you tell him about us?"

"Nothing. I came home from San Francisco devastated. I didn't need to say a word."

"I think we should talk."

"Do you really want to? I thought you wanted me out of your life as soon as possible."

He did—or at least he thought he did. "We slept together. You can pretend it didn't happen all you want, but I can't. We live in the same town. We are going to run into each other over and over. We need to figure things out."

"You could go back to San Francisco. Then I wouldn't have to worry about bumping into your stupid face every time I left the house."

He almost smiled at her childish name-calling. There were only two women who could ever make him smile. Ruby was one of them, but Belinda was the first. "I'm not moving back. Ruby likes it here. I've never seen her so happy."

"She could have been happy anywhere. Why here, Carter? You know this is my town. You had to know how difficult it would be to live where I am."

"You are not my only tie to this place. My best friend and his family are here. I spent every summer break here during college. I want my child to grow up here." He shook his head. "I never thought you would move back to Durant. I had a private detective track you down. I thought you lived in the city."

"That was four years ago. Why did you have me tracked down?"

He paused for a moment, not sure if he should answer her question. "I wanted to know how you were."

"Bullshit," she snapped. "You could have called me, or come after me. But you didn't care enough to. Just admit it, you were glad when I left. I was never going to fit into your world."

"Damn it, Belinda, I know things were hard for you in San Francisco, but I never wanted you to leave. You never told me my parents were cruel to you. You never gave me the opportunity to fix things. You just left!"

"That's right I left! How could we have fixed the unrepairable? We were strangers. We married too fast. We were going to fail no matter what."

"You don't know that!" He turned away from her, unable to focus his thoughts when his emotions were so out of control. "I don't want to fight with you."

"We never fought! We never talked. That was the problem with us. You never said a word to me."

"I never had the chance. I knew you for four weeks before we got married. We only stayed married for six. How the hell did you expect me to tell you everything?"

"I can't do this now." She shook her head. "I can't be around you. I'll send Ruby back over so you can get on with your day."

"No." He grabbed her arm. "We need to settle this."

"Yeah, but it's not going to happen today." She walked off. He watched her go knowing that letting her go was a mistake.

CHAPTER 9

Coldhearted snake . . .

Grilled cheese was on the menu for tonight's dinner. It was all Carter could manage, and he barely got that on the table. He had burned his sandwich to a blackened crisp he had been so distracted, but he made damn sure Ruby's sandwich came out okay. He wanted everything to be okay when it came to his daughter.

He felt guilty again as he sat across the table and watched her eat the orange-colored processed cheese food and white bread. It wasn't good for her. He knew that, but he was a hopeless failure when it came to cooking. He never had to do it before. Her nanny had prepared all of Ruby's meals before the move, but now she was gone and he found himself barely treading water. He thought about hiring somebody to do the cooking and cleaning. Somebody to take a couple of things off his overloaded plate.

He didn't want to. He shouldn't have to. Millions of

single parents did it on their own. They didn't even have the option of hiring somebody. He should be able to handle one well-behaved five-year-old. He made this move as a way of showing her that he wanted to be the one to take care of her. But sometimes he wondered if that was a good thing for her. If feeding her crap and keeping her cooped up in his office with him after school was going to hurt her in the long run.

"Are you happy, Rube?"

She looked up at him and nodded before taking another bite of her sandwich. "I had fun this weekend."

"I did, too." He paused, not sure how he should phrase his next question.

"Do you have a headache, Daddy?" She frowned up at him.

"No, baby. I was just thinking."

"Oh. I think, too. Thinking very hard makes my head hurt."

"Mine, too." He nodded. "When you think, do you ever think about having a mommy?"

She looked pensive for a moment. Then she looked up at him, as if she was unsure what to say. "My mommy's in heaven. I can't see her no more."

"I know, but do you think about having a new mommy?"

"Like your wife?" she asked cautiously. "She could be my mommy."

"No." He shut his eyes for a brief moment. Kicking himself for not expecting that response. "Not Belinda. She's not going to be my wife anymore. I was thinking I might like to have a new wife one day, and that lady would be your new mommy."

"No, thanks." She went back to chewing her sandwich. "Can I have ice cream for dessert?"

"Yes, but you have to take a bath first."

"Okay." She hopped off her chair and threw the

remaining corner of her grilled cheese in the garbage. "You turn on the water and I'll go get ready."

He watched her trot off. He ought to start dating. Maybe a new woman would take his mind off Belinda. Maybe if he became intimate with another woman he would stop lusting after the one who'd walked out of his life so long ago. He shook his head. He knew that wasn't going to happen. In four years nobody had caused him to take a second look, nobody had piqued his interest. No other woman could make him feel as out of control as Belinda. He wondered what it was about her that kept him from moving on.

The phone rang, forcing him out of his thoughts.

"Lancaster residence."

"Hello, dear. It's your mother. I was just calling to see how you were faring in Nowhere, New York."

Carter stiffened at the sound of her voice. He had been trying to get in touch with her for days. "I've been trying to call you and Father for days. Haven't you gotten my messages?"

"I was away in Catalina for a few days and I left my cell phone at home. I can't speak for your father. He doesn't keep me abreast of his daily activities anymore, and I'm fairly sure I don't want to know what he's up to anyway."

Carter had been ready to grill his mother about what happened with Belinda, but something about his mother's voice, the change in her tone when she spoke of his father, made him pause.

"Is everything all right between you and Father?" His parents had always been a united front. He had never heard his mother speak poorly of his father before.

"Yes, yes. Everything is how it always has been. Now, how are you settling in that little town of yours? DuPont is it?"

"It's Durant, Mother, and you know I like it here. I've always liked it here."

"I know. It was like hell trying to get you to come along on breaks. I at least thought you would be like the other kids your age and want to go skiing in the Alps or partying in the French Riviera, but instead you chose to spend your holidays with somebody else's family in a town that nobody has even heard of."

"Does it hurt to be such a snob all the time?"

"I'm not a snob," she sniffed. "I just have exceedingly good taste."

He could picture his mother sitting in her professionally designed dressing room. Her white hair cut into a sleek bob, her thin body draped in designer clothing. She wasn't a woman who exuded warmth, but she did know what she wanted and she somehow made the rest of her circle want it, too.

"If you say so, Mother."

"I do. How is my grandchild? I know you wanted to move away from San Francisco but did you have to take her away, too?"

"I did it for her, and she's happier than I have seen her in a very long time."

"I guess that's something. Let me speak to her. She must miss her grandmother terribly."

"Yeah, in a minute. I need to ask you something first."

"What is it?"

"Did you and Father offer Belinda money to leave me?"

Silence.

"You've been divorced for over four years. Are you telling me you have spoken to her recently?"

"We're not divorced and yes, I have spoken to her. She's here in Durant."

"Excuse me?"

"You heard me, Mother. We're still married. She lives

here in Durant and you never answered my question. Did you offer her money to leave me?"

"Your grandfather was a senator. Our bloodlines can be traced back to the *Mayflower*. What did you think was going to happen when you bought home that busty, exotic-looking shopgirl? Did you think that she was just going to be accepted? Did you honestly think we were going to be happy you'd bought home some gold digger a little over a year after you threw away your marriage to the perfect girl? You father and I worked very hard to make you into a man we could be proud of, and by bringing that girl home you threw all of that work into our faces."

"Belinda was important to me. She doesn't come from old money. She doesn't have an overpriced Ivy League education, but she was sweet and loving and she was the woman I chose to spend the rest of my life with. I thought my mother would have supported me. I thought my mother would have seen how happy she made me. I thought my mother would have gotten the chance to know her and see how smart and funny she was before she decided that she wasn't good enough."

"You may not have seen it, but I know her type. Your type and her type are not supposed to mix."

The hairs on the back of his neck went up. "What the hell is that supposed to mean?"

"It means you're a Lancaster, damn it. And we expect you to act like one. I thought this move across country was just a phase but now I see that you did it just to be with her. I'm not sure what kind of hold she has over you but—"

"She's my wife, and she loved me. That's all you should have cared about."

"I love you, and like it or not I only had your best interests at heart."

"You had your best interests at heart. You didn't give a damn about what I wanted."

He hung up, unable to speak to her for another moment. It was no wonder that Belinda had left him. If she'd stayed, his parents would have tried to destroy her. Why hadn't he noticed that? Why hadn't he seen that Belinda wasn't as happy as he'd thought she was?

A loud clap of thunder shook the small cottage that Belinda was sitting in. She was at the home of Flossie Waters, a local artist who handmade exquisite beaded necklaces. That was the best part of living in Durant. There was never a shortage of creative people, and Flossie's colorful necklaces were just the kind of thing the shoppers of Size Me Up would like.

"Look at that sky. The good Lord is about to shake something up out there, isn't he?" Flossie said in awe.

Belinda looked out the window at the darkened sky then back to Flossie and smiled. She had met the New Orleans native by chance at the supermarket a few weeks ago when she had admired a bracelet she was wearing. Ever since then Belinda had been trying to get Flossie to agree to sell her pieces at Size Me Up. "I didn't even know it was going to rain today," she said as a purple streak of lightning illuminated the room.

"That's the way spring is. Sometimes it rains for no good reason."

"I guess so." Belinda smiled at her. "So what am I going to have to do to get you to agree to let our store carry your jewelry?"

"I make these things because I like them. Not to make any money. I don't want it to feel like work."

"But you wouldn't even have to make any more. You have dozens of pieces already made. All you would have to do is give me a few of them to put out in the store. Your work is so lovely, Flossie. I think the world should see it."

Flossie was silent for a moment. "Can I think about it?"

"Of course." Belinda stood up, her hand extended. But instead of the shake she was expecting, Flossie placed a beautiful coral-colored beaded necklace in her hands.

"This doesn't mean yes, girl. It's just a thank-you for appreciating something that nobody ever has before."

Belinda smiled. "You shouldn't thank me. I've always had damn good taste." Another boom of thunder shook the house again, startling both the women.

"You'd better go on home, young lady. This hill is a muddy bitch in bad weather, and we've been after the town to fix the potholes in this road since last winter. You've got about fifteen minutes before the rain comes."

They said their good-byes and Belinda rushed out to her car, the wind whipping her dress up around her waist. Thankfully nobody was there to see. Flossie's cottage was located on the outskirts of Durant, on top of a very steep hill. Belinda understood why the few residents of the neighborhood had chosen to build there. All of Durant was visible from this spot, and in calm weather it must have been a beautiful view. But right now the only thing Belinda wanted to see was the inside of her store.

Her cell phone rang just as she started her car.

Ellis.

"Hey. I'm just leaving Flossie's house."

"Did she agree to let us sell her stuff?" she asked hopefully.

"Not yet. But she gave me one of her pieces. I'm so excited to show it to you, Elle. You'll finally understand what I've been going on about."

"I don't ever doubt your taste, Belinda. Since you've taken over all the buying for the store, our merchandise has gone from good to freaking fabulous. I've been so busy with the bridal salon lately I haven't even noticed how amazing the store looks. You know how much I appreciate you going into business with me. There would be no store without you. I can't do this without you."

"You can kiss my feet when I get back to the store, Ellis. Why are you sucking up to me now?"

"Because I'm afraid that I might lose you."

"Why?"

She was quiet for a moment. "Because your mother came into the store today. She said that you told her you were thinking about moving to Spain. And then when I called Cherri to ask if she knew anything about it, she said you told her you were thinking of going abroad."

"My mother came to the store to see you?"

"No, she came to see you. She had your father with her. They are worried about you. Since Carter came back we've all been worried about you."

"I'm fine, Ellis," she lied. She wasn't fine. She was far from it. "I can't believe you are all talking about me like I'm some kind of mental patient about to have a breakdown. Nobody questioned my sanity when I dyed my hair blond and got a perm. And you were right there by my side when I decided to give myself a bikini wax and gave myself second-degree burns. But now just because some guy shows up in my life you are all treating me like I'm about to go off the deep end."

"You looked really, really bad with that hair. Don't ever do that again. Like ever."

"Ellis!"

"What?"

"What do you want?"

"Nothing. I'm just saying hi."

"Hi. I'll be back at the store in an hour. We can talk then."

"We can't. I have a doctor's appointment. I won't be back in today. I feel like I'm with you all the time but I never see you. It's been this way for a long time."

She could hear the sadness in Ellis's voice. She could feel it in her own chest. Their friendship had changed so much in the past few years. She missed her friend. She hadn't realized how much until that moment.

"Yeah, I—" A loud clap of thunder startled Belinda. "Listen, Elle, I've got to go before this rain starts. I'll call you tonight after I close the shop."

"Yikes. It looks like it's going to be a bad storm. I'll talk to you later."

They disconnected and the first drops of rain hit Belinda's windshield as she pulled off. Those few drops turned into a harsh downpour; her wipers were useless. Belinda's pace down the hill was slow and painful. She thought about pulling over, about stopping until the rain cleared, but she knew that the road would only get worse.

Her wheels slipped on the unpaved road. The new tires she needed came to the front of her mind, but before she had time to castigate herself for not buying new ones her back left wheel hit something hard. Her car slid, the road too muddy to provide any traction. She came to a stop unharmed but she knew all was not right. Half of her car was in a ditch. Foolishly she pressed on the gas, trying to pull it out, but she knew there was no way she was going to make it out on her own.

"Fuck." She threw open the door and got out of the car, the rain immediately drenching her. She could barely see in the downpour, but it did register that her tire had blown.

She wasn't getting out of there anytime soon.

Carter turned his wipers to their highest speed. He was glad he'd opted for the sturdy SUV when he'd moved to New York instead of the smaller luxury car he had been driving for years in San Francisco. He remembered how much snow Durant got in the winter from his visits at Steven's house in between terms. He was excited for it. Ruby had never played in the snow before. He couldn't wait to bring her sledding for the first time. He couldn't wait to watch her build her first snowman and experience her first Christmas in a place where it really got cold. It was another reason he wouldn't be leaving Durant.

A flash of red caught his eye as he drove that windy road, and even in the harsh rain he knew what it was. He recognized it. He was drawn to it. There wasn't another shade of red like it in the world. He pulled over, barely throwing his car in park before he jumped out.

The cold hard rain pelted him, but he barely noticed the chill. He was too busy thinking about her. "Bell, what happened? Are you hurt?"

She turned slowly to look at him, her clothes and hair plastered to her body. He could barely make out her face, but he knew she was upset. He could feel it, and the need to make it better overwhelmed him.

"Not you," she groaned.

"It's nice to see you, too," he said, actually meaning it. She had been in his thoughts nonstop since their last meeting. Since he'd talked to his mother, since he'd found out that there was more against their marriage than he'd ever realized. "Why are you standing out in this mess?" he shouted at her through the rain and the wind.

"My car!"

He looked over to her old gold-colored Mercedes. It was funny how he hadn't noticed it before, only her. But it was precariously perched on the side of the road. Halfway into the muddy ditch. He knew it was moments from sliding all the way in. And there she was heading back toward the driver's-side door. He grabbed her arm just as her heel slipped on the wet gravel. She struggled for a minute, but he looped his arm around her waist and lifted her off her feet and toward his SUV.

"But my car!" she shouted at him.

"Leave the damn car!"

He mentally shook his head, unable to believe that she was still driving the same car as when they had met. They had talked about getting her a new car just before she left him, but she never seemed too thrilled about the idea. It had belonged to her mother. It was her first car. She was very fond of it then, even now it still seemed she was. It made him wonder if she felt the same way about everything in her life. If she still liked to hold on to things. He wondered, probably foolishly, if she was holding on to him. She could have divorced him by now, but she hadn't, and for some reason that made him feel hopeful.

He opened the rear door on the driver's side and pushed her in, following close behind her as a gush of wind threatened to knock him over. She glared at him. Those unforgettable eyes flashing at him. The temperature in the car went up ten degrees. The windows fogged up. They were totally alone for the first time since they'd last made love. He couldn't help but be aware of her. He could be blindfolded and in a darkened room and he would still know she was there. He felt her in his chest.

For a moment all he could hear was the rain pelting his car and his own beating heart. The sky had somehow grown darker in the few seconds they had been inside. Originally he had thought that it was going to be one of those storms that lasted for a few minutes and then dried up, but he was afraid things were only going to get worse.

She kept staring at him with those hot angry eyes. Maybe he deserved her heat, her anger. But he couldn't help but feel some of his own toward her. He couldn't help to think that she gave up on them too soon.

He reached over into the back of his car and pulled out two towels and a blanket to distract himself momentarily from his thoughts of her. The pink blanket belonged to Ruby. She still fell asleep in the car on longer rides. As for the towels . . . He'd learned never to be without them after she had gotten sick after eating too much cotton candy at the fair. Being a father to Ruby taught him always to be prepared for certain things, but as his eyes traveled to the woman he was still married to he realized he was totally inept at dealing with her. Still, he reached for Belinda, unable to stop himself. He pulled off her soaking-wet blazer. Beneath it she wore a little cream-colored dress. It was so wet and molded to her body he could see her underwear through it. She wore a yellow bra. A sweet sexy yellow bra on her bad-girl body. The urge to yank down her dress and peel her out of it was overwhelming. He wanted a glimpse of her. He needed another taste of her, but he controlled himself. He used all his power to control himself.

"What are you doing?" she asked as his eyes continued to roam her body. Goose bumps broke out all over her chilled skin. He ran his hand down her arm, in an attempt to make them disappear, but he got distracted by how hot her soft, damp skin felt.

"I'm getting you out of this jacket before you get sick."

She made a low sound in her throat. It almost sounded like a moan. "I need to call a tow truck."

"I'll do it for you." First, though, he reached down and freed her feet from the insanely high heels she wore. They were gray with little pointy spikes lining the front. "Are these your stay-the-hell-away-from-me shoes?" Her toes were cold and for a moment he held her foot in his hands, stroking them to warm them.

He made the mistake of looking into her eyes. They were wide. There was still some innocence in Belinda. At first he had been attracted to her because of her outrageous in-your-face sexiness, but he had wanted to make a life with her because there was a sweetness to her. And kindness and thoughtfulness and he had felt like he had finally come home when he was with her.

"I can warm my toes myself." She suddenly jumped away from him as if she had been bitten. It was a good thing, too. The heat in the car had jumped another ten notches. "I've survived the past four years without you just fine, you know."

"I know," he said softly. "You've never needed me. Have you?"

She blinked at him for a moment, seeming a little stunned by his words. He turned away from her in that moment, unable to look at her and have coherent thoughts at the same time. He blindly handed her a towel and pulled his now wet cell phone out of his pocket to call for help.

"It's going to take an hour for a truck to get here," he said when he got off the phone. "Maybe more. They don't want to risk the truck getting stuck on this road in the rain. Let me take you home. The tow company will call when they have the car."

"No. I want to be here when the truck comes." She opened the car door, but a strong gust of wind shut it again.

"You are not getting out of this car."

She looked at him, the towel draped over her head. "Does that tone of voice work on your daughter? Because it sure as hell isn't going to work on me."

"Maybe a good spanking will work." He shrugged out of his wet suit jacket and tossed it in the back of the car. "I'm not sure why you are so hardheaded. The weather is bad. If you aren't going to let me take you home, then you're going to be stuck with me in this car until a truck comes."

"I'd rather be stuck in a car with a big hairy spider than with you."

"You're so damn testy today." Unable to help himself he reached for her arm and tugged her across the backseat until her soft body was neatly tucked into his. She tensed for a moment at the contact, but then she relaxed. He didn't know if she was feeling what he was, but a memory flashed across his mind. Of them sitting like this on his couch. They weren't speaking then. They needed no words, or at least he didn't. Back then, having her close to him always seemed to calm him.

"I'm having a bad day," she said after a moment.

"Want to tell me about it?"

"No. You're ninety-seven percent of the reason I'm having a bad day."

For some reason her nasty little remark caused him to chuckle. "You were so sweet to me when we first got married. What happened?"

"See, that proves how much you didn't know me. I was always this bitchy." She nestled her head into the crook of his shoulder. Her hand rested gently on his stomach.

He pressed his lips to the bridge of her nose as his thumb swiped down her check. "Why are you crying, pretty girl?"

"I'm not crying. It's the rain."

"Rain isn't hot, but tears are."

She looked up at him, her green eyes shining with tears, her hair slicked back away from her face. She was so damn stunning. *Beautiful* wasn't a strong enough word to cut it. "Why are you here?"

"I had a meeting. A client was thinking about building a house up here, but after seeing how shitty this road gets in the rain I think I'm going to talk her out of it."

"No. Carter. Why are you here in Durant?"

"I told you why. I want Ruby to grow up here."

She shook her head. "There has to be another reason. I can't believe that."

Looking at her he almost didn't believe it himself. But it was true. At least he thought it was true. He wanted Ruby to grow up here. "I never kept Bethany from you," he said, surprising himself. "I told you that I had been in a long-term relationship for years."

"But you didn't tell me that you had a wife before me."

"No. I am guilty of that. But I never thought of Bethany as my wife. We were only married for three days before I got it annulled. I didn't love her."

She rested her head on his chest again, and he was glad for that. He didn't have to see the hurt in her eyes anymore. "Tell me the whole story."

"We were childhood friends," he started slowly. "Our parents vacationed together. We spent holidays together. We had dinner once a week at their house. It wasn't until my sophomore year of college that I realized our parents kept throwing us together for a reason. I'm not sure how it happened but we started dating. Bethany was a pretty girl and she was sweet and I liked her so it wasn't a hardship to be her boyfriend. We dated off and on for years. Most of it long distance until one day my father called me into his office and told me it was time I settled down with Bethany."

"So you just did it?"

"No." He thought back to that time in his life and remembered how much he hated himself then. "Not at first. I balked at the idea. My whole entire life they had dictated my every move. They chose my friends and sent me away to boarding school and handpicked my college. I balked when they wanted me major in finance and go into the family business and I was ready to tell my father to shove it then, but he told me that if I didn't marry Bethany, his merger with her father's company wouldn't go through. I had no idea that my father's business was in trouble, but it was. My father told me that they had given me everything; it was time I gave back to them. Two weeks later we were engaged. We dragged out our engagement for two years and then our mothers started planning the wedding and the whole thing got so out of control that neither of us knew how to stop it."

"You didn't want to disappoint them," she said softly.

"No. Neither of us did. When we got married it was the wedding of the decade and I had resigned myself to living the rest of my life with a woman I didn't really love. But three days into our marriage Bethany had the guts to do what I didn't. She told me that she wanted out. She went to Europe for a year while the fallout over what we had done blew over. I had no idea about Ruby until they showed up at our door that day. If I had . . ."

"You would have never consented to the annulment."

"No, but I'm almost glad that it happened the way it did. Bethany made me realize how stupid I was for going along with their plans. I promised myself that I would only be with someone because I wanted to be with her. Not because my parents thought I should be with her."

"I guess you showed them by marrying me," she laughed bitterly. "You had to know they were going to have a huge shit fit when you brought me home."

"I wasn't thinking about them, Belinda. Trust me, when I was with you my parents were the farthest thing from my mind."

"Whatever happened to Bethany? Ruby told me she passed away."

He nodded. "In a car accident. She was taking Ruby to the doctor for her six-month checkup and some asshole in a pickup truck hit them. Bethany died on impact, but Ruby was in the hospital for weeks." A lump formed in his throat. "I almost lost her."

"Is that how she got the scar on her arm?"

He nodded.

"Carter, I'm so sorry."

She pressed herself against him a little harder, holding him a little closer to her. "You want to know why I didn't come after you? I was angry with you and I was angry at Bethany for keeping my daughter away from me and I was overwhelmed at the thought of being responsible for somebody else's life. And just when I started to fall in love with my kid, just when I was getting used to everything that had come my way, the accident happened. And I was a single father with a sick baby. Ruby had to come first in my life. She still has to come first in my life."

Belinda reached up and grabbed his face between her soft hands. She kissed him, and he closed his eyes and let himself be kissed. It wasn't explosive like their prior kisses. It wasn't even heated. It was just a slow soft kiss from a woman he thought he would spend the rest of his life kissing.

"Belinda," he breathed when she broke the kiss. "I don't know how I can feel such conflicting things about you."

She looked up at him with curiosity.

"Half the time I don't want to let you go. The other half I want to throw you off a cliff."

"Ass!" She pinched him hard on his chest and pulled away from him.

He wouldn't let her go. He pulled her closer and dropped a kiss right on her pouty lips. "Kiss me again, Bell."

"No. I don't know what I was thinking. I'm not even attracted to you anymore."

"You're not?" He slid his hand up her dress, settling it on the back of her soft thigh. "You could have fooled me. You sure are good in bed for a woman who isn't attracted to me anymore."

"I was out of my mind in that moment," she said. He took the opportunity to slide his hand a little farther up to her behind. It felt just as good as he had remembered.

"Were you?" He sprinkled gentle kisses around her mouth, dragged his lips across her jaw until he reached that spot on her neck that he liked to bury his nose in.

She went totally slack then. He almost felt like liquid

himself. She was warm and soft and sweet smelling. And he wanted her so bad his teeth hurt.

"I was. I hadn't had sex in four years. You can't blame a girl for wanting to crawl out of her skin."

"What?" He lifted his lips from her skin. "You haven't been with anybody in all that time?"

She looked away from him. An embarrassed flush coming over her skin. "Just you."

He didn't know what to call the feeling that swelled in his chest. Relief. Pride. Happiness.

"Why not?"

"Because in the back of my mind I knew I was still married to you."

She was his. She was still his.

He took her face in his hands and looked into her eyes for a long moment. He wanted to smash his lips into hers and kiss her hard and pump inside her until he forgot his own name, but he didn't. Their last time had been like that—too fast, too frenzied, too much, too soon. He regretted that. She was the kind of woman a man needed to take his time with.

He moved closer to her, letting her know what was about to come, giving her the chance to pull away, but she didn't. She accepted him willingly, like their coming together was an inevitability. Her mouth was welcoming, her lips sweet, her skin soft and still a little damp from the rain. It was a slow kiss, because all he had thought about at night was her and this, and he'd promised himself that when he got close to her again that he would do this right, that he would show her how good it could be.

She moaned into his mouth, causing him to grow so hard he wanted to burst from his pants, but he ignored the urge to free himself and focused on her. His fingers slid up to the top of her pretty underwear, the tips slipping inside, slowly tugging them down. She broke their kiss, frowning at him in curiosity, but her lips were pink and kiss-swollen and her hair was tousled and she was so damn beautiful that it would kill him if she asked him to stop.

"Let me touch you. I need to touch you. Please, Bell."

She looked unsure for a flash of a moment, but then she nodded, lifting herself up so he could slide the little piece of fabric off her body. He was rewarded with skin, the smooth rounded flesh that fit in his hand so nicely.

"You're so beautiful." He lay her down on the seat, her dress bunching up to her waist as he did. He had loved seeing her completely naked, he'd loved seeing all of her skin, but there was something about seeing her half clothed that was erotic to him, too: covered up but naked. He couldn't decide if he wanted to look at her or touch.

"Come here," she whispered, reaching for him, sliding her fingers into his hair.

Touch won out.

He kissed her and her legs parted for him but he didn't enter her. Instead he placed his hands between her thighs, stroking her. She was more than ready for him, but when he touched her, she whimpered, the sound so arousing it nearly caused him to explode. He touched her again, a longer stroke, a little firmer this time. She moved against his hand, clearly not wanting to be teased anymore. He sank his fingers into her, rubbing her as he stroked inside her, showing her with his fingers what his body was planning to do to her next. Their kisses turned hard and hot and hurried. Frantic, almost, and soon she was shuddering against him. He lifted his lips from her mouth so he could look down at her. He always loved to look at her after they had finished making love. She was so unguarded then. He could see every feeling in her face. But he didn't get to process her emotions for too long because she reached for him, rubbing him through his pants with one hand as she undid his belt with the other.

"Damn it, Bell," he hissed as she slid a hand into his boxers, the feeling almost too good. "I need to be inside you."

She nodded and then said the sexiest words he had ever heard: "What are you waiting for? I'm right here."

She unzipped his pants, tugging them down as he brought himself closer to her. Her legs hooked around him, and he fully pressed against her. She was ready for him and the anticipation of that wet heat around him almost caused him to lose it.

"Now, Carter."

He obeyed her order . . . and just as he began the slow slide into her, honking penetrated his ears, bright lights shone into his car, and for a moment he couldn't process what was going on.

"Shit. The tow truck is here," Belinda said, pushing him away. "Shit!" She looked at him, her face pained. "What the hell are we doing? What the hell am I doing?"

"It's okay, Bell. The windows are fogged up. They can't see what we were doing."

"It's not that." A horrified looked crossed her face. "You came here to divorce me. Divorce me! We can't keep doing this. It's screwing with my head. I need to move on with my life and you need to move on with yours. We need to be done."

"You think I expected this, to still be so attracted to you?"

She shook her head. "Send me the papers, Carter. Please. Just send them."

And with that Belinda slipped on her shoes, straightened her clothes, and walked away from him without another word.

CHAPTER 10

Ain't nothing but a hound dog . . .

"Daddy?" Ruby called to him from her tiny desk in the corner of his office.

"Yes, babe?" He looked up to find her head down, most of her attention absorbed in the drawing she was in the middle of.

"Can you buy me an iPhone?"

"What?" He shook his head. He thought he knew his daughter, but she never ceased to surprise him. "What do you need with an iPhone?"

"I could play games on it. You don't let me play on your phone anymore. But if I had my own phone then I wouldn't want to play with yours."

He blinked at her for a moment. She made a very sound argument. "I don't let you play with mine because the last time I did you sent fifteen picture messages to my old boss."

She looked up at him, kind of exasperated, like she

didn't know what the hell she was going to do with him. "I don't know why you got so mad. I didn't mean to. I was trying to send the pictures to Grandma. She said you should get me my own phone, and that way we could talk to each other anytime we wanted. She said that she's sad I moved so far away."

Carter inhaled. He wasn't speaking to his mother, still bothered by the fact that she'd gone out of her way to make Belinda feel like she didn't belong, but he couldn't let that interfere with her relationship with Ruby. In her own odd way, Bernadette Lancaster loved her granddaughter. He wasn't surprised his mother would suggest he buy a five-year-old an expensive cell phone. "I'm sorry, Ruby. I know you miss your grandma, but I'm not buying you an iPhone."

"Okay." She went back to her drawing. "Daddy?"

"Yeah, Rube?"

"Can you get a TV for your office then?"

He looked up from the plans he was drawing and gazed at her, her little face so serious. She was bored. She never complained about being there for two hours almost every afternoon, but he should have known that construction paper and coloring books weren't enough to keep any child occupied for so long. Sometimes he thought it might be better for her to go to the after-school program and be with the other kids. He sent her when he had meetings he couldn't reschedule, but most days he was selfish and kept her with him. It was one of those parenting moments when he wasn't sure if he was doing the right thing or not.

He had so many of those lately.

"How about we go to the store this weekend and see about getting you a tablet? You could read books and watch movies and play games on it. It will be like your own little computer."

"Can I go on the Internet?"

"No."

She shrugged. "Okay."

She went back to her drawing and he went back to his until he heard, "Knock, knock."

Molly poked her head in his door and smiled at him. She had been stopping by his office more and more the past couple of weeks. They even had lunch together in the break room a couple of times, but he still hadn't agreed to dinner. He liked Molly but he didn't want to date her.

"I was heading out to class and just wanted to drop in and say good night before I did."

"Good night, Molly. Have a good weekend."

"You, too." He thought she was about to leave but she stepped farther inside his office. "You got any big plans this weekend?"

"Big plans?" He shook his head. "Just plans. I think I'm going to take Ruby to the electronics store and maybe to the movies."

He glanced at his daughter, who was staring at him, and winked. She gave him a soft smile before she went back to coloring.

"Oh, that sounds nice. And hello, Ruby. I nearly didn't see you there."

"That's because you were too busy gawking at my daddy."

"Ruby!" he scolded, but he was more than a little surprised that she'd said anything to Molly at all. She was coming out of her shell. He would have been inordinately proud if she hadn't been so rude.

"Well, don't you have a mouth on you, little Miss Ruby," Belinda said, walking in. "I'll have to admit I'm a little relieved to hear it. You were far too polite and well behaved for a normal child. I was starting to think you were a robot." She smiled at Ruby, her green eyes sparkling.

He was surprised to see her in his office. He didn't think he would see her so soon after their afternoon in the back of his car. She'd asked him to send the divorce papers but he hadn't. He couldn't bring himself to. Not after what had almost happened between them.

"How are you, beautiful girl?"

"Good." Ruby grinned widely at Belinda, seeming happy to see her.

"You should apologize, though. It's okay to be a little sassy sometimes, but it's not okay to be unkind."

Ruby nodded, looking contrite. "I'm sorry, Molly."

"That's okay," Molly mumbled as she focused on Belinda. The two women looked at each other, checking each other out in the way only two women could.

"I'm, Molly. I work here. I'm Steven's intern."

"Hi, Molly. I'm Belinda," she said, giving no explanation as to who she was. "Nice to meet you."

Molly glanced at Carter and then back at Belinda as if trying to figure out their relationship. He might be reading too much into it, but it seemed that Molly was a little more interested in who Belinda was than she should be.

"It was nice meeting you, too. I need to get going. Good-bye, Carter. Let me know if you want to do something this weekend."

Belinda crossed the room, stopping at his desk. She gave a quick look at the door before she bent to speak into his ear. "I think Miss Perky Blond Intern has the hots for you."

He grinned at her, trying to ignore the feeling of her warm breath on his skin. She was arousing without even trying. "Are you jealous?"

She searched his face for a moment, all traces of humor melting away. "Damn. I'd almost forgotten how beautiful your smile is."

She was the beautiful one. He took a moment to study her but he didn't need to because he'd barely taken his eyes off her since she walked into his office.

She was in bombshell mode again in a body-hugging red dress and little denim jacket. She was always in bombshell mode, but today he had an especially hard time pulling his eyes off her. She was too much for him to take in. Lush breasts, tiny waist, an overabundance of curves. She never hid it. She was never afraid to show herself off to the world. Belinda wasn't a woman who hid herself in corners. She wasn't quiet. She wasn't understated. She was the opposite of everything he had ever known or wanted. He had spent so many years being angry that he had forgotten those little things that had made it impossible for him to live without her.

"I'm sorry if I overstepped my bounds with Ruby a few minutes ago," she said awkwardly, and he realized he had been staring at her just a little too long. "I had no right to ask her to apologize. She's your child."

"No. You should have." He managed to pull his eyes away from Belinda long enough to give his daughter a pointed look. "She was rude."

Belinda gave Ruby a small smile before she turned back to Carter and lowered her voice. "She's just a little territorial over her daddy. Or maybe she has exceedingly good taste. If she doesn't like the woman you're dating, maybe you shouldn't date her."

"She likes you. What does that tell you?"

"Of course she likes me." She raised her chin haughtily. "I'm not trying to get in your pants."

"Really?" He felt like teasing her a little. He dropped his voice, wrapped his arm around her waist, and pulled her close so that his lips touched the curve of her ear. "Should I remind of you of what happened in my car a few days ago?"

Her eyes shot up to his and she shook her head. "You started it!" She tried to pull away from him, an embarrassed flush creeping up her face.

"I can finish it, too. Just say the word."

"No," she hissed. "I came here to divorce you. Do you have the papers here?"

He looked at his desk drawer where he kept the papers, but he made no move to retrieve them. It would make sense for him just to pull them out, for her to sign and go on her way, but . . .

This whole thing seemed wrong.

"How about we try some idle chitchat for a couple minutes first?" He took her small hand between his and just held it for a moment before he turned it over and stroked his thumbs over her palm.

"Stop." Her eyes went wide.

He ignored her request and continued stroking. His fingers brushed against her pulse. Her heart was racing. "What's the matter, Bell?"

"Your kid is here," she said, her voice just above a whisper as she pulled her hand from his. "You're supposed to be divorcing me. What the hell are you trying to do?"

He knew Ruby was here. He could feel her eyes on them. It was because of her he was going to stay sane and push back those thousands of feelings that ran through his chest when Belinda was around. It was because of Ruby he was going to try to ignore the urge he had to kiss her.

"Tell me about your store. You own it with your best friend. Ellis, right? How is she?"

"You remember?"

"How could I forget? You two went to prom together, and she made your dress."

She smiled at him, the thick suffocating tension between them melted. "And I wondered if you were listening to what I said on our dates or just staring at my boobs."

"A little of both," he admitted. "Speaking of dates, are you seeing anybody right now?"

She was quiet for a moment. "Why are you asking? You already know I was faithful."

Faithful. She said the word like they were still a couple. Like they were still really married. She wasn't his wife anymore. How could she be? Six weeks together and four years apart did not make a marriage. They were strangers now. Familiar, connected strangers. "You kind of wish when your wife leaves you that she has been lonely and miserable without you."

"I can never tell when you're joking." She shook her head.

"Just because you haven't been with anybody else doesn't mean that you aren't seeing anybody. We were *together*," he said seriously. "I need to know that there isn't someone else."

"There's nobody."

"Ah." Relief coursed through him. "So I can sleep soundly tonight."

They were quiet for a moment, awkwardness invading the air as they stared at each other.

"Do you have the papers here?" she asked, breaking the silence.

"No." He lied to her for the first time. "I have them at home."

She exhaled, seeming relieved. "Mail them to me. Send them to the store." She looked over at Ruby. "I didn't want to do this in front of her anyway. It seems wrong."

"It does." He rubbed his now throbbing head before he turned to his daughter. Her little face was scrunched in concentration as she tried to figure out what was going on with the adults in her world. He stood up, causing

Belinda to take a step back. "Ruby, Belinda's here to take you out."

Ruby's eyes lit up. "You are?"

"I-I am?" She gazed at Carter with curiosity, but then she turned to Ruby, who looked so damn hopeful that she crumbled. "I wanted you to take you guys to check out the new frozen yogurt place in town."

"Frozen yogurt is a poor substitute for ice cream," Ruby said, leaving her desk.

Carter was about to scold his daughter for repeating another thing she had clearly heard from an adult, but Belinda put her hand up to stop him.

"Is it now?" She raised a brow.

"Yes, Grandma says that frozen yogurt is what fat people eat when they are trying to convince themselves they are being healthy."

"Well, baby doll, I could take you for ice cream but the Fro Yo Fortress has thirty-seven different yummy toppings. You could put gummy bears and cheesecake and M&M's on your yogurt if you wanted to. If I take you for ice cream, all you get is sprinkles."

"I'll go for frozen yogurt. I've never had it before. I don't even know what Grandma is talking about."

"Good choice. Wait for us by the door. I need to tell your father something." She walked over to him, stood on her tiptoes, and spoke into his ear. Her breath tickled him, her breast pressed against his arm, and for a moment he shut his eyes as her nearness assaulted his senses. "What the hell are you trying to pull here, Lancaster?"

"Nothing. I shouldn't have told you that I wanted you to stay away from her. It was wrong and I'm sorry for doing that. I would like to be your friend, Belinda. If we are going to live in the same town we might as well try to get along."

"Is it possible?"

"I don't know, but it seems worth a shot."

His phone rang and he glanced at the clock, remembering he had scheduled this call. "You two go on without me. I have to take this."

She nodded and gave him one long last look before she walked out the door with Ruby. He'd never thought the day would come when he would see his wife and his daughter together. He wondered how many times he would see it before it all ended.

Belinda glanced at the top of Ruby's messy hair as they left Carter's office. She couldn't believe that this was happening. Somehow something had changed between them. She wasn't sure what. Maybe his explanation was what she needed to move on. She was still hurt by his omission. She still regretted her foolish decision to marry him, but she wasn't angry anymore. She could picture him in that hospital with his very hurt baby. She could imagine the loss he'd felt when Bethany had died and the huge amount of responsibility that settled on his shoulders the moment she did. She could forgive him for not trying to save their marriage. She could finally forgive herself for the same reason.

She hadn't been in the neighborhood when she stopped by. She had been at the store going through the motions, trying to pretend that her every thought wasn't occupied by Carter. She kept thinking back to the other day, when they were stuck together in his car, when they were so close to making love again, and a little piece of her had spent the day missing him. She was obsessing about him. And it had to stop.

There was no need to drag out this divorce. She decided to take charge of her life and go to his office and sign the papers. She was supposed to be figuring out what the hell she was going to do with her life. Not reliving the past with a man she should have never married.

When she showed up at the office she had planned on quickly signing the papers and then leaving to go home and plan her next move. But the Lancasters had thrown a wrench in her plans. Carter suddenly didn't seem so hell-bent on ending their marriage—and then there was Ruby, who looked so serious and kind of cute sitting at a minia-ture wooden desk with a tiny little rolling chair. From that alone Belinda knew that Ruby spent a lot of time in her father's office. It seemed Carter was the type of man who liked to keep his child close, but Belinda wondered if that was the best thing for Ruby. Being cooped up in an office all afternoon seemed kind of boring. But she didn't dare say anything to Carter about it. It was none of her business. Besides, what did she know? She could barely keep a plant alive, much less give advice on how to raise a child.

"So, kid. Who was the lady you weren't very nice to in your dad's office?" Belinda asked, remembering the fit-looking blonde who looked like she wanted to have a side of Carter for dinner.

She seemed like Carter's type. Sweet face. Big blue eyes. Looked like she ate organic food, jogged for fun, and did Pilates on a regular basis. She was the exact op-posite of Belinda.

"Molly," Ruby responded like it was a dirty word.

She laughed. "I take it you don't like her?"

"No. She keeps asking to cook for my daddy."

Ah, so little Miss Ruby was jealous. "You know, your daddy is a very handsome man. Ladies are going to want to cook dinner for him and take him out and even kiss him. It's never going to stop. You might as well get used to it."

"He told me he wants to date." She frowned.

"Oh?"

"I told him I was gonna think about it."

Belinda suppressed a smile. Talking to Ruby was like talking to an adult, only Ruby was a little smarter than most of the adults she knew. "Your daddy never dated in San Francisco?"

She knew she was prying. She knew it was wrong to pump information from a five-year-old, but she was curious about his past four years.

"No. He was at work all the time."

"But not anymore, right? That's why you came to Durant?"

She nodded. "He still works a lot but now he lets me work with him. I draw pictures of houses just like him."

"You shouldn't work so hard. You'll get gray hair."

Ruby shrugged. "I'll get some dye."

Ruby slid her small hand into Belinda's as they approached the sidewalk, causing Belinda to jump.

"What are you doing?"

"Holding your hand." She looked up at her as if it was obvious.

"I know that, but why are you holding my hand?"

"Because grown-ups are supposed to hold kids' hands when they cross the street."

Duh, Belinda.

"I guess you're right." She allowed Ruby to slide her little soft fingers between hers. It was a weird sensation. She had never held hands with a child before. It was something she'd never thought she would do because she wasn't particularly fond of children.

But Ruby was okay. Her hands were clean and she didn't seem like a nose picker. Besides, it was good practice, she told herself as they made it safely across the street. Cherri's baby was going to grow up and she was planning to be a super aunt. Hand-holding and all. She needed to get used to spending time around kids.

They walked into the Fro Yo Fortress, which was actually not very fortress-like at all with its strawberry-printed walls and cotton-candy-colored seats. A plethora of tattooed, pierced, and multicolor-haired college students staffed the registers. Belinda watched as Ruby took it all in.

"Hi, guys!" A green-haired girl walked up to them. "Welcome to the Fortress. We currently have forty-five yummy flavors available. Our newest is tiramisu. My all-time favorite is peaches and cream topped with piecrust and graham cracker crumbs, but you can go wild and when you're finished bring it to the front. We'll weigh and you'll pay."

"All right, baby doll." She looked down at Ruby. "You heard her. Go crazy."

Ruby rested her head on Belinda's thigh. The contact jolted Belinda. "I don't know what to do," she said quietly.

Crap. Belinda felt that stupid tiny little tug in her chest as she looked down at her. "It's okay." She ran her hand over Ruby's messy curls. "We'll do it together."

Ten minutes later Belinda and Ruby snagged a booth in front of the window. She thought Ruby was going to get bubble gum or cotton candy or some kind of kid-friendly flavor but she got exactly what Belinda got. Strawberry yogurt with fresh fruit on top.

"Do you like it? You know you could have gotten candy on it if you wanted to. You didn't have to get fruit."

"I know, but I like it like this. Thank you for buying it for me."

"You're welcome. You know, I've never been out with a kid before. What do you want to talk about?"

"You and Daddy," she said immediately.

"Oh?" She couldn't tell the kid no. It seemed wrong to keep her completely in the dark. She had to be curious. "What do you want to know?"

"Daddy says you aren't going to be his wife much longer."

"No. Not very much longer."

"Why not?"

She blinked at Ruby. How could she explain why she and Carter were getting divorced when she could barely understand it herself?

"So he can date other ladies."

Ruby shook her head. "I think you should stay his wife then."

"Ruby . . ." She laughed uncomfortably.

"Hey, Belinda." Douglas Jackson stopped at their table. He was one of the guys she had dated the past year. They had only been out once. One unforgettable time. Mr. Jackson was the founding member of the I-Like-To-Grope-Boobies-When-I-Go-In-For-A-Kiss club. Belinda had nearly slapped the taste out of his mouth that night.

"Hey, Douglas," she said, turning her attention back to Ruby. She had no wish to converse with the man.

"I haven't seen you for a while. How've you been?"

Apparently he was as bad at reading body language as he was at being a good date.

"I'm fine." She wanted to leave it at that, but her good manners wouldn't allow her to stop there. "And you?"

He grinned at her and leaned over, pressing both of his hands on the table. "I've got a lot of things going on; if you come out with me again I can tell you about them."

Belinda stared up at him. He couldn't honestly think that she would ever, *ever* go out with him again after the last time.

"She can't go out with you," Ruby said. "She's married to my daddy."

They both looked at Ruby. Belinda wondered if it would be too much if she kissed the little girl's feet.

"You're m-married?"

"Yup, and this is my stepdaughter, Ruby."

"Oh." He stood up straight. "Hello, Ruby. Aren't you a cute little chunky thing?"

Belinda's hackles went up. "Don't call her that."

"Call her what?"

"A chunky little thing. What the hell is wrong with you? Nobody meets you for the first time and says, *Hey, Doug. Aren't you a cute little balding thing?* Or *What a great beer belly you got going on there.* Can't you just say it's nice to meet you and not comment on her weight or looks? If she were a boy you wouldn't have done that. If she were a boy you would have said *Hey, champ*, and left it at that. But that's the problem with this world. People say stupid things without thinking of the long-term implications. She's perfect as she is, chunky or not, and I don't need you or anybody else making her doubt that."

"Whoa." He put his hands up in defense. "I knew you were feisty but who knew you would turn into a mama bear? I didn't mean anything by it. Congrats on the marriage."

He walked out and Belinda sat there still feeling her blood boil. Why couldn't she ever control her mouth? It wasn't like Ruby needed defending . . . but she did. Only it wasn't Belinda's place to do so. It was like her brain and her voice were never fully connected.

A little warm body pressed against her, distracting her from her mental berating. Belinda looked down to see Ruby kneeling next to her in the booth.

"What are you doing?" She was horrified as she watched Ruby lift her arms.

"Giving you a hug."

"Ew no. Don't touch me. You've got kid germs and you're all sticky."

Ruby ignored her, wrapping her arms around Belinda's neck. "You just got really mad."

Ruby patted her back, and for some reason Belinda felt comforted.

Comforted by your soon-to-be-ex's five-year-old. You need mental help.

"Yeah, I shouldn't have."

"Why did you?"

"Because when I was a kid people use to call me chubby and chunky and fatty and pudgy and every other name in the book and I didn't like it. I don't want people to do that to you."

Ruby kissed her cheek and patted her back once more. "It's okay, Belinda. Eat your yogurt."

Belinda did eat her yogurt, with Ruby leaning against her side like it was totally normal, like Belinda wasn't a near stranger to her, like she wasn't the woman who was about to divorce her father. It almost felt comfortable.

Which was wrong. There would be no more bonding. No more outings. No more liking the kid. She had a life to get on with. And she was going to start right now.

CHAPTER 11

Just the way you are . . .

"I would kill for this dress," Maggie, one of the salesgirls, said to Belinda as they dressed a mannequin a few days later.

"It is kind of amazing," Belinda agreed. "When I saw it I knew we had to carry it in our store. Never in a million years would I have put pink and tangerine in the same dress, but the way this designer did the color blocking across the waist and bust is exquisite. Normally I try to only carry female plus-sized designers, but this guy knows a woman's body."

"Does he want to be a woman?" Maggie asked with a raised brow.

"No." She smiled. "I was surprised to find that Alexander is one hundred percent straight. His father was a tailor so he learned how to sew, but then he started to make clothes he wanted to see his girlfriends in."

"Did you say Alexander?" Maggie left Belinda and

went behind the counter. "This box came for you yesterday from Alexander Dreyer. Is that the same guy?"

"Yes." Belinda took the box from Maggie. "I wonder
what this is. He already sent me all the stock."

The bell over the door sounded, alerting them that
somebody was entering the shop. It wasn't a customer,
though. Carmina, Cherri, and Cherri's son Joey walked
through the door, both adults holding large coffees in their
hands.

"*Mamá?* Cherri? Were you together?"

"Yes, Pudge," Carmina said as she kissed Belinda's
cheeks. "We had breakfast this morning at Sunny Side
Up. Have you ever had their pancakes? They have many
different kinds, chocolate chip, and blueberry—they even
have French toast pancakes. And they come with eggs
and hash browns. It was so much. You shouldn't go there
very often though, Pudge. The food will sit in your tummy
all day and you will get sleepy. You always get sleepy
after you eat too much." Carmina ran her fingers through
Belinda's hair. "Your hair looks very good today. Have
you tried the conditioning masque I gave you?"

"Not yet," she said distractedly as she glanced from her
mother to Cherri, who looked more innocent than usual.
"Do you two have breakfast together often? Or was this
something you just decided to start doing."

"I don't have a mother to talk to, Belinda. And now
that I have Joey I just wanted to talk to somebody who
has been through this before. You don't mind, do you?"

"No. Of course I don't." She was being paranoid. It
made sense that Cherri would want to speak to an experienced mother about things. But she secretly wondered if her
friends and family were up to something. "Do you know
Maggie, *Mamá*? She's one of our new sales associates."

Maggie smiled. "It's nice to meet you, Mrs. Gordon."

She turned back to Belinda. "Do you want me to put this box in your office?"

"No. I want to open it now. Maybe Alexander sent me a sample. I would love to carry more of his work. I found this great new designer," she explained to Cherri and her mother as she ripped open the box. "What the hell?"

She stared at the wispy pieces of fabric that the box contained.

"What's in the box?" Cherri asked.

"Garters." She pulled out the black lace. "And tiny panties. And . . ." She looked up at them. "A leopard-print bustier. There's a note, too."

"Don't leave us hanging, Pudge!" Carmina clapped her hands. "This is so exciting. What does it say?"

" 'After we met I couldn't get the image of you wearing this out of my head. Please don't take this as a come-on, but as a token of my appreciation for your perfect beauty.' " Belinda snorted and tossed the note back in the box. "This guy is so full of it."

"I think you should try it on," Maggie said surprising her.

"What? No way."

"Oh, come on, Pudge. Let us see what the nice man sent for you. It's nice to be a muse, no?"

"Yeah," Cherri added. "The store just opened. You won't get any customers for at an hour. Try it on and if you really like it, maybe you can send him a very personal thank-you."

"Cherri!"

"Oh, don't be such a prude," Carmina said. "I don't know why Americans are so uptight about these things."

"I'm not uptight! I don't know what has gotten into you all today."

"Just go." Her mother shoved the box toward her and pushed her toward the dressing room.

It had been a long time since she had played dress-up,

Belinda thought as she took her dress off. It had been a long time since she had worn lingerie. She could still remember the last time she did. It was for Carter. He bought her a blush-pink chemise and little matching underwear. She remembered how he looked at her when she put it on for him and how he stared at her as he peeled it off five minutes later. She felt sexier in that soft pink than she ever would in leopard print and black satin.

Hollowness filled her for a moment. If she didn't know any better she would think that she missed him. But that couldn't be right, especially after their last tense meeting. They were totally wrong for each other and they proved it each time they were in the room together.

"Belinda?" she heard Cherri call.

"I'm coming. I'm coming. Let me just put my shoes back on."

"No, it's not that. It's—"

"What?" Belinda opened the dressing room door and posed with her hand on her hip. Maggie, her mother, and Cherri stared at her with open mouths. "Damn, I know it's a little tight in the chest but I don't think it looks that bad." It was Cherri's head that swiveled first. Belinda turned, too, to see Carter, the man she was just thinking about—the man who was always on her mind—standing there.

Carter stood outside the doors of Size Me Up. He hadn't meant to come here, he wasn't planning on it, but Belinda had been on his mind constantly since he last saw her. He kept seeing in his mind her half-naked body sprawled across his backseat the afternoon of the rainstorm, and he kept remembering how she felt and how she responded to him. He might have been able to ignore all that—he knew his attraction to Belinda was something that was never going to go away—but he also kept seeing her walk hand in hand with Ruby. He kept thinking about how natural they looked together, how happy his daughter had been when she returned to him that afternoon. She was bubbly.

It was almost like he was seeing someone else's kid. If half an hour with Belinda could do that to her, he thought about how life might have been if she stayed, if they had raised her together. And a little bit of that anger toward Belinda that he thought he set aside had resurfaced.

If she had stayed, their lives could have been so different.

He walked through the doors, still not sure what he was going to say when he saw her. He had been past the shop countless times since he had moved here, but he'd never been in. He hadn't known that it was Belinda's store until she gave him her card. But even if she never told him, he would know. He could see signs of her all over the place, from the paint colors to the soft scent of lavender. It all read Belinda.

"Oh. Hello."

He heard and noticed the three women and the small child who were staring at him.

"Hello." He recognized the blonde immediately. She was with Belinda that day in the park. He could tell by the stunned look on her face that he was the last person she'd expected to see there.

"I came to speak to Belinda," he said, not knowing what else to say.

The blonde and the equally tall, dark-haired woman exchanged looks. His memory triggered. Carmina Del Torro. Now Mrs. Gordon. Belinda's mother. He had never met the woman. He had planned to. They were planning to fly out to New York, just three days after Belinda left.

He stared at his mother-in-law for a moment. She was very beautiful: tall, elegant, slender, all the things Belinda said she was not. But he could see Belinda in her mother.

The same cheekbones, same eyes, same softly rounded nose.

"Belinda?" the blonde called. The three women looked at the dressing room door and then back at him.

"I'm coming. I'm coming. Just let me put my shoes on."

"No. It's not that. It's—"

"What?" Belinda opened the dressing room door and came and posed with her hand on her hip. Leopard and black satin, garters and stockings on a too-lush curvy body. He had seen her in far less, but his mouth watered. *Shit.*

His thoughts evaporated.

His pants grew a little tighter.

"Damn, ladies. I know it's a little tight in the chest but I don't think it looks so bad that it calls for speechlessness."

"I don't think it's tight in the chest," he said after a moment. "I think some people would pay good money to see you in that."

She looked up at him, her mouth dropping slightly, an adorable red flush covering her cheeks.

"You do look fabulous, Pudge," Carmina said softly.

"Yes, she does." The third woman rushed forward, took a silky pink robe off a hanger, and tossed it to Belinda. "But this would look so nice over it."

Belinda put it on, shooting all of them dirty looks. "While I sincerely appreciate all of your compliments, I would have appreciated it more if one of you would have said, *Hey, Belinda, don't come out here half-naked. Your estranged husband is here to see you.* But no, everybody suddenly develops a huge case of the shut-ups," she grumbled.

"I need to speak with you," he said, smothering a smile.

She nodded, tightly tying the belt of her robe. "My office is a good place." She stopped in front of her mother, who was staring at him with open interest. "*Mamá,* this is him. This is Carter."

"Carter," Carmina said, studying his face. "It's so nice to finally meet you."

"You, too, Mrs. Gordon."

"And this is Cherri, my other best friend. And this is Maggie. She works here."

"Nice to meet you both." He nodded at them and then turned his gaze to Belinda.

"My office is just down the hall."

He followed her, trying not to look at her bottom as she walked. But it was hard. He knew what she was wearing underneath and he liked the way it wiggled as she went.

"Stop staring at my ass," she said through clenched teeth.

"Not going to happen."

They entered her office. He closed the door behind them and then pushed her against it. Her eyes went wide again, but he ignored the surprised look on her face as he undid her robe.

"No need to cover up for me, Bell." He pressed his lips to her throat. "You know I've seen it all before."

"Carter," she groaned, but she didn't push him away as he slid his lips along her skin.

"This thing has to come off," he said as he went for the hooks on her bustier.

"Do you know how long it took for me to get this thing on?"

"Don't care. I want it off." He kept undoing the tiny hooks, revealing her skin inch by inch. She never attempted to stop him; just looked at him with a slight frown.

"My mother is out there. And my best friend and her baby. And one of my employees. They've probably got their ears pressed against the door."

He grinned, kissing down the seam of her throat, while his fingers worked to undress her. "That's probably why you should stop talking and let me do this."

He finally reached the last hook of the bustier, freeing

her of the confining thing. All she was left in was her silky robe, garters, and those little black lace panties. But as much as her body drove him to distraction, it was her face he couldn't stop staring at. She wanted him just as much as he wanted her. He could see it in her eyes. She never could hide it. It was one of the reasons he fell for her in the first place.

"You're the only man who has ever looked at me like that," she said in wonder.

He pressed his face closer to hers, close enough so that his lips brushed hers. "Like what, Bell?"

"Like you . . ."

"Like I?" She didn't have to say it. He already knew, even if she couldn't find the words. He looked at her like she was perfect for him, like he loved her. He had tried to convince himself long ago that his feelings had died, that she was just some woman who had passed through his life, but apparently he was wrong.

Just being around her again, he was feeling that same pull he'd felt four years ago.

"Never mind." She shook her head, then closed the distance between their mouths and kissed him.

"Why were you wearing that thing? It left marks." He ran his hands over her torso, his thumbs soothing her slightly inflamed skin. "You don't need to wear a bustier. You're sexy enough as it is." The backs of his fingers brushed the undersides of her breasts, her nipples tightening in response.

"That feels good." She swallowed as her eyes drifted shut. "Someone made it for me. Unfortunately the designer underestimated my girth. Lucky for me, the guy I married prefers his girls a little chubby."

"Hmm? Chubby?" He shook his head. "Chubby is not sexy. You're not thin but you are curvy and warm and you feel good. You're the way a woman should feel."

He cupped her breasts, pressing a kiss to each of them. She moaned. "Why are you here today?"

"I just came to say hi. Wanted to see if I could feel you up a little before my next meeting."

"Hi," she said back, smiling with pleasure. "I wish you would have called to let me know this. I would have planned my day a little better."

"You would have avoided me."

"I totally would have." She cupped his jaw in her hands and brought his face to hers. She kissed him that time and he was happy to let her take charge of it. He had been turned on the moment he saw her walk out of the dressing room, but her kiss brought him over the edge. He closed the small gap between them, bringing her naked chest against him and deepening their kiss. He cupped her thigh in his hand, bringing her leg around his hip.

This wasn't enough for him. He needed more from her. He needed to feel closer. But then he remembered where they were, and why he was here.

To talk about ending their marriage.

But he was never going to get enough of her. Never. There was no putting her out of his mind, no calming of their extreme magnetism.

She broke the kiss, returning to sanity before he did, and rested her head on his chest. They stood together for a long time, just holding on to each other, their breathing unsteady. This kept happening. Every time they were alone together things spiraled out of control. And as miserable as she had made him he didn't want to give her up, give up the way she made him feel.

She felt like home to him. And there was no way he could just give his home up.

"I'm going to have to order a shit ton of those bustiers for the store. If they turn you on that much, imagine what they'll do to regular men."

"It's not the bustier. It's you in the bustier. Put on a garbage bag and I'll come after you the same way." He kissed her lips once more. "Be glad your mother is out there or this meeting would have ended differently."

"I wish it had. I'm going to be uncomfortable for the rest of the day now," she complained.

He raised a brow at her. "You're going to be uncomfortable?" He took her hand and placed it on his pants where he throbbed painfully. "How the hell am I going to hide this?"

She gave him a bashful grin and pulled him closer, wrapping her arms around him. "My poor baby. I wish I could fix it for you."

"You can," he said seriously. "You can come home with me right now."

She blinked at him, and he could see the thoughts on her face. She wanted to, but something was holding her back. "You're supposed to be divorcing me."

"I'm also supposed to floss twice a day but that's not happening right now, either."

"What's that supposed to mean?"

"It means that you're gorgeous and before I die I'm going to get you in a bed and make love to you until one of us can't see straight."

"You sound so sure of yourself," she said softly.

"I'm not, but I'm sure I haven't got you out of my system." He kissed her once again and forced himself away from her. "This isn't over."

It would be easy to send the papers, but he was fooling himself to think it would all be over once she signed them. The thoughts wouldn't stop, the feelings wouldn't die.

He knew it couldn't end them. Not yet. There was still hope.

CHAPTER 12

Baby on board . . .

"Knock knock."

Belinda looked up from the catalog of classes she was studying to see Ellis standing just inside her office door.

"Hey, Ellie. You've finally unchained yourself from your needle and thread?"

"Yeah." She walked in and plopped herself on Belinda's couch. "Come sit next to me. I need to talk to you."

Belinda studied Ellis's face for a moment. She looked as weary as Belinda felt. She was pale, and her face was a little puffy. Ellis had been working nonstop for the past year. Brides were now on waiting lists for one of her dresses. Belinda sometimes worried about her friend, but Ellis seemed to love every minute of it. She was happier than Belinda had ever seen her.

"Are you okay, Ellie?" Belinda reached out and touched her forehead. "You look kind of sick."

"That's what I wanted to talk to you about. I told Mike

that I wanted to hire a full-time seamstress to help. That part-time work I've been hiring out isn't enough to cut it. We are going to need another full-time employee. Mike says we have enough to hire her but he wanted to make sure it's okay with you before we start the search."

"Of course it's fine, Ellis. If you need somebody, you get them. You don't need to ask me."

"I do. We're partners, dummy."

"I thought Size Me Up Bridal was separate from the clothing store. That business belongs to you and Mike."

"Nope. You own forty percent of that, too. So you really can't go running off."

"But, Ellis," she said seriously. "What if I need to?"

"I heard Carter was here this morning. I also heard that you were wearing only lingerie that Alexander sent you. I'm not sure if I like that one of our suppliers is sending you panties, but if it gets us a discount, let him. Maggie told me his dresses flew off the racks today." She shook herself. "What were we talking about?"

"Carter. He showed up here, undressed me, felt me up, and warned me that we weren't finished yet."

"He undressed you?"

"Yes. I really think we're going to have to get Alexander to make some lingerie for us. I have never seen that man more determined to get me out of something before."

"Start with a dozen and then we'll go from there. PS—What the hell goes on around when I'm not here? Do you have sex with him?"

"Not today, but I've slept with him once already. And what I didn't tell you is that last week when my tire blew, Carter was the one who found me and he stayed with me until the tow truck came, and we fooled around like horny teenagers on spring break. When we are near each other we just lose our damn minds."

"Is that such a bad thing? He came here, Belinda. He

could have gone anywhere else in the world but he came here where he knows you have strong ties. And he hasn't divorced you yet. If he didn't want you he wouldn't be here. Maybe you should think about getting back together with him."

"No." She shook her head. "It won't work. Sex is the only thing we do well together. We are from two different worlds."

"Are you? It doesn't seem so to me. He's here. He put his daughter in school here. He gave up a higher-paying job to be here. He's in your world now. Or at least he's trying to be. I know you. I know when things get overwhelming you want to run, but going away is not going to solve your problems."

"I just need space away from him to think, and as long as I'm here I can't do that. This town is too small."

"Well, how much time do you need to think? A week? A month? Belinda, I'm going to need you more than ever this year."

"What's the matter?" She looked into Ellis's eyes. "What happened?"

"I'm pregnant," she whispered.

"What?" Belinda wasn't sure why she was shocked. Ellis was a married woman. Her husband couldn't keep his hands off her. She just hadn't expected Ellis to actually venture into motherhood so soon.

"I know. This is a crazy time. We're so busy here and we're renovating our house. And there's the small fact that I told my husband that I never, ever wanted to have kids. And now I'm pregnant. And I'm scared shitless."

"Mike doesn't know you're pregnant?"

"No." She shook her head. "Don't tell him. I just found out myself the other day. I kind of planned this without running it by him."

"Ellis! Are you fucking crazy?"

"Shh! And yes, I am. But I know Mikey wants to be a father. I can tell by the way he looks at Colin and Cherri's boy. It'll make him happy."

"So why didn't you just tell him you were ready?"

"Because he has given so much up for me. He quit his job. He borrowed an obscene amount of money from his father to buy this building for me. He loves me more than I deserve and I want to do this just for him. I want to give him a little piece of him." She shook her head. "Does that make sense?"

"Yes." She nodded, her heart feeling heavy. She knew what it felt like to love somebody so much that she wanted to give up a piece of herself for him. "I know you want to make your husband happy, but are you sure this is what you want?"

She nodded, and suddenly her eyes went teary. "I want to be a mommy. I want to have his baby."

"Okay then." Belinda nodded. "I'm here for you. I'm happy for you."

CHAPTER 13

It's a hard-knock life . . .

"Ruby, let's go!" Carter barked at his daughter for the tenth time that morning. He had finally slept the entire night through after weeks of hardly sleeping at all, but he woke up an hour late, which meant Ruby woke up an hour late and he had to get her to school. He had a meeting in the city with one of his parents' oldest friends. At first he didn't want to take it. He wanted to leave that world behind him, but designing a house for Mr. James Westmore was a big project for Steven and his little firm. It was a good way to grow their business, and if he was going to make it on time he needed to be on the road in twenty minutes.

"Ruby, let's go." She was dragging her feet this morning. He swore he had never seen her move slower. It was hard to get her going in the morning; he often wondered how other single parents managed. The thought of hiring help crossed his mind again but he disregarded it. He was going to raise his daughter. He refused to be like his parents who had never taken him to school or put him to bed. He was going to spend time with his kid even if that meant he had to bark at her sometimes. "Put on your shoes."

"But, Daddy—"

"Shoes!" He walked away from her, snatching her book bag off the counter. "Where is your homework folder? I told you a million times to put it back in your book bag after you're finished with it. We have to go on a mad hunt for it every morning, which all could be avoided if you would put it back when you're done with it." He tossed a bottle of water and a banana that was starting to turn brown in her backpack for snack and made a mental note to stop by the store on his way home from work today. "You manage to wake me up at six o'clock on a Saturday morning but when it's time to go to school you sleep the sleep of the dead."

He found her folder, grabbed the sweater Belinda gave her, and turned back to her—only to see her standing there in the same spot he had left her.

"Is there a reason you aren't moving?" She only had one shoe on. A brush had not visited her hair that morning and she had toothpaste smeared on her face, but he couldn't waste any more time. "You know what? I don't care why you're not moving. You're going to move now." He scooped her up, grabbed her missing shoe and her backpack, and headed out the door. Her school was ten minutes away and she was already late for it. He hated being late and Ruby hated being rushed.

He didn't say another word to her as he placed her in the backseat. When he went to strap her in she blocked his hand and grabbed the seat belt. "I can do it by myself."

She was pissed at him and he was irritated with her but that was the way of parents and children sometimes. He watched her buckle herself in, silently willing her to move faster, and then got in the car and peeled out of the driveway. They were really late for school. There wasn't a single school bus in sight, not a parent milling around. He pulled into the fire lane.

Shit. He would have to sign her in now, which would take another five minutes. He was kicking himself for not setting an alarm, but he'd never needed one before. He would have to make sure he set one from now on.

He threw his car into park and rushed around the back. She still had one shoe on, her face was twisted in anger, and she looked an absolute mess. His irritation melted away. She was a five-year-old, doing what five-year-olds did. "Come on, babe. You're late."

She unbuckled herself, shoved her foot in her shoe, and got out of the car without his assistance. He didn't even try to hold her hand as they walked the few steps to the front door. The secretary greeted him with a knowing grin and handed him the late-arrival clipboard.

"Thank you. We woke up a little late this morning."

"It happens to the best of us."

He liked this school. He liked the people here. It was so different from Ruby's former private school. Everyone was so much kinder here. He turned to his daughter, seeing that her arms were folded across her chest and that she still had that mulish expression on her face. He bent before her, smoothing his hands over her wild hair and scraping the toothpaste off her cheek. He kissed her forehead and then both her cheeks. "I'll see you this afternoon."

"You didn't give me breakfast," she said, her voice full of hurt.

"Oh, baby, I—"

"I don't want it now! My tummy hurts." She walked away from him and stomped down the hallway to her classroom.

"I can get her some cereal," the secretary said behind

him. "I know you're running late. Don't worry about her. We'll take care of her."

"Thank you." He got to his feet. Guilt was kicking the shit out of him. He was tempted to cancel his meeting, pull her out of school, and make it up to her, but he couldn't do that. He was just going to have to do better by her tomorrow.

Carter made his meeting on time, but the whole drive down to the Upper West Side he kept thinking about Ruby. He tried not to. He knew she would be fine at school but she stayed with him. He could see her little angry face in his mind. He could still feel her hurt, but he pushed that all aside when he arrived at his meeting. Mr. Westmore was a close friend of his parents and he wanted Carter to design the weekend home he wanted to build on top of Forster's Ridge, right on the outskirts of Durant. When he walked in, he thought that Westmore was going to be a difficult picky client, like the ones he was so used to dealing with in San Francisco. He wasn't. He made no demands. All he required was that Carter meet him at his main residence so he could get a feel for his family's personal tastes.

"I think I have a good idea of what you and your family would like." Carter packed his briefcase after spending two hours in the comfortable but upscale home. "I've never designed a log cabin, especially one of this size, but I think we can do some amazing things. I'll call you at the end of the week so we can review the first set of plans."

"That's good, son. I'll drive up with Mildred next week. We'll have dinner. We would love to see Ruby again. I haven't seen her since she was a baby."

"She's five now." He smiled at the mention of his little girl. "Five going on fifty. Sometimes I wonder who the parent is."

James nodded. "Raising girls is tough. Your father tells

me you moved to this side of the country in order to spend more time with her."

"I did. San Francisco was great for my career but it wasn't great for her."

"That's admirable."

"It was the right thing. Now if you'll excuse me. I have to head back upstate. I have to get back before school lets out."

"Go. Go. We'll talk later."

Carter thanked Mr. Westmore and left the building. If he got on the road right away he would have just enough time to pick Ruby up from school, but if he hit traffic he would be late and he didn't want to risk that. He already had some making up to do. He pulled his iPhone out of his pocket to call her school to ask them to put Ruby in the after-school program just in case he didn't make it. He hated to do that to her, but sometimes it couldn't be avoided.

There were four missed calls. All from Ruby's school. "Fuck."

Today was a bad day for her to get sick when he was so far away. He prayed that she was just a little sick, a tummy ache, a rash, something that wouldn't require an immediate trip to the emergency room.

"Hello, this is Carter Lancaster," he said when the secretary picked up the phone. "Ruby's father. I see that you called."

"Yes, Mr. Lancaster. I don't know if you were aware but today was an early release and there is no after-school program. Is there somebody coming to pick her up? She's been waiting for half an hour."

"She's tried on nearly every dress in the store," Maggie whispered to Belinda as she walked up to her flustered-looking salesgirl.

"Who?"

"The same lady who was here before you and Mike went to the bank."

"Seriously?"

"Yeah. That's why we called you. I don't think we can take much more of this."

"Ick." The customer, a busty bleached-blond female, came rushing out in one of their sexiest black dresses. "It doesn't fit. Nothing in this whole damn store fits me. I came here because everybody keeps telling me that I would be able to find clothes here. This place is just like every other overpriced boutique in this town."

Belinda's hackles went up. "Hello, miss. I'm the owner of this overpriced boutique and I'm here to tell you that if you want everyday low, low prices you can head to the Walmart in Kingston. If you want good-quality fashion you've come to the right place." She walked forward, surveying what the customer was wearing. "Of course nothing fits you. We have the same problem. Big boobs, big butts, small waists. Size Me Up tailors clothing to fit your body. This dress would be amazing on you if you let us take it in at the waist."

"I don't have time for that! My party is tonight and my ex is going to be there with his new girlfriend and I have to look fantastic or else the bastard wins."

Belinda sighed. "Well, why didn't you just say that?" She turned to Maggie. "There is a black corset in the underwear section with gold detailing. Can you grab it for me?" She looked back at her customer. "Shoe size?"

"Ten."

"Got it." She pulled a pair of strappy black stilettos off the shelf, then dangly gold earrings and a beaded gold necklace to complete the look. "Turn around," she ordered the customer when Maggie brought her the top. "And breathe in." She fastened the woman into the corset, handed her the jewelry and the shoes, and told her to finish getting dressed.

The woman did. When she went to the mirror to look at herself, she had nothing to say.

"You look like a modern version of Marilyn Monroe, honey. Make sure you curl your hair tonight and wear red lipstick. His girlfriend will look like dog food next to you."

"I take it back. You're worth the money."

"You're damn right. Maggie, ring her up and give her my card." She extended her hand to the customer. "Belinda."

"Rhett."

"Nice to meet you, Rhett. I do wardrobe consultations. You call me next time you're having a crisis."

"I will. Thank you."

She turned away from Rhett to nearly run into Mike. "You're scary-good at that."

"At what?

"Being bossy and telling people what to wear."

"Some people find cures for diseases. I, however, can put together one hell of an outfit. If only I could put together my personal life as well."

"You will, and speaking of your personal life—your husband is on the phone. He says it's urgent."

"Urgent?" She walked away from Mike immediately and into her office to pick up the phone. "Hello?" She couldn't imagine what urgent matter he would need to discuss with her or why her heart rate had sped up when Mike told her that he was on the phone

"Bell?" She could tell by the strain in his voice that something wasn't right.

"What's the matter?"

"It's Ruby. She's stuck at school. I forgot it was an early

dismissal and there's no after-school program. Please, Bell. Can you pick her up for me?"

Part of her wanted to laugh at the absurdity of his request. The man who once told her he didn't want her anywhere near his daughter was asking her to pick her up from school. But she couldn't laugh at him. She could hear the panic in his voice, the guilt. Carter was raising her alone. She could only imagine how hard it must be. "I'll go right now."

"Thank you," he breathed. "Thank you. I'll call the school and let them know you're on your way."

Ruby was sitting in a chair by the office door when Belinda walked in. Her little face was scrunched and stormy. Something pulled painfully in Belinda's chest looking at her.

"Hey, baby doll."

Ruby looked up at her, pinning her with those gray eyes that looked so much like Carter's. "He forgot about me again."

"He didn't forget. He's just stuck in the city," she lied. For some reason she felt the need to defend Carter. Or maybe she was just trying to soothe Ruby's hurt feelings. Nobody should feel like they were forgotten.

"He's not here," she said stubbornly.

"I'm here." Belinda, not sure what to do, approached Ruby and ran her fingers through her tangled curls. "I'm going to take you back to my store for a little while and then we'll go to my house and make cookies and I'll let you sit in my big bed and watch whatever you want on TV till your daddy gets back. It will be fun. I promise."

Ruby looked at her for a long moment, and Belinda knew she was no substitute for the girl's father.

"I'm sorry, Ruby." She slid her hand down to cup Ruby's soft cheek. "You know he would be here if he could."

She nodded, but Belinda could tell she didn't believe her. She felt very sorry for Carter at that moment. It was going to take a lot to make up for this one.

"Let's go, honey." And this time she took Ruby's hand as they left the office.

"This is my store, Ruby," she explained to the stonily silent child when they entered the store. "I get to help other ladies play dress-up and my friend Ellis makes dresses and she fixes everybody's clothes so that they will fit. It's a great job. I get to work with my friends."

Ruby said nothing to that. She hadn't said a word since she got in the car.

"My office is down the hallway. My friend Cherri painted the walls for me so it looks like 1920s Paris."

Still nothing. Not that Belinda expected much of a reaction, but she wanted Ruby to say something, anything. She hated that she looked so upset.

Fix it. Fix it!

The voice inside her kept telling her to do so. But she really didn't know how. For the first time in her life she didn't know how. She could outfit an army of women in forty-five minutes but she wasn't equipped to deal with an upset child. Or any child, for that matter.

Ruby walked two steps ahead of her with her oversized pink backpack on her back, her head down as she made her way to the back of the store. Belinda watched her with a sinking stomach.

"Whose kid is that?" Ellis, appearing from nowhere, whispered.

"Carter's. He's in the city." She shook her head as she looked at miserable Ruby's back. "It's a long story."

Ellis followed them down the hallway to Belinda's office. They both watched Ruby as she slung her backpack on the floor, and then they looked at each other. She was hoping that Ellis would have some insight to offer, but she only looked as lost as Belinda felt.

"How do you make a kid feel better?" Belinda whispered to her best friend.

"I don't know."

"What do you mean you don't know? You're knocked up. Doesn't some kind of mommy gene kick in or something?"

"It hasn't kicked in yet. Maybe I'm like my mother. She was never fond of small children. I swear she didn't like me until I was ten. You should probably call your mother. She loves little kids."

She couldn't call her mother. She didn't want to explain why she had Carter's kid.

"Can't call her. We are going to have to handle this. Ruby," Belinda called tentatively. "This is one of my best friends in the whole world, Ellis. This is her store, too. She's the one who makes the dresses."

"Hi, Ruby." Ellis gave her a soft smile. "I could make you a dress if you wanted. I could make you a princess gown."

"You can?" Belinda shot Ellis a look.

"Got asked to make a flower girl dress. Then the wedding got canceled. It would take no time to fit a dress on Ruby."

"Would you like that, baby doll?" Belinda asked the pouting child. "Do you want a princess dress?"

"I'm not a princess. I'm nobody! I'm nothing!"

"Ruby, no . . ."

"He keeps forgetting about me. He forgets to give me money for trips, and he forgets to buy me shoes and feed me breakfast. He forgets about me all the time. I hate it. I hate—"

Belinda dropped to her knees in front of Ruby and

cupped her angry red face in her hands before she could finish her sentence. "You are not a nobody. You are wonderful." She kissed her forehead and her tiny nose, and the light sprinkling of freckles that dusted her face. "Your daddy knows that. He loves you, Ruby. He loves you so much." She picked up the small girl and cuddled her close.

All the fight seemed to have left Ruby's body in that moment and she went limp in Belinda's arms.

"He didn't do it on purpose, Ruby. He would never leave you on purpose. You are the most important thing in his life. You know that, right?"

She nodded, her eyes filled with unshed tears.

"He's raising you all by himself, and raising a kid is hard without a mommy to help. I know you're mad and you have every right to be, but try to cut him a little slack."

"Okay," she sniffed as a tear escaped her eye.

"You can cry if you need to. It's okay."

If was as if she needed permission. She let a few tears slip, her chest softly heaving. Belinda could tell that Ruby wasn't a regular crier. She was pretty tough kid with no mother and a father who was trying to make up for it all.

"Don't cry on my clothes, Rube." Belinda wiped her tears away with her thumbs. "Tears stain this kind of fabric and this dress cost way more money than you have in your piggy bank. You might have to get a job to pay for it."

Ruby gave a watery laugh and snuggled into her chest. Seeing her smile caused Belinda to release a breath she didn't know she was holding. Seeing Ruby so hurt had affected her, made her want to make everything better.

It was an odd feeling, one she didn't want to examine too closely. Ruby was Carter's child. Carter's. The one he made with the wife he didn't tell her about.

"Thank you for coming to get me."

"So polite, even when you're royally pissed off." She kissed her forehead. "I like that about you." She sat Ruby up on her lap and ran both her hands through Ruby's messy curls until they were neat and fluffy. "I'm going to take you back to my house now. I think maybe you could use a rest. I just need to tell Ellis that I'm taking the rest of the day off."

"It's okay with me," Ellis said, making her jump. Belinda had no idea her friend was still there or how long she had been staring at them with that curious expression on her face. "I'll see you tomorrow."

CHAPTER 14

The long road home . . .

Carter pulled up to Belinda's townhome for the second time. He couldn't help remembering his last visit there, and for a moment he regretted coming here to pick his daughter up. He should've had Belinda meet him somewhere. He should have gone to her store. Anyplace but here. The combination of his feelings for Belinda and the guilt over his daughter was enough to kill him.

It had been a week since he'd gone to her store, a week since he last touched her, and for a moment he thought time and distance from her would help clear his mind, would put him back on track. But every time he left his house he found himself searching for a glimpse of her. Every redhead he saw reminded him of her.

And today when he was at a loss Belinda was the first person he called. He didn't think to call Steven, whom Ruby had known longer than Belinda, and that troubled him. It told him he was in too deep with Belinda again already. She wasn't his wife anymore. Not really. She had walked out on him during the hardest time of his life. And as much as he felt for her, he couldn't trust her not to walk out on him again.

He sat in the car for a few moments trying to gather the strength to get out. Ruby probably hated him. He didn't blame her. He was an hour and a half later than he'd expected to be. Traffic had been hellacious. An early Yankees game turned the highway into a parking lot, and the whole three-and-a-half-hour car ride home he thought about how he was going to make this one up to Ruby. He had messed up a lot in the time that he had her, but he had never left her stranded at school. This was one he couldn't forgive himself for.

He might have to break down and buy her that iPhone she wanted.

Or a pony.

He finally got out, slowly walking to the door, his legs protesting after being stuck in the car for so long.

What was he going to say to her? How was he going to explain this one?

Belinda opened the door before he even got the chance to knock. She was barefoot, her body encased in a blue dress that hugged her in all the right places. Seeing her waiting for him at the door made him flash back to their married days when she used to greet him at the door when he came home from work. Then she used to throw her arms around him and kiss him deeply. But now things were different. Seeing her familiar face waiting for him caused a twinge in his chest.

"You look like shit," she said in greeting.

"I feel like shit."

She smiled softly at him as she stepped aside to let him in. He brushed against her as he entered her place and caught a faint trace of her scent. Orange and ginger. The same exotic smell she'd used when they met.

"Can I get you something to eat or drink?" she offered politely.

"I'm fine, but thank you." He wanted to get his daughter and get the hell out of there. Being around Belinda made him feel like he was walking through a fog. Her nearness combated with his common sense and he needed to think clearly now. He needed to focus on his daughter. "How was she? I hope she didn't cause you any trouble."

She shook her head. "Of course not. She's a good kid."

They both fell quiet for a moment as awkwardness surrounded them. It seemed that neither of them knew how to behave around the other in that moment.

"Where is she?"

He looked around Belinda's town house just so he had an excuse to pull his eyes away from her face. He hadn't had a chance to look at it the last time he was there. He'd come storming in, brimming with emotions he didn't know how to deal with. He was too pissed to notice the smaller details last time. But the place suited her. It was boldly decorated with brightly colored paintings on the wall, but it was homey at the same time with overstuffed furniture and shelves filled with books and photos of her friends and family.

It looked like a home. It was so unlike his, so unlike the one they'd shared four years ago. She didn't get the chance to put her touch on that place. He wondered what it would have looked like if she had.

"She's upstairs in my bedroom watching *The Adventures of Milo and Otis*."

Her comment caught him off guard, and he set his eyes on her face once again. "You rented *Milo and Otis* for her?"

Her cheeks went slightly red and she folded her arms beneath her breasts, pushing them into his eye line. She studied his face carefully as if she was bracing herself for a blow. "No, I own *Milo and Otis*. I also own the entire collection of Muppet movies. You got a problem with that?"

He almost lost his train of thought as his eyes lingered on her chest for a moment, but he remembered their conversation and forced his eyes back to hers. "I never thought you would develop a love for kids' movies."

"I didn't develop a love for them. I've always loved kids' movies," she said quietly. "I just never told you because I wanted you to think I was smart."

"What?"

"I didn't want you, fancy-pants San Francisco architect, to think you'd married an immature weirdo."

Everything inside him paused in that moment. "You honestly think that knowing that would have changed how I felt about you?"

She was quiet for a long moment, an expression crossing her face he couldn't name. It looked suspiciously like sadness.

"I don't know what I thought then." She shook her head and gifted him with a sassy smile. "But now I don't care what you think. I will no longer hide my love for a movie about a pug and a cat from any man."

He wanted to laugh away their exchange but he couldn't. She didn't have to hide that from him. It bothered him that she hadn't felt good enough for him then. It made him mad at his parents all over again.

"Do you want me to get Ruby for you now or do you need a minute to relax?" she asked, distracting him from his thoughts of her. "I know you've had a rough day."

He hadn't been expecting her kindness. He thought she would be irritated or smug, but she acted like babysitting the child of the man she wanted to divorce wasn't out of the ordinary.

"I'm ready to take my punishment."

She lifted her hand and gave his arm a squeeze. "Don't beat yourself up too much, Daddy."

She left him standing by the couch. His eyes followed her as she ascended the staircase. The thoughts of her he'd just had flew out of his head as he watched the way her hips gently moved. He noticed the way her dress clung to her curves and how her bottom looked so perfectly round. Memories of them together flashed in his mind. He remembered how good she felt cupped in his hands, the long nights they shared wrapped in each other's bodies. He remembered how happy he thought they were, but a murmur of soft voices at the top of the stairs pulled him from his thoughts.

His baby girl was about to make an appearance. He almost didn't want to see her. He was a grown man. He had dealt with all kinds of ruthless assholes in his field and yet he was scared to face a little girl's anger.

"Come on, baby doll," he heard Belinda say.

Baby doll. When Ruby had returned from getting frozen yogurt the other day she couldn't stop talking about Belinda. About how her nails were painted with white tips and how her shoes made noise when they clicked on the floor and about how she called her baby doll and yelled at some man for calling her a chunky little thing.

His wife and daughter descended the stairs together, Ruby practically glued to Belinda's side. He noticed a slight difference in Ruby. Her hair was no longer a tangled mass; instead it was bouncy and glossy. Her face was clean. Her clothes were still mismatched but for the first time in a long time Ruby looked neat. It was obviously the work of Belinda. He appreciated what she'd done—hell, after today he owed her big—but he felt uneasy about how quickly Ruby was growing attached to Belinda. Frankly, it bothered him that Belinda seemed to like his child so much. Why couldn't it have been like this four years ago?

"Hi, Rube." He held out his hand to his daughter when she neared but she wouldn't take it. She just rested her head against Belinda's thigh and glared at him.

He no longer just felt like he was the world's shittiest father. He *was* the world's shittiest father.

He squatted before her. "I'm so sorry, baby. I was in the city with a client and then I got caught in traffic. You know I would never forget you on purpose. You don't know how bad I feel."

Ruby said nothing, only looked at him like he'd betrayed her. Suddenly he felt like he was the child and she the adult. He had disappointed her, and that was far worse than her anger.

"You don't have to forgive me," he went on, "but I wish you would say something to me."

"Go on." Belinda nudged Ruby closer to him. "You've only got one daddy."

"I want to stay here until the movie is over. It just started."

How could he tell her no? He owed her this one little thing. He glanced up at Belinda, who nodded her permission. "Okay. You just let me know when you're ready to go home."

"Give him a hug," Belinda ordered.

Ruby looked up at her and frowned but Belinda didn't say a word; she just raised both her brows and silently restated her order.

Ruby sighed and loosely wrapped her arms around him. It wasn't a real hug and he couldn't take that so he lifted her up, squeezed her tightly, and kissed her chubby cheeks before he let her go.

"I love you, Ruby."

"I'm going upstairs now."

Not hearing her say it back was like a kick in the chest. He wanted to keep her there, to force her to say it. Instead he watched her go with the sinking feeling that it was going to take a lot to make this up to her.

Belinda saw misery wash over Carter's face as he watched his daughter walk away from him. Seeing him like that made her chest ache. No matter what had happened between them, he was still a good father.

And she took no joy in seeing him so hurt.

"She cried, didn't she?" He took his eyes off Ruby's retreating form and looked at her.

Belinda nodded. She wanted to lie to him but she couldn't. "Only a little bit, though."

"She never cries, not even when she gets hurts. I seem to fuck up everything when it comes to her."

"You don't." She took a step toward him but caught herself. She wanted to comfort him, to make him feel better, but she knew she shouldn't. She wasn't his wife anymore. At least not in the way it counted. "Ruby's hurt. She thinks she's not important to you."

She couldn't miss the shocked expression on his face. Immediately she regretted her words. The last thing she wanted to do was open up a can of worms, but she kind of understood how Ruby felt. There were times when she felt unimportant, too, and it wasn't a good feeling.

"I love her," he said simply after a long pause. "It hurts. I love her so much it hurts. How could she not know?" he said in wonderment.

"She's just a baby, Carter. She may act like a tiny grown-up but she's not. She isn't able to understand how hard it is for you raise her alone. But she will one day."

He blinked at her and she knew her words were inadequate at that moment. But they were true. Ruby was going to have a very hard time finding a man who loved her half as much as her father.

"Give me your jacket," she ordered as she shook herself from her thoughts.

He was rumpled. His tie barely on. His hair a mess from running his fingers through it. She felt that familiar beat of attraction race through her. She tamped it down.

"I shouldn't. We're going to be leaving soon." He seemed to regain control of his emotions in that moment, his naked pain fading away as if it had never been there. Once again he looked at her with that expression she could never read.

"You've got about an hour to kill. I put the movie on right before you pulled up. I think you should make yourself comfortable."

Carter gave her a stiff nod and slipped out of his suit jacket. He still smelled good and clean and familiar—as if it hadn't been years since she'd smelled his scent. Unconsciously she held his jacket to her chest, feeling the warmth his body had left behind, and he stood before her staring at her. It took a moment for her to snap out of it, to realize that they were staring at each other, to notice that she was hugging his jacket to her.

It was weird for him to be in her space, in her home. There was a time in her life that she never thought she was going to see him again.

"We should sit," she finally said. "Here. On the couch." *Could you sound any more like an idiot if you tried?*

He nodded and sat down on the far end of the couch. She sat on the opposite side, as far away from him as possible. Her brain seemed to stop working correctly when he was near. She welcomed the two feet of space between them. It gave her the presence of mind to put down his jacket.

"I'm not a leper," he said softly as he pulled off his tie and loosened the top two buttons of his shirt. She got a little peek of chest hair and the large Japanese-style dragon tattoo that snaked across his chest.

"What?"

"I don't smell. I know I was sitting in the car for a long time but I don't think my deodorant has given up on me yet. Has it?"

"No, of course not." Her attention snapped back to his face. She had been staring at him again. "Let me get you something to drink."

She bolted up from her seat in a vain attempt to escape his overwhelming presence for a little while. He caught her hand and with a gentle tug pulled her down on the couch beside him. "Goddamn it, Belinda."

"What?"

"I don't like this. I don't like that you are so nervous around me. I'm not going to hurt you."

It's too late. You already have.

"How do you expect me to act? The last time we were on this couch together we were having hot monkey sex."

He flashed her a wicked grin, but it faded away all too quickly and she was sad to see it go. "I wouldn't call it that."

"What would you call it then?"

He shook his head and then surprised her by lifting his hand to briefly touch her cheek. "I was unkind to you that day. I regret it. I regret so much when it comes to you."

Pain, sharp and breath-stealing, streaked through her chest. Of course he regretted her, regretted their time together. She wished she could say the same thing about him, but she honestly couldn't. "Why did you ask me out?"

"I wanted to have sex with you." His answer was honest. There was no hint of a smile, no humor in his voice, and she respected him for that.

"You were attracted to me."

"I usually don't want to have sex with people I'm not attracted to."

"Oh." He had her there. "I didn't think I was your type."

"I was going to walk past your store that day."

"What?"

"The day we met. I was going to walk past your store but I saw a glimpse of you in the window. I don't know what made me do it, but I walked in just so I could get a better look at you. I don't know how to explain this. I've never been very good with words, but when I saw you, it was like everything inside me snapped to attention. The hair on the back of my neck stood up straight. If it were simply attraction I could have kept walking by, but when I looked at you I knew that I would regret it for the rest of my life if I didn't speak to you."

She was stunned. This was the sweetest thing he had ever said, the sweetest thing anybody had ever said, but it took her only seconds to remember that he had lied to her. That he had hurt her. That he never really wanted her in the first place. "And now you regret it for the rest of your life because you did."

He didn't respond to that. "I didn't have a good time on our first date with you just because I found you beautiful—and you are beautiful. You know that, don't you?" He looked into her eyes. "I liked you. I liked talking to you."

"If I recall, I was the one who did all the talking on our first date, throughout our entire relationship."

"I liked hearing you talk. I liked your voice. I liked how it made me feel."

She wanted to believe that. She wanted so much to believe that. To believe that she hadn't married a man who had no feelings for her at all, but she couldn't because in the end, even with all her talking, they were still strangers. He didn't know anything about her, only the woman she pretended to be while she was with him. "You already got in my pants this month, mister. You can stop laying it on so thick."

He shook his head. "I shouldn't have said anything."

He was shutting down. She could see his expression closing off, and she wanted desperately to stop it. But why? She wanted him out of her hair, out of her life. She shouldn't care if he never spoke to her again. But she did. She wanted to know more from him. "Why did you ask me to marry you?" she blurted out before she saw him completely close down.

"Because you loved me," he said without hesitation.

"You seem very sure of that." She frowned.

He nodded. "You don't give your love away. I knew that the moment I met you. And yet you love very deeply. I could feel your love, Bell. There were times when I was overwhelmed by it."

"Damn it, Carter." She shut her eyes before the tears could come. "I wanted us to work. I had dreams for us."

"What happened to them?"

"They died," she said truthfully. "I have to go." She stood up, needing to get away from him. It was too much for her. Too much emotion for one day. But she realized she was in her house. That his daughter lay upstairs in her bed. She couldn't flee him for long. "I have to go check on Ruby."

She walked into her bedroom to find Ruby lying on her side not watching the television but staring at the wall. She was still so upset, which bothered Belinda more than she wanted to think about. "Hey."

"Hello."

"Don't you like the movie? It's one of my favorites."

"My tummy hurts."

She could hear the pout in her voice. On any other kid she might have found it irritating, but on Ruby . . . She crossed the room and sat on the edge of the bed. "Is there anything I can get you to make it feel better?"

"I saw on TV that Pepto-Bismol is good for nausea,

heartburn, indigestion, upset stomach, and diarrhea. I can take that. I think I got some heartburn."

Oh, good God. Something inside Belinda cracked. She lay next to Ruby, cupped her small face in her hands, and peppered kisses across her freckled nose. Ruby shut her eyes and accepted her affection and Belinda didn't know what she was more surprised by: the fact that Ruby seemed to need it or the fact that Belinda needed to give it. "You are very dramatic, little one, but really freaking cute." She gave her one last kiss on the cheek and pulled her close. Ruby snuggled into her and for a few minutes they were quiet.

"Squeeze me," Ruby ordered.

"Like this?" She wrapped her arms around Ruby tightly until she heard the little girl sigh in contentment. "I can squeeze you like a pimple, little girl. I'm just hoping you don't pop."

"Thank you," Ruby sighed.

She finally understood why women wanted to be mothers. For this. To hold a child. And for the first time Belinda wondered what it would feel like to hold a child created with a man she loved, one who came from her body. It must be a powerful feeling.

This feeling was nice, too. She enjoyed Ruby, enjoyed the few hours they had spent together today. Too bad this little girl didn't belong to some other man. Her past with Carter always made things impossibly hard.

She looked down at Ruby, smoothing the hair from her face. "Ruby, I want you to do something for me?"

"Yeah?"

"I want you to forgive your father."

Carter only sat on the couch for a few moments before he followed Belinda upstairs. She was still running from him. Four years and nothing had changed. Except him. He wasn't content to let her walk away this time. She asked him half a dozen questions but he had one of his own.

Why did you love me?

She was the only person besides Ruby who had ever uttered those three words to him. Not even the first woman he'd walked down the aisle with. But she had, and he wondered why.

He walked down the long hall that led to her bedroom and stopped as he approached the door. Belinda had his daughter's face in her hands. She was kissing her freckles and he wasn't sure who captivated him more: Belinda, who looked so natural giving her love to a child, or Ruby, whose eyes were closed, her face upturned, soaking in Belinda's affection like she was starved for it.

Shit.

He'd suspected for years that Ruby wanted a mother. Now he knew it was more than a want. It was a need. He couldn't do it all. He loved her more than anything in the world but his love alone wasn't enough. Ruby deserved to have the love of two parents.

He knew things weren't over with Belinda. But as much as he craved her nearness, her warmth, he wasn't sure he trusted her with Ruby's heart. She had walked away once and it nearly killed him. He couldn't risk her walking out on Ruby. He couldn't let her get hurt.

"I want you to forgive your father."

"He broke his promise," she whispered.

"What promise?"

"He said we was moving here so he could be with me more. He forgot about me today. I don't want him to forget about me like he forgot about me when we lived in California."

"He loves you. He loves you more than anything or anybody else. I know he forgot you had a half day, but he didn't forget about you. He could never forget about you.

He made a mistake, baby. We all make mistakes. One day you'll make a mistake or two and your daddy will forgive you, because that's what daddies do. They forgive. We all forgive and now you have to, too. You'll feel better after you do."

"Being mad always makes my tummy hurt."

Belinda bent down and smoothed a kiss to her forehead. "Then don't be mad anymore."

She nodded. "Grandma says being angry gives you wrinkles."

"Does she?"

"Yes. She said if you get wrinkles then you need Botox." Ruby reached up to touch Belinda's forehead. "She said ladies get it right here."

"Your grandmother is a wealth of information, isn't she?"

"She tells me lots of things. Sometimes I don't know what she's talking about."

"I think a lot of people feel that way about her." She pulled herself away from Ruby and sat up. "I think we'd better go downstairs now."

"Can I stay here for five more minutes? I like this bed. You think Daddy will buy me one?"

"No to the bed. Yes, you can stay here, but don't be too long. Your father is tired. I think he wants to take you home."

"Okay."

Carter unfroze then and backed out of the doorway. He knew there was no way he could get downstairs without Belinda hearing so he ducked into the bathroom just a little farther down the hall, and when she was near enough he grabbed her hand and pulled her inside the room with him. She let out a little frightened yelp but when he shut the door and backed her against the door her expression changed. Her pouty lips parted in surprise and something flashed in her eyes.

He wanted to call it attraction, but it had to be more than that. If she felt an ounce of what he did, then the word *attraction* seemed wholly inadequate. He pressed his body into her soft curves, holding back a groan when their bodies connected. He'd missed this. He'd missed the connection that he had never felt with anybody else.

"What they hell are you doing?" she asked when he pressed himself into her.

"Be quiet and let me hold you. I need this from you right now."

"Be quiet?" She wrapped her arms around him. "I thought you liked to hear me talk?" Her sassy comment and that gorgeous red raised eyebrow caused him to smile.

"I'd rather not hear you talk before I kiss you."

"Who says I wanted to be kissed?"

"Who says you have a choice?"

"Oh." She smiled bashfully. "Do you still want to have sex with me?"

He nodded once, still surprised that she was the only person in the world who could get him to be nakedly honest. "Just because you smashed my heart into a million pieces doesn't mean I stopped wanting you."

"Smashed your heart, huh? I wasn't aware you had one."

"Belinda," he warned.

"I know, that was really a bitchy thing to say. I know you have a heart. I can see it when you're with your daughter."

"Bell . . ." Her words stung. A lot. More than he thought they could. Hadn't she known how much he loved her? Maybe she didn't and that was his mistake. He didn't even know how much he could love until Ruby came into his life. He was so unsure about them, about their future, but he wanted to make that up to her, he wanted to show her how much he felt for her.

"If you would kiss me already I wouldn't have the chance to say such stupid mean things."

"You want me to kiss you?"

"I'd rather have that hot burly guy from *True Blood* kiss me, but you're the only one here."

He shifted his hands to cup her face, running his thumbs over her high cheekbones. Her eyes went wide again as if she wasn't expecting his gentleness. He pressed one very soft kiss on her lips and stepped away.

"Thank you for taking care of Ruby today. You don't know how much I appreciate it."

She couldn't hide the disappointment on her face. She wanted more from him. He wanted to give it to her, but he knew he couldn't. Once he started with her he couldn't bring himself to stop. "I like her. If you ever need somebody to babysit, I wouldn't mind. My parents wouldn't, either. I know you don't have much help with her, but if you needed us we would be there for you."

He was surprised by her offer, touched by it even, but he knew it was one that he couldn't accept. Not until he was sure of where their relationship was heading. "That's very kind of you, but I don't think that's a good idea. I don't want Ruby to get too attached to you."

"Oh. Whatever." Hurt flashed in her eyes but she covered it quickly. "I didn't really want to babysit for a five-year-old. I was only offering to be nice."

She turned away from him and walked out of the bathroom and he knew he had said the wrong thing. He never meant to hurt her. But he couldn't allow her to hurt Ruby, either. If her leaving had nearly destroyed him, he couldn't imagine what it would do to his baby girl. He needed to know that they would be forever before he let Ruby fall in love with her.

He went to follow her, to explain himself, but he ran into his daughter when he stepped out of the bathroom. "Hello,

Ruby." She was the other woman he had hurt today, and seeking her forgiveness was more important right now.

"Hello, Daddy."

"Are you ready to go?"

She nodded once and slid her small hand into his. His chest felt lighter with that small action. He scooped her up and kissed her hair. "Can I take you out for dinner tonight? Or are you still not talking to me?"

"I'm talking to you," she said resting her head on his shoulder. "But I want you to cook spaghetti tonight."

"Of course I'll cook you spaghetti." He walked down the stairs. "Do you want anything else?"

"I want Belinda to have dinner with us."

Her request shook him, and for a moment he didn't know what to say. "I meant did you want anything else for dinner. Belinda can't eat with us tonight."

"Tomorrow night?"

"I don't know, baby." He didn't want to tell her no. But he couldn't tell her yes. "Let's ask her later."

"Okay." For that moment his answer was good enough.

Belinda was waiting for them at the bottom of the stairs. She held Ruby's book bag, her sweater, and a container full of cookies in her hands.

"You're giving me all the cookies?" Ruby asked.

"Of course I am. I made them for you."

"You baked for her?" Carter asked.

Belinda looked at him briefly before she smiled at Ruby. "It was no big deal. They came from a mix. All I had to do was add eggs and stir."

"You put lots of butter in them, too. They taste very good, Daddy."

"I'm sure they do, Rube. I want you to thank Belinda for taking such good care of you today."

Ruby stretched her arms out, silently begging for

Belinda to hug her. Belinda looked unsure for a moment and glanced at him. "My hands are full."

Carter felt like the world's biggest asshole. There were few people Ruby responded to. There was no way he could deny her this. "I'll take your things." He did and when her hands were free Ruby wrapped herself around Belinda, holding her tight.

"Thank you for taking care of me."

"You don't have to thank me." Belinda hugged her briefly. "I had fun with you today. Be a good girl for your father." She set her down and looked Carter in the eye. The hurt was still there and it was unmistakable. "I haven't received the papers yet."

He nodded. "You will," he said, lying to her. He wasn't going to send them. He needed to figure out a way to get her back.

CHAPTER 15

Stuck in the middle with you . . .

Three days later Belinda and her father walked into Durant's community center. Three years ago it had been rebuilt, turning a once aging building to a place where the people of Durant could truly come together. During the day it was a place the elderly hung out to play cards, swap gossip, and share sips of Irish coffee out of the big thermoses with them, but in the afternoons it turned into a school, with classes on photography, computers, art, and fitness.

And that's why they were there. Belinda had been thinking about it for weeks now, about finding a way to better herself. But all of her big plans seemed to fall by the wayside the day Carter came back into her life. She was mad at herself for letting him change her plans, the way she lived her life. So when her father called her and told her that he had signed up for woodworking and introduction to Spanish classes and asked if she wanted to join him, she jumped at the chance.

Her Spanish was good, thanks to her mother speaking it to her as a child, and there was no way in hell she was going to take woodworking, but Cherri was teaching a beginning painting class across the hall from her father's class and her father had promised to take her out to dinner after class each week. Something about seeing Ruby and Carter together made her appreciate her father more. He wasn't openly affectionate with her like Carter was with his daughter, but she had no doubt he loved her. She knew that he was still trying to make up for her first twelve years when she had seen him more on TV than she had in their home.

"Why woodworking, Dad?" she asked at they walked down the hall toward their classes.

"Pops used to make things for the house. Tables and cabinets and stuff. I've always wanted to do it, too, but he never taught me. He always made sure I was out practicing ball. I guess he was right in a way. Ballplaying worked out for me, but I still want to learn. I want to make a rocking chair one day. We had two when we were kids. My parents used to sit out there after dinner and just look out into the yard. My mama still does it, even though Pop has been gone for twenty years. You think your mother would like one of those, Junior?"

"Yes. She would love it. That's a really sweet thought, Dad. Are you learning Spanish for *Mamá*, too?"

"I really just want to know what the damn woman is saying behind my back."

She shook her head, remembering her mother's colorful language. "You don't want to know."

"No," he nodded, "maybe I don't. But I'm going to retire soon. I've talked to a travel agent. I'm going to take your mother on a big trip to Europe."

"But you hate Europe."

"I do. Especially those damn pretentious French and don't get me started on those Germans."

"Dad!"

"What? I'm from Texas. No place on earth is more beautiful. I wouldn't mind retiring down there, but I know your mother. She would never be happy down there. She gave up a lot for me. She gave up her career. She moved from the city to Durant because I asked her to. She sacrificed having a big family like she wanted because of me. It's my time to do something for her. I'm just hoping we don't kill each other before that time comes."

"What do you mean she sacrificed having a big family for you? You didn't want any more kids?"

"No, I wanted bushels of them. But when we went to the doctor we found out that it was me who had the problem. Too much time in hot tubs nursing my knee caused my count to go low, if you know what I mean."

"I do," she said softly, hearing the heaviness in his voice. "I'm sorry about that."

"Why?" He ruffled her hair. "I got my Junior. I would like some grandkids, though. No pressure. But since you're it, it's all up to you, kid." He grinned at her. "I'll come get you after I'm done. I was thinking we could try that new pizza place. They stuff their crusts with cheese."

"Okay. Don't tell *Mamá*, though. She'll drag me to the nearest gym by my ear."

"I won't." He grinned at her. "But don't pay her any attention. You're built like the women in my family. And there ain't nothing wrong with that."

She left her father, glad that he had invited her to come. She'd learned more about him in those few minutes than she had in years. Her parents really did love each other. They had more than passion. They had compromise. They sacrificed for each other. It made her briefly think about

Carter and her, but she pushed away those thoughts. He still didn't want her around Ruby. There would be no saving them, even though in her most private thoughts she wondered if there might be a chance they could.

She walked into Cherri's class to find her standing in the back of the room pulling out supplies. It had been months since Belinda had seen Cherri without her son. It was almost odd. Since Cherri had Joey, the boy seemed like an extension of her.

"Hey, baby cakes!"

Cherri looked up and smiled brightly at her. "I'm so glad you came! I just saw your name on my list a few minutes ago."

"My dad is taking a few classes across the hall. So we are going to enrich ourselves together."

"Your dad is taking classes?"

"Yeah. He told me that he's going to retire soon. I think he wants to be able to fill his days. He's taking woodworking and Spanish."

"Woodworking! My father-in-law is teaching that class. You should see him, Belinda. He's so excited he went out and bought a jacket and suit coat. Not that he's going to wear either of those things for long. But—"

"Excuse me," a little voice said. "Is this the paint class?"

"Yes, it is, honey," Cherri said. "Come on in."

Belinda turned around to see her classmate only to find Ruby standing just inside the doorway with her head full of messy curls, her oversized pink backpack on, and her small eyes wide with worry.

Damn it.

She couldn't avoid father or daughter, it seemed, but Ruby she didn't want to avoid. She only wished her father weren't so dead set against them being friends. It bothered her a lot. So much so that it was all she had thought about that evening. She wasn't sure why she couldn't let it go.

Carter was right. Ruby shouldn't get attached to her and she shouldn't get attached to Ruby. That's what was happening. She was growing ridiculously fond of the kid.

"Ruby? What are you doing here?"

"Belinda?" Ruby hurried across the room to her. She didn't stop until she had reached her, until she had wrapped her little arms around her and rested her head against her hip. Belinda stiffened at first, remembering Carter's wishes, but that only lasted a second. She relaxed and ran her fingers through Ruby's messy curls. "I was very nervous."

Belinda lifted her up and set her on the counter. "Why, baby doll? Why are you here? Where is your father?"

"He's at work. He said that they had classes and fun things to do after school for kids at the community center. And he asked me if I wanted to come here sometimes instead of sitting in his office. So he let me pick a painting class."

"That's a good thing. Why are you nervous?"

"Because I had to take the school bus here. I never rode on a bus before. Daddy always picks me up from school. My teacher made a big kid bring me here, but I wasn't sure if this was the right place and that's why I was nervous."

"Don't be nervous." She kissed Ruby's forehead. "You're here and you're going to learn to paint from my friend, Mrs. O'Connell. You're going to have fun. I promise."

"Hi, Ruby. I'm Mrs. O'Connell, but you can call me Cherri, since you know my very good friend Belinda." Cherri made brief eye contact with Belinda before she looked back at Ruby. "And since you are the first one here, you get to pick your easel and your supplies first."

"That's Carter's kid," she said when Ruby went to pick her easel.

"I figured," Cherri said as she glanced back at Ruby. "Ellis tells me you bought her to the shop."

Belinda nodded. "Carter got stuck in the city. He needed me to go get her."

"Hmm . . ."

"What? Why do you have that stupid smirk on your face?"

"Nothing. Oh, look. More students are starting to file in."

Belinda turned to survey her other classmates. They were all children. "Cherri, is this painting class just for kids?"

"No. It's for all ages." She turned away from Belinda. "But you are the oldest student I have and it's too late for refunds."

"Belinda!" Ruby called to her. "Sit next to me."

The clock had barely moved since the last time he had looked at it. Only two minutes ago. His leg jiggled non-stop. He tapped his fingers on his desk. He had too much nervous energy to focus on the work he was supposed to be doing.

He had let Ruby go. It shouldn't have been a big deal. He had called the school that morning to make sure that the bus would get her to the community center. He had spoken to her teacher, who assured him that she would have a buddy to drop her off at her art class. He had called the community center to make sure she had arrived. Ruby was there, they told him. She was checked in as soon as she got off the bus.

She was fine. He wasn't. Before they moved he had barely seen her, trusting her care to somebody else, but all that had changed. For the past few months Ruby was barely without him. He missed her more than he thought possible. But this was good for her, to be away from him, to be with other kids. To do things that she liked to do.

Twenty-two minutes until he had to leave for pickup. He wasn't getting any work done. He got up and ventured across the hall to Steven's office. Molly, his intern, was with him going over a set of blueprints.

"These are good, Molly. But you might want to think about the placement of this bathroom. Some people are fine with having one right off the kitchen, but kitchens are gathering places and nobody wants to hear anybody doing their business while eating their pork chops."

"What if I move the bathroom to the other side of the laundry room? That way the plumbing lines don't need to be moved."

"That's great thinking. Good work. You should get an A in this class."

"Thanks. I'm going to miss being here after the semester is over."

"You can always work here for free over the summer. We won't kick you out."

Molly smiled at him. "I'll think about it. I've got to head out to class. I'll see you in the morning." She stepped away from his desk and spotted Carter. "Hi, Carter." She gave him a shy smile. "I didn't see you standing there."

"I didn't mean to intrude. I just came to talk to Steven."

"No worries. I'm on my way out." She lightly set her hand on his arm. "I'll see you tomorrow. Maybe when I'm finished with this class I can take you and Steven out to dinner to thank you for all you've taught me."

Carter shook his head. "You don't have to thank me. Steven is your teacher here."

"But I want to. Let me know what date works best for you." She walked out then.

"Damn," Steven said, shaking his head. "The girl has it bad for you. Clearly she has no taste, because of the two of us I'm more charming and way better looking than you."

"I know," Carter said, drily. "I often find myself daydreaming about what our future children would look like."

Steven chuckled. "What's up? I haven't seen Ruby today."

"She's taking an art class at the community center. She took the bus there. She's never taken the bus."

Steven left his desk and clapped Carter on the back. "She's all right, man. I took the bus to school every day from kindergarten on. My father was a bus driver. She's fine."

"I know that, but—"

"You have got to spend some time away from your kid once in a while. Come out with me this weekend. You're single or soon to be. Right?" He smiled slightly. "I haven't heard you say anything about Belinda lately. What's going on there?"

Carter sighed, feeling heavy. "Long story short I don't want to give her up, but I'm not sure we're going to work out."

"Why aren't you sure?"

"Because she keeps asking me for the damn divorce papers. And then there is Ruby. She's gotten so close to Belinda. What if Bell decides she really doesn't want this and walks out again? I can't let Ruby grow to love her, just to have her walk out on us."

"It would be like losing another mother." Steven nodded with understanding. "Have you talked to Belinda about getting back together?"

"Not really. I have this annoying little problem. I can't seem to keep my hands off her whenever were alone."

"You're stuck on this girl. We both know that you can't live in the same town with her if things are going to be like this. You're going to have to figure out how to make this work or one of you is going to have to leave."

He nodded. It would have to be him. It would be unfair to expect her to move away. Her life was grounded here.

"Why are you still single, Steven? You're thirty-five. Don't you want kids? Haven't you dated every woman in this town already?"

"I was engaged once, remember?"

"Yeah, but you never told me what happened. I only met her once, but she seemed perfect for you."

"She was. On paper. Nice girl. Good family. Beautiful, but something was missing, and it took me a long time to realize it was love. Rene was just some woman I was going to marry. She wasn't the woman I wanted to spend the rest of my life with. I wasn't stuck on her. And I kept thinking about you and Bethany. I didn't want to end up walking down the aisle with a woman who was all wrong for me."

"You knew Bethany was all wrong for me? Why the hell didn't you say something?"

"We weren't so tight then. It wasn't my place to say anything."

"I know we haven't kept in touch over the years like we should, but I'm here now. Let's not let that happen again."

He nodded. "That's why you're going to come out with me on Saturday. You need to clear your head and I need to meet some new women."

"I'll think about it. I need to find a babysitter first."

"My mother can watch her. Or one of my sisters. She'll be fine. You have no excuse."

"Okay, Steven. I'll be there. I've got to go get Ruby. I'll see you tomorrow."

Fifteen minutes later Carter walked into the buzzing community center. There were kids everywhere, outside playing kickball, inside at the indoor pool, in the gym line dancing. There were adults, too, he found as he walked down the hallway where Ruby's class was being held. They were in classes of their own. He passed pottery makers and what appeared to be quilters before he walked up to Ruby's room.

It was empty except for three people. The tall blonde he knew as Cherri, Belinda, and his little girl. Cherri and

Belinda were talking and Ruby sat there quietly on her stool with her head resting on Belinda's stomach. Belinda was absently stroking Ruby's curls.

There was no point in keeping them away from each other, he realized. Ruby was already attached. She was craving a woman in her life, and Belinda was the one she chose.

"Am I late?" he asked walking in. "I'm sorry, Ruby. I thought the class got out at five forty-five."

"No, Mr. Lancaster," Cherri said, turning toward him. "You're not. The other kids belong to the kids' club enrichment program so they all leave together to go to their next activity. Since Ruby is just signed up for this class, you pick her up here."

"Good." He breathed a sigh of relief as he lifted his daughter up. "Hi, honey. Did you have a good time?"

"I had lots of fun. I like painting." She looked back at Belinda, whom he had avoided making eye contact with. "Belinda is taking this class, too. Did you know that, Daddy? Cherri is her best friend. Cherri paints things and people give her money for it."

"That's very cool, Rube."

"She's talented, Mr. Lancaster." Cherri gifted him with a beaming smile. "Look at her work. She has amazing skill for a five-year-old."

Carter glanced at the easel to his right. There was an oddly shaped red flower that he assumed was a rose. Ruby had always liked to draw. She loved art. That was something she had gotten from her mother, who had majored in art history in college. "What a beautiful rose, baby. We'll have to frame it."

"Um." Belinda cleared her throat. "That one is mine. Ruby's is the sunflower."

He looked over to the next easel to see a vibrant yellow sunflower, complete with seeds. He had assumed that an older child had done it when he first saw it. "Wow, Rube. This is so beautiful! I can't believe how talented you are."

She blushed, her cheeks turning pink. "Belinda tried really hard, Daddy, but she can't paint like me yet. Mrs. O'Connell said that she was going to have to practice some more."

"Yeah," Belinda said, standing up. "I can't paint as well as a kindergartner."

"You're good at other things, honey." Cherri patted her back. "Mr. Lancaster—"

"Carter, please."

"Carter." Cherri nodded. "I think Ruby should paint more than just in my classroom. She has a great eye for color already, and if she practices I think she could do outstanding work."

"You want to paint more, Rube? We can go to the art supply place this weekend and get you some things."

"Yes, I like painting. I think I should help Belinda learn."

"That's a very sweet offer." Cherri grinned at Belinda before she looked back to him. "You don't have to go to the store, I have some supplies in my car that I can give her today. Would it be all right if I take her to get them now?"

"It's fine." He set Ruby on her feet and watched her walk out hand in hand with Cherri.

He was left alone with Belinda again. He finally fully looked at her. She was wearing a black smock over her little grass-green dress and a mulish expression on her face.

"I didn't know she was going to be in this class, Carter. But I'm not going to drop out of it. And you can't ask me to stay away from her while I'm here," she said with so much conviction his damn heart squeezed painfully. "I won't hurt her like that. I refuse to."

He leaned forward and settled his lips against hers. It

was the only rational thing he could do in that moment. The sizzle was there immediately, but he didn't react to it. He kept his kiss light, trying to thank her for her sweetness without words. "I'm not asking you to give this class up," he said against her mouth. "You clearly need it."

"Rub it in," she said, grinning against his mouth. "I know my painting sucks."

He slid his hands along her jawline and gently pulled her face toward his. "Come here. I want to feel you against me."

She did as he asked, her expression wary but her body willing. He wrapped his arms around her, pulling her closer, tangling his fingers in her thick red hair. "I'm sorry for what I said to you the other day. I didn't mean it that way. Thank you for being so sweet to her."

"I couldn't be mean to her if I tried. She's a great kid, Carter. You've done an amazing job with her." She looked up into his eyes. "And that's why I get so pissed at you every time I'm with her."

"What?" He blinked at her. "Why?"

"Ruby was supposed to be my baby. Our baby. I feel like I was cheated."

Her words brought him up short. "You could have stayed," he said without anger for the first time. "We could have raised her together. She would have been ours."

She shook her head. "No. Not with Bethany there. Bethany was her mother. Ruby was her baby. She was the baby the two of you made. If Bethany had lived, I would always be the stepmother. Not her mother. Not like I would have wanted to be. It may have been selfish but I wanted to be the one who had your first child."

"So what are you saying? That you couldn't love a man who has children already?"

"No." She shook her head. "Of course not. If you had told me about Bethany before, things might have been different. But things aren't different. You had a life before me that I didn't know about. We didn't know each other before we got married. And if we did I wouldn't feel like I lost out on something good."

"But, Belinda, I—"

"Bill Junior?"

Belinda's father was standing just inside the door. Belinda tried to pull away from him, but at first he didn't let her go. He couldn't. This conversation wasn't over yet. She wanted children, a family. She had wanted those things with him. It was something they hadn't talked about in their short time together. But it was something they could talk about now. He could give her those things. She was right, they didn't know each other then, but they were learning about each other now. He could get to know her now. They could make things work.

"I've got to go, Carter."

"Okay." He cupped her face in his hands, pressing a soft kiss to her mouth before he let her go.

Her eyes widened in shock and she darted a glance to her father but he didn't care if Bill saw. He would be seeing a lot more of them together. Belinda was his wife. He was going to get her back.

CHAPTER 16

A night to remember . . .

Belinda's doorbell rang just as she was putting on her mascara. She frowned at the clock, knowing it couldn't be Cherri or Ellis at her door. They were all going to meet at the restaurant separately to have a girls' night out. Full of fruity drinks and lots of blabbing. They were going to have a night like they did before the girls got married, before Cherri became a mother. Before Ellis got pregnant. Before life had changed so much for them. She was looking forward to it. She missed her friends and the way they used to be together. Not that she wished she could go back to that time. Ellis and Cherri were so happy. But it would be nice, for one night, to go back to a simpler time.

The doorbell rang again. Sighing, she tossed her mascara on the vanity and trudged downstairs to see who was there.

Please let it be anyone but Carter.

She'd had about enough of him. Unfortunately her

body was buzzing for his touch. It missed him. Her brain, however, wanted him as far away as possible. She still couldn't believe that he had kissed her in front of her father. It was no rushed kiss, either. No caught-in-the-moment embrace. It was deliberate. Like he was trying to tell her something.

Whatever it was, she wasn't sure if she wanted to hear it.

She made it to her door just as the ringer rang for the third time. "Oh, Pudge! I was standing outside forever. Ringing and ringing and ringing. I never thought you would answer. It's still quite chilly at night and I didn't bring a heavier coat."

"What can I do for you, *Mamá?*" Belinda asked when her mother took a breath. She stepped aside to let her mother in, noting how great she looked in jeans and a button-up blouse.

"I just came to see how you were. Your father sees you more than I do these days." She frowned as she studied Belinda from head to toe. "Are you going out tonight?"

"Yes?"

"And you are wearing that?"

"Yes." Belinda put her hands on her hips. "What's wrong with it?"

"Nothing. I like you in purple, but that print is a little bold? No? Maybe you should wear black?"

"Why, *Mamá?*" She raised a brow. "Because black is slimming?"

It took a long time before her mother answered. "What's wrong with wanting to look slimmer?" She briefly touched Belinda's cheek. "Are you going out with Carter tonight?"

"No. Why?"

"I just was wondering. Your father told me that he saw him kiss you."

"Yes. He did." She waited for her mother to continue, curious to know why she was really there. After years of silence about Carter, was her curiosity finally getting the better of her?

"It wasn't the first time, was it?"

"No, *Mamá*. It wasn't."

"Are you getting back together?

She shook her head. "I don't know, *Mamá*, I really don't."

Her mother searched her face for a long moment as if she was trying to search out some truth. She wished her mother would just ask or say what she wanted.

"Oh. Okay. I have to go now." She turned to leave.

"What? I thought you came here to talk."

"Talk? I talk all the time. Your father says I never run out of words. I think that's why he is taking the classes at the center, so he can have two more hours a day with me not talking."

"But, *Mamá* . . ."

"What, darling? I just wanted to see you. That's all." She kissed Belinda's forehead. "Come by for dinner next week. You can bring him if you want. And the little girl, too. I want to know him."

"But we're . . ." She stopped herself from denying they were a couple.

He was weakening her. Before he came back she'd been determined to find a new path in life, not travel down an old one.

"Do you think I would get back together with him without telling you?"

"I don't know what to think, Pudge." She shook her head. "You didn't tell me when you got married. You didn't tell me you weren't divorced. You don't tell me anything."

She walked out after that, and for the first time in her life Belinda wished her mother had more to say.

"Are you sure you are going to be okay here tonight?" Carter asked his daughter for the third time. He was leaving her at Steven's sister's house for the night, for a sleepover with Steven's nieces, with three other little girls, one of them Ruby's age.

"Yes, Daddy. We're gonna watch a movie, and then we are gonna play with dolls, and Mrs. Cameron said we could make ice cream sundaes, too."

"It sounds like fun. But if you feel sick or scared or you just want to come home, you call me and I'll come get you."

"I know, Daddy. You told me," she said, sounding a bit annoyed with him.

"Yes, Daddy," Steven said from behind him. "The kid is telling you she's going to be fine. Let's go. The band starts playing at eight."

He held in a sigh, kissed his daughter's hair, and followed Steven out. He had never left her overnight before. He was almost feeling a bit of panic, not that he would ever admit it to anyone. It was irrational. Steven's sister was a preschool teacher. She had three daughters. Her husband was a police officer, and he had known the woman for over fifteen years. Ruby was in good hands. He just felt uneasy about leaving her overnight.

"What the hell happened to you, man?" Steven asked, smacking him on the back as they made their way to Steven's car. "You're worse than a woman."

"Wait until you have a daughter."

Fifteen minutes later they walked into Rubio's. It was a modern lounge type of place. Restaurant during the day, nightclub in the evenings, catering to Durant's after-college crowd. Not a two-for-one beer special or beat-up pool table in sight. The band, complete with a brass section, was setting up onstage.

"You look like a man who needs a drink," Steven said. "It's been a long time since we've been out drinking together. You still a scotch-and-soda man? First round is on me."

"I think I'll just have a beer," he said as he turned to survey the crowd. "It's been so long since I've been out."

He looked around him, trying to remember the last time he had been single. It was right before he met Belinda. Steven had flown in for a few days and they had gone out to a place similar to this. Filled with mostly late-twenty- and thirty-somethings, looking to have a relaxing time. He hadn't found anybody who sparked his interest that night and he knew tonight would be the same. The only girl he wanted was probably at home tonight.

"Trying to decide who we should sit with?"

"No—" he started, but then he saw her. The only girl he ever wanted was coming his way.

"Ick." Ellis rubbed her tummy. "I don't think I should have eaten all that food. My stomach is pissed at me."

"That blue cheese garlic bread was good, though," Cherri said. "I could have eaten a whole loaf by myself."

"It was good. I think it was the buffalo chicken quesadillas that did it. I don't think the baby likes spicy food."

"No?" Belinda asked. "I thought jalapeños, extra hot sauce, and the pepper you added to it were going to sit well with you."

"Mike warned me before I left not to overdo it. I told him that I knew my body better than he did, but he was right. I hate it when he's right." She frowned.

"I'm assuming you told Mike you were pregnant. The man hasn't stopped smiling for the past two days."

"Yes." She rubbed her belly again. "I was going to tell him on our anniversary but the dumb man ruined the surprise by telling me he wanted to talk about having kids. I had no choice but to tell him."

"I hope you have a girl, Ellis," Cherri said. "That way your baby can marry my baby and we can control their lives forever." Cherri leaned over and squeezed Ellis's arm.

"Next time we'll plan on getting pregnant together. It would be so much fun."

"Next time? Fun?" Belinda shook her head. "She hasn't even popped this kid out yet and you're planning another?"

"Duh." Cherri rolled her eyes. "We can buy baby clothes together and plan our nurseries together and get extra fat together. Fun."

"For whom exactly would that be fun?" Belinda asked, looking at her two best friends. "Then I would be forced to deal with two always hungry, crazy, emotional pregnant ladies. And frankly, I don't think my nerves are good enough for that."

"You could get knocked up with us," Ellis stated with a shrug. "Then we can be three hungry pregnant moody bitches." She groaned. "Just don't eat jalapeños."

Pregnant. Her last conversation with Carter came to mind. She had never voiced it before, not even to herself, but she wanted a baby and her own family. For some reason she had stopped thinking that was possible.

"I'll go to the bar to get you some seltzer," she said, standing up. "Try not to toss your cookies on the table." She then studied Ellis, who was rubbing her small belly. "Would you rather go home?"

"No. I don't want to go home! We are going to dance and laugh and stagger into the house after ten PM. You know I can't stay up that late anymore. And this baby is taking it out of me even more. I haven't seen *The Daily Show* in months."

"Girl, DVR it," Belinda said. "I haven't made it past ten thirty in two years." She sighed and looked back at her friends. "What the hell happened to us?"

"Life."

She nodded and then headed toward the bar. Life happened when you least expected it.

A hand reached out and grabbed her wrist just as she was about to approach the bar. "Are you just going to walk right past me?"

She stiffened upon hearing his voice.

Damn. She'd been determined not to think about him tonight. She wanted to hang with her girls and pretend that she was carefree.

But 99 percent of her cares were standing right in front of her.

"If I didn't know any better I would think you were stalking me."

"I was thinking it was the other way around." He pulled her closer, his arm wrapping around her waist, his hand settling on her hip possessively. Like he had the right to. Like his hand belonged there. She felt those damn tingles again. "I've been thinking about you all day," he said into her ear, his warm breath tickling her skin. "I've been missing you."

Damn.

It had always been bad, but lately every time she was near him, she felt something. It wasn't just the extreme attraction, the sizzle that never failed to make them cook. There was something soft there, too. Like butterflies. Like how she felt with her first crush. It almost felt like being in love again. Which was a stupid feeling, because she was pretty sure she had never stopped loving him.

"I wish I didn't have to miss you so much," he said, making her heart thud painfully.

But this time it felt a little different.

Shit.

His lips brushed the skin just beneath her ear, leaving the softest of kisses. "I want you to meet somebody."

He turned a little, lifting his lips from her skin, leaving her feeling almost bereft. It was then she noticed that there was another man standing there. Steven Oliver. She knew him but she didn't. She had been friendly with his younger sister in school. His mother even shopped in her store, though they had never spoken.

"This is my best friend and business partner, Steven."

"I know exactly who this man is," she said, willing herself not to be embarrassed by what Steven had just witnessed between her and Carter. "We've been avoiding each other like the plague for the last four years."

"You have?"

"Of course we have," Steven said with a smile on his face. "We act like we are perfect strangers. It's awkward living in the same town with your best friend's estranged wife. I wasn't sure whether to hate her or ask her out."

"I probably would have said yes if you asked me out. You're cute." Belinda nodded, glad that Steven broke the tension.

Steven shrugged his grin, growing a little naughtier, a little wider. "I had to ignore her totally, because if I had asked her out we probably would have fallen in love and made beautiful little brown babies, because you know how much more charming I am than you are. And you would have been pissed at me. I've seen you in a fight. I've seen you knock a guy's tooth out, and since my teeth are my best feature I stayed away."

"I'm glad our friendship means so much to you, Steven. Thank you," he said drily.

"No problem." He extended his hand and brazenly studied her. "It's nice to finally get to meet you. Now that I see you up close, I know why he hasn't been able to get you out of his system. You are amazing to look at."

Belinda smiled at the compliment. "You sure you don't want to go out with me?"

"You busy tomorrow night?"

"Good-bye, Steven." Carter shook his head at his friend and gently led her away from him. "Let me buy you a drink."

"No. More alcohol is the last thing I need, especially around you. I've had one tonight. That's enough."

"What happens if you have two?" he asked, his eyes suddenly curious.

"I'll probably end up trying to have sex with you in the bathroom."

"Excuse me?" His eyes bulged a little. He was so cute when he was surprised.

"I'm going to give it to you straight, Carter." She walked up to the bar. "I get stupid when you are around. My head loses all common sense. My stomach gets all fluttery and my panties . . . well, you don't want to know the state of my panties."

"Well, actually I do."

She ignored that little remark and continued. "The simple fact of the matter is that I'm trying to stay away from you and it's hard. I don't want to want to sleep with you. I don't want to fall back in love with you. So you're going to have to leave me alone." She waved at the busy bartender failing to get his attention.

"I thought you weren't drinking."

"I'm not. I came to get Ellis some seltzer. She's not feeling well."

"No?" He signaled the bartender, who acknowledged him. "Are you going to leave?"

"She doesn't want to. It's just indigestion. She's pregnant and spicy foods no longer agree with her."

"You know it's too late, right? You know this is going to happen between us. Why are you trying to stop it?"

She turned to him and forced her eyes up to his. "Why did you kiss me in front of my father? What the hell were you trying to pull?" She shook her head. "I had plans, you know. I had all these plans and a path set out. You're screwing that up for me."

"Really, Bell? What plans did you have? Because it

looks to me like you've been stuck for the last four years. Like your life, at least personally, has gone nowhere."

"Shut up." His words stung, but they were true. She had been stuck on sit and spin since she walked out on him. "You don't know what the hell you're talking about."

"I do. Because I have been stuck, too. Why do you think I'm here? I couldn't wait any longer for you to come back so I'm here. I'm here with my daughter. I'm changing my life. Is it too much to ask you to change yours?"

"Yes" was all she said before she walked away. Yes. It was too much. As much as she loved him, their marriage wasn't good for her. Because she always had the feeling she wasn't good enough for him. And that left her heart feeling a little bruised.

"Hey, where's my seltzer?" Ellis complained when she got back to the table.

"Sorry," Belinda muttered. "Carter is up there. I got all . . . flustered."

"Carter's here?" Ellis sat up straight, looking out into the room. "Where? Why am I the only one who hasn't met him? Even Maggie has. It's not fair."

"I'm sorry that my husband has yet to barge into my life while you were with me. Maybe next time I marry a stranger I can be more considerate and have him stalk me around your schedule."

"Meow," Ellis said. "Is he really stalking you?"

"Not intentionally, but he's every freaking where I go."

"We know that, but if you didn't have feelings for him," Cherri said softly, "you wouldn't be bothered by his presence."

"Of course I have feelings for him! I love him!"

Ellis and Cherri exchanged looks.

"What? Why do you look surprised? You think you could stop loving Mike or Colin just like that?"

"No, honey. Of course not," Ellis said. "We just never thought you would admit it."

"He loves her, too, Ellis." Cherri glanced toward the bar. "You should see the way he looks at her."

"I know he hurt you, Belinda. But if you two are in love, then why can't you be together?"

Because he broke my heart. And it hurt too damn much.

"I'm having my quarter-life crisis right now. Last year it was Cherri's turn. The year before it was yours. I would like my chance to be crazy and irrational without you two judging me."

"Somebody is cranky," Cherri said to Ellis.

"Somebody needs to get laid," Ellis said back to her.

Belinda wondered if it was possible to smack two people at the same time.

"Look! He's coming this way." Cherri grinned.

"Fantastic." Ellis clapped her hands. "Maybe she'll get lucky tonight."

"I hate you both."

"Good." Ellis nodded. "That means we're family. All families hate each other sometimes."

"You wanted a seltzer?" Carter approached them, setting down the glass of fizzy water in front of Ellis, but instead of looking at her and Cherri he kept his eyes on Belinda. He didn't have to speak to her to understand what his eyes were saying.

Why did you run away? Are you scared?

The answer was yes. With a capital Y.

"You must be Ellis. I'm Carter. It's nice to meet you." He nodded his greeting to Cherri.

"Well, damn, Belinda. You never told me he looked like the guy from *Mad Men*."

"He's beautiful." She made a vague motion in Carter's direction. "That's why I married him. I'm incredibly shallow."

Carter slid into the booth, not giving her any space, his big body pressed against her side. They couldn't be in the same room, the same space, without touching. She couldn't be on the same planet with him without thinking about him. She was screwed. Seriously screwed.

"I married her for the same reason," he said, his eyes roaming her face. "We don't talk. We just stare at each other and admire our magnificence."

Belinda rolled her eyes, but her friends laughed.

"It's good to meet you, Carter. And thank you for my seltzer." Ellis extended her hand. "It's nice to put a face to the name of the guy our friend has never told us about."

"Belinda never talked about me?" He glanced at her. "I would have sworn you ladies had a stack of voodoo dolls of me in a drawer somewhere."

"Nope." Ellis shook her head. "If she had told us, trust me, we would have. But not a word from Miss Tight Lips over there. I didn't know you two were married until you showed up here a few weeks ago." Ellis rested her hand on her chin and looked from Carter to Belinda. Belinda knew her best friend. She knew when Ellis was up to something. She just didn't know what.

"Now it makes sense why Belinda never had a boyfriend for the past few years and why she turned down so many dates. She was married to you. I've known Belinda most of my life and I've never known the girl to be a saint, but she has been almost nun-like in her chastity these past few years. What about you, Carter? Have you dated a lot since your separation?"

"Ellis," Belinda hissed. She kicked out, hoping to connect with Ellis's shin.

"Ouch," Cherri yelped instead. She frowned at Belinda as she rubbed her aching leg. "Are you wearing those stupid spiky shoes? I think I'm bleeding."

"You are not!"

"I could be!"

"It's all right, Bell," Carter said in a calming voice that made her want to punch him. He draped his arm over her shoulder, pulling her closer so he could soothingly rub her arm. "I haven't dated, Ellis. I've been too busy raising my daughter and growing my career."

"That's understandable." She nodded. "I met Ruby. She's a great kid. But everybody gets a little lonely sometimes. What about sex? You don't have to date anybody to have sex. Have you been having a lot of sex since you and Belinda split?"

Belinda felt her face grow hot as mortification swept over her. It was a question that had crossed her mind a few times, too, especially since she'd spilled the beans that there hadn't been anybody else but him in all this time. But she didn't want Carter to have to explain himself in front of her friends. What the hell had gotten into Ellis?

If this was payback for keeping Carter a secret from her, it sure as hell was effective.

"Uh-oh, Ellie," Cherri said. "She looks kind of mad."

"I know. Her cheeks are all red. What do you think it will take for smoke to come out of her ears?"

"Ellis, I'm going to hurt you," Belinda warned. "Like, seriously hurt you. You are not going to have any hair left when I get finished with you."

"I'm pregnant." She folded her arms across her chest and raised her chin. "You can't beat up a pregnant lady."

"Yeah, but I can knock your teeth out."

Ellis waved her hands back and forth. "I'm shaking in my boots, Belinda."

Carter watched as Belinda's eyes sparked with anger. He had only seen her look at him that way. It made him smile. It was nice to see her pissed at somebody else for a change.

"You should be scared." Belinda lunged across the table and pinched Ellis's arm.

"You bitch," she said rubbing her arm. "That hurt."

"It was supposed to!"

Carter suppressed a laugh. Belinda was pretty damn cute when she was mad. Still, he didn't want her to kill her best friend. It was odd seeing her interact with her friends this way. They were more like sisters. It was the way they spoke to each other, the way they bickered and openly teased that told him they were more than just friends. She was so natural with them, so unguarded. In San Francisco he hadn't seen her like this. Whenever they went out she stuck by his side, only speaking when directly spoken to. He had foolishly thought she was shy then, but now he realized how uncomfortable she'd been there. It wasn't like his family had gone out of their way to make her feel welcome.

They had never spent time doing what she wanted to do or with her friends. Belinda kind of morphed into a member of his world, and seeing her now he knew that she wasn't that kind of person. The more he saw her here with her friends and family, the more he understood how they could have never lasted in San Francisco.

Of course they hadn't lasted. They didn't have a shot.

Then.

He didn't believe that now.

"Hey, what's going on here?" Steven walked up, grinning. "If I had known there was going to be a catfight I would have come over a lot sooner."

"Steven Oliver." Ellis glanced at Belinda and then back at Steven. The woman had mischief in her eyes. "Rumor is that Carter is your best friend. So you must know something about his sex life. Has he been hooking up a lot since he and Belinda took their little break?"

Belinda reached across the table again, but this time

Carter had caught her arm and lifted her up away from the table. "Let's go, firecracker."

"What are you doing?" She struggled until he set her on her feet.

"The band is starting to play. Let's dance."

"But I don't want to dance with you."

"Too bad. We need to dance off some of your aggression. If you get arrested tonight then I'm never going to hear the end of it from my mother." He pulled her out on the dance floor, grabbing her by her hips to keep her near him.

"Your mother can kiss my ass."

"You have my permission to tell her that next time we see her."

She opened her mouth to retort but seemed lost for words. She was fighting the fact that he was coming after her, that he was going to get her back. He was tired of fighting himself, deluding himself. The only time he ever felt right was when he was with her.

"We've never danced together before," he said before she could collect her thoughts. They moved easily together despite her unwillingness. He led, keeping up with the fast-paced tempo of the band. She followed, brushing her sweet little body against his. The dance floor wasn't crowded. The room wasn't hot, but his temperature went up.

"I didn't think you could dance."

"Why? Just because I come from an uptight, stuffy. WASP family doesn't mean I can't dance."

"I guess not." She looked up and smiled at him for the first time that night. "You're actually pretty good."

"My partner inspires me." The song ended, the band went into a slower song, and as if it were the most natural thing in the world, Belinda inched herself closer to him, looping her arms around his neck.

"I've never seen you in anything but a suit since you've been here." She studied him for a long moment. "You look good in jeans."

"Did I just hear you pay me a compliment?"

"Don't look so shocked. Your ass looks good in them and I've always been an ass woman. You don't have to wear a suit all the time in Durant, you know. This town is laid-back. I think people assume you're some kind of narc when they see you all buttoned up."

"You don't like me in suits?"

"No, it's not that. When we met you were wearing a suit. I've got a thing for men in suits." She shook her head. "But under the suit and your neat haircut, there's a bit of a rebel. You're like an enigma. You confuse the hell out of me."

"I'm not so confusing and I'm definitely not a rebel. I've followed too many rules in my life."

"You didn't go into the family business. You married me. You left your high-paying job and moved across the country. You've got tattoos."

He shook his head, unable to agree with her. "You think I'm a rebel? I spent most of my life doing what was expected of me. I let my parents pick my college. I married a woman I didn't love just to please my parents. I'm not a rebel. I just decided I was done living the life everybody else wanted me to live. I needed to prove I was my own man before I started to hate myself more than I already did."

"You shouldn't hate yourself. They guilted you," she said to him. "That's what parents do. They guilt you and they bug you and they suck the life out of you. My parents do the same thing to me. I'm their only child. They like to spend inordinate amounts of time with me. They come to my job and show up at my house uninvited. They drive me to drinking but I don't stop them from being smothering because I feel guilty."

"What do you have to be guilty about?"

"Oh, lots of things. I ran away from home when I was eighteen. I never got my bachelor's degree. I moved to the other side of the country and I married you, a man I barely knew, and didn't tell them about it until two weeks after it happened. Do you know what my mother said when she found out? 'Oh, Belinda. How could you?' She never calls me Belinda. Only when she's upset. My mother who is a fountain of words had nothing else to say about our marriage but that. She had been planning my wedding since birth and I robbed her of that and took myself far away from her, and I feel guilty for that. So I will go fishing and pretend I like beer and listen to my mother blab on for hours about nothing to make up for my mistakes."

He thought about what she'd just said for a moment. It was his idea to elope. He had asked her to marry him on a whim. He had never thought about robbing her of her dream wedding. He never asked her if she wanted one, because he'd had a big one the year before. His guilt was just as heavy as hers. He needed to make up for it, too.

"Why didn't you tell them about us right away? Why didn't you tell your friends about me?"

"I don't know," she said quietly. "I think I was afraid of us failing. It happened so fast and at times you seemed a little too good to be true. I was scared I was going to wake up one day and find out that you used to be a woman or that you had six wives in four states, and that I would hear nothing but I-told-you-sos and feel like a big fool."

"And then you found out that I had one former wife and parents who were horrible to you."

"And I felt like a big fat fool anyway. I guess I should have told them. The outcome would have been the same."

"I'm sorry, you know." He cupped her face in his hands and kissed her eyelids. "I'm so sorry about everything."

"Stop apologizing."

"I will." He kissed her forehead. "When I stop feeling sorry."

"Carter . . ." Her eyes teared.

"I think you should know that I haven't been with anybody else."

"What?"

"Hey, you two!" Ellis came dancing up. "The song has changed twice already. You two look kind of nutty swaying slowly in the middle of the dance floor while everybody else is shaking their rumps."

Carter looked around him. Sure enough, everybody else was keeping up with the fast-paced tempo of the song. He hadn't noticed. He was too wrapped up in her.

"Go away, preggers. We're talking."

"Well, excuse me." She looked back at Cherri. "Shake your tail feather with me, honey. I think we've lost her for the night."

"There's been no one else? No one? Not a hookup with a colleague. Not a quickie with a client? Nothing?"

"We're married. I never forgot that."

"I've been dating," she blurted. "I started right after our anniversary. I've never been with anybody else, but I went on a few dates."

He didn't like hearing that, but he nodded. What could he say? He had waited so long to come after her. "It's okay."

"I know it's okay. I'm not apologizing. I'm just letting you know. We're supposed to be getting divorced."

"I'm not divorcing you, Bell."

"You're not?"

"No. I—"

"You should date, Carter," she cut in. "You should go out and date other women and play the field."

"Bell." He shook his head. "I'm don't want—"

He was cut off again but this time by a man, grabbing Belinda's upper arm.

"Hey, buddy. Mind if I cut in?"

"I mind, Theo!" Belinda shot back, shaking the guy's hand off her. "I don't want to dance with you."

Carter stiffened, trying to place Belinda away from the man. But she wasn't having it. She wasn't backing down, either. She must have known him. He was tall, probably an inch or two taller than Carter. He wore a backward baseball cap, and a DURANT U FOOTBALL T-shirt stretched across his substantial gut.

"Why not? You've been dancing with this clown for fifteen minutes and you don't know him. I've known you half your life. You can't dance with me for five damn minutes?"

Belinda rolled her eyes. "I don't know how many times I have to tell you this. Just because we lived on the same street growing up doesn't mean you have any claim on me."

"I was the only guy who liked you when you were a fat ugly teenager and now you won't even give me the time of day."

The hairs on the back of Carter's neck went up. His hands balled into fists. "What did you say to her?"

"Stay out of this," Theo said, his eyes flashing as he looked at Belinda. "I don't know what happened to you, but you turned into such a stuck-up frigid bitch. It's no wonder all your friends are married and have families and you are the only one who doesn't. Come off your perch. You're not as hot as your mother is anyway."

Carter stepped forward but he didn't have a chance to put his hands on the guy because Belinda went after him, grabbing his shirt with one hand, her other hand balled into a fist. She swung at him, not a girlie slap, but a full-on jackrabbit punch. The guy's head snapped back. Spittle flew from his lips. He stumbled backward.

"I may have been a fat kid, but I was never ugly. And the next time you call me a bitch you're going to be missing a tongue. Go home, Theo. You're drunk. And you better hope I don't tell your mother about this. I know she would hate to have a thirty-year-old disrespectful jackass living in her basement. Let's face it, Theo, you don't want her pissed off because you don't have any other place to go."

"I can't believe you hit me, you crazy b—"

She lunged at him. "Say it again."

Carter grabbed her by the waist and lifted her away from the man and out of the bar altogether.

"What the hell are you doing?"

"I'm getting you out of here before you maim somebody." He set her down in the parking lot.

"But Theo had it coming. Did you hear what he said to me?"

"I know, champ." He cupped her face in his hands and kissed her. "He had it coming and you clocked him pretty good, but I wanted to hit him. You didn't even give me the chance."

"Did you want to hit him?" She lost the aggravated look on her face. "Should I have played damsel in distress and let you beat him up for me?"

"Yes. It would have been nice."

"Yo, Carter!"

He turned to see Steven rushing out of the bar. "Get her out of here now. That asshole is pissing mad and looking to stir up some more shit."

"He's all talk." Belinda waved her hand dismissively. "He's not planning on doing anything."

"You hit him. In a room full of people," Steven said. "If the cops are called you're going in."

"Shit." She looked back to Carter and then shut her eyes for a moment. "Your mother would just love that.

Wouldn't she? Instead of paying me off, she'll probably pay to have me offed."

"I wouldn't put it past her, but let me take you home just in case."

"I shouldn't have hit him. I just don't like that he thinks he can talk down to me just because I turned him down. I don't know why he thought it was okay to try to degrade me."

"It's not okay. It's not okay for him to talk to you like that."

"You guys need to go," Steven said impatiently. "I'm going to try and smooth things over. Just get her out of here."

"What about you?"

"I'll take Belinda's car. Ellis is getting her stuff out of the coat check. Just get her out of here now! I'll talk to you later."

He didn't hesitate a second longer, he just grabbed Belinda and pulled her toward his SUV.

"He's not going to do anything. Let me go back in there and talk to him."

"No. No more arguments. Let me take you home."

She exhaled, getting into his car without another word.

He started it up and pulled onto the road. "Who is that guy?"

"Theo Wassell. He's the first guy I ever went out with."

"Why? He's an asshole."

"Yeah," she said softly. "He always kind of was one, but he asked me out. Nobody else had asked me out so I said yes. He's the kind of guy who goes in for a kiss and tries to suck your brains out. But I went out with him a handful of times, and I let him try to suck my brains out a handful of times. Then the last time I did he wasn't content to just kiss and grope me. He pulled out a condom and when I said no he got nasty with me. Ever since then he's been pissed at me. Trying to get with me or back at me at every shot. I shouldn't have hit him. I know it was wrong but he had it coming. He's had it coming for a long time."

"I don't get it, Bell. If you looked anything then like you look like now, then those boys in your high school were totally fucking stupid. I would have fallen over if you walked through my high school."

She looked up at him and smiled beautifully. "You went to an all-boys' high school, baby. I would hope I could have caused a little hiccup there. I was a very awkward teenager and my mother was so damn gorgeous. She still is, but she decided that she was going to take an active role in my education when we moved here. Both my parents worked a lot before we came to Durant, which left them feeling guilty. Which meant they chose to spend every waking moment of my adolescent years with me. My mother was in my school a lot. She volunteered to chaperone dances and she helped out in home economics class during our sewing unit. She ran every fund-raiser, including the car wash. Durant's high school isn't that big. Everybody knew who my mother was and everybody couldn't help but compare me with her. I didn't survive the comparison."

"My parents were the opposite. When your parents were smothering you, mine sent me across the country to school. For a time I thought they sent me away because they hated me."

"And now?"

"I'm not sure much has changed." He laughed, but it sounded bitter to his own ears.

"That's not true. They offered a lot of money to keep you away from a gold-digging hussy. If that's not love . . ."

Carter pulled into her driveway, put the car into park, and leaned over to kiss her without warning. She closed her eyes and let herself be kissed. He took his time, like she was new to him, like he hadn't already kissed her a thousand times. Part of her felt like she was sixteen and had butterflies; part of her felt like she was falling in love for the first time all over again. It was how all kisses should be. But it wasn't enough. She wasn't content to just kiss him anymore. She wanted to lie beside him, to feel him on top of her, inside her. She was tired of all the barriers. Emotional ones. Physical ones. She just wanted to be with him. Doubts be damned.

"I would have slept with him," she said when he lifted his mouth from hers. "I would have slept with him if he kissed anywhere as good as you."

"Who? That asshole from the bar?" He grinned at her in that boyish way she was fond of. "I'm glad he didn't. I want to be the only one who kisses you like that."

"Come—" His cell phone rang just as she was about to ask him to come inside and spend the night with her.

He glanced at the clock on the dashboard then frowned and pressed the Bluetooth button to answer it. "It might be about Ruby. Hello?"

Ah. Ruby. Somehow she had forgotten all about the little girl.

"Hi, Daddy." Her voice came clearly through the speaker. "It's me, Ruby."

Belinda watched Carter's face soften. "Hi, baby. Are you okay?"

"I'm fine. I just wanted to talk to you. I never slept in nobody else's house before and I wanted to make sure you wasn't sad without me."

"I miss you a lot, Rube. But I'm okay. Are you okay?" Belinda could hear a little worry in Carter's voice. "Do you want me to come get you? I can be there in a few minutes if you need me."

Ruby came first, she was reminded in that moment.

She always would, and Belinda was glad about that. It made her respect him so much more.

"I miss you," Ruby said in her soft voice. "But I don't need you to come get me. I just wanted to talk to you."

"I'm here. Talk to me."

"Can you come get me at twelve o'clock tomorrow? Mrs. Cameron is gonna take us to get manipures and she said I had to ask you if it was okay. But she said to ask you in the morning because you might be sleeping, but I knew you wasn't sleeping because you like to stay up late and watch TV."

Carter smiled. "You're right. I do. It's okay with me if you get a manicure tomorrow. I can pick you up at noon."

"Thank you, Daddy."

"You're welcome, Ruby."

"I'm going to go to sleep now. Mrs. Cameron said it's not right for children to be up past ten PM."

"Okay, baby. I love you."

"I love you, too. Good night."

"Good night." He hit the button again, disconnecting. "She said she doesn't need me. It's her first time sleeping away from home and she's not scared and she doesn't want me to come get her and she doesn't need me. I kind of feel like crying a little." He grinned at her but there was a little bit of sadness in his eyes.

"She said she didn't need you to get her. Not that she didn't need you." She kissed his cheek, knowing that she had been wrong earlier. She'd said she couldn't fall any more in love with him. She had been wrong. Because she tumbled a little deeper into it tonight.

"Thank you for bringing me home, Carter." She went to open the door but he stopped her.

"I don't want to say good night yet, Bell."

"And I don't want to fall in love with you again."

"So don't." She thought about saying no, about making excuses, but the truth was she didn't want to say good night, either. She didn't want to spend this night without him. "Stay with me tonight."

She got out of the car and he was right behind her. She felt his warmth on her back, and she smelled the spicy scent of his aftershave as she fished around for the spare key she kept tucked behind her light.

"You shouldn't keep a key there," he scolded softly. "I don't like you living by yourself. It's irrational. I know this town is safe, but I can't help but think that if something were to ever happen to you, it would be my fault because I wasn't there to protect you."

"I'm fine," she said softly, feeling kind of choked up.

"I know." He linked his fingers with hers as soon as she opened the door. "I still thought about you, though."

She walked through her living room, past the couch, and they went directly upstairs to her bedroom. She couldn't sit on the couch and pretend that this wasn't the place they were both thinking of. He looked at her for a moment and then around her bedroom before stepping completely away from her.

"It's nice here. I like your house. It feels like a home to me."

"Really? I like it here, but it's a little too cookie-cutter for me. Every unit in this complex is the same. I would like a house one day. One of those little cottages like they have on Lafayette Drive. They have so much character and not one of them looks the same."

"I live on Lafayette," he said absently. "One Thirty-Two. My place has plenty of character, but it doesn't feel like home. I can tell so much about you by looking at this place." He picked up a small picture frame that she had picked up at a gift shop in Nantucket. "I can tell that you like to travel and that you love your friends and that you lovingly handpick each thing you own. And even if none of it matches it somehow all oddly fits together." He walked over to her and kissed her nose. "I missed that about you when we were together the last time. I was with you but I didn't know you like this."

"I didn't let you know me. I was so busy trying to be perfect for you that I lost a little bit of myself. I had to go, Carter. You know that. If I hadn't I would have ended up hating myself and you would have ended up hating me."

He nodded. "Maybe. But we're here together now." He wrapped his strong arms around her. "Getting to know each other." He kissed her. She felt him grow hard against her and just like that the sizzle they always had, the burning for each other, turned into fire. She gripped the back of his head, pulling him closer, taking steps backward toward the bed. Clothes were too much. They were bothering her. She wanted to feel his skin. She wanted to lose herself in him for a few blissful minutes.

He broke their kiss abruptly and gently set her away from him. "We're going to sleep together tonight."

"I know." She reached for him. "Drop your drawers."

"No. We're going to sleep. That's all, Bell."

"What?" She shook her head bewildered. "Why?"

"Because it's always sex with us. Even the first day we met. I want to prove to you that we can really be friends. That we can really get to know each other."

She blinked at him.

"This is important to me, Bell. Please."

She nodded. She could have refused. She could have sent him on his way. She could have seduced him. But she didn't do any of that.

"I'm going to get ready for bed then."

She went about her nightly rituals while he slipped out of his clothes and waited for her in bed.

She washed her face, brushed her teeth, and moisturized her skin, so aware that his eyes were on her. When she finished she slipped into bed beside him. As soon as his leg brushed hers she got a flashback to when they were first married, and those feelings of anticipation and excitement came over her. Back then, she couldn't believe she had married him, that she'd found someone who had the power to make her feel so much. Things weren't much different now. She still felt the rush, the anticipation, the wonderment.

She touched his dragon tattoo, trailing her fingers over its curved form and feeling the solidness of his chest.

"Tell me how you got this again."

"Hmm?" He was looking at her through half-closed eyes, in that sleepy aroused way that always managed to turn her on. He took her fingers from his skin and kissed them. "I have a hard time paying attention when you're touching me."

"Your tattoo." She pressed her lips to his pec and spoke against his skin. "I want to know how and why you got this one."

He let out a slow breath. "You kissing me is only going to make this conversation more difficult."

"Talk to me." She smiled.

"It was a stupid reason really. I was eighteen. I had just come back from boarding school and I wanted to get the most badass tat I could think of. And this dragon seemed pretty gnarly at the time."

"It looks like it hurt." She kissed his tattoo, right on the dragon's face.

"It hurt like a bitch and is ugly as hell."

"You don't like it?"

"Nope. It's big and angry. It kind of represents how I felt back then."

She touched the anchor on his bicep. "And what about this one? What does it represent?"

"My grandfather. He was in the navy. We were close, even though he lived in Connecticut most of the time. He used to come rescue me from school when I was a kid and take me to Mets games. He had money, but he wasn't like my father. It was just a circumstance of life for him. He never let it dictate who he was. He was the most down-to-earth person I knew."

"And you got this to honor him." She kissed the anchor and then climbed on top of Carter. His eyes widened and he let out a short breath, but he didn't stop her. Instead he ran his hands up her thighs.

"We're not supposed to be having sex. We're just spending time together."

"I'm not having sex with you. We are spending time together. I'm just on top of you."

"You're not wearing any underwear." He grinned lazily at her.

"Oh. I guess I could see how that could be troubling for you." She stroked her hands up his sides, running her hand over the simple R tattoo. "This one is my favorite."

"I got it when Ruby was still in the hospital. It was on a whim. I wanted her at my side. I was so afraid that she wasn't going to make it that . . ."

She could see that he was getting emotional, so thoughtful and sweet, a side she'd seen only tiny glimpses of when they were together before. "You wanted to keep a piece of her with you." She leaned over until their chests were touching, and took his face in her hands, just looking at him for a moment as she ran her thumbs over his cheeks. "I'm so glad you have her. She's made you such a good man."

"I miss you, Bell. I don't want to do this without you anymore."

She closed the distance between them and kissed him. She missed him, too. She wasn't sure she could go back to life without him.

* * *

It was almost strange to be in bed after all these years. Strange to have her curvy body on top of his, strange to feel her gentle kiss on his mouth. They had been through so much since he came to Durant. So much anger and hurt that he almost couldn't believe that she was willingly giving herself to him, that her guard was all the way down, that she was loving him again. He had missed her so much after she first left. His bed had felt empty. His house had felt empty. His chest. For weeks he couldn't bring himself to change his sheets because her smell still lingered there. He had been too stupid to call her to go after her, too prideful. Too angry. He was so mad at Bethany and mad at Belinda and bewildered by Ruby that he felt like he was drowning. It was a bad time in his life; the only time that was worse was when he was sitting in the hospital with a baby he wasn't sure was going to survive.

Now she was back in his life. In his arms, and for once he felt balance.

She broke their kiss, sitting up to pull her nightie off over her head. She was fully naked for him and even though they had been intimate many times since he had come here, he had never seen her fully undressed. He couldn't help himself: He stared at her. The sight of her nude, straddling him, with her loose red hair falling over her shoulders was nearly enough to take him over the edge. He hardened even more.

And when he looked into her eyes he noticed that she was looking down at him shyly, a flush creeping up her cheeks.

"What is it?" He sat up, causing their chests to touch and her nipples to scrape against him. She closed her eyes at the brief contact, and he knew that she was just as aroused as he was.

"I'm nervous," she admitted to him, her tongue coming out to lick her lips.

He kissed her quickly, unable to stay away from her mouth. The glimpse of her pink tongue made him want to lick the moisture from her lips. "Why are you nervous, baby? We've done this before. In fact we're quite good at it."

She grinned at him. "I don't know. It feels like my first time all over again."

"Oh, Bell." He shook his head. "My first time was nowhere near as good as this. In fact, if I had a girl as sexy as you my first time, I could have died right there on the spot and been a very happy, very satisfied seventeen-year-old."

"Carter . . ." She rested her head on his shoulder. "This feels important to me, like if we do this we can't go back."

He grabbed her face, pulling it up so that he could look in her eyes. "This is important and you're right, we can't go back. I don't want to."

He rolled them so that she was on her back. He buried his face in her neck, kissing her there as he ran his hands down her body. He didn't want her nerves getting the best of her. He didn't want her second-guessing them. She was his wife. They were meant to be together. He had to prove that to her.

"You have to trust me," he whispered in her ear, before he lifted his face to look into her eyes.

She stared at him for a moment, a hundred emotions flashing through her eyes before she nodded. She didn't trust him. Not yet. He hadn't realized how much he had hurt her, but the fact that they were together in her bed was a step in the right direction. He just had to prove himself.

"Trust me." He leaned down to kiss her and just before

his lips met hers, she sighed, her body relaxing beneath him. "Let me make love to you tonight."

"I always wanted you to." She smiled again. "You're the one who said you just wanted to sleep tonight."

"Sometimes I can be a very stupid man," he said as he moved down and bent to kiss her stomach. "But in my defense, you seduced me."

"Seduced you? Me?"

"You got naked and climbed on top of me. You knew what you were doing." He kissed her thigh, shifting her body so he lay between her legs, and then licked inside her. "I wanted to show you that it's more than sex between us, that I want to be with you because you are you." He licked inside her, deeper this time. She let out a sound that was in between a gasp and a groan. He groaned himself. She tasted sweet and familiar. He sucked on her nub, eliciting a cry of his name. He stayed there playing, taking his time, bringing her to the edge and then pulling back. She moved against him, panting, begging, cursing him. Each sound she made spurred him on.

"Please, Carter." She lifted her head and looked down at him when he removed his lips. "I'm ready."

His lips traveled up her body to her belly, where he dipped his tongue into her belly button. Her fingers curled into his hair and tugged.

He looked up at her, the slight pain making him pause and turning him on at the same time.

"Now. I want you. Now. Please."

"It's been four years. I want to take my time. Let me." He shifted himself up her body a little more, stopping at her breasts. He covered one with his hand and tested the weight; the other he covered with his mouth. He tugged on one nipple with his teeth and rolled the other between his fingers.

She came, shuddering so hard that her back came off the bed. His manhood twitched between his legs, jealous that it didn't get to experience her orgasm.

"So sensitive." He kissed her heartbeat, lifting himself slightly to settle between her welcoming legs. She wrapped them around his waist, rubbing her wetness against his hardness. He slid inside her, unable to take being apart from her anymore, gritting his teeth at the intense sensation of being encased in her wet warmth. "Oh, God, Bell. You feel too damn good."

"Don't hold back." She moved against him. "I need this from you."

He didn't hold back. It was impossible. She wouldn't let him. She wasn't passive, grabbing onto his hips as she pushed herself toward him, meeting his every thrust. He had been too long without her; being with her now made him realize that he couldn't go back, he couldn't half live anymore.

"Carter." She dug her nails into his skin, and he could feel her orgasm building. It was almost enough to drive him over the edge, but he held on, stroking her slower, kissing her harder, tilting her hips so he could slide deeper into her. She cried out as she came, sinking her teeth into his shoulder. That caused him to explode and lose his breath, his mind, and the little bit of empty space he had in his heart.

"Hell," she panted. "Or maybe I should be saying heaven and thanking God." She kissed his shoulder. "That was good. Now be a dear and make me a sandwich."

He blinked at her, and her mouth bloomed into a beautiful full smile. This is what he loved about her. She could be so serious, so intense in her lovemaking, but then she could be playful and sweet. The only woman he knew who could make him smile so much. He kissed the corner of her mouth, to thank her for that, to thank her for giving him back something he had been missing for so long. He would do anything to keep her that way. "I'll make you a sandwich." He kissed the other side of her mouth. "Just as long as you promise me you'll eat it naked."

"Of course I'm going to eat it naked. Make sure you make yourself one, too. You're going to need sustenance, because we're going to do that again, but this time a little faster."

He rolled onto his back, taking her with him, loving the feel of her soft weight on top of him. "I'm not a machine, you know. I need time to recover."

She lifted her chest away from his so that she could look down at him. "I know very well that you are a man. If I wanted a machine I could use the one in my dresser drawer."

He cupped her breast, rubbing his thumb across her nipple. "You have one?"

"I call him Elvis. What did you think I did without you?"

"Cry?"

She smiled at him and then lowered her mouth to his. He could feel himself hardening again.

"I want to be in charge this time," she said against his mouth.

"I thought you were in charge the last time."

"I'm sorry"—she slid her lips along his jawline, kissing every inch—"but you're really going to have to suffer this time. But I'll be nice." She kissed her way down his neck to the hollow of his throat, where she licked him. "I'll give you plenty of time to recover." She glanced at the clock. "Is three minutes enough? Think you can make and eat a sandwich in that time?"

"Forget the damn sandwich." He guided himself into her. "I'm ready for my punishment now."

* * *

The sun on her face woke Belinda from a deep sleep. It wasn't the man wrapped around her with his hand on her breast and his lips on her ear.

"I don't want to get up," he said, his voice rough with sleep.

She said nothing to that, but she agreed. She didn't want the night to be over.

He kissed the back of her neck. "I would try to make love to you again, but I think you took everything I got, girl." He gave her bottom a little smack. "It's going to take me three days to recover from last night."

"Only three?" She turned in his arms to find him smiling at her. "I must not have tried hard enough. I was hoping it was going to be at least a week."

He laughed, the sound of his soft chuckle sending tingles along her skin. "Thank you," he said, giving her a long slow kiss.

"What's your favorite color?" Belinda found herself asking Carter when their kiss broke, not wanting their night to be over yet.

He looked at her for a moment as if he was trying to determine if she was serious.

"I could say the green of your eyes or the red of your hair, but you would say that I was full of shit so I'm going to stick with blue." He gave her an easy smile. "But I really don't have a favorite color."

"I like to wear a lot of colors. So I don't really have one, either," she told him. "I think every color has its place. Like sunflowers are supposed to be yellow, because yellow makes you happy and they wouldn't look right in purple. And strawberries are supposed to be red to make them look so succulent and little girls should wear baby pink because it's the only color that can capture their sweetness. You must think I sound like a crazy person."

"I don't," he said seriously after a moment. He was

staring at her mouth intently, which not only caused tingles to go up her spine, but made her wonder if he was paying attention to her rambling. "Each color does have a place. They are supposed to make you feel. Can you imagine how shitty life would be if we only saw in black and white?"

"I think it would be shitty only if we saw color and then it was taken away. We wouldn't know how beautiful color was in the first place, so we wouldn't know what we were missing. Take dogs, for instance. They don't see color like we do, but they're not any less happy for it. My aunt Mimi's dog has just about the best damn life I have ever seen. I would gladly trade places with him. She takes him for weekly massages. Can you believe that? I'm pretty sure he doesn't give two shits about the subtle differences between plum and eggplant."

"No." He grinned. "Probably not. I wouldn't care so much, either, if I hadn't taken a class in color psychology when I was getting my degree. I thought it was total bullshit until I had to redesign a school based on it."

"That have classes on that?"

"Yeah. It was interesting, too. We learned that white always makes people think of innocence and purity, that purple sparks people's imaginations, and red inspires passion. At the school we did we had the cafeteria painted powder blue because that color is supposed to make a person feel tranquil. Before it was painted red and purple and the principal told us that the kids were nuts after lunch. But with the blue they calmed down. Purple and red are great colors, but three hundred passionate and imaginative kids in a cafeteria wasn't working."

"Oh, boy. I can only imagine."

Carter's eyes made a quick sweep over her face. "I think that's why I'm so damn drawn to you. There are so many colors on you to look at." He stroked his thumb across her cheek. "Red hair, and green eyes, and this warm tan skin. I feel a whole bunch of things when I look at you."

She blushed.

Damn it.

"You're good, Lancaster." She inched closer to him even though there was hardly any space between them. "I think you must have been reading up on how to pick up ladies because that BS was just too smooth."

"Took an online class," he said without missing a beat. "It's called How to Hit on Your Estranged Wife. I did surprisingly well."

"Of course you did. You were always a smarty-pants in school, weren't you?"

He nodded. "Did you like school? For some reason I always get the feeling you didn't."

"It was hard for me," she admitted to him for the first time. "I wasn't smart. I was average. I had to work really hard to get Bs. It didn't help that I was best friends with Ellis, who is a freaky genius. I just didn't understand why we had to learn so much stupid math and science, when there was all that art and music and drama out there. I've used the color wheel many times since I left high school but I never once had to find X."

"You're creative." He stroked his hand down her hair. "You can't paint for shit, but you're one of the most creative people I know. That doesn't mean you're not smart. You're one of the smartest people I know. I wouldn't have married you if you weren't," he said with absolutely no trace of humor.

"Stop picking on my painting skills," she said, trying to ignore the achy feeling in her chest upon hearing those words. She had always felt like such a screwup. But maybe she wasn't. Not in all ways.

"I hated school, too." He shrugged. "It wasn't hard for me, but I hated it all the same."

"That's because you were away from home." She felt sorry for the boy he was. His young life had been a lonely one, and it changed how she thought of him. "Don't you think it would have been different if you got to go to school at home?"

"I'm not sure. My parents' house never felt comfortable to me. For so long I thought I was a misfit because I couldn't seem to make a connection with either one of them. I thought home was supposed to give me this certain feeling, but it didn't. It wasn't until I came to Durant when I was in college that I got that feeling."

"It was Steven's family who gave you that feeling. Why didn't you stay in Durant then? Steven was here. He never left this place. You could have been his partner years ago."

"I went back to San Francisco because I had to. My family expected it from me." He turned to look at her. "Why did you run after college? You love it here. I can tell. Why did you leave it?"

Run. It was the right word to use. She certainly had run away from this place.

"I guess I was trying to find myself. I think I'm still trying to."

"You don't know who you are?" He seemed so surprised by that. She thought he would have figured that out about her a long time ago. "I think you do. I think you are just looking for that thing to fill you up and make you feel whole. I think a lot of people are."

"Are you still looking for that thing to make you feel whole?" she asked him, needing to know.

"I had to look at my life really hard after Bethany died and I almost lost Ruby in that accident. I could literally lose everything—my job, my money, my house—but the only thing that would truly be a loss is if I didn't have my kid, my family. That puts things in perspective for me.

There are things that I want in my life, but it's the people that I need."

Well, damn.

"I need to be here." She looked away from him, unsure why his words left her feeling so hollow. "But a week in Antigua once in a while wouldn't be a bad thing."

"You like Antigua?"

"I've never been," she admitted. "I collect pictures of tropical places. Thailand, Bora-Bora, Mexico. I have a scrapbook that I keep them in. Sometimes when things are gloomy I take them out and look at them. I have this one picture of Antigua at sunset that pulls me every time I look at it." She sighed. "It seems like the perfect place to be trapped with a hot naked man. Maybe I missed my calling. Maybe I should write romance novels that take place in tropical settings."

Carter grinned at her again before he leaned over and kissed her cheek. "You're very cute, Ms. Gordon."

More warmth spread through her with his kiss. She wanted to live in that moment forever. They were talking. Not arguing. Not rehashing their failed past. They were talking for the first time. She realized that they could. That there could be more to them than passion and sex, and too much emotion.

Give him a chance.

Give yourself a chance to have what you always wanted. But don't rush. Just don't rush.

"Is there a place you've always wanted to go, Carter?"

"Yeah, to the Poconos."

"Say what?"

He laughed, his deep chuckle going through her. "You know, that place with the champagne-glass hot tubs. I've always wanted to go there. Take a pretty girl, put on some Barry White, play in the bubbles."

"Carter, that is so cheesy! But kind of adorable. I thought

you were going to say Zurich or Prague or some other place pretentious rich people like to go."

"Hey, I'm not pretentious and I've been to Prague and Zurich when I was a teenager. I really would like to go to Disney World, though. I hear Epcot is damn near magical."

"Disney World is magical. At least for me. Ellis hates it. I think it has more to do with waiting in line than anything, though. We could go—" She stopped herself, feeling a little bit of insecurity creep up.

But he already seemed to know what she was going to say. "I would like to go with you." He kissed her softly on the bridge of her nose, and held her closer while they lay in silence for a few minutes. "Just let me know when you're ready, Bell."

She was starting to think about the future. Their future together. It scared her. She didn't want to fail at love again.

"I don't want to leave this bed, baby, but nature is calling my name." He rolled away from her, getting out of bed, his beautiful naked body causing her hormones to act up again.

His phone buzzed from her nightstand.

"Can you grab the phone, Bell? It's probably Ruby."

He walked into the bathroom, shutting the door behind him as she reached for the phone. "Carter's phone. Belinda speaking."

"I wondered how long it would take before you got your hands on him again."

For a moment Belinda was at a total loss for words. Carter's mother. Bernadette, the only woman in the world who could make her feel worthless. She hated that she had given her the power to make her feel like shit. She refused to let that happen again.

"Well, hello to you, too, Mommy dearest."

"He's fixated on you. I don't know why, but he is. That's what this move was about, but I know my son. He doesn't love you. He only thinks he does. Your relationship didn't work then and it's not going to work now. You are simply just not good enough for him. I'm not saying this to be unkind. I'm just telling you the truth."

"And I'm telling you, you're an uptight bitch and I simply don't care what you think."

Carter walked out of the bathroom then, naked as the day he was born. "What's the matter?"

She handed him the phone and left her bed. Suddenly she felt damn vulnerable with no clothes on. "It's your mother." She found her discarded nightgown on the floor, near his underwear. She tossed his boxers at him.

"Bell?" Carter grabbed her hand. "What happened?"

"Talk to her. I'm sure she'll tell you."

"I'll speak to you later." He disconnected and pulled on his boxers. "What did she say to you?"

"You know. The usual. How I'm not good enough for you and that you'll never love me."

"Belinda." He pulled her close. "I don't care what she says. I'm going to have it out with her."

"What's the point? She's never going to think I'm good enough."

"She hurt you and by doing that she hurt me and she can't get away with that. She has to understand that you're it for me."

"Pudge?"

"Bill Junior?"

"Oh, God, no." She heard her parents' voices. In her house. Uninvited. When there was a half-naked man in her bedroom.

"Are those your parents?" Carter's eyes went wide, and

he looked just as dumbfounded as she felt. "What are they doing here?"

"Hell if I know! You think you can climb out of my window without breaking your neck?"

"No!"

"Oh, come on! Well, how about the closet. Get in my closet." She tried to pull herself away from him, but he wouldn't let her. He kept his hand planted firmly on her waist.

"I'm not hiding. We're married and you need to talk to your parents about boundaries."

"Pudge?" Her mother poked her head in the door, her eyes going wider than Belinda had ever seen. "Oh. Oh! You have company."

"She has company? This early? Is it her friend Apple Blossom?"

Her father burst into the room to see Carter standing there. Standing with her, with his hands on her body.

"It's you," he said grimly. "I'm going downstairs. I'll be in the car."

"Oh, but Bill . . ." Carmina called after him. He didn't turn back and Belinda was infinitely grateful that her father didn't want to be in the same room with her and her nearly naked kind-of husband.

But it appeared her mother wasn't going anywhere. She was staring at them with open interest.

"Hello, *Mamá*. You remember Carter?"

"Of course." Carmina studied him for a very long moment, her eyes traveling all over his cut body. "He is very handsome, Pudge," she said almost approvingly.

"Yeah. He's much better than those other dogs I've brought home."

"You never brought him home," she said sharply. For a flash of a second she saw her mother's anger; then her face cleared and she looked like her normal self. "We came over because I got a call from Patrice last night. She said her boy came home very upset because you smacked him when you were out last night."

"I did. He had it coming. He said some nasty things to me."

"She said she knows and that you were right to smack him, but Theo told her that you disappeared last night with a strange man and you know how much I worry about you and I wanted to see if you were all right because if you went home with a strange man all types of things could have happened to you. You could have been taken by a serial killer and we would have found little pieces of you all over the county."

"Mamá!"

"I'm glad to see that you went home with not such a strange man but your husband who you have been married to for a very long time but have never bothered to bring him home to meet me."

Guilt. Guilt. Guilt. Guilt. Guilt.

"I—"

"How was the food at the restaurant last night? What did you eat? I hear they make excellent duck."

"I—uh. Huh?" Her head spun as her mother changed topics with lightning speed.

"What did you eat last night?"

"I had a Cobb salad."

"Are you eating salad?" Her mother nodded approvingly. "That's good. I know your father has been taking you out to dinner after your classes. He came home smelling like sausage two weeks ago. He had the nerve to be upset with me for frying candy bars when he fills you with enough cheese to start a dairy. Did you eat cucumbers on your salad last night, Pudge? You know you cannot eat cucumbers. They make you horribly gassy. You are like me that way. I can eat a bucket of chicken with no problem but you put a cucumber in front of me and I blow up like a hot-air balloon. Same with bananas. I belch and belch, which is sad because I really like bananas."

"Mamá!"

"What?" She blinked at her. "Talking about one's gas is unacceptable? Well, keeping your secret husband away from your mother is, too, so there." She looked at Carter. "What upsets your stomach?"

Belinda opened her mouth to tell Carter that he didn't have to answer that, but she wasn't quick enough.

"Surprisingly grapefruit, which is okay because I don't like grapefruit. My Ruby does, though. She likes me to peel them so she can eat them like oranges. I don't know how she does it."

Carmina nodded sympathetically. "It's very acidic, but it can be good for you, too. But you can have oranges or lemons to get your vitamin C. I know!" Her eyes lit up. "We can go to the farmers' market together. They have fruit the size of a small child's head! The lady who sells them swears to me that there are no pesticides or chemicals in them but I'm just not sure. It seems unnatural for fruit to be so big. I keep hearing about these GMO things on the news. They make it seem like we are going to have zombie fruit walking around and killing our farm animals. Would you like that, Carter? We can go to the farmers' market. They have it on the green every Wednesday and Saturday until one. We can go and get fruit for your Ruby. My husband doesn't like fruit but he'll eat it if I pack it in his lunch. He gets very hungry, you know. All that barking he does at the boys on his team. Thank goodness we didn't have a son. We would have had to use half our savings just on food. It's not that Belinda didn't eat a lot as a child, but she was a girl and her body couldn't handle as much. So we will go on Saturday morning? You have to go early or all the good fruit is gone."

Belinda was having a hard time believing that this was happening. That her mother was standing in her bedroom talking about fruit with Carter when he wasn't wearing any clothes.

"Ruby would like that. It's okay if I bring her, right?"

"Of course you can bring her!" Carmina's face lit. "Such a beautiful little girl."

"Hey!" Belinda said. "Wait a minute."

They both ignored her. "It's a date," Carter said.

"Lovely. I have to go. Your father is probably having a coronary in the car. I'll have to make it up to him. He's been asking me to make him egg salad but I hate making it."

"Me, too," Carter said as if they were old friends. "They stink up the house and I always end up with shells in my salad."

"Yes! I'm excited for our date, Carter." She leaned over to kiss both his cheeks and then she kissed Belinda's. "I'll see you later." She left them alone.

"Did you just make a date with my mother? In your underwear?" She heard what had just taken place. She saw it with her own eyes, but had her mother just invited her estranged husband on a fruit-buying trip? Seriously?

"Yeah. I think she's delightful." He yanked her closer and kissed her mouth, like nothing had happened. "Come shower with me. I want to take you to breakfast before I have to get Ruby."

She relented. Rather easily. Her parents knew what she had done. There was no going back. She might as well enjoy him today.

CHAPTER 17

Same song, different meaning . . .

Belinda lay on the floor of Cherri's nursery with little Joey sleeping on her chest. She wasn't sure why she'd come here after she had gotten her car back and she and Carter had parted. Her original plan had been to go back home, shower, nap, and ponder the direction her life had taken in these past few weeks, but after she got home she realized that she didn't want to spend the day alone in her house—that her house felt kind of empty.

She kind of missed him and she didn't want to.

"The lass looks good with a baby on her bosom, don't she, lad?"

Belinda opened her eyes to see Colin, Cherri's husband, and Magnus, her father-in-law, standing over her. It nearly hurt her eyes to stare at father and son. Both were well over six feet tall, burly, and ruggedly handsome with deep Irish brogues that made many women swoon.

"She does," Colin said. "I've been sent to rescue you

from my boy, but you seem to have charmed him. He's been a hyper little bugger lately."

"Yup, just like his father," Magnus said, slapping his son's back. "Just wait till he starts walking. I thought I was going to have to start putting a little bourbon in your bottle just to get you to settle at night. Lucky for me a little Guinness did the trick."

Colin grinned at his father and shook his head. "Maybe we just need Belinda. What are you doing every night around seven?"

"It's the boobs," Cherri said, walking in. Colin wrapped his arm around his wife, tucking her close to him. "Men go gaga for them."

"It's true." She rubbed the sleeping baby's back. "It's a gift."

"You men want to head out and grab up some lunch?" Cherri asked.

"What do you want to eat, love?"

"What would you like, Belinda?"

"Cake or doughnuts. Or a cakey doughnut with chocolate. You know what? Just surprise me."

"We'll swing by the bakery on the way," Magnus said. "Girl after my own heart. You know I've got my own little place downstairs, girlie. You could move in with me. I could even give you a baby if you want. We could make some beautiful kids together. Colin could use another sibling. Isn't that right, lad?"

"No." Colin kissed his wife's forehead and gave his father a little shove out of the room. "You stay away from her, Pop. I have no urge to call Belinda mommy."

The exchange between father and son made Belinda smile. She imagined that's what her own father wanted, a son who looked and walked and talked just like he did. It was nice to see them together. She knew Colin and his father didn't always get along so well. "So you really like having your father-in-law live with you?" She looked up at Cherri, who had a small smile on her face.

"I love having him here. Our family wasn't complete without him."

"I wish I could love my mother-in-law like you love your father-in-law. I might still be happily married." She shook her head. "That's bullshit. Bernadette was a royal bitch but I can't totally blame her for the failure of my marriage."

She blamed herself for so many reasons. But the biggest reason today was allowing Bernadette Lancaster to plant that seed of doubt in her mind. She loved herself; after years of battling with her self-confidence, she had learned to love herself just the way she was. But it still bugged the hell out of her—no, it hurt her to hear Bernadette say that she would never be good enough for her son. It hurt her to know that somebody would always be betting against them.

Cherri sat down on the floor beside Belinda. "What brought this subject on?"

"I spoke to her on the phone this morning. Of course that was after I had hot sex with her son all night and before my parents barged in on us. She basically told me that I was never going to be good enough for her son and that our relationship will never work."

Cherri shook her head, reeling from that information. "First of all, yay for hot sex! Second, what did you say to that? And third, what do you mean your parents walked in on you?"

"I called Carter's mother a bitch. Which part of me feels bad about but most of me feels great about. I've always tried to play nice with her because I didn't want to cause a strain between Carter and his mother, but now I don't care. I'm too old and respect myself too damn much to let somebody bully me. And yes, my parents showed up

this morning just after Carter pulled on his underwear. I
don't think they were too pleased to see me shacking up
with my estranged husband, but they said surprisingly
little to me about it—which worries me. My mother did
invite Carter to go to the farmers' market with her on
Saturday, though."

"Are you going to go?"

"I wasn't invited."

"Oh." Cherri blinked at her. "So I take it you and Carter
got back together last night?"

"No." She shook her head. "I don't know. I love him,
but I'm not sure if I can go back down that road with him.
There's still so much hurt between us."

Cherri nodded. "There's a lot you have to overcome.
Maybe you should just have sex with him."

She stared at Cherri for a moment, surprised. "You
think so? You don't think I should just forget the past and
be with him?"

"I like him, Belinda. I don't want to like him, because
he lied to you. By not disclosing such a huge part of his
past he lied to you. But I see him with his kid and I can't
help but like him. And if I'm so confused about him and
I'm an outsider looking in, I can't imagine how you must
feel. So I say yeah, why not? Have sex with him. Date
him. Learn what it's like to be around the guy he is now
and not the man you used to know. This is your time.
Take it. Colin and I got married very quickly, too, so I
know what it's like to marry a man that you aren't sure
you know all that well, but we were friends first and you
didn't have that experience with Carter." She grinned at
her. "Just don't do what I did and get pregnant." Cherri
gazed at her son and touched his dark curly hair. "Forget
I said that. Getting pregnant was the best thing that ever
happened to me. Get knocked up if you want to."

"Don't give that talk at high schools, honey."

"I won't." She grinned at her. "But you're old now and you'll be a good mother. And I know you want to have babies. I can see it all over your face."

"It's your fault. I didn't think about any of this stuff until you and Ellis both got married."

"You're lying to yourself, Belinda. You got married four years ago. You can't tell me that having a family wasn't always on your mind."

Belinda sighed heavily. Cherri was right. Her own family was something she had always wanted.

"Daddy?" Ruby called to him. He was lying next to her in her small bed. They had just finished reading one of Ruby's favorite books, *The Paper Bag Princess*, for what had to be the hundredth time. They did this every night now. Just spent time together in her room, sometimes not saying anything at all.

"Yeah?"

"Why don't you got no brothers and sisters?"

"Why don't I have any brothers and sisters? I don't know, babe. My parents just didn't have any more children."

She was quiet for a moment. He could see that she was processing something in that little head of hers. "Mrs. Cameron is Uncle Steven's big sister. She says she has four brothers and sisters and her kids are sisters. She says she likes having a big family."

She wanted a family, too. She didn't have to say it, but he knew that she wished it was more than just him and her. "Her family is very fun. When I was in college I used to hang out with Uncle Steven's family a lot. I even spent Christmas there."

"Did Santa bring you presents at his house?"

"I was a grown-up when I did, so no, but Uncle Steven's mom used to give me a bunch of presents. She made me sweaters and cakes. They're nice people. I can understand if you want to spend time with them."

She nodded. "I'm going to ask Grandma why she didn't have no more kids next time I talk to her. She says she misses me, Daddy. She wants to see me."

He nodded, afraid to say anything because he didn't want Ruby to realize how unhappy he was with his mother at the moment. She didn't want him with the only woman he had ever truly wanted, and that bothered him more than he could express.

This was their second chance. He wasn't going to allow his mother to make him unhappy anymore. If it was just him he might have been able to cut her from his life, but he couldn't. He had Ruby, and Bernadette was a good grandmother. She loved Ruby, and he couldn't keep her away from her only grandchild.

"She says she's been very sad without me."

"I know." Guilt burned in his gut, but he didn't regret the move. Durant was better for her. For them. "You'll see Grandma again. Maybe this summer. She talked about taking you into the city."

"Are you going to come with us?"

"No." He kissed her forehead. "That's going to be just time for you and your grandmother. And now, since you had your first sleepover, you'll be fine going away without me."

"But I still want you to come. I never been to the city before."

That statement lifted his mood. She was growing up but she still liked to have him around. He wondered how much longer it would last. "It's not summer yet. We can talk about it more when the time comes. Okay?"

"Okay." She yawned.

"Time to go to sleep. You stayed up late last night."

"I know. Children need their rest."

"I'm going to take you to the park tomorrow after school to ride bikes. So sleep well tonight."

"I'll try." She reached up and touched his face. "You look tired, too."

"I am, baby. I'll see you in the morning. Good night."

"Good night."

He left her and went directly into his bedroom. He was tired. He'd almost smiled when Ruby mentioned it. His kid was far too perceptive. He just hoped that she had no idea why he didn't get much sleep last night.

"Where do you want to eat tonight, Junior?" Belinda's father asked her as they hung outside their respective classrooms waiting for their classes to start. It was their second week at the community center. And just like last week, she waited for him to mention Carter, but he said nothing. It worried her.

"I know you like that sushi stuff. You want to have that?"

She frowned at her father for a moment. "You hate sushi."

"Yeah." He shrugged. "Can't believe they have the nerve to charge people for some damn raw fish, but you like it and I got to pick last week. I guess I should ask you to do things you like sometimes. I forget, you know." He shrugged. "You could also talk to me about . . . things. And I'll shut up and listen. I'm not like your mother, but you can talk to me, too. Over dinner."

Belinda took a step forward and wrapped her arms around her burly father. It was probably one of the nicest things he had ever said to her. "I want sweet potato fries and chicken fingers."

"Okay. Okay. What are you hugging me for?" He awkwardly wrapped his arms around her and patted her back. Her father didn't show his affection like this. He was more of a good-sturdy-slap-on-the-back guy. He was so unlike Carter was with his little girl, but she wasn't complaining.

"Because you love me."

"You're my kid. If I didn't there would be something wrong with me." He let go of her, apparently having his fill of public affection. "We can go to Dishin's Diner. They'll even put cheese on your sweet potatoes if you want."

"Sounds good."

Belinda spotted Ruby walking down the hallway. She immediately thought about the girl's father—whom she had been thinking about nonstop for the past few days. Cherri's advice gave her something to think about. She should enjoy him. But the more she was with him, the more she wanted to be with him, and that scared her because a big part of her didn't trust him. A big part of her was still heartbroken by him.

As Ruby got closer, Belinda could see her more clearly and she knew something wasn't right. Her face was scrunched. Her cheeks were red, her mouth turned down. Belinda left her father and met her in the middle of the hallway.

"Ruby, are you okay?"

She shook her head, her eyes filling with tears.

Belinda crumbled. Crying children made her uncomfortable, but this one broke her heart. "What's the matter with my baby?" She lifted her into her arms and kissed her cheeks.

Ruby broke, tears streaming down her face, sobs racking her chest. She was crying so hard her breaths were coming in little shallow spurts, causing Belinda to think she was about to hyperventilate.

"Honey . . ." Belinda shut her eyes feeling her own tears threatening. "Please calm down a little. I don't like to see you so upset. Please tell me what happened to you. I want to make it better."

"I had a very bad day at school."

"Is everything all right, Bill Junior?" Her father walked up and placed his huge hand on Ruby's small back. His brow creased with worry. "What can I do?"

"Ruby had a bad day at school." She pulled the child closer. "She was just going to tell me about it."

"I got in trouble."

"Why?" she asked cautiously.

"Because I told Elroy to go to hell."

"You did?" Belinda exchanged looks with her father, not sure how to react to that statement. "Tell me why you said that."

"I said it because I was mad. We was making Mother's Day cards and Elroy said I shouldn't make one because I don't have a mommy. He said she died because I was ugly and fat and because nobody liked me."

"He said what?" It was like the air had been sucked right out of her chest. She knew kids could be cruel. They were cruel to her, but this kid . . . *Nasty* didn't begin to cover what the little twerp was. She pulled Ruby's chin up so that she could look into the little girl's eyes. "You should have knocked his teeth out! Telling him to go to hell is the least of what you should've told him. You should've told him to kiss your—"

"Junior," her father said softly, a tiny hint of warning in his voice. "Try again."

She sighed, knowing her father was right. She had no business telling Ruby any of that stuff. "It's never wrong to stick up for yourself, baby doll. Never, never, never. Elroy was wrong to say that to you and he was very mean and while it's not nice to say bad words, none of us is mad at you. You know your mommy died in an accident. She's probably looking down at me very jealous because I get to hug you and she can't. You can't believe what that boy says about you. You are beautiful and sweet and smart and I like you very much."

"I do, too," Bill said. "The boy that said that to you . . . his name is Elroy?"

"Yeah. He's always mean to me."

Belinda felt helpless. Ruby wasn't even her kid but she wanted to fix this for her. She wanted her to stop hurting. She wanted to make it so that she never felt this way again. But she couldn't. And if she could feel these kind of feelings for a kid that wasn't hers, she could only imagine how Carter felt, or any parent whose child was being hurt.

"Daddy, I have to fix this," she said as Ruby buried her face in her shoulder and cried.

"You do, Junior. You do what you think is best."

She kissed Ruby's wet face half a dozen times trying to think of anything she could say that could help, but nothing seemed good enough. She wanted to be good enough for Ruby. "Ruby, would you like to come to the mall with me for a little while and then maybe I can take you out to dinner? Would you like that?"

She nodded, tears streaming down her face.

"Stay with my father for a minute. I'm going to call your daddy." She handed Ruby over to him. He brought her in close, shielding most of her small body with his arms. It was a protective gesture. Her father was a man who was meant to have many children in his life. She was sorry that he didn't.

She walked away from them, stepping into the classroom where Cherri was teaching.

"Hey, chica," Cherri greeted her.

"Hey. I think I'm going to take Ruby out right now. She had a bad day at school. Some little asshole is teasing her about her dead mother."

"I know a ten-year-old who can break his legs if you want."

"Save his number for me. I need to call Carter." She excused herself to the back of the room and dialed the number she had committed to memory without even trying.

"I was just thinking about you," he said by way of greeting.

"Carter, Ruby had a rough day at school."

"What happened?" The edge in his voice was unmistakable.

"She's not hurt, some boy said something stupid to her, I'll tell you about it later. But I don't think she's up for art class tonight."

"I'll be right there."

"No. Please, let me take her with me to the mall. I think I can cheer her up. We'll meet you for dinner."

"Okay, Bell. You can take her. How about Mina's for dinner? I'll be there at six."

"Okay, Carter. Thank you for letting me take her."

"Thank you for wanting to."

CHAPTER 18

Let's do it again . . .

Carter stared out the window of his office, feeling the chill in the air even though he was inside and all the windows were closed. He was supposed to be working on revising the plans for a new house that was going to be built in the center of town. The client wanted a replica of a Victorian on the outside, but a completely modern open-concept space on the inside. Normally he loved this kind of job. At his old firm he had designed office buildings and malls and condo complexes that were large, cold, and emotionless. Here he got to design homes, spaces people would grow and love in. But today he wasn't feeling up to it. It was very gloomy for mid-April. A heavy rain looked as if it was going to start any moment now and he just wanted to go home.

Home.

He nearly smiled at the thought. He liked his little house and his neighborhood. He felt so much more comfortable in Durant than he did in the place where he had grown up. It could be he just needed a simpler life, and a simpler house.

"Hey." Belinda walked in.

Or maybe it was she who made this place feel more like home.

She was in jeans, cherry-red heels, a tight white T-shirt, a black leather jacket, and red lipstick.

He swiveled his chair toward her, just so he could take her in. He hadn't seen her in two days. Not since he had dinner with her and Ruby at Mina's. Before that, another two days had gone without a glimpse of her. She was avoiding him. He knew what had happened. His mother had called. Her parents had shown up that morning, the outside world had infiltrated their little bubble, and her doubts had crept in. He told himself to give her time, that it was going to take time for those old wounds to heal, but he wanted to be back with her. He had moved back to Durant for that reason. He could admit that to himself now. He wanted to start over with her and he didn't want to wait any longer.

"Hey. Did you know my heart skips a damn beat when I see you in a white T-shirt?"

She grinned at him, crossing the room and not stopping till she was close enough to wrap her arms around him. "You like what I'm wearing? Ellis calls this my rebel-without-a-cause look."

"I like it very much, especially the way your butt looks in these jeans."

"It looks big."

"Then you can call me Sir Mix-A-Lot, because, baby, you got back."

She threw her head back and laughed. He loved her laugh and her smile; she was growing easy around him again.

"You're so corny sometimes."

"You bring it out in me." He slid his hands beneath her shirt, just so he could feel her skin, and steal a little bit of her warmth. "I was hoping to see you today. I was going to go to your store but you came to me."

"I did." She fiddled with his collar. "You're not wearing a suit."

"You told me not to."

"I love it when you listen." She flashed him a quick grin. "I can't stop thinking about Ruby. How has the rest of her week been?"

"She's been fine. You didn't tell me how upset she had been when you talked to me on the phone."

"No." She gently ran her fingers over the skin that was exposed at his neck. "If I was ready to break the kid's legs I know you would have gone ballistic."

"I would have."

"That's why I wanted to calm her down first. Mother's Day has got to be brutal for her. I just wanted to do something that would take her mind off her bad day."

"So you bought her three dresses, two pairs of shoes, a tutu, and a Justin Bieber poster."

"Little girl's clothes are so cute nowadays. I could have bought half the store." She shrugged. "And it's not my fault your kid has shitty taste in music."

"You made her happy. I'm not sure I could have managed it that night. The truth is, I don't know how I would have handled it seeing her that upset. Since we moved here she hasn't seen her grandmother and there has been no woman in her life. And that night she needed a woman."

She needed Belinda. He watched them together at dinner. Ruby was practically attached to her side, sucking up every little piece of affection Belinda had to give. And Belinda gave it so freely, so naturally that it made Carter uncomfortable. It made him angry that Ruby had missed out on so much. He couldn't blame Belinda for it all. He chose to stay away from her.

"That kid isn't still bothering her, is he?"

"No." He smoothed his hand over her cheek, trying to wipe away the worry on her face. "I got a phone call from Elroy's father that night apologizing for his son's actions. And the next day Ruby came home with an apology letter and a brand-new box of colored pencils."

"What?" She scrunched her head in confusion. "Did you call the school after dinner?"

"No. I was going to email her teacher but I got Elroy Senior's phone call first."

"How did all that happen so quickly? If you didn't call . . ."

"Your father. Apparently Elroy's father works at Durant U as the assistant volleyball coach. I guess your father had a talk with him."

"He probably threatened to crush his bones."

"I'm sure he did. Why do you think he did that?"

She shut her eyes and leaned against him. "I'm sorry he interfered. I'm not sure why he did that. He barely knows Ruby."

"He doesn't. But what he did doesn't bother me. It's nice to know that there is somebody else here to look out for my kid. I've been alone at it for a long time. Of course, he took the steam out of my pissed-off father righteous anger, but in the end as long as Ruby got what she needed I'll be fine."

"My dad doesn't deal with emotional girls. He just wants to make whatever is bothering them stop."

"All fathers are like that." He pulled Belinda closer, closing the tiny gap between them. "I miss you." He feathered kisses along her neck. "Come to my house today. Stay over."

She thought about saying no, but she couldn't. She

missed him, too. The past two days she thought about him and Ruby and how empty she felt when she was home alone that night. "What time does Ruby go to bed?"

"Between eight and eight thirty."

"I'll be over at nine."

"What?" He pulled away from her and looked into her eyes. "Why then?"

"Because you obviously can't sneak out and leave your kid alone to play at my house."

"No." He shook his head. "I wasn't asking you to come over to have sex. I was asking you to come over to be with us."

She shook her head. "But what would Ruby think about me sleeping over? I don't want to give her the wrong idea."

"What wrong idea?" He frowned at her. "That I'm crazy about you and am tired of being without you. Damn it, Bell. I want you back in my life."

"I'm here. But I just don't think we should be rushing into anything. We might not work out and I don't want Ruby getting hurt. The last thing she needs is to have another woman leave her."

"I agree with that, but you aren't going to leave her. We are going to make this work."

"It's not that easy. You just can't expect us to get back together and act like a married couple again. There's too much shit between us for that."

He looked weary at that moment. His eyes searched her face, and she couldn't help but note the sadness in them. "What do you suggest we do then?"

"Date." She pressed her lips to his cheek. "We'll have lunch together a few times a week and go to the movies and make out and make love in the backseat of a car like horny teenagers."

"And we'll keep it—us a secret from my daughter."

She looked up at the stony tone of his voice. He wasn't

happy with her, but this was the way it had to be for her. She couldn't jump into this blindly again. She couldn't fail at this love a second time.

"Carter . . ."

"I don't want to sneak around."

"We won't be."

"Then what would you call it?"

"Dating! I can't be the first person you went out with and didn't tell Ruby about?"

"There has been no one, Belinda. Not a single woman. Not one date."

"Why not? Why haven't you had dinner with another woman in four years?"

"Because I'm married to you!"

"But you're not. Not really. We were husband and wife for six weeks. We've been apart for four years. You should have gone out with other women. You should have seen what's out there. You were right when you said we were stuck. We are. If you really want this to work we can't be like we always were. We have to try something new. You should try something new. Somebody new."

"Today is Molly's last day." Steven walked into Carter's office holding a card, seeming oblivious to the tension between Belinda and Carter. "My mother mailed this card to me, because she thought I would forget to buy one for her. I'm thirty-five years old. You think she could trust me enough to buy a card for my own damn intern."

"You forgot to buy a card, didn't you?" Carter said, taking his eyes off her and looking to his best friend.

"I'm a man. We don't buy cards unless it's our woman's birthday or anniversary. And even then I don't understand the point of them. They're just expensive pieces of paper that you look at once and then throw away."

"I think it's the thought that's supposed to count, Steven. Not the actual card itself."

"Yeah and I think this whole greeting card thing is a racket by some big corporations to get your money. Like if you don't buy this five-dollar piece of paper you don't care. It's bull if you ask me. But sign the damn thing anyway." He dropped the card on Carter's desk. "I need to give it to her before she walks out of here in five minutes."

Carter frowned at him. "Who shit in your cereal this morning?"

Steven shook his head. "I ran into Felicia Daniels this morning. Well, 'ran into' is the wrong expression. She ambushed me."

"Felicia? That's the girl you always had a secret thing for?"

"What?" Steven said sharply. "Are you crazy? That woman had been a huge pain in my ass since middle school. The only thing I have for her is loathing. Can you believe that she wants me to design her house? She's moving back here! I thought I would only have to dodge her around the holidays when she's here to visit her family but now she wants me to work for her."

"What happened between you two? I've never seen you have such a strong reaction to a woman."

"Woman?" He shook his head. "She's a pain-in-the-ass, manipulative she-devil." He motioned his head toward the card. "Will you sign the damn thing already?"

Carter quickly wrote good luck and signed his name so he could hand Steven back the card. "Are you going to take the job? We could always use the work. And if she's asking you to design her house she must have money. You don't do average family homes."

"She's got the money," he said through gritted teeth. "She's a writer." He stalked out of the room without answering his question.

"Whoa," Belinda said, staring after him. "He's a moody one."

"He's got woman problems. But don't we all." He rested his hands on her hips. "Now back to you and this crazy idea of yours."

"It's not crazy!"

"You're right." He dropped his hands from her body and folded his arms across his chest. "It's nonsense. Complete and utter nonsense."

"Carter, I—"

"Hey, Carter!" Molly walked in this time. She was smiling and also oblivious to the tense situation she had walked into until she spotted Belinda and stopped short. "Oh, I'm sorry. I didn't know you were busy."

"I'm not." Carter flicked a gaze at Belinda before he focused on Molly. She had the pink card in her hand that Steven had just asked him to sign. "I was just having a little chat with my *friend*. What can I do for you?"

"I just wanted to say thank you for the card and gift certificate. It was very generous of you and Steven." She looked at Belinda for a brief moment as if she was expecting her to leave the room. "I also wanted to know if you'd like to have dinner with me on Saturday. I'm done with my internship as of ten minutes ago. I know you were too professional to agree to go out with me before, but since I don't work for Steven anymore, there is nothing to stop us from spending a little time together."

Carter looked at Belinda for a long moment before he looked back at Molly. She knew he was annoyed with her, but he looked hurt. She hadn't wanted to hurt him. She just wanted to protect herself, her heart. She had to. "I'm single. I guess there's no reason we can't see each other. Is there?" He paused for a moment as if waiting for Belinda to stop him, to say something. But she couldn't. "I can have dinner with you, Molly."

"I can babysit!" Belinda said with false cheerfulness. Her stomach ached. Her heart hurt. It shouldn't. This was her doing. She was keeping him at arm's length. She had told him he should have dated while they were apart. She encouraged him. But why then did it bug the hell out of her that he had agreed to go out with another woman?

"Really?" Molly grinned at her, genuinely smiling at her for the first time since they had met. "That would be awesome. Thanks." She looked back at Carter. "I'll cook for us."

Belinda took a step back. A step away from them. She wanted to slap both of them, but she couldn't. She had asked for this. "I'll let you two make plans. I'll see you later, Carter."

Carter locked eyes with her, looking regretful, looking almost miserable, and that left Belinda wondering if she had just made a colossal mistake.

"I miss coffee," Ellis said taking a sip of the decaf tea Belinda had made her. "I never thought I would miss it so much."

"You can't have any during your pregnancy?" Belinda asked her from across her dining room table.

She shook her head. "The doctor said that I could have one small cup a day and for a while I tried it, but eight ounces of coffee doesn't work for me. Once I had a little sip I would crave more, and knowing I couldn't have more made it worse. If I don't have at least two cups of my Sea Salt Caramel Mocha coffee I turn into a raging bitch. My poor husband. I'm cheating on him in my mind. I'm having really graphic dirty dreams about coffee. Vivid dreams. I'm fantasizing about it. He thinks that when I space out that I'm just tired. I'm not tired. I'm daydreaming about coffee."

Belinda grinned at Ellis, who'd stopped by on her way to the grocery store that morning. They had promoted Maggie to assistant manager. She had only been there a few months but the girl knew her stuff and had past experience. They were slowly giving her more responsibility at Size Me Up, including allowing her to open the store on Saturday. Mike was going to be there for a couple of hours just in case, but they wanted to see what Maggie was capable of on her own. Ellis was going to take some time off when she had her baby and Belinda . . . She wasn't sure where her life was going to take her, but it was nice to be able to trust somebody else with the store.

"You're cute. You know that, Ellie?"

"Yes, thank you, I do," Ellis said with a raised eyebrow. "What's up with you the past couple of days? You're being sweet to me." She touched Belinda's forehead. "Are you feeling okay?"

"No," she said honestly. "I told Carter that I wasn't ready to get back together yet and that he should try dating other people."

"Why the hell did you do that?" Ellis reached over and smacked her arm. "You're in love with him."

"I don't know why I said it. Maybe because I thought he wouldn't actually go out and ask a woman out. But five minutes after I told him that, Steven's intern comes waltzing in there and asks him out."

"You should have slapped her."

"I offered to babysit."

Ellis cradled her forehead in her hands. "I used to think you were so smart. I used to look up to you, but now I'm seriously doubting my devotion to you because that is just about the stupidest thing I've ever heard."

"You looked up to *me*?"

"Yes! You taught me how to be sexy and how to feel good in my skin. You made me realize that it was okay for me not to be a lawyer. You made it okay for me to follow my dreams because you weren't afraid to search for yours. You told me it was okay to let myself fall in love with

Mike even when it was the last thing I thought I should do. Not to mention you run the store so well I'm not even sure you need me at all. You've done so much for me, now it's time for me to do something for you." She smacked the back of Belinda's head. "Take your head out of your ass and get your man. He moved all the way here for you. He loves you."

"He lied to me!"

"So what? He failed to reveal a three-day marriage he had the year before he met you. That was four years ago. You've got to get over that."

"There's also the little fact that his parents hate me so much they tried to pay me to leave him."

"So, nobody's relationship with their in-laws is perfect. You've got to forgive him, because if you can't you're going to spend the rest of your life alone and stuck on him."

"Ellis . . ."

She stood up. "You can't move on from him. All these years. And you can't blame him for something you did yourself. You kept this marriage from me for years. You kept it from your family and sometimes when I think about it I get pissed off, but I love you. I could spend the rest of my life being mad at you, but what good would that do me? I'd rather spend the rest of my life with you as my best friend."

She was right. She was right and that scared the crap out of Belinda. She was afraid of a future with Carter but she was terrified about what her life would be like without him. "Sure, it's easy to be rational and sensible when you're happily married and have a baby on the way."

"You're more stubborn than a jar with a stuck lid." Ellis kissed her cheek. "I've got to go grocery shopping before my husband divorces me for starvation. But I love you, you big pain in the ass. Stop making that man suffer. Everybody will be happier for it."

"I'll think about it," she said as she walked her friend to the door. Carter was all she had been thinking about since he showed up nearly two months ago. Letting go of the past was so hard, but she needed to forgive. She needed to live in the present.

Ellis opened the door. "Yes, do. Come shopping with me next week? I need new shoes. My husband has gone all-controlling man on me and won't let me wear pointy high heels anymore."

"He won't let you?" That surprised the hell out of Belinda. Ellis wasn't one to be controlled.

She smiled brightly. "Let me rephrase that. My feet are starting to swell and I can't spend all day in heels anymore."

"Ew. Mom shoes. Of course I'll be there to help you pick out your first pair."

Just as Ellis stepped her foot out the door, a little dark-haired creature rushed in. Ruby flung her little body toward Belinda. She was surprised to see the child but she caught her in her arms as she stumbled backward.

"Belinda," she groaned dramatically. "It's been *forever*."

"Ruby," she groaned back as she hugged the little girl close. "You're such a drama queen. But I missed you, too."

She had missed the little girl and it was quite annoying. Bad enough that she couldn't get Carter off her mind—but she had a thing for his kid, too.

"You should call me on the phone sometimes," Ruby said earnestly. "That's what friends do, you know."

"I guess they do." Belinda looked over at Ellis, who was watching them. She gave her a knowing smile and waved at Belinda before she walked out. "I didn't know you were coming to visit today."

"We are going to buy fruit with your mommy today and Daddy said that you wasn't coming. And I told him I wanted to see you and he said he wanted to see you, too, so we are going to buy fruit and then take you out to lunch."

"You're taking me out to lunch?"

"Yeah, I wanted to go to frozen yogurt again but Daddy said no because that's not real food and since I ate a Pop-Tart for breakfast he says I gotta eat a vegetable at lunch. But I only like corn. So then he said we were going to eat Mexican food because they've got salsa and guacamole there and those got vegetables in them. I like salsa," she said thoughtfully. "But not when it's spicy. It burns my mouth."

"I love you, Ruby." She kissed Ruby's cheek. "You're so freaking cute."

And before Belinda could fully process what she had just said, Ruby replied, "I love you, too." Just like she had been saying it forever, just like it was the most natural thing in the world.

Damn.

She sure as hell couldn't take that *I love you* back. She couldn't. She loved the kid.

Carter was there when she looked up.

Double damn.

She was in trouble now.

"Ruby, go to the bathroom and wash your hands before we go," Carter told her. "Use lots of soap."

"Okay." She slid herself out of Belinda's hold. "Grandma says a lady should always freshen up before she eats."

Ruby left them, and as soon as she was out of sight Carter came at her. She shut her eyes waiting for him to say something, to bring up commitment, to gloat, to say anything about what had just taken place, but he didn't say a word. He just hugged her close and kissed her forehead. "I hope you don't mind that we dropped by. She wanted to see you."

"You think she really loves me?" she asked quietly,

almost hating herself for doing so. "Or do you think she said it because I said it first." She shook her head. "I always forget the first rule of relationships is to never say *I love you* first."

"You're ridiculous," he said with a sigh, right before he kissed her. "Of course she loves you. She's five. She's too innocent and honest to say she loves you if she doesn't."

"You think so?" She searched his face. "I don't know why she loves me."

"Because you're lovable." He cupped her face in his hands and kissed her again. She shut her eyes. She had probably been kissed by him thousands of times but her knees still went weak.

Damn.

"What are you doing?" they heard a little voice say.

Belinda froze.

Shit. Busted!

She looked down at Ruby, who was staring up at them curiously, and stammered as she searched for the right thing to stay.

"I'm kissing Belinda," Carter said simply.

"Why?" She blinked at her father.

"Because she's pretty and I like her."

"Oh. Okay." She shrugged like it was no big deal. "Can we go now?"

"Yes." Belinda took her hand. "We can go."

Carter ginned at her, a triumphant I-told-you-so kind of grin. He might be right: The revelation that they were more than just friends may not have been earth-shattering to Ruby. But it felt like that to her. She felt like they had just gone down a road that they couldn't turn back on.

CHAPTER 19

So sick of love songs . . .

Carter had never been to a farmers' market. There were dozens of little stands stretched out across the green, selling fruit, organic meat, pastries, and myriad other food-related items. There was even a grilled cheese truck that sold gourmet grilled cheese to the huge line of hungry shoppers. It was a lot to take in. It was yet another reason to love Durant, but he was too preoccupied to pay attention to all that was there. He was too busy looking at Belinda, who sat on a nearby bench with Ruby on her lap. They were just talking. About everything. About nothing. Ruby loved Belinda. Ruby was happiest when she was with her.

Carter realized that he had made a mistake with her. He had gone too slow. He had given her the chance to think too much. Because she was keeping him away from her. She had told him to see other women. He hadn't planned to. He hadn't been with anyone else since they'd said their vows but when Molly walked in, when she asked him out right in front of Belinda, he couldn't say no.

He should have. He had wanted to. He didn't like Molly like that. He wasn't attracted to her. He didn't want to lead her on, and by saying yes he was. He hated himself for that. He'd gone to bed every night since then hating himself for what he'd done. He needed to cancel this date before he ended up hurting her.

"Pudge! Is that you?" Carmina waved her arms and smiled beautifully at them as she left her car. "Oh, Pudge, I'm so glad you came."

Belinda came to stand by him. A slight frown crossed her face.

"What's the matter?"

"Nothing."

"Yes, something. Tell me what's wrong."

She sighed. "She's yelling 'Pudge' in front of all these people? I wished she would just call me Belinda sometimes."

He wrapped his arm around her waist. "You know she doesn't mean anything by it."

"I know, but she never thinks, either. She never thinks about how that nickname bugs me."

"You're not pudgy."

"Compared with her I am." She rolled her eyes. "Ignore me. I'm hormonal."

He kissed her cheek. "I know. You're always hormonal around me. I'm going to start taking it personally."

"You should." She glanced down at Ruby, who was paying attention to everything that they said. "And stop kissing me. You're not my boyfriend."

She pulled away from him and took Ruby's hand as she walked away to greet her mother, which reminded him that they weren't a couple. "Hello, *Mamá*."

"Hello, Carter. How are you?" She looked at her daughter and squeezed her face. "My pudgy Pudge. I'm so glad you came today. I wasn't expecting you to come. You need to eat more fruit and vegetables so I am glad you did. Well, maybe you shouldn't eat too much fruit because fruit turns to sugar and you know sugar gives you a little bit of a round belly." She rubbed Belinda's tummy. "But that's okay. Fruit is good for you. So many vitamins. I saw on the television that people put greens in their smoothies. Like kale and spinach. It looks yucky to me, but all those yucky things are so good for you, no? Plus with all the other fruit in there you don't even taste the green stuff. I think we should try to get some greens for you today. It would give you so much more energy and then you would want to exercise more. And the exercise will help you slim down for your big day."

"She doesn't need to slim down," Carter said.

"What big day?" Belinda asked at the same moment.

"Carmina." Bill Gordon walked up behind his wife. He was the last person Carter expected to be there that day. "Stop bugging the girl. She's fine how she is."

"Of course." She kissed Belinda's cheeks again. "I just want her to look her best. Oh, hello, you gorgeous girl!" Carmina bent to scoop Ruby up. "I nearly didn't see you there. How are you, sweet pea?"

"I'm fine, thank you. Are we going to buy fruit?"

"Yes." Bill took Ruby from his wife. "We are going to buy fruit and bread and cakes and whatever else we want." Bill gave his wife a long hard look. "We are here to have fun. Not to worry about anything else." He took Ruby and walked away, and in that moment Carter's respect for Bill Gordon went up a little more.

Twenty minutes later they were a quarter of the way through the market. Carmina chattered her way through the stands, saying so many words that at times he found it hard to keep up with her, but in a way he found her charming.

Belinda didn't. She hadn't said much since her parents had arrived. Belinda was the most confident person he knew, but he wondered if her mother's comments bothered her more than she let on.

He walked up beside her, catching her fingers in his hand. "Are you okay?" he asked her quietly. She locked eyes with him nodding briefly, pulling her hand from his. And once again he was reminded that she didn't want Ruby to think they were a couple. That she didn't want to get back together with him yet. It was a punch in the gut. Every time she put distance between them it was like a hard punch that took his breath away.

They stopped at a little stall that sold handmade soaps. Carmina pulled her husband to the manlier selection. He heard her said something about sweaty feet and locker rooms but he couldn't pay attention to her because he was too busy looking at Belinda with his little girl.

They were hand in hand again, as they had been most of the day. It wasn't as if Ruby needed her hand held inside the market—her hand just seemed to merge with Belinda's every time she was near her. If he didn't know any better, he would say that they were mother and daughter.

Belinda picked up a pink bar of soap, sniffed it, and then held it down for Ruby. "Smell this one, Ruby. I'm thinking about buying it. Do you like it?"

She nodded and took the pink brick from her hand. "I like it. But it doesn't smell like you."

"No?" Belinda raised a brow. "What do I smell like?"

"I don't know. Something else. Like something good. I like that smell better because every time I smell it I think of you."

"My sweet girl." Belinda bent down and pressed a kiss to Ruby's head. Watching her do that—watching her be so natural and comfortable in her affection to his child—

made a little knot form in his stomach. How could she say she loved Ruby, how could she get so close to her and not want to be permanently in her life? Ruby was already attached, couple or not; if Belinda were ever to walk out on her, she would be heartbroken.

"Lancaster," Bill called. "Take a walk with me. I want to look at some bait."

"We can all go, Dad," Belinda said, giving him a cautious look. "I can't wait to see what kind of gross things you want me to put on my hook."

Bill's face softened for a moment as he looked at his daughter. "I didn't invite you, Junior. There's a reason for that."

"You want to surprise me with bait? You don't have to. You know I'll just crawl out of my skin if I don't know what you have for our next fishing trip."

"You'll survive, Bell. Your father and I are going to pick out some good bait."

Bill nodded once and walked away. Carter followed him, almost not wanting to, but knowing the conversation they were about to have was long overdue.

To his surprise they did head to a stand that sold all kinds of fishing gear. Bill hadn't said a word yet, he just walked over to the fishing poles and picked up a small pink one. He studied the tiny rod, which almost looked ridiculous in his large hands.

"Do you think this is a good starting rod for a five-year-old?" he asked him.

"I don't know, sir. You know more about fishing than I do."

"You're right. I also know more about my daughter and I know the last time she was involved with you she came home with a crushed heart."

There it was, out on the table, just like that. He could

try to defend himself. He could tell him about Bethany and about Ruby's accident and why it took him so long to come back, but he didn't.

"I know. I was wrong and I'm sorry about that."

Bill looked up at him. He pinned him with intense eyes that were nearly the same as his daughter's. "I should kill you. I should snap your neck and bury you in my backyard. I would do it. I would do it because you asked her to marry you without meeting us, without a phone call. You had a wedding without inviting us. We've got one damn kid. One kid who means everything to us and you didn't even have the common decency to have a simple conversation with me."

"I'm sorry."

"You're damn right you are! You've got a girl. How the hell would you feel if you didn't meet her husband? If you didn't give her away?"

"Like shit, sir. Worse than that. I would feel like somebody stabbed me in the chest."

"I could have forgiven you for that if you had at least made her happy. But you broke her heart. You didn't come after her. She came back here broken and miserable. She didn't get out of bed for two days. She cried for you, and just for that I should kill you."

"But you won't."

"No. I saw you at the park with your kid the other day. I saw the way you are with her. I saw that you were *with* her. I wasn't there a lot when Belinda was little. I wasn't around until she was twelve, when I looked at her and realized that I didn't know my own kid, when I realized that she wasn't happy. I know about you. I know you used to work all the time. I know you stopped because you were missing out on your kid's life. I respect you for that, because you figured out how much of an asshole you were long before I did."

"Ruby's my life," he said softly, not knowing what else to say.

"Belinda is mine. I know sometimes my wife and I interfere more in her life than we should, but I feel so damn guilty for missing out on so much of her childhood and we're trying to make up for it. Now you've got to make up for missing out on her life, too. She doesn't deserve to be let down by the people she loves anymore."

"I know. I love her. I want her back in my life for good."

"I see the way you look at her when she's not looking. You've got the look of a man with his balls in a vise grip."

"Isn't that what being in love feels like?"

"Yes. My damn wife has the temper of a bobcat and talks more than a women's chorus on a coffee break, but she's got me. Bill Junior's got you. What are you going to do about it?"

"I want to marry her again. Life is too damn hard without her."

He turned the fishing pole over in his hands. "I want grandkids. And if I kill you I'm pretty sure I'm not going to get any so I'm going to allow you to marry my daughter again, but if you break her heart again, I'm not only going to snap your neck—I'm going to break every single bone in your body."

"I understand." He nodded. "There's only one problem."

He raised his thick brows. "What's that?"

"She doesn't want me back yet. She says I need to date other people."

"Does she now?" He smiled. "That's my Junior. Stubborn as hell. I know exactly how to fix that."

CHAPTER 20

Stormy weather . . .

Carter glanced at Ruby through the mirror as she stared at him while he shaved. Her arms were folded over her chest, her lips turned down. Her forehead was furrowed. She was pissed.

He tried to ignore her death glare but it was hard. She looked kind of cute. Plus she had every right to be mad at him. "Are you all packed, baby girl?"

"I'm not a baby and I'm not packing."

He put his razor down, took a deep breath, and turned to face her. "Why are you so mad, Rube?"

"I don't want you to go out tonight. You said when we moved here that you was gonna stay with me. I want you to stay with me."

"I'm sorry, but I have to go out tonight." He was sorry. He had to go out tonight. He had to do this to get Belinda back.

Growing up, Carter could never go to his father for advice about anything—especially women—but Bill Gordon seemed to have a fountain of information to share with him about the women in his family.

Sometimes, son, you've got to give a woman exactly what she is asking for.

And that's what Carter planned on doing. Giving Belinda exactly what she was asking for.

"I do stay with you more. And we talked about this. I told you I was going to start seeing ladies my age."

"No you didn't! You asked me if it was okay. I said you could date Belinda. I didn't say you could go on a date with another lady."

"Well, it's good thing that I'm the adult and you're the child, because I don't have to listen to you. I'm going out tonight and you're going to spend the night with Belinda. So get your stuff packed or I will pack it for you."

"Fine!" She turned to leave, but he heard her mumble something under her breath.

If he thought she was going to back down he was sorely mistaken. He had fallen in love with one incredibly strong woman and raised another. There was an early grave in his future. "What did you say, young lady?"

She turned around, her little face red with anger. "I said she's your wife. You aren't supposed to date people that are not your wife."

She was right and he should have never told her they were married. Belinda was right. Ruby was confused by their relationship. He thought she understood about them but how could she? She might act like a wise old woman but she was just five years old.

"Do you know what a divorce is, Ruby?"

She nodded. "It's when people get unmarried."

"Yeah." He didn't know what else to say to her or how to say it to her. The simple truth of the matter was that he was married to Belinda. He still thought of her as his wife.

He still loved her. There was no moving on. There was no life without her.

He had a plan. He could see their future. He just had to get through tonight.

"Well, Belinda and I were unmarried for a very long time; that's why you haven't seen her until this year. I have a piece of paper that says she's my wife but she's not my wife really. We haven't lived together or had fun together or talked in a very long time. Belinda and I are friends. We like each other very much, but we aren't married like most people are."

He watched her as she tried to process his words. Her face was scrunched with confusion but he knew that no matter how much he tried to explain it to her she wasn't going to get it, get Belinda's and his relationship, because he didn't get it himself.

"I'm sorry, honey." He picked Ruby up and kissed her cheeks. "I wish I could make you understand but I don't know how."

"My tummy hurts." She rested her head on his shoulder. "I don't like being mad at you."

Belinda opened her front door as soon as she saw Carter's headlights shine through her front window. She was ready for her sleepover with Ruby. She had bought all the fixings for ice cream sundaes. She'd rented movies and bought pizza and buttered popcorn. She even got a special night-gown and slippers for the occasion. Tonight was going to be fun. She kept telling herself that all day. All she had to do was ignore the little ache in her chest and the knowledge that the only reason she was able to keep Ruby tonight was because Carter had a date. Foolishly she'd forgotten that she'd agreed to do this, or she had pushed it out of her mind. Maybe it was the trip to the farmers' market, or the fact that he took her and Ruby to the movies the next day that made her think that he was no longer going to see Molly. But he'd called her later and asked her to keep Ruby. Not for a few hours but overnight. Overnight.

While he was out with another woman.

Another woman that she had practically forced him to go out with.

Father and daughter approached her but instead of the happy faces she expected they both looked kind of miserable, and Carter had this weariness in his eyes that made her heart squeeze.

"Hey, baby doll."

"Hi." Ruby dropped her bags on the floor and hugged Belinda's leg, resting her head on her thigh for a long moment.

"What's—" Carter caught her eye and shook his head. She dropped her question. "Ruby, put your things in my guest room. I made it up special just for you."

"Can we lay in your bed and watch TV tonight?"

"Of course, but I bought all the things to make ice cream sundaes. Don't you want to make them first?"

"No, thank you. My tummy hurts."

She let go of Belinda and headed upstairs to put her things away. Which left Belinda alone with Carter. He looked so . . . sad. It made her want to wrap her arms around him.

"We had a rough evening. She wouldn't eat her dinner."

"It's okay. I have food here. Why is she mad at you?"

"For so many reasons." He took in a deep breath and locked his sad-looking eyes on hers. "Do you think I should cancel tonight?"

"Is she that mad? I usually don't advocate backing down with five-year-olds, but I'm not in your shoes."

"This is not about Ruby. This is about me and you. Do you want me to cancel tonight?"

Yes. Yes. Yes. Yes. Yes!

But she couldn't say that. She couldn't tell him that she was horribly jealous or that she hadn't slept well since he had asked her to take Ruby overnight. Or that when she did sleep she saw him with Molly in her dreams. "You go have fun," she told him instead. There was that fake cheerfulness in her voice again. And in that moment she hated herself for it. "I know you don't get to do grown-up things very often. It's rare you get to eat in a restaurant that doesn't have paper place mats and kids' meals. You go and enjoy yourself."

"I love restaurants with paper place mats and kids' meals. I like having my little girl with me."

"We'll be here when you get back," she said, suddenly feeling the need to cry. "Go out tonight. She'll be fine. We'll be fine."

"I know." He took a step toward her and pulled her into his arms. He did nothing but hold her tightly against him for a few moments, his nose buried in her hair. "Bell."

She shut her eyes, holding him back, loving the way he felt pressed against her, not sure she could go the rest of her life without him or even a few more days. "What is it?"

"Nothing." He let her go. "Thank you for keeping her tonight."

Belinda sat on the edge of Ruby's bed and looked down at the sleepy child. It had started to pour in the last hour. The rain was pounding against the windows; streaks of lightning made the room flash bright purple. It was one of those spring showers that made it hard for Belinda to sleep.

"Are you scared of the storm?" She leaned down and pressed a kiss to Ruby's cheek.

"I like storms. I like to lay in bed and listen to the thunder."

"Do you?"

"Yeah, I like it when the thunder shakes the house.

Sometimes I scream, but I'm not scared. Sometimes it's just fun to scream."

"You're very brave. Much braver than I am." She lay down next to Ruby, taking her small hand in hers. Even though she was feeling shitty, it was nice having a little girl around. It was nice not having her house feel so empty. This is what she wanted. A child. It had taken her so long to figure that out, but she wanted to be a mommy. "So you're going to be okay up here by yourself tonight? I have to go downstairs into my office for a little while."

"Don't worry about me. I had a long day. I'm going to go to sleep."

"Good girl." She smiled at her mature answer then kissed her again, ready to leave her and work on the ordering for the next week.

"Belinda?"

"Yes?"

"Can I live here with you?"

Totally taken aback by the question, she stared at Ruby. "I—um . . . What about your father? You can't leave him. Who will take care of him?"

"I can live with you some of the time and with him some of the time. He could live here with us, too, but I don't think he wants to live with you. He went out tonight. He didn't tell me with who. But I know it was with that stupid lady."

"Don't call her stupid," Belinda scolded softly. "It's not nice."

"I don't like her. She pretends to like me so my daddy will pay attention to her. If he marries her I'm moving away. She can take care of him."

"Don't say that. You don't mean it. You're just mad at your father. You want him to be happy, don't you? And if you left he would be a miserable sad lump."

"I know," she sighed. "He needs me. Can we have pancakes for breakfast?"

"Of course, love."

She left her a few minutes later, going downstairs to her den. She wanted to check out the jewelry of a new local artist and get a head start on accessories for the upcoming season, but after twenty minutes of staring at pieces on the computer she couldn't concentrate anymore. She kept thinking about her conversation with Ruby and Carter's miserable face when he dropped her off earlier. It was a little after ten. He had been gone for four hours. She didn't want to think about what he was up to.

She turned off her monitor and sat on the old couch she kept in the den. She should just go upstairs and go to bed, but she knew that sleep would elude her. Her mind was too busy and the raging rain was unsettling. Ruby was handling it better than she was. She envied the child. She also worried about her. She had told herself that she didn't want to confuse her, that she was keeping Carter away so that she wouldn't think they were a couple. But it was too late. Ruby was already attached. She was already attached. And she'd sent him out with another woman tonight. He could hit it off with Molly. He could decide that being with his estranged wife was too hard, too painful. She could lose him and it would be her fault.

There was no way she could continue to be in Ruby's life if Carter found love with another woman. It just wasn't possible, and the thought of not seeing that little girl anymore killed her.

A loud rumble of thunder startled her, causing her to look out her sliding glass doors. A purple streak of lightning raced across the sky—and that's when she saw the man standing at her door. She screamed.

"It's Carter." He yelled through the door. "Let me in."

She didn't move for a moment. The shock of seeing him there made her feet immovable.

"Bell. It's me. I'm sorry I scared you. Please open the door."

She finally unfroze enough to move. She slid the door open, feeling a blast of humid air as she did. "What the hell is your problem? You can't be banging on my door in the middle of the night! Are you trying to give me a heart attack? Do you want me to kill you? Why can't you use the front door like normal people?" She stepped away to let him in. "You'd better be glad I didn't have a weapon. I might have bashed your brains in or—or—or . . . I don't know but it would have been bad."

He frowned at her. "Are you done with your rant yet?"

She nodded, her heart still racing—but it was no longer heavy. He was back. He was with her. "I think so." She touched her chest. "I'm just waiting for my heart to jump out of my throat."

"I tried the front door, but obviously with all the thunder you didn't hear the bell so when I saw the light on down here I figured you were in your den. I didn't mean to scare you. I'm sorry."

She nodded. "You're soaking wet." She walked a few steps away from him and into her laundry room where she kept the extra towels and blankets. "Give me your clothes."

Carter tried to suppress his smile when he saw Belinda walk away from him in a huff. She was adorably disgruntled in her pink-cupcake-printed nightgown.

"Give me your clothes." A blanket and a towel were tossed unceremoniously in his face, and it took him a while to process what she was saying. "Clothes. Take them off so I can put them in the dryer. I'm not going to let you sit on my furniture with a wet behind."

He did as she ordered, noticing that she kept her eyes off him as he stripped down. All evening he had been jumpy, unsettled. He had wondered if he was doing the right thing but as soon as he saw her, as soon as he was in the room with her, his unsettled feeling melted away.

This was where he was supposed to be.

"Wrap the blanket around you and go sit down."

He didn't listen immediately. Instead he stared at her while she bent over to put his clothes in the dryer. Her bottom looked extra sweet in her bubble-gum-colored pajamas. "Stop staring at my ass and go sit down."

Busted. But he didn't care. Still, he obeyed her barked-out order and wrapped the blanket around his cold damp shoulders. "I don't know why you don't have the blinds down over these doors. I don't like the idea of just anybody looking in here and seeing you." He pulled them shut.

"I'm the end unit. Nobody ever looks in here unless they are my creepy estranged husband." She reappeared from the laundry room. She deposited herself on the couch and looked up at him. "Why are you here, Carter? I hadn't expected to see you until morning."

He sat beside her, not giving her any space. He needed to feel her warm body beside his. He had gone too long without feeling her heat. "I wasn't sure how late I was going to be so I asked you to keep Ruby just to err on the side of caution."

She looked up at him. She was trying to keep her face neutral but he could see the little bit of underlying sadness in her expression. Good. He wanted this night to be hard on her, as hard as it was on him.

"So how was your date?"

"We went to that tapas place downtown. I had duck quesadillas. They were made with goat cheese. It was a very interesting combination."

She nodded. "Anything else?"

"There was a three-piece band playing. We danced a little bit."

"Did she order dessert?"

"She invited me back to her place."

She shook her head. "I know I asked but I don't want to hear any more."

"I went. There was a bottle of wine already chilling when I got there. She made chocolate cake."

"Carter, stop."

"She kissed me and for a moment it felt odd. I haven't been kissed by another woman in four years. She wanted me. She started to pull off my tie."

"Shut up, you bastard." She tried to move away from him, to get up, but he caught her wrist. She was going to hear this.

"I was going to sleep with her. I had my clothes off. I was in her bedroom."

She slapped him hard, with her hand half closed. The throbbing sting made his eyes water, but a little burst of joy filled his chest. He grabbed her other hand and pushed her back on the couch. Her eyes were brimming with tears. She was angry and hurt—more so than he had ever seen her. He should have felt guilty, but this was exactly where he wanted her to be. He wanted her to confront her feelings.

"Why are you so angry? Why are you crying?"

She struggled against him. "How dare you? How dare you come into my house and tell me you almost had sex with another woman?"

"I'm not sure why you're so mad. You don't want to be with me."

"I never said that. I told you to go on a couple of dates. I wanted us to be even. I really didn't expect you to go crawling into bed with another woman at the first opportunity."

"I didn't! I'm here, Belinda. I moved my life, my child

here because I love you, damn it. I thought I came here to divorce you but I came to get you back. I've always loved you and now I love you more than ever. You were right before, I didn't know you, but now I do and you're the only woman I want, the only person I can see myself spending my life with."

She let out a guttural sob that tore right through the center of his chest.

"I didn't almost sleep with her. I didn't even go out with her. I was with your father and Steven. We had dinner at Flannigan's Pub. I love you." He kissed her face. "I love you. I love you. You have to know that."

"I—I don't even know where to begin." The tears streamed down her face. "You never said that to me before. You've never said you loved me."

"I'm sorry." He cupped her face in his hands. "I'm so sorry for that. I love you. I. Love. You. And I will tell you that every day."

She nodded, swiping at her eyes. Her tears were just rushing out. He had never seen anybody look so happy and sad and beautiful before. "What the hell were you doing with my father?"

"This was his idea. He said you were just like your mother, that you're stubborn and that I should give you exactly what you asked for."

"You bastard!" She swung at him but he caught her hands and pulled her close. "You put me through all of this to make a point?"

"Yes. I had to. I want to be with you. Always. No more games. No more waiting. I need my wife back."

She stared at him for a long moment. Her eyes hot. Her body tense. He didn't know what did it. What caused the change. But suddenly her eyes softened. Her body relaxed beneath his touch. "Okay," she breathed. "Okay. I'm yours."

He pulled her to him. His lips needed to be on hers. He

needed to taste her. She was his. Finally his, and he had never felt better.

The heat exploded between them instantly. She was pawing him, touching his damp skin, bringing him closer. He placed himself between her welcoming legs, sliding his hands beneath her nightgown, needing to touch her as much as she needed to touch him.

She suddenly broke their kiss and looked up at him, her eyes filling with regret.

"What is it?" If she backed out now, if she told him she couldn't be with him, he didn't think he could take it.

"I hit you." She touched his sore cheek, and a fresh wave of tears seeped from her eyes. "Again. I've got to stop doing that."

"You've got one hell of a swing, too, but I'm not mad at you. I deserved it." He kissed her wet eyelids.

"I'm so sorry. I feel horrible."

"Don't." He slid his nightgown up to reveal her breasts. "But if you want to make it up to me, you'll let me have sex with you every day for the rest of our lives, or until you get old and saggy and I find somebody younger and hotter."

"Ass," she laughed and lifted her head off the couch until her lips met his. "I've missed you so much, Carter."

"You won't have to miss me anymore. You are stuck with me."

An hour later he and Belinda lay naked and wrapped up in each other on the couch. He knew his body was heavy on top of hers but he couldn't bring himself to move. He was finally going to have his wife back. His heart had stopped beating when she walked out on him four years ago and now he felt it surging back to life. He didn't want to let her go even if it was for a few minutes.

"We've got to get up, Carter."

"I'm squishing you."

"No." She twined her fingers through his wet hair. "I don't want Ruby coming down here and finding us like this."

"No, you're right." He sat up and found his underwear. "What are we going to tell her?"

"Nothing. Not yet. She's very confused about us and I'm not sure if she could process all of this right now. She was really upset this evening."

"I know, and if she knows we're together it will make her happy."

"Don't you think that will send her the wrong message? I don't want her to think that we got back together just because she doesn't like Molly. Our relationship is more complicated than that. I think we should just ease her into us."

"How do we do that?"

"We start spending more time together. We show her that we love her but let her see that we are in this relationship because we make each other happy. Not only to make her happy."

"But I want to make her happy. She's the most important thing in the world to me."

Belinda stared at him for a long moment and for the life of him he couldn't read her expression. But then she took a step forward and kissed him softly. "I know that, and that's why you make my knees go weak." She gave him a soft smile. "Come on, let's get you cleaned up before bed."

They left the den together, their fingers locked, their palms touching. He loved the way her smaller hand felt in his. He never held hands with another woman before. The thought had never occurred to him, but with her it felt right. On their second date when she curled her hand into his he knew he loved her. She made him realize that he needed things he never had before.

"Are you hungry?" She looked at him sideways. "Or

did you fill up while you and my father were laughing at me and being big fat stupid jerks."

"Are you ever going to forgive me for that?"

"It depends." She gave him a sassy smile. "How much jewelry can I get out of you?"

"So, so much." He grinned back. "I love you."

She didn't say it back; instead she smiled shyly at him. "I'm not used to hearing you say that."

"I think I've only told Ruby that, but I feel it. I felt it the first time I kissed you."

She blushed, embarrassed by his words, but he didn't care. He would just keep telling her until she was comfortable with it. "So are you hungry? I've got pizza and ice cream here just for the sleepover."

"Pizza sounds good right now."

She led him into her small kitchen, where he watched her turn on the oven. She liked to cook. He would build her a top-of-the-line kitchen in their new house. They could build the house from the ground up together. That was another mistake he had made in their past. She'd moved into his house. His city. His world. They didn't build a life together. The thought of doing that hadn't occurred to him before.

"Ruby tells me you make a mean spaghetti dinner."

He grinned at her. "It's edible." He grabbed her by her hips, pulling her into him so he could gain access to her sweet-smelling neck. "You're very edible, too."

She moaned a little. "She says it's her very favorite thing to eat. You'll have to make it for me. I don't think I've ever told you how hot I think men are who cook."

"Belinda?" Ruby called from just outside the kitchen door. "Who are you talking to?"

They both froze as Ruby walked into the kitchen, rubbing her eyes with her fists.

"I'm talking to your father."

"I thought he was out." She narrowed her eyes at him. "I thought you was on a date. Why are you in your underwear? Why are you holding Belinda like that?"

"I—I . . ."

He and Belinda exchanged looks. They were busted. Thoroughly and completely busted.

"He got done with his date early," Belinda started as she pushed him away, "and he wanted to come and check on you but I didn't hear the door at first so your father had to stand outside in the rain for a little while. His clothes got soaked so I put them in the dryer. I don't have any clothes for him to put on so he's got to sit in his boxers."

"Oh," she said slowly. She didn't believe them. Belinda didn't exactly lie but she wasn't telling the truth, either, and Carter didn't want to lie to his daughter.

"I think we should tell her," he said quietly to Belinda.

"Okay." She lifted Ruby up on the counter and kissed her cheeks. "There's one more thing I need to tell you. I've decided that I don't want your father to date other ladies. I want to keep him for myself. I like him a lot and I want to see both of you a whole lot more."

Ruby was thoughtfully quiet for a moment. "Are you going to have a wedding? Can I be the flower girl? Are you going to live with us?"

Belinda blinked at her, clearly taken aback by her rapid-fire questions, but they were valid. They were about their future. They were questions that Carter wanted to know the answer to himself.

"I just want to date him for a little while. I know that's confusing because we are married but your daddy and I screwed things up so we kind of have to start over. I'm going to be like his girlfriend. Do you understand that?"

"Yes. Can I go on dates with you and Daddy?"

"Yes, some of them." Belinda nodded. "Sometimes we'll go out to dinner or the movies without you."

"Your mommy and daddy can watch me or Uncle Steven's sister can watch me."

"Yes. That sounds like a good idea. You're okay with this? Right?" She looked at Carter for a brief moment. "You're okay with sharing your father with me? Sometimes you'll see him kiss or hug me, but you know you'll always be his best and favorite girl."

She nodded. "I love you. I want you to be my mommy. I want you to be in our family forever."

Belinda's eyes widened slightly as Ruby's words hit her. Ruby wanted a mother. She needed one, but Carter wondered in that moment if all of it was too much for her. He knew they couldn't rush back into marriage, that he couldn't just expect her to be his wife again, to be Ruby's mother, but they would be there one day. One day in the near future. Maybe they were wrong to tell Ruby about them so soon. Maybe they needed to have a conversation about where they were going first.

"I love you, too, Ruby. Very much." She hugged Ruby closer, shutting her eyes as if she were savoring Ruby's words.

"Can we still have pancakes for breakfast tomorrow?" she asked with her head on Belinda's shoulder.

Belinda smiled. "Of course. Now go back to bed. We'll be up later."

After more good-night kisses Ruby went back to bed, leaving Carter alone with Belinda again. "She took that well. Do you think we did the right thing by telling her?"

"I don't know." She pressed a kiss to his cheek. "I'm just hoping she likes my pancakes."

It was nice to just sleep with a man, Belinda thought as she rested her head on Carter's chest the next morning. He pushed his hand into her hair, cradling her head, keeping her close so that she could hear the steady beat of his heart. She had missed this. She had missed him in her bed, in her life, in her heart. They were back together.

Not because she was sure that things were going to work this time around but because it was too hard to be without him. He had grabbed hold of her heart four years ago and never let it go. She knew she might be able to find another man, to date again. She might even find a man whom she might want to share her life with, but she knew she wouldn't love anybody else. He'd ruined her for other men.

"What are you thinking about?"

"Pancakes."

"She'll like your pancakes." He chuckled. "I promise. They have to be better than mine anyway. Last time I made them I served them to her burned and raw at the same time."

"Gross. That's like child abuse."

"Most of the time I cook for her I keep a lookout for the cops because I'm pretty sure the stuff I feed her is a crime against food and humanity."

"I can cook." She kissed his chest. "I can teach you how." She was quiet for a moment, absently stroking his hard stomach. "I'm scared shitless, you know. She wants me to be her mother, Carter. I love her. I love her so much. I want the world for her, but what if I fail her? What if I suck at being a mother?"

"You've got it." He kissed her forehead. "Those thoughts right there are what being a parent is all about. At least for me. Most days I'm wondering if I'm screwing her up. If she's going to need a lifetime's worth of therapy. Every day I ask myself if I suck at being a parent."

"You don't," she assured him.

"And you won't. All you have to do is love her. That's all she wants."

Carter made it all sound so simple, but Belinda knew that this was one thing in her life that she couldn't screw up.

* * *

"Belinda?" Ruby called to her the next week as they were walking hand in hand to her parents' house. "What's a French kiss?"

Belinda looked down at the child, feeling her heart jump into her throat. She and Carter had been back together for almost a week. Not much had changed for them, except that they spent more time together. She would pick Ruby up from school and they would hang out until Carter came home from work. They would all eat dinner together and she would go home just as Ruby was getting ready for bed. Carter had asked her to stay almost every night, but she only slept over once and left before Ruby woke up. They had argued about it. She felt weird about being there with him, like sleeping with him every night would change things, rush them. She didn't want to rush this time.

She wanted to ease her way back into being his wife, into being Ruby's mother. But she wasn't sure that was going to happen. When it came to Carter she always seemed to jump in with both feet.

"Belinda! Are you going to tell me what a French kiss is?"

Holy shit.

"Why do you ask?" she said, trying to keep the panic from reaching her voice.

"Because I heard some big kids talking about it on the bus when I was going to painting class this week and I wanted to know."

"Painting class was on Tuesday. Why didn't you ask your daddy?"

"Because he gets mad when I ask him about kissing." She frowned. "He won't tell me what sex is. He got real mad when I asked him. But I know people do sex, because that's how babies get here. I just don't know how they do sex."

Belinda didn't know if she'd rather be struck by light-ning or swallowed by a sinkhole in that moment, but any-thing was preferable to answering the little girl's questions about sex. She didn't want to know how Ruby found out about sex. She supposed it was the way most little kids heard about it. It was impossible to shield them from life. And if she freaked out, she was sure Ruby would remem-ber that more than any answer she might give.

"French kissing is when people kiss with their tongues," she said, answering the girl's question, hoping that she would be satisfied.

"That's gross!"

"Yeah, and if anybody does that to you, you knock his teeth out."

"I will." She frowned, truly offended. The door swung open before they even approached. Carmina stepped out, wearing an apron, her long hair elegantly swept on top of her head, a little flour smudged on her cheek. She looked like she was doing a high-fashion Betty Crocker ad. "Pudge. I didn't know you were coming today!" She looked at her watch. "It's just before lunchtime and you brought Ruby with you. It must have been an early dismissal at school today. Is that right? Some sort of teacher meetings. I know other parents hated them when you were a child because they had to scramble and find places for their children but I never minded. Remember we used to go out for lunch on those days and for a little shopping? You used to love to go shopping with me when you were Ruby's age. You loved shoes. I swear you walked better in heels at six than most models ever do. Especially that Miranda Phil-lips. Always looked like a horse to me when she did run-way. I hated runway. Speaking of runways, did you see *Project Runway* this week? I'm so glad they got rid of that whiny little crybaby one. You know who I'm talking about. No talent. Everybody thinks they know fashion nowadays! But I love that Tim Gunn. You think I could get him to go shopping with me? Bah! Your father would have a heart attack if he saw how much we would spend. He doesn't like me to have new things. I'm just his servant." She brushed her hands off on her apron. "Come inside. I was making cookies for your father. You can help. Hello, beautiful Ruby. I'm happy to see you again." She bent to kiss Ruby's cheeks.

"Hello, Mrs. Gordon. I had a half day and Belinda picked me up from school because Daddy had a meeting in Rhinebeck this morning."

"Rhinebeck is lovely. I wanted to move there but my husband said no, because he didn't want to drive an hour to work. So we are here, but Durant is nice, too. Come, come. Why are you still standing outside?" She stepped aside and ushered them in. "I didn't expect to see my only child today. I have not seen you in a while, Pudge. I thought when you moved back here that we would be seeing each other all the time, but I guess busy ladies can't make time for their old mothers. Not even a phone call. My life has been very sad these past few weeks."

"You're laying it on kind of thick today, aren't you, *Mamá*?" She kissed her mother's cheek.

Carmina looked Belinda directly in the eye. "I have one child. One. I know more about the next-door neighbor's daughter than I do about my own." She turned away from her in a huff. "Did you eat lunch, Ruby? I have hamburgers in the freezer or I could make you spaghetti. There is roast beef for sandwiches, but I don't think many children like roast beef. Pizza sounds good, no? Pudge, we have everything. Make us a pizza."

An hour later a pizza was made and consumed and freshly baked chocolate chip cookies sat on the stove cooling. Carmina and Ruby talked the whole time about everything and nothing while Belinda sat there and watched the two interact. They seemed to be enjoying each other and Belinda was glad for that, but she felt a little left out. Her mother who had endless words barely had any for her today.

Carmina was upset with her.

"Ruby," Carmina purred in her lispy accent. "Go upstairs and wash up. Belinda's room is up there, too. I haven't changed it since she was a little girl. See if there is anything you would like to play with."

Ruby looked to Belinda. "Is it okay?"

"Why are you asking her? I'm her mother. Of course it's okay, *gordita linda*. Go."

Gordita linda. It meant "pretty little fat girl" in Spanish. Belinda cringed. Even though it was a term of endearment, she didn't like it.

"*Mamá?*" she started softly. "I know you don't mean anything by it, but would you mind not calling Ruby that. I don't want her to be sensitive about her weight. A boy at school has already teased her about it."

Carmina waved her hand dismissively. "I'm not teasing her. She is a beautiful chubby baby. And that fluff will melt off her. I can tell. She's not like you. You were never able to slim down."

"Is there anything wrong with me not slimming down?" she asked, fed up with the little pokes at her weight. "Do you wish I had?" She shook her head. "You don't have to answer that. I already know. You can't stand to have a short, dumpy, funny-looking daughter. You never could."

"You've got it wrong," she snapped. "What I cannot stand is to have a child who lies to me."

"Lies to you? I never lied to you."

"Keeping Carter away from us wasn't a lie? Being married for four years and not saying a word about it is not lying to us? And even when he comes here and comes back into your life you still don't say anything to me about him. I had to invite him out just to get to know him."

"You could have asked me about him. But you never did. Even when I came home devastated you never said a word. I thought you didn't want to know."

"I didn't say anything because I wanted to keep the peace. I wanted to keep you here with your family. You have always been running from us."

"That's because it was damn hard to grow up with you. They tortured me in school before we moved here and you had no idea. They called me rat face, and Shamu. They said I was adopted, that you found me in a Dumpster, that I couldn't be your kid. That Bill Gordon and Carmina Del Torro couldn't possibly make such an ugly kid. You had no idea what that was like. You had no idea what it was like in high school when boys were telling me that they'd rather have sex with my mother than me. And I could never talk to you about it. You didn't understand. You'll never understand not being perfectly beautiful. You want to know why I left? Because I couldn't find my own identity until I got away from yours."

"You should have told me. You should have talked to me! I would have understood and even if I didn't, I would have tried, but you never talk to me. You always treat me like I'm some kind of idiot. Everybody treats me like I'm some kind of idiot. But I'm done trying to keep the peace. You want to know what I think about you and Carter? You broke my heart when you ran off and got married and didn't tell me. But that's not what bothers me. You should have stayed with your husband. Marriage is forever. You think things were easy for your father and me? With him traveling half your life and me working and raising you alone? But we stuck together because those vows are sacred and if you weren't going to take them seriously you should have never said them in the first place."

"You think I didn't take my vows seriously?"

"No. If you did you would have not hidden him from

us. I know you. You were expecting it to fall apart then and you are doing the same thing now. You didn't even tell me you were back together. I had to get to know your husband without you."

"We just got back together. You have no idea—"

"He's a good man and he loves his little girl and he loves you and you should have given your marriage a chance instead of running away. You should have given me a chance to be your mother instead of running away. Your life may not have turned out the way I dreamed but I still wanted to be a part of it, damn it. You owe me that."

"I don't owe you anything." She left the room, heading up the stairs to find Ruby, but she didn't have to go far because the little girl was standing at the top of the stairs.

"Were you yelling?"

"Yes, baby." She picked up the little girl and squeezed her, needing to take comfort from the child. "We yell in my family sometimes. Don't be worried. We do have to go now. I have to go back to the store for a little while. Do you think you would like to help me at work for a few minutes?"

Ruby nodded then pulled away slightly to touch Belinda's cheek. "Does your tummy hurt? My tummy hurts when I get mad, too."

Carter's cell phone buzzed as soon as he stepped foot in his office. He had just come from a long meeting with a new client. They wanted to turn an eighteenth-century church into a home without taking away the building's charm and they wanted his help to do it. Carter had never taken a job like that one, but he thought the idea of making something old new again was cool. Walking through the church, he could see the possibilities. His job sometimes mirrored his life. He was now walking around seeing the possibility in everything.

He took the phone from his pocket to see that the call was coming from his house. He answered immediately.

"It's me, Daddy."

"Hi, you. How was school today?"

"It was fine. Are you very busy right now?"

"I just got back to my office." He frowned at the tone of her voice. If he didn't know any better he would say Ruby sounded worried. "What's wrong?"

"I think you should come home right now."

The hairs on the back of his neck stood straight. "What happened?"

"Belinda is sad. You need to come home."

"Okay. I'll be there."

When he walked in the house he found Ruby sitting by the door waiting for him, worry etched all over her face. He scooped her up and kissed her brow, not liking to see her this way. "Tell me what happened."

"I don't know. We went to Mrs. Gordon's house and Belinda made us pizza and then I went to play in her room and then I heard them yelling and then we went back to Belinda's store and I helped her do her work, but then we came home and Belinda went to lay down in your room. She said I could lay with her, but I called you so you can lay with her. I think she's very sad."

"Thank you for calling me, baby. That was a good thing. I'll take care of this. You don't have to worry."

He set Ruby on her feet and went to his bedroom. Belinda was lying on her side, her face to the wall, but he could tell just by the way she held herself so tightly that she was miserable. "Bell?"

He kicked off his shoes and climbed on the bed, taking her in his arms.

She turned into him and that's when she broke. "It's okay, sweetheart." He didn't bother asking her what was wrong. He just held her and murmured soft things in her ear until her tears subsided.

"Thank you for coming," she said.

"Ruby called. You know I couldn't say no."

"No. I mean thank you for coming to Durant. I don't want this to fall apart. You know that, right? I'm going to try really hard to keep us together. When I married you I really did want this to be forever. I took our vows seriously. I never wanted us to fall apart. I'm not sure why I didn't tell my parents about us. Maybe because I thought I wasn't good enough. That I couldn't measure up, but I know myself now. I like myself now and I like how I feel when I'm with you."

He shook his head, trying to absorb her frightened words. "I know that, Bell. We wouldn't have lasted then. It was nobody's fault. We needed this time apart. We'll be better now." He gathered her close and kissed her forehead. He believed that. If things didn't work out this time, they never would. And he couldn't see his life without her.

CHAPTER 21

I'll always love my mama . . .

Belinda stood at the jewelry counter of Size Me Up, watching Ellis as she straightened the same rack of dresses for the third time. She seemed in a daze, every few moments stopping to rub her belly. She wasn't very far along in her pregnancy, but Belinda could see the change in her friend. She was slowing morphing into another person and it amazed her. She'd met Ellis as an awkward twelve-year-old girl. She had seen her go through horrible relationships. She was there with her when she opened this store and married the man of her dreams. And now she was watching her best friend become a mother.

They had been through so much.

"Hey, preggers." She walked from behind the counter. "I didn't think pregnancy brain took over this early. What are you thinking about?"

She gave Belinda a soft smile. "Mike says I've lost my mind, but in a cute way. I've got baby on the brain. I read something that said my baby had webbed fingers and toes until the end of my second month! Can you believe that? It's like I have a little alien growing inside me. I can't stop looking up the stages of pregnancy. I have this crazy need to know what's going on inside me at all times."

"I'm sure that's normal. Are you scared that something might go wrong? I know I would be. Does it feel weird to have something growing inside you?"

She found herself thinking about that lately, about what it meant to be a mother.

"I am scared. I'm scared shitless. I know there are so many things that can go wrong. I don't know my family history because I was adopted. There are so many things I want to know but can't ask my mother. I have contact info for my real mom, but I don't want to talk to her. I'm so glad that she gave me to Walter and Philippa, but I'm mad at her, too. I feel my baby growing inside me and I can't imagine giving it up. Now I just wonder after feeling life grow inside her, how she could give it up." She rested her hand on her belly. "Ugh. Ignore me. I thought I was over the adopted-kid issues. Being pregnant just brought a whole bunch of shit up." Her eyes grew misty. "Damn." She swiped at her tears. "I'm a mushy emotional wreck. I hate it! This baby is turning me into a goober."

"I think it's sweet." Belinda hugged her. "It's better than you being a raging bitch."

"I'm tired and hungry and horny all the time. And Mike loves it. He walks around all day with a goofy smile on his face as if to say *I did that.* I want to smack him."

"I'm happy for you, Ellie." She was, and jealous of her, too. Ellis had done everything right. Belinda wondered if life could ever be that way for her.

"Thank you." She pulled away and looked at Belinda. "I've been so preoccupied with my stuff lately I don't know how you're handling yours. What's going on with you?"

"My mother and I got into a huge argument. We haven't spoken since." Belinda was too bothered by her mother's accusations to call and apologize. And Carmina . . . she was just as stubborn as her daughter.

Carmina never understood her. As mother and daughter they were almost mismatched.

"About what? You and your mother never argue."

"A lot of things. Stuff that had just gone unsaid for too many years."

And Carter. But Belinda didn't want to voice that, because a big part of her knew that her mother had a point. She had run from her marriage.

"Hey, Bell. Hello, Ellis." She looked up to see Carter walking in with Ruby. She may have run from her marriage, but it seemed like her marriage wasn't going to let her get away.

She looked at her husband and his daughter for a moment. Her little fingers were locked with his. The thing she loved most about Carter was that he loved his kid and wasn't afraid to show it.

"Hello, Ruby. Hello, Mr. Suit and Tie," Ellis said with a grin. "You've got to come over to have dinner with my husband and me and Cherri and Colin, too. We need to check you out if you are going to be involved with my best friend."

"Just name a day."

Ellis looked back at Belinda and gave her a slight nod of approval. Ellis liked Carter. So did Cherri. Belinda had her doubts, but knowing her friends liked him helped soothe them. "I'll set things up with Belinda. I've got a client coming in soon. I'll see you both later."

"Hi, baby doll. I didn't expect to see you here today." She glanced at the clock on her wall as she rose and approached, scooping a sleepy-looking Ruby into her arms. It was just after two. School didn't let out for another hour. "Especially not at this time of day."

"The school nurse called and asked me to come get Ruby. She's says she's got a headache. I would take her home, but I have to meet a client in ten minutes. Do you think she could stay with you until I got back?"

"Of course. That's what I'm here for."

He leaned in and gave her cheek a long lingering kiss. "Thank you." He kissed her other cheek and then her lips, never afraid to show affection in front of Ruby. "I appreciate this."

"You don't have to thank me."

"I just want an excuse to kiss you. If Ruby is up to it later, can we take you out for dinner?"

"Only if we can go for burgers."

"Deal." He kissed her again and then Ruby's forehead. "I love you both."

He loved her. She believed it this time. She felt his love. Maybe that's why she was so afraid of things falling apart.

"Does your head hurt, baby?" She rubbed Ruby's back.

Ruby snuggled into her a little deeper and then looked up at her, her expression guilty. "No."

"No?"

"I think I just needed a day."

Belinda almost wanted to smile at her very adultlike excuse, but Ruby wasn't one to fake sick. Something was up.

"What's the matter?"

"We was gonna make Mother's Day books in school this afternoon. My teacher said I can make one about my grandma, but I didn't want to so I told the teacher I needed to go to the nurse. Everybody else in my class has a mommy. Bianca even has two mommies. But I don't have any."

"It makes you sad," Belinda said, not knowing what else to say. "I'm sorry you had a rotten day." She kissed her forehead and held her for a few moments. It was times like these, when she held Ruby close, that she got so mad at Carter, that she felt robbed. Ruby should have been hers. Theirs together. As much as she loved her, in the back of her mind she would always know that she wasn't hers, that she was the child her husband had with somebody else.

"Cookies might make me feel better."

"Oh, really?" Belinda laughed. "Well, Miss Thing, if you want cookies you're going to work for them."

"But I don't got no homework tonight."

"You're going to work here in the store. I hope you know how to balance the books and pay bills."

Ruby shrugged. "I can try."

"So that's the kid of the hot guy who came in while you were trying on the underwear," Maggie, their new assistant manager, said to Belinda as they watched Ruby attempt to fold the camisoles they'd just gotten in. "I was wondering how you knew him. If I knew he came in here looking for a babysitter I would have pushed you out of the way and thrown myself in front of him."

Belinda looked at Maggie and laughed, surprised by her candor. Maggie was a relatively new hire but she was great at her job, and the more she got to know her the more she was beginning to see that her quiet assistant manager was sassier than she thought. "Back off, girl. That hot guy just happens to be my husband."

Maggie's eyes went wide. "I didn't know you were married."

"Nobody did. We were estranged for a while, but we're trying it again. So you might see Ruby around here from time to time."

"She's really cute. She looks so determined to fold those camisoles."

"I know, and we're going to have to steam every single

one of those again before we sell them. I would stop her, but I like a girl with a good work ethic."

"Don't stop her. When I was a kid my father was a housepainter. He used to take me on jobs with him sometimes. I knew that I must have been more of a hindrance than a help but I sure did feel important when he took me to work with him."

Belinda couldn't help but note the fondness in Maggie's voice when she spoke of her father. "Are you two close?"

"He passed away a couple of years ago. I've been trying to get closer to my mother since then. We haven't always gotten along, but now that my father is gone she is all I've got. So that's why I'm taking her away for Mother's Day. I don't want to regret not spending time with her."

Guilt snuck up on Belinda and kicked her hard in the butt. She had argued with her mother. They weren't speaking and while she tried to fool herself into thinking it didn't bother her, it did. She could be like Ruby with no mother at all. Or like Maggie, trying to make up for lost time. Mother's Day was coming and she really didn't see herself spending that day without her mother.

The bell over the door sounded, causing Maggie and Belinda to turn to the customer who walked in. "I've got this," Maggie said to her and walked away to greet her.

Belinda went to Ruby, who was still diligently folding while she sat on the bench in the shoe section. "It looks like you've been working hard over here." She smoothed Ruby's hair out of her face and kissed her forehead.

"I like to work." She nodded. "I'm going to help Ellis sew, too."

"Don't work too hard. I might not have enough cookies to pay you."

"I'll take a check."

"Ruby Lancaster." She sat next to her on the bench

laughing and pulled her close. "Where did you come from?"

Ruby blinked at her. "San Francisco."

"Are you sure it wasn't from outer space? Because you sound just like a grown-up."

"Yeah. Grandma says Lancaster ladies have to be so-phisticated."

"Sophisticated? You know what the word means?"

"No, but I think it means old."

"You do have an old soul." She kissed her cheeks, un-able to help herself. "And that's why I love you."

"Belinda!" Maryanne, one of her regular customers, walked over to them. "I didn't know you had a daughter. She's adorable."

"Thank you but she's not my . . ." She stopped herself, unable to complete her thought. She didn't want to say that Ruby wasn't her daughter but she wasn't. But she could have been, and that little bit of hurt and longing snuck up inside her. Ruby was Carter's daughter and if things didn't work out with him, she would lose her. She didn't want to think about losing her. "This is Ruby," she said to Mary-anne. "I'm training her to work here so she can run the store when I go on vacation with her daddy."

"I'm folding clothes," Ruby said quietly.

"Wow. It's so nice that you want to help your mommy. I can't even get my kids to put their shoes away. I've got to head to the back. I've got a fitting with Ellis. Good-bye, ladies."

Belinda watched her go, feeling a little hollow after the exchange. "Are you ready for some cookies now? I think you've earned them.

She took Ruby back to her office where she kept her secret stash of fudge-dipped graham crackers. "You know," she started as she pulled the treat out of her desk drawer, "I don't share these with just anybody, so you should feel extra special. I almost fought Ellis for taking one. She's having a baby and all she wants to do is eat cookies."

"Ellis is going to be a mommy?" Ruby asked as Belinda sat beside her on the couch.

"Yes, her baby should be here a little after Christmas."

"Oh," Ruby said. Belinda could hear the heaviness in her voice.

"What's wrong, baby doll?"

Ruby leaned against Belinda, shutting her eyes. "I don't know what my mommy looks like," she said softly. "I don't remember her. It makes me feel bad."

"You were just a little baby. Of course you don't remember. You don't have to feel bad. We could get some pictures. Don't you have another grandma and grandpa? Can you call them and ask?"

"They died, too."

"Damn, kid. You're ripping my heart out today."

"You're not supposed to say damn. You gotta put money in the cuss jar." She slipped her hand into Belinda's. "That lady thought you were my mommy today."

"She did. I didn't want to tell her that I wasn't your mommy," she admitted.

"That's because you love me, right?"

"Yes. More than my Jimmy Choo shoes and that's a lot. You should be honored."

"You take care of me."

"I try."

"And you talk to me."

"Because you are so easy to talk to."

"You could be my mommy if you wanted to. And when Mother's Day comes I could make a book of things I love about you. I want you to be my mommy," she told her for the second time. "When is that going to happen?"

"Oh, God, Rube." Belinda didn't know what to say to that. She felt a little cheated again. Like Ruby should have been hers. It was irrational because she loved her more than she thought she was capable of. But she hadn't been there at her birth. She didn't get to see her first steps or first Christmas. She didn't get to carry this child in her body and experience what Ellis was experiencing. As much as she loved Ruby she was never going to have that. Because that honor had gone to another woman. Carter's first wife. It made Belinda feel like she was always going to be in second place.

"You're going to make me cry, kid. That's the nicest thing anybody has ever said to me. Being a mommy is a big job and I'm glad you want me to take it, but I don't want you to forget about your mother, either. I know how much she loved you. I know she would be here if she could. I'm going to have a talk with your father. Even though she's not here, she's still very important."

Ruby looked up at her, her little face scrunched as she took it all in. "Okay." She wrapped her arms around Belinda and squeezed. "Can we go shopping? I've got to buy Grandma a Mother's Day present. Daddy said he would mail it to her. I even have my own money. Uncle Steven gives me money sometimes when Daddy isn't looking. He says a girl needs her own spending money."

"That's right, Ruby," a familiar voice called. "A lady should always have her own money."

"Grandma!"

Belinda looked up to Carter's mother standing just inside her office. A cold chill ran down her back.

What the hell is she doing here?

Bernadette Lancaster had not aged at all in the past four years. Still perfectly slender. Still beautiful. Same perfectly coiffed hair. Same tasteful classic clothing. Same critical gaze she always gifted Belinda with. Being an icy bitch did wonders for one's appearance.

"Hello, darling. I came to surprise you." She smiled brightly and genuinely as Ruby scrambled off the couch to her. "I missed you so much. It was killing me not to see you on Mother's Day." Bernadette closed her eyes and hugged Ruby close.

The affection took Belinda off guard. The Bernadette she knew never smiled like that. She never had a kind word. She never seemed happy to see anybody, even her own son. Maybe that was the power of Ruby. The kid could melt anybody.

"I missed you, Grandma." Ruby turned to look at Belinda. "Grandma, this is Belinda. This is Daddy's wife. I told you about her on the phone."

She nodded briefly at Belinda. "Yes, darling. I remember her. Miranda, how are you?"

"Her name is not Miranda," Ruby frowned. "It's Belinda, Grandma. I just told you."

"It's okay, Ruby. Sometimes, very old people have problems with their memory. You're looking well, Bernadette," she said loudly. "Give my compliments to your doctor. You hardly look like you've had anything done at all. Next time I would tell him to go easy around the eyes. You don't want to end up looking like a snake."

Bernadette froze for a moment, surprise crossing her face. The last time they had met, Belinda had been reserved, trying so hard to make this woman like her that she hid her true self. But those days were over, and she refused to be treated or feel like shit.

"Thank you, dear," Bernadette said, recovering. "You are looking well yourself. Pleasingly plump as I remember. When I walked in and saw you in that green dress, with the way my granddaughter was sprawled all over you I almost mistook you for one of those beanbag chairs."

"Like father, like daughter. I think being sprawled all

over me was one of the things your son liked best about me, too."

Ruby frowned at them in confusion and Belinda remembered that there was a small child in the room and she couldn't say what she wanted to say. It was a shame, though. She had so much she wanted to say.

"Does Daddy know you're here?"

"No, I'm surprising him, too."

"But you came to my store first?" Belinda narrowed her eyes at the woman.

"I wanted to speak with you, but now that I see my beautiful grandchild is here, our conversation can wait."

"There's nothing to talk about. I'm not going anywhere."

"But I thought we was going to go shopping," Ruby said. "Grandma can come with us."

"Yes." Bernadette kissed her granddaughter's cheek. "I would love to go shopping with you and Belinda. She's always had such *interesting* taste." She looked into Belinda's eyes. "I do have to compliment you on this store, Brenda. It's more elegant than I imagined. Not a stripper pole in sight."

CHAPTER 22

Nobody does it better . . .

Carter pulled into his driveway to find an unfamiliar car parked next to Belinda's. He didn't think much of it. It was probably Ellis or Cherri, there for a visit. He was glad Belinda felt comfortable enough to invite her friends over. He knew that they had to start over, build a home together, but for a little while he had hoped they could stay here. He didn't want to move Ruby again so soon after they had come here. He wanted to keep her life as consistent as possible. It was a conversation that he should have with Belinda. He kept meaning to talk about what their future plans were going to be but the time never seemed right.

He opened his door, greeted by the smell of cookies and the sound of female voices.

"Yes, dear, the cookies are indeed delicious, but do try not to eat anymore. They'll go right to your backside and frankly you already look as if you are walking around with two hams strapped to your behind."

It was his mother's voice. She had come to Durant. He should have known she wasn't going to accept them getting back together, but he was glad she was here. He had a hell of a lot to say to her.

"Well, Bernie, I'd rather have these here hams than that flat thing you got back there. How do you even sit down comfortably? It's like you're sitting on bone all day. Do be careful or you'll have to carry around one of those unfortunate hemorrhoid doughnuts with you, and I don't think they make those in very many colors. They'll clash with your ensembles horribly. But I'm sure you can avoid that fate with a trip to the plastic surgeon. He fixed those nasty bags under your eyes; I'm sure he can stick some fat in your butt," Carter heard Belinda say as he walked into the kitchen.

It was a beautiful, perfectly mean setdown and for a moment he just watched as the two women who were sitting side by side stared at each other. His mother then did something he never expected. She threw back her head, opened her mouth, and laughed.

Belinda laughed, too. They laughed together. Carter did not know how to handle this scene.

"Daddy!" Ruby jumped off her chair and ran to him. He picked her up and kissed her hello.

"Hi, baby."

"Grandma's here," she whispered. "She surprised me."

"I see."

"She and Belinda are being weird."

"I can see that, too."

"They're confusing me."

"I feel the same way, Ruby." He put her down and cautiously approached the two women, not sure what the hell was going on.

"Hello, son!" His mother stood up and hugged him. A full-on motherly hug. It was unusual for her. He had always been greeted with a dry peck on the cheek.

"Hello, Mother. What are you doing here?"

"I came to see you. Marimba and I took Ruby shopping and then we made cookies together. Can you believe that she bakes? And all this time I thought she only had one talent. I guessed they trained her well on that bunny ranch."

"Mother," he hissed.

"What? That was a compliment!"

"I need to speak to you outside."

"It's okay, Carter." Belinda wrapped both her arms around his mother and squeezed the slender woman. "Bernie and I have been getting to know each other," she said loudly. "It's important for a woman of her advanced age to spend time with loved ones. I want to make this time count before her memory starts to slip away." She looked at his mother, her voice going even louder. "Don't worry, Bernie. I'll make sure we put you in a decent home. We'll even visit you once or twice a year."

"What a kind girl you are, Belladonna." She patted Belinda's hand. "And to think just six short months ago you were still on the streets picking up men."

"What the hell is wrong with you two?"

His mother actually looked . . . Relaxed. Happy even. This is not the woman he'd last seen in San Francisco.

"It really is okay, Carter," Belinda said softly as her arms came around him. "We're getting along. We had fun today."

He shook his head, unable to believe what he was hearing. His mother had tried to pay Belinda to leave him. She was cruel to her. She told him that she didn't want them together, and now suddenly everything was fine.

Bullshit.

"Outside, Mother. Now."

"Carter. Not now. Please," Belinda appealed to him.

"If not now, when? She cannot get away with what she did."

"It's okay, Belinda." Bernadette squeezed her arm. "He's right." She looked at Carter as he led the way.

He took her outside, to the back of the house far away from the open kitchen windows.

"This is a lovely little town, Carter," she said before he could start. "I see why you like it so much here. Your neighborhood is adorable, all these little cottages. I feel like I'm in another era."

He stared at his mother, dumbfounded. Nothing was ever good enough. Not his college major, not his choice in friends, or clothes, or wife. And especially not this place, where all the things she hated converged.

"What the hell is wrong with you? Why are you here?"

"I just wanted to see Ruby."

"That's complete bullshit and you know it!"

She seemed startled by his profanity but for once he didn't care. "The last time you spoke to Belinda you told her she wasn't good enough for me and that our marriage wasn't going to last. And then you show up here. Where do you get off telling my wife that she's not good enough for me? How dare you hurt her like that! If you came here to try to interfere or pull us apart, you've got another think coming. I'll cut you out of my life. I won't let you see Ruby again."

"Carter!" She looked horrified.

"I'm serious. I won't allow her to be around somebody who can be cruel to somebody she loves. I don't want her to learn that it's okay to hurt people just to get your way. She loves Belinda—"

"I know that! I know she loves her." Tears flashed in her eyes. "I saw them together today. I came here to warn her away from you, but then I saw how she was with Ruby. They're—they're connected. And if I didn't know that Ruby had come from Bethany I would have mistaken her for Belinda's daughter. She's not the same child who left

San Francisco. She's not only happy, she's loved. I could never interfere with that. I could never hurt Ruby that way. I'm just going to go back and tell your father that I approve, and we should just leave things alone."

"Father sent you?" He hadn't spoken to his father in months, not because they weren't speaking but simply because they had nothing to say to each other. Most of his life they had spent communicating through Bernadette.

"Well, yes, but I wanted to see how Ruby was anyway. I missed her terribly. And you, too, Carter. Being with Ruby and Belinda today made me realize that I've been so focused on trying to mold you into the perfect Lancaster man that I never really got to know you. We aren't close, and I don't want to die and regret not knowing my only child."

He didn't know what to say to that. He wasn't expecting to hear that from her. "I love her, Mother."

"I know, and now I see why you do. She's vibrant. You need that in your life."

"Grandma! Daddy! Belinda said that you two need to stop fighting because she's hungry and somebody needs to take her out for dinner."

"Oh, dear!" Bernadette turned to her granddaughter. "We mustn't keep her waiting much longer. We don't want her chewing on the furniture."

Belinda watched Carter for a moment as he sat on his couch watching TV. She knew he wasn't paying attention to what was going on because his mind was elsewhere. Probably on his mother, who had shown up out of nowhere and taken Ruby for the night.

She went to him, resting her head in his lap so that she could look up at him. He had changed into jeans and a T-shirt. His five o'clock shadow had made an appearance. His eyes were sleepy and thoughtful looking. She could stare up at him like this all night.

"What are you looking at?" He ran his fingers through her hair, scratching her scalp and causing her to moan.

"You're cute. I think I'm going to write about you in my journal when I go home."

"You're pretty cute yourself." He ran his fingertips over the skin just above her breasts. Tingles ran through her limbs at his touch. "Especially in this little dress. Do you sell this in your store?"

"Why, you thinking about buying one for yourself?"

"No. For my other wife. What the hell was going on with you and my mother today?"

"Nothing. We were getting along. I thought that's what you wanted."

"How could you even attempt to be nice to her after what she did to you?"

"First of all, I wasn't nice, thank you very much. And second, she's your mother and the grandmother of your child, whom she happens to love very much. I can't hold on to that. It's not good for Ruby."

"No," he agreed as he dropped a kiss on her lips. "It wouldn't be good for her, but you are." He kissed her again, slower this time, and she shut her eyes to savor it. "And you're very good for me. Thank you for today."

"Don't thank me. I actually had fun with her today. Don't get me wrong, she's still a total bitch, but she's witty as hell and has a wicked sense of style. You should have seen the shoes she picked out today to go with her cocktail dress. Black with a four-inch silver heel." She moaned again. "Shoe porn. You'd better be glad you weren't there. I would have jumped your bones right in that store."

"Is that all it takes to get you going? Remind me to take you to a shoe store soon."

"I'm free tomorrow. How are you feeling, Champ? You missing your baby already?"

"Get out of my head." He tweaked her nose.

"She'll be fine, you know. It's just overnight."

"I wanted to say no so bad."

"That would have killed Ruby."

"I know. My father sent her here to handle me. Like our relationship is some kind of dirty work to be disposed of."

"I just don't understand why he hates me so much. The way he looked at me when you first introduced us . . . He didn't even have to say anything, I just knew I wasn't good enough."

"It's not you. It's me. When things fell apart with Bethany, both of our parents were extremely upset and embarrassed. Bethany's father said it was my fault, that I chased her away and he threatened to back out of the deal, because he thought my family couldn't be trusted. To this day I'm not sure what my father did to make the merger go through. But he was mad that I strained things almost irrevocably with the Spencers. Even after that I think he thought he could shape me into his clone. And then a year later I come home with you, whom he hadn't met and vetted and approved of. He was mad because for the first time in my life I made a decision without any kind of input from him."

"But you became an architect. You didn't go to his alma mater."

"I really wanted to be an artist and I went to a school he approved of."

"Who could be disappointed in an Ivy League graduate?" Belinda nodded. "I didn't know you wanted to be an artist."

"I did. I liked to draw, but thankfully it was just a phase. I love what I do, especially now. I get to see people enjoy the places I create."

"I learn something new about you every day."

"I learn something about you, too. You need to call your mother."

"I should, but I don't wanna."

"Why not?"

"I'm just not ready. My relationship with my parents is so weird, they went from never being there to always being there and smothering me. I don't know how to handle them. But at least my father kind of gets me. My mother never did. She's mad that I keep stuff from her, but I just never knew how to talk to her."

"In her defense I don't get you, either, but here I am."

"Shut up."

"It's true. So what she doesn't get you? So what she calls you Pudge? She loves you. That's clear. You two have a hell of a lot better relationship than my mother and I."

"I think she wants to fix it. I saw the way she looked at you tonight. She does love you."

"Don't change the subject. Call your mother."

"I will, if you forgive yours."

"I'll work on it. I love you," he said. "You know that, don't you?"

"I do," she told him. He told her often but for some reason each time she heard it, it was like a little shock to her system. After all those *I love yous* she had said to him when they were first together, after all that time wondering if he ever loved her, he was now saying it freely. She believed him, but just like the first time together she wondered if this was all too good to be true. Something might happen that let him slip through her fingers.

"Are you going to stay over tonight?"

She took her hand in both of his and kissed his fingers. "Wild horses couldn't drag me away."

"I want you to stay more during the week."

She knew that. She knew he hated it every time she walked out the door, but she wasn't ready to stay with them all the time yet. It just seemed so soon. "What about if I promise to stay over on the weekends?"

"I didn't want to disrupt Ruby's routine, but we can come over and stay at your place if you don't like sleeping here."

"No." She shook her head. "I like it here. I like your little house. It could use some better furniture and a couple of paintings on the walls, but it's so cozy here."

"Then what is it?"

She shut her eyes and took a deep breath, afraid to tell him what she was really feeling. "If it doesn't work this time, if you break my heart again, I won't be able to survive it."

"Well, shit." He smiled. "I thought you were going to tell me something big."

"Carter! It's not funny."

"I know," he said softly. "I want to be married to you. I want to build a life with you, a home. I want to have babies with you. I want us to be us. What is it that you want?"

"I want the same things. Ruby asked me what French kissing was last week. And she wanted to know how people do sex! And today she asked me when I was going to become her mommy. I had answers for none of those, Carter. None! Except the French kissing. I told her what that was, but my point is, I'm not sure I'm ready for all of this. It's happening so fast."

"I know, Bell, but that's just the way it is with us. I wish I knew what I could say to make you feel better about us. I wish I could tell that I'll take it as slow as you like and wait until you're ready but I'm going to be thirty-six soon. I found the love of my life and now I want to build a life with her. What's the holdup?"

"I don't know," she lied.

I don't trust you not to break my heart.

"I'm going to try," she said, meaning it. She had to let go of the past, of that hurt that still clouded her heart from time to time.

"Thank you." He cupped her face in his hands and gave her a long kiss. "I love you so much."

"Kiss me again," she ordered and he obeyed.

"Do you want to do something tonight?"

"No. I want to stay in this house with you and only put clothes on when the pizza delivery man shows up."

"That sounds like a better plan," he said into her mouth. "Shut the blinds. I don't want to neighbors to see us."

CHAPTER 23

My girl . . .

Carter watched as the black Mercedes his mother had rented for her trip pulled up in front of the house. He had missed Ruby. She had only been gone for twenty-four hours but he missed her a lot. The house almost felt different without her. Belinda had been there and he loved having her all to himself for a few hours, but that didn't stop the constant thoughts about Ruby. The worry he always got when she wasn't around.

The car pulled to a stop and Ruby jumped out, running at full speed toward him. "There's my kid!" He caught her and kissed her curls, relieved to have her back in his presence.

"Daddy! Grandma took me to the toy store and she said I could get whatever I wanted but I didn't want no dolls because I don't like playing with dolls because they don't do nothing. Grandma got me a scooter instead! But it came in a box and Grandma didn't know how to put it together, she said she never put anything together in her life, so she gave a man fifty dollars to do it. But she said I couldn't ride it until I got home. Can I ride it? Please?"

"I don't know." He looked at the pink scooter Belinda was helping his mother take out of the car. "You've never ridden a scooter before. I think we need to get you a new helmet and knee pads first."

"But I just want to try it. Can I?"

"Oh, come on, Carter," Belinda urged. "Just let her take it up the block once before we leave for dinner. We can pick up the pads after."

He sighed, uneasiness creeping up inside him. It was the same uneasiness he felt when she rode a bike, roller-skated, and walked for the first time. "Okay. Just up the block and then we need to head out to dinner with Grandma."

He set her down, watching her as she jumped on the scooter and pushed off. "Slow down, Ruby!"

"Relax, son." His mother came up beside him. "She's just having a little fun."

"You shouldn't have bought her that without asking me first. Ruby!" he called after her when she had whizzed past her fourth house. "That's far enough. Come back!"

She obeyed and turned around and came back toward them, going faster than before.

"She's amazing on that thing," he heard Belinda say.

"She's going to break her neck." As soon as he said the words, the scooter started to wobble, Ruby quickly losing control. He watched her fall, her little arms flailing as she went down.

"Ruby!" He went after her. She wasn't moving. Her eyes were closed and her body still when he reached her. "Ruby," he choked out as he knelt beside her. His heart was pounding so hard he could barely breathe. "Open your eyes."

"Ow." Her eyes popped open and she stared up at him. "I hurt my butt."

"Baby doll," Belinda said, bending down to pick Ruby up. "You wiped out. You have to slow down. Okay?" She kissed Ruby's forehead.

"You shouldn't move her," Carter warned. "She could be really hurt. She could have broken something."

"I'm fine, Daddy," Ruby said. "It doesn't hurt no more."

"She didn't break anything." Belinda waved off his warning and set Ruby on her feet. "You're okay. Right?" She lifted Ruby's shirt to check her back. "You might have a sore bottom tomorrow, but you'll be fine."

How could she be so calm about this? "She could have hit her head, or damaged her organs."

"Didn't you ever fall off a bike or out of a tree when you were a kid?"

"I think we should take her to the hospital just in case."

"No, I don't think we should. She's fine, Carter. It was just a fall. You need to calm down before you scare her."

"I don't really care what you think," he snapped. "She's my child, not yours. I didn't ask for your opinion. I'll do what *I* think is best."

Belinda paused, shock, then hurt, then anger crossing her face. "You're right. She's not my kid. She's the baby you had with the wife I didn't know about." She shook her head and then bent down to kiss Ruby. "There's an ice pack in the freezer if you need it. I'm going home. Call me if you need me. I'll see you later." She walked away from him. He knew he had gone too far.

"Carter," his mother scolded softly. "You shouldn't have said that."

"I know. Okay. I know. Bell, wait." He caught up with her just inside the house, grabbing her hand.

She snatched herself away from him. "I *really* don't want to talk to you right now."

"I'm sorry."

"Are you? Because you pulled that she's-not-your-kid card pretty damn quick."

"So you're just going to run away."

"Yeah, I'm pissed right now and don't want to have an argument fifty feet away from *your* kid and mother. How the hell can you tell me last night that you want to be a family with me and then when it comes time for me to actually do some mothering treat me like my opinions don't matter? If this is going to work you are going to have to share her with me. Fully. Not just when you need someone to babysit."

"Wow." He took a step away from her. "If this is going to work? You're doubting us already."

"How could I not? Everything was always your way or no way the first time we got together."

"I never made you do anything you didn't want to do."

"No? We got married when you wanted, where you wanted, and how you wanted. We moved into your place. Hung out with your friends. We lived your life. You never once asked me what I wanted."

"You never said anything!"

"You never asked. You never bothered to even ask what I wanted. And I never said anything because I wanted you to be happy. But now I'm telling you that if this is going to work I have to be allowed to have some input in her life. I don't just want to be your wife. You've got to let me be her mother or this is not going to work."

He was quiet for a moment as her words sank in. She was right, he knew she was, but it had always just been him and Ruby. He had almost lost her once and every day since then he had been terrified of really losing her. He had lost Belinda before and that was nearly unbearable, too. He couldn't risk her walking out. She made him happy. This had to work.

"I'm sorry. Please don't go." He cupped her face, softly kissing her lips. "I'm not used to having someone here. It's been me and her for so long, but you're right. I'm going to try. You've got to try, too. You can't walk away every time I piss you off. Because I'm pretty sure I'm going to be pissing you off a lot."

He felt her relax. "I know. I need to stop walking away from you."

"Oh, good. You've made up," Bernadette sighed as she walked in with Ruby. "I'm not up for going out tonight. Come along, Belinda. I feel like Chinese, you like to eat. I'm sure you know where to get the best takeout from."

Carter linked his fingers with hers as they walked up to the restaurant the next evening. They were going to have a nice dinner with Bernadette to celebrate Mother's Day and her arrival.

"I kept passing this restaurant on my way to work and I thought it looked nice," Carter said to her. "Have you ever been here before?"

"No," she said distractedly. She couldn't focus today. She hadn't slept well last night. She kept thinking about their argument, how quickly Carter had thrown it in her face that she wasn't Ruby's mother and how quick she was to bring up past hurts. Maybe those hurts weren't past. Maybe they were something she would never be able to get over.

"I have coupons."

"Do you?"

"Yup, buy two entrées, get one free. I had to dig in the garbage behind my office to get them. I find the best stuff in that Dumpster. Where do you think I found my couch?"

"What?" She looked at him, giving him her full attention.

"You've been quiet all day."

"I'm fine. I just didn't sleep well last night."

"I know," he said softly. "I felt you toss and turn all night."

"I kept you up. I'm sorry."

"No. I'm sorry." He kissed her forehead. "You know that, don't you? I love you. I need you in my life."

"I know, it's just—"

Ruby ran up to them then, leaving her grandmother's side. "Can we get frozen yogurt for dessert? I want Grandma to try it." She slipped her hands into theirs, connecting them all.

"It's up to Belinda," Carter said. "I'm not sure she's feeling well."

"Really, Belinda?" Ruby looked up at her with worried eyes. "Are you sick?"

"I'm fine." Belinda brushed the curls away from Ruby's face with her free hand. "Of course we can go."

She decided then to snap out of the funky mood she was in. She loved them both and that was a stronger feeling than any old hurt she had experienced.

They were shown to a small private room in the back of Carlotta's Grille, which surprised Belinda. If Carter wanted this intimate a dinner, she would have cooked for them at home.

"You must be trying to impress your mother with this private room, but Bernie would have been fine with a bucket of chicken and a couple of beers at home." She wrapped her arm around Bernadette's slender shoulders. "Isn't that right, Grandma?"

"I would have been perfectly content with a quiet dinner at home, Bertha, but this private room suits me just fine. Anything to spare the general public from your atrocious table manners. We chew with our mouths closed, dear. And use napkins instead of sleeves to wipe our mouths."

"Belinda Jane Gordon!" Carmina's voice caused her to whip around. Her mother never used her name, much less in complete form.

"*Mamá?* What are you doing here?"

"Your husband invited me, but I really came to find out what the hell this is." She held out the box that Belinda had shipped to her house just the day before.

"It's your Mother's Day gift. You said you wanted a new cashmere sweater, and I got you one."

"No, you had one mailed to my house. You didn't give it to me. You didn't call me on Mother's Day. You sent a text message to my phone, which you know I can barely use. You didn't call me, even though I went through twenty-seven hours of labor and got stretch marks on my hips bringing you into this world. What the hell has gotten into you?"

"We're not speaking! Of course I didn't call you."

"You are the one who is not speaking to me. I am not the one who is not speaking to you."

"Oh, yeah? Well, why didn't you call me?"

"Why didn't you call me?"

"Because you're both stubborn pains in the ass," her father said. "Carmina, you have been sulking around the house for over a week. Junior, you need to talk to your mother. I'm sick of this crap." He walked over to Bernadette. "I'm Belinda's father. Bill Gordon." He extended his hand. "We're not always this loud and poorly behaved. Sometimes we are but not always."

"Don't be so nice to her," Carmina said. "She was mean to my baby! She tried to pay her to leave her son."

"Why do you care if she was mean to me?" Belinda shot back. "Wait a minute. How do you know she was mean to me? I never told you what happened."

"You're Bill Gordon," Bernadette said in shock, ignoring them completely. "You're the baseball player. You played for the Mets. My father adored you." She looked at her son. "Why didn't you tell me?"

"Was it important?" Carter asked.

"Of course it's important!"

"Oh, boy," Ruby said. "Everyone is confusing me again."

"I know, sweetheart." Bill picked her up and kissed her cheek. "Junior, Carmina, go outside and talk. We are going to have a nice dinner if it kills us. Carter, find us some damn drinks, and you, Princess Ruby, talk to me about your weekend."

Everybody stared at him. Nobody moved.

"Hustle, people! I'm not going to tell you again."

"I should have never married such a bossy man," Carmina huffed. "I should have married that Italian male model who was so sweet to me and used to write me poetry. He would never tell me to hustle!"

"Woman," he warned.

"Let's go, Pudge. I mean Belinda. Let's go before he starts barking at us like the players on his team again. I really have no idea how I put up with him for so many years. I should be granted sainthood or if not, they should at least name a school after me. The Carmina Del Torro Gordon School for Long-Suffering Wives or some such."

Belinda followed her mother out of the restaurant, truly amazed that she was babbling on even now.

"It's such a nice evening, no? It's warm for May. I didn't even have to wear a sweater tonight. I—"

"*Mamá!* Stop talking about nothing and talk to me. You said I kept everything from you. Maybe I did because you never stopped long enough to listen."

"I never know what to say to you. I never know how to talk to you. I love you, Pud—Belinda. I love you so much but I never could connect to you as a child. You were always so much smarter than me. So much quicker than me. You were like this serious little human who was nothing like me. I always thought I was going to have a girl who was just like me, who was bubbly and tall and wanted to do the things I liked and be just like me but I didn't have one. I got this little round red-haired being who was so different from me that at times I wondered if I had the wrong kid."

"I knew I was a disappointment to you."

"You aren't! You are different. But you are not a disappointment." She cupped her face in her slender hands. "You are so much smarter than me. All I had were my looks. If that photographer hadn't found me in my village I would still be there. I would be married to a shop owner. I would have never gotten out, but you are so much more than I can be. You run a business. People depend on you. Ellis tells me she wouldn't have Size Me Up without you. And then I see you with Ruby. I see you love her like she was your own. I see you connect with her like I could never connect with you, and that's why I got so mad that day. I didn't understand how after knowing her for only two months you could be more in tune with her than I ever was with you. I never knew that the kids were being horrible to you when you were a child. Your father was the one who picked up on that, and he was barely home. I didn't know the boys in high school were saying such things to you. I didn't know that my being around made your life worse and not better."

"No, *Mamá*. That's not what I meant."

"I know, but that's what happened. I was so mad when you didn't tell me about Carter, but I wasn't mad at you. I was mad at myself for failing you so much that you would want to keep him from me, too."

"You didn't fail me." Her eyes filled with tears as the guilt attacked her heart again.

"You were twelve years old and hurting and I didn't see that. I didn't know. You are so beautiful and you don't even know it and that's my fault, too. There's nothing wrong with your body. There's nothing wrong with you. I just knew how hard it was for me when I was working. Everybody was always watching what I put in my mouth. They always were pressing me to be slimmer and I hated them for it. And I didn't realize that I was doing that to you. I'm sorry, Belinda. I'm sorry I made you feel unbeautiful. That was the last thing I ever intended."

"I'm sorry, too. I'm sorry I kept things from you. I should have tried harder. I'm going to try harder."

They hugged for a long time. For the first time in her life Belinda had heard exactly what she needed to from her mother.

"Can I still call you Pudge sometimes?"

"Yeah, it sounds weird when you don't."

"Thank you for inviting my parents tonight, Carter," Belinda said to him on their drive home. "It was good for everyone to finally meet."

They had had a nice dinner, not one moment of awkwardness, no strained silences. His mother was at ease, joking with Bill, chatting with Carmina about clothes. It was unlike any family dinner he had before, and that surprised him. It made him regret the way he and Belinda got married. No family, no friends, just them in city hall with no celebration. He was going to have to do it again. The whole thing, right down to the proposal.

He was going to ask Belinda's father for his blessing. "I've never seen my mother so happy." He reached over to take Belinda's hand. "It's almost like she's somebody else's mother. I thought she would hate it here."

"She asked me if she could stay in the guest room tonight. She wants to spend more time with Ruby before she goes back to school in the morning."

"What did you tell her?"

"That it was okay with me, but then again it wasn't my house and she could sleep in the driveway for all I cared."

"Ouch."

"She got me back good," she said, smiling. "She said it was better sleeping in the gutter, which is where I clearly came from."

"I'll never understand you two."

"You shouldn't even try."

He pulled onto his street, feeling the weekend starting to catch up with him. "We're going to have to talk about where we are going to live soon. I want to have a home with you. No more your house–my house. Okay?"

"Okay. Let's talk about it tomorrow. I'm exhausted," she started then stopped. "Is that a Town Car in the driveway?"

Carter looked to see that there was a car in their driveway. Even though it was just getting dark, he could see that there was a uniformed chauffeur in the driver's seat. His stomach dropped. He knew who was in the back of that car, and it was last person he wanted to see. Still, he parked in front of his house and opened the passenger door to let Belinda out. He needed her at his side for this.

"Come on, Bell." He linked his fingers with hers, sealing their hands together.

The Town Car's window rolled down and there sat John Lancaster. His father. The man had never come to visit him his entire life. And now he was here in Durant. That could only mean one thing.

"Hello, Father."

"Son." He nodded. "Belinda. You and your wife are going to have dinner with your mother and me tomorrow at eight PM. I've rented a suite at Mohonk Mountain House. I'll see you then."

He nodded again, at his driver this time, and the car pulled off before Carter could say a single word.

Bernadette's car pulled up a moment later. She rushed out of the car to his side. "Please don't tell me that was your father."

"Grandpa was here?" Ruby asked. "He didn't say hi to me."

Carter scooped Ruby up and kissed her forehead. Unlike his mother, his father never tried to make a connection with Ruby. He wasn't sure the man even recognized her existence. "That was Father and don't worry, Rube. The man is a mean old bastard."

CHAPTER 24

A change is going to come . . .

"We don't have to do this," Carter said to Belinda as they walked up to his father's suite.

"I know," she said, squeezing his hand. "But I'm here just to see this place. There are plenty of hotels in Durant and yet your father chooses to rent a two-story suite in a Victorian castle. That says something about a man."

"That he likes to spend more on an overnight stay than most people make in six months?" He shook his head. "If you really want to see this place, I can bring you back and we can stay here for a couple of days. I don't feel good about this. I don't like to be summoned like some kind of child."

"We'll go if you want to, Carter. I'm here for you. Just tell me what you want."

"Carter. Belinda."

They looked up to see Bernadette coming toward them. Long gone was the relaxed look she had worn these last few days, but it wasn't replaced by her normally icy exterior. Today his mother looked pinched. Anxious even.

"Hello, Mother." They walked over to her and she surprised him by hugging him tightly. This open affection between them wasn't the norm, but he was okay with it. It was a sign that things were changing between them. "How are you?"

"I don't know what he wants. He won't tell me."

"Are you staying here with him?" Belinda asked.

"No. I got here about an hour ago. I've just been walking the grounds."

"Well, let's not wait any longer," Carter said. "We'll see what he has to say and get the hell out of here."

They walked up to the suite, the door answered by a hotel servant before they could even knock. "Please come in. Dinner will be served shortly."

Carter might have been blown away by the luxurious suite if he could've taken in his surroundings. The only thing he could focus on was his father descending the spiral staircase from the second floor. He was dressed down for him. No suit, just a pair of tailored khakis and a dress shirt. But Carter wasn't fooled by his casual wear. The last time his father had summoned him was when he pushed him into proposing to Bethany. He'd been wearing a similar outfit then.

"Please, all of you sit." He motioned to the table set up in the middle of the room. "I have chosen some excellent wine for this evening."

"What's the occasion, Father?" Carter took a seat across from him. "You want to toast our long and happy marriage?"

John Lancaster said nothing to that, but his eyes hardened. "Red or white, Belinda." He nodded and out of nowhere came another servant with bottles in hand.

"I'm fine with just water."

"Drink some wine," Bernadette said. "Trust me, girl. You're going to need it."

Belinda looked at Bernadette, and the two women shared a quick smile. Neither Lancaster man missed this exchange and while Carter found it pleasing, he could tell his father found it distasteful.

The first course was brought out. Potato-and-leek soup, which was consumed in strained silence. No attempt at small talk was made. This was not the warm family dinner that they had shared the evening before. They were all just waiting to hear what John had to say.

When the soup bowls were taken away and the veal brought out, Carter knew he couldn't be silent anymore. He hated veal and his father knew that. He probably ordered it just to put him off.

"Why are you here?"

"I sent your mother to talk some sense into you and bring you back where you belong, but obviously since she can't do anything right, I have to do it myself."

"John," Bernadette gasped. She couldn't hide the hurt on her face.

"You wasted your time. I'm not coming back. There's nothing you can say that's going to convince me."

"You'll be disinherited if you don't." He cut into his veal, while the rest of them stared at him.

"I've made plenty of money. I don't need yours."

"You say that now. You think you're in love, but love doesn't last even if it does exist. You'll get tired of her." He glanced at Belinda. "She won't hold up much longer and you'll be stuck. It was a blessing when she left. Even if things didn't work out with Bethany there were other women, more appropriate women you could have aligned with."

"Marriage is not a business venture." His jaw clenched,

the need to escape overwhelming but he felt just like he did when he was younger: pissed off and powerless.

"Maybe not, but I expected my child to have a better life than I had, not a worse one. You've always been a screwup, ever since you were a child, a disappointment really. Too stupid to take the path laid out for you. All of that rebellion and what did it get you? A job building houses? You were meant for more than that. You were meant to be great, but instead you're just average. My average disappointment that I can barely tell my friends about. How pathetic. You can't even keep your women satisfied. They keep leaving you."

"You're no freaking prize yourself," Belinda said. All eyes turned to her. "What do you have? Money? So what? Nobody respects you. Nobody even likes you. From my perspective you're the pathetic one. You come all the way across the country to tear your son down. Does it make you feel like a big man? Is your manhood that small that you have to compensate by making everybody else feel even smaller?"

"Belinda," Carter warned. "This is not your fight."

"It is my damn fight! How can you sit there and just let him degrade you like that? He's shit, Carter. He's the disappointment. He couldn't even be bothered to say hello to Ruby. He has no purpose in our life. No power. And if you're not going to tell him to take his money and his insults and shove them up his ass, I will." She looked at his father. "Excuse me, Mr. Lancaster, for acting like the crass unsophisticated woman you always thought I was. But my father is from Texas and where he comes from there's a saying they like to use: Go fuck yourself!"

She threw her napkin down and stormed out of the room. Carter sat there for a moment, still taking in what had just happened. He hated his father, he was annoyed with Belinda, but mostly he was mad at himself. There were so many times he wanted to tell his father to go fuck himself, but he couldn't do it. Because whenever he was around him, he felt like that kid who was never good enough. Belinda fought his fight, and that made him feel like less of a man than ever before.

"I need some air." He left the suite not sure what direction his wife went in and for a moment not caring. He just needed to get away.

Belinda had stormed off into a small bedroom. She had been so angry, she walked through the first door she saw. She could have kept her mouth shut. She should have controlled her temper but she couldn't just sit there and watch that man tear down her husband. She had probably embarrassed him with her behavior and she was sorry for that, but she couldn't be sorry for what she'd said.

She heard the door open and close behind her. "I totally ruined my storming out by coming into this bedroom. I'm going to have to storm out in the other direction next time."

"I think it was perfectly well executed."

She turned around to see her father-in-law there and not her husband.

"I can see why he likes you." He walked toward her, backing her against the dresser. "My son is more like me than anybody knows. I was never attracted to the slender society girls I grew up with. My first love was one of my mother's maids, a beautiful curvy girl from the islands." He touched Belinda's face. She cringed, knocking his hand away, ready to punch him, but he caught her fist in his hands. "I wasn't foolish enough to marry her, though."

"Get. Off. Of. Me." Belinda felt her blood pressure go up.

"I have a proposition for you. Leave him. I'll set you up nicely."

"What the hell is wrong with you? This is not about money! I don't need your money and I sure as hell don't want it."

"You could come away with me. I can keep you happy, Belinda. You wouldn't have to work again. You would just have one purpose in life."

"To be your whore?" she asked in disbelief.

"You are keeping my son from his destiny. I put him down so I can build him up. He's smart. He calm and he doesn't blow under pressure. He's my only child. I need him to take my place. A Lancaster has been at the top of my company for the past one hundred years and I can't allow a girl with big tits and a tight dress to ruin that for him."

"So you're suggesting I run away with you to save him."

"If you loved him, you would do that for him."

Belinda didn't see Carter come up behind his father until it was too late. He grabbed the older man by the jacket and slammed him against the wall, causing the whole room to shake. "My wife." His fist pounded into his father's face. "She's my wife. It's bad enough you tried to chase her away and now you're trying to steal her from me." He punched him again, blood spurting from John's nose this time. "You stay away from her. Away from us."

Belinda grabbed him. "Enough, Carter."

His hand was raised to hit his father again, but Belinda grabbed him, stopping him before he killed the man. He would have killed him, too, if she had let him. He'd walked into the room to come after her, to take her away from this place, only to find her with his father, her body pressed against a dresser.

His mind went blank then. He turned back into that angry boy who used to get into fights and take his temper out on anybody who came his way.

"It's okay, Carter."

"He had his hands on you."

"I know, but I'm fine. I think we should go now." She led him away and he saw his mother in the doorway, tears streaming down her face.

"I'm so sorry, Carter. Belinda. I have no words."

"You're going to divorce him," he told his mother.

"I—I . . ." She nodded. "Can I come live here?"

"I want you here." He kissed her face. "We're done with him."

"What's that white stuff in the middle?" Ruby asked Belinda a few weeks later. She was helping to cook dinner, or trying to help. Sometimes she got in the way, or made a mess, or dropped eggshells in things, but Belinda didn't mind having her around while she cooked. And she had been cooking every night in Carter's old-fashioned kitchen. She had made it a point to stay with them after the final meeting with his father. He had been quiet since then, obviously hurt by his father's brutal betrayal, and she just wanted to show him that she was there for him. That they were a united front.

"It's ricotta cheese. Any good lasagna has ricotta in it."

"It looks gross." Ruby frowned.

"Then don't eat it. You'll have to cook your own dinner and you can't reach the stove but I'm sure you'll find a way to manage." She winked at her, causing Ruby to grin and reveal her teeth that hadn't quite grown in yet.

"I'll eat it. I like the way you cook. It's much better than the way Daddy cooks."

"Thank you, baby doll."

"I like that you stay here with us now."

"Do you?" She ran her fingers through Ruby's shiny curls. "You aren't sick of me yet?"

"No. Not yet. Maybe when I get older I'll get sick of you, but right now I love you."

She smiled at Ruby and bent to kiss her forehead. "I love you, too, kid. I hope I don't get sick of you until you're thirteen. But then I'll trade you in for a younger cuter model."

"Where are my two favorite ladies?"

"In the kitchen," Ruby yelled. "We're cooking dinner for you!"

"That's why it smells so good in here." He kissed Belinda's cheek and then bent to kiss Ruby. On the outside he looked like the same old Carter, but she could tell that he was still off. Things had become a little strained between them. Ruby might not have been able to tell, but she knew. She just didn't know how to fix it.

"Dinner smells amazing. Can I help you with anything?"

"Actually, would you mind keeping an eye on the lasagna? I've got to run to the store and pick up some garlic bread."

"I'll get it. You should have told me to pick it up on my way home."

"I didn't want to bother you at work. I know you were busy today."

"And so were you." He grabbed her by the waist and pulled her into a hug. "You do a lot for us. I don't want you to think I don't notice that."

She nodded, hugging him tightly, wishing she could snap him out of this mood.

"Come on, Ruby. Let's get some bread for Belinda."

"No, thank you. I want to stay here with Belinda."

Carter's face turned to stone, and Belinda knew that Ruby had hurt him. He had been a little sensitive about Ruby lately. And Belinda realized that she had to take a step back. She wanted to be an equal parent, but she knew that Ruby was still Carter's only child and he needed to feel that bond with her. Especially now that all hopes of having any sort of relationship with his father had died painfully.

"Go with your father. You've been with me all day. I could use a few minutes alone."

Ruby shrugged. "I wanna stay home with you."

She shook her head. "Go with your father. If you stay here I'm going to make you dry dishes. If you go with him you can probably get him to buy you candy."

"But—"

"Ruby . . ."

"If she doesn't want to go she doesn't have to, Belinda. Stop trying to convince her otherwise. I'll go by myself. It seems like everyone prefers you anyway."

There was no denying the sharpness in his voice. Even Ruby noticed it and looked up at him with surprise.

Belinda's first instinct was to snap back at him, but she didn't want to argue with him in front of Ruby.

But this wasn't her fault.

"Okay," she said softly.

He grabbed his keys off the counter and walked out the door.

"I'm sorry," Ruby said immediately. "I didn't mean to make him mad." Her eyes went big with panic. "I'm sorry."

She lifted the child off her feet and hugged her tightly. "Relax, baby doll. You're not in trouble, but I think you hurt your daddy's feelings. He wants to spend time with you. Just you and him. It's just been you and him all these years, so it hurts his feelings when you don't go to him because he loves you more than anybody else on the planet. Do you understand?"

She nodded.

"Why don't you go get washed up for dinner?"

Ruby ran off as soon as she set her down. She was alone, feeling completely at a loss for a moment. But then the front door opened and she was surprised to see Carter rushing toward her.

"I'm a dick." He cupped her face in his hands and stroked her cheeks with his thumbs. "I'm sorry." He pressed his lips to hers. "I was . . ."

"You were hurt. I'm not trying to come between you and her."

"I know. I just can't shake what happened."

"I know. I can't imagine how you must feel." But she had an idea. He was barely talking to her anymore, so in his head that some days she barely reached him.

"I'm sorry, Bell. I don't want to fuck this up. I love you too much."

"It's okay." It was going to take time, but she wasn't sure how long they could survive this.

"There's a house for sale on my street," Cherri said to Belinda a month later. "Four bedrooms, three bathrooms. Two-car garage. It needs a little work, though. Are you prepared to take on something like that?"

"I don't know." She looked back at Ruby, who was a little way behind them trying to kick a soccer ball from the middle of Elder Park to the parking lot. "We haven't talked about it much. Our first time looking at houses will be on Saturday, but I think I would be open to renovating a house. We could put our stamp on it together."

"Ellis and Mike just finished the process. Their house looks great. I'm sure they could help you find a good contractor."

"Yeah, I'll ask her about it later."

"Belinda?" Cherri stopped pushing her son and placed her hands on her shoulders. "What the hell is up with you?

You should be excited. You're buying a house with the guy you love."

"I am."

"Then what's your deal?"

She wasn't exactly sure. Things had mostly gone back to normal with Carter, but there was still that little bit of distance between them. It was almost like he blamed her for the break with his father. She knew that wasn't strictly true. But she really had been the catalyst, the biggest and final thing that came between them. Carter claimed to hate his father, but she knew that he loved the man, or had once upon a time. All Carter wanted was for him to respect his decisions.

"My mother keeps asking us when we are going to get married."

"You're already married."

"I know, but I think she would rather that we have a wedding before buying a house. She says we always do things backward."

"You do. But is that what you want? Do you want a big wedding?"

"Would you judge me if I said yes?"

"Hell, no. Ellis and I have been planning your wedding in our heads even before we knew about Carter. Ellis has sketches of big extravagant dresses for you that she keeps in a book."

"That's nuts."

"We never claimed to be sane. That's why you love us."

"It's true. I shouldn't need a ceremony to feel like we're married but I kind of do. Last time didn't feel real because I didn't have my family there. I didn't have Ellis there. I didn't know you then, but you're my best friend, too, and I needed you there to make it real."

"So tell Carter that you want to get married again. Tell him you want your wedding."

"If I have to tell him then it won't be genuine. He should want to walk down the aisle with me. He should want to do this in front of our family and friends."

"I'm sure he does, but men are stupid. You have to tell them these things."

"Okay. I will. I'll talk to him tonight."

"Belinda." Ruby ran up to them and grabbed hold of her hand. "You think we could get a dog when we move to our new house?"

"I don't know, babe. That's something we'll have to ask your father about."

"I don't think he likes dogs very much." She looked up at Cherri. "Maybe we could borrow your dog sometimes so Daddy gets used to him."

"Rufus would love to have a little girl to play with. I would bring him to the park with us but he loves my husband too much. He barely leaves his side."

"I think Daddy gets sad sometimes that there are no boys in the house. He needs a boy to play with."

"You think so?"

"Yeah, you could have a baby for him."

"Excuse me?" she said as she heard Cherri snort.

"You could have a baby for him, or we could get a boy dog."

"Oh, Ruby." Belinda ruffled her hair. "You are either the sweetest child on the planet or a master manipulator."

"Can we get frozen yogurt today?"

"Yes, but after you eat your lunch."

"Okay." The ball slipped out of her grasp as they approached the parking lot. She let go of Belinda's hand to chase after it.

"Ruby, don't run out in the parking lot."

"I just want to get the ball. Your daddy just bought it for me."

"Ruby!"

"That truck is backing out quickly, Belinda," Cherri warned as Ruby ran farther out into the parking lot.

"I know. Ruby Lancaster, you stop right there!" She ran after her.

"I'm coming." She ran right behind the pickup. Belinda was right behind her. "I just—"

Belinda grabbed her arm, yanking her out of the way, but she wasn't quick enough because she heard Cherri scream at the same moment she felt the impact of the truck.

CHAPTER 25

The first to say good-bye . . .

Carter didn't remember the drive to the hospital or even getting out of the car. He didn't remember walking down the hall in the emergency room. He didn't remember any of the words that the nurse had said to him while she showed him the way. All he could think of was Ruby. Ruby was hit by a truck. It was happening again. His nightmare was repeating itself. He had almost lost her once. She had three surgeries. She was hooked up to a ventilator. She had tubes coming out of her nose. He wanted to die then. It was the worst time in his life, and he knew he couldn't survive seeing his baby hurt again.

"There she is, Mr. Lancaster."

He walked into the room slowly. Slowly because he almost didn't want to see her, because he couldn't bear seeing her hurt again. It was too much. Her face was turned away from him. She looked pale, but whole, not the almost lifeless being he saw the last time this happened. Her arm was in a sling and wrapped tightly in a bandage. It wasn't as bad as he thought.

He thanked God for that. Thank God. Thank God. Thank God.

He approached her slowly, afraid to touch her, afraid that she was like a mirage that was going to break apart, disappear through his fingers if he touched her. But he wanted to touch her and hold her and squeeze her. He wanted to never let her out of his sight again.

"She's okay," he heard Belinda say from behind him. "Most of the damage came from me."

He turned around to look at her. She had her cell phone in her hand. She didn't look like herself. Her eyes were wide, remorseful, regretful, and he knew whatever took place was her fault.

"How did this happen?"

"She dropped her soccer ball in the parking lot and she ran after it. There was a truck pulling out and I went after her. I grabbed her arm to pull her away from the truck and I dislocated her shoulder in the process." She went to Ruby's bedside, smoothed her hair away from her face to kiss her forehead. "I didn't mean to hurt her. I just wanted to get her out of the way. Thank God that truck slowed down when it saw me. It just barely tapped her." She cupped Ruby's cheeks and kissed every inch of exposed skin on her face.

Ruby opened her eyes. "You keep kissing me and kissing me."

"I know. I'm not going to stop, either. I'm glad you're okay. You scared me."

"I'm sorry. I didn't mean to. Is Daddy here yet?"

"Yeah, Cherri must have gotten ahold of him. He's right over there."

"Hey, Rube." He approached her, gently taking her little hand in his. "How are you feeling?"

"I'm okay. The doctor gave me medicine for my arm. Can we still go get frozen yogurt?"

"Yes. We can have whatever you want."

Later that evening Belinda had given Ruby a bath and put her to bed. She kissed her probably a thousand more times since she left the hospital. She was going to be fine, but Belinda's heart still raced when she thought about it. The child had taken ten years off her life today.

It could have been worse. It could have been so much worse, but it wasn't. Ruby was safe in her bed, in one piece, and hopefully she had learned her lesson from all of this.

She went to the kitchen where Carter was cleaning up after dinner. The day had finally caught up to her, and so had the soreness that was starting to throb throughout her body. She had been hit by the truck, too. Her thigh and hip had taken most of the impact.

She went to Carter, whose back was turned to her, and wrapped her arms around him, resting her face on his wide strong back. He stiffened at her touch. She felt it immediately but she didn't move away at first. Her body didn't want her to.

"Is Ruby settled?"

"Yes. The pain medication the doctor gave her this afternoon made her sleepy. She asked why you didn't come say good night to her when I did."

"Go lie down," he said with frost in his voice. "I'll go alone."

She stepped away from him, pulling him around so that she could see his face. "You have been short with me this whole evening. If you have something to say to me then I wish you would say it."

"Just go to bed, Belinda. You don't want me to say what I want to say to you."

She put her hands on her hips, not backing down from him, refusing to walk on eggshells. "Say it, damn it."

"How could you let her run out into a goddamn parking lot? I trusted you with her! Your only job was to keep her safe and you couldn't even do that right."

She recoiled at his words, feeling almost breathless. "You sound just like your father. I can't do anything right? Am I your wife or your babysitter? I never meant for her to get hurt. I tried to stop her. I told her not to go. She didn't listen. I went after her. What else did you want me to do?"

"Learn how to handle her in the first place. Learn how to be a damn parent."

"Fuck you, Carter. That could just as easily have happened to you. She's five years old. She ran after a ball, but she's okay. She's alive."

"By the grace of God. She's never been hurt with me. Maybe I've been stupid. Maybe I shouldn't have let you near her."

"Don't go there. Don't you dare go there. You came after me. You wanted this."

"Well, maybe I don't. Maybe I can't trust you. She could have died today. You would have been the cause of that. You would have lost the most important thing in the world to me. And that's got me thinking that maybe I don't want you around her at all."

She had thought she had been hurt by him before. He kept his marriage away from her, he kept part of his life a secret from her, but that was nothing compared with how hurt she felt right now. He didn't want her around the most important person in his life and that meant he didn't want her around him, either.

"Fine," she said calmly even though calm was the last thing she felt. "I'll go."

"No!" They both looked down to see Ruby standing in the doorway. Her little face was red and twisted with anger, and her eyes were full of tears. "No. You won't go."

"I'm sorry, Ruby." Tears stung at Belinda's eyes, blinding her, but she refused to let them slip in front of Ruby. "I'm so sorry, baby. This is not your fault. But I have to go."

She left then before her tears could slip out. Before she broke down in front of them.

"You get her back!" Ruby screamed at him. "You go get her back right now!"

Shit. What the hell had he just done? He didn't mean it. He didn't mean any of those things he said to her. He was mad. The last few weeks were finally taking their toll on him. He kept thinking about the last time Ruby was hurt. He kept thinking about her fighting for her life. He kept thinking about the weeks he spent at her bedside. He kept thinking about afterward, when he had to raise her alone. He kept thinking about how mad he was at Belinda then. Belinda who left him. Belinda who threw away their marriage when she was supposed to love him.

He kept thinking about the past and because of that his future just walked out the door.

"You go now!" He took a step toward his daughter, reaching for her, not sure what else to do in that moment. He had never seen her so upset. This was his fault. He had screwed up a lot in his life, but he had never fucked up this bad.

"I'm sorry, honey." He tried to hug her, but she shoved him away. She pounded on his shoulder with her fist.

"You're not sorry. You were mean to her. You made her go away. You made my mommy go away."

The sobs came then and he grabbed her, wrapping his

arms tightly around her to stop her from struggling against him. "I'll get her back," he promised her. "I'll get her back."

He had to, because life was too hard without her.

"Are you sure you're okay, my Pudge?" Carmina asked as she stroked Belinda's hair. "Mommy can stay tonight it you want."

"I'm okay, *Mamá*. You don't have to stay."

She had been back in her condo for a week now. It had been a week without Carter, a week without Ruby. Without the little girl who followed her around like a shadow, and tucked her little fingers into hers when they were out. Without the little one who totally changed her perspective on life. She missed her. She had missed Carter, too, but she missed Ruby like she missed a limb. It was just hard to function without her.

She hadn't expected to fall in love with a kid. She hadn't expected that the need to care for somebody else would satisfy her, but it did. She knew these past few months that she wanted to be a mother, but she never knew that she needed to be a mother; that it would be this important to her. But it was.

She needed her kid back, but how could she have Ruby in her life when Carter didn't trust her with Belinda? He said that he didn't want Ruby around her if she couldn't keep her safe. It was bullshit. She would die for Ruby and if he couldn't see that, if he didn't know that by now, there was no helping him.

"What about me?" Ellis said, rubbing her growing belly. "I can stay over. I won't hug you and kiss you like your mother, but I can help you do other stuff like set his clothes on fire. Or I could have his legs broken. I'm good at stuff like that. I used to be a lawyer. We wouldn't even do jail time."

She smiled at Ellis's violent streak. "All I have to do is call my father," she said. "I think he's itching to put a beat-down on him."

"Is Carter still calling?" Carmina asked.

"Yes. He only called ten times today. I think he's getting tired. He called sixty times that first day."

"Have you talked to him?" Ellis asked.

"No. There's nothing for me to say. He doesn't trust me with her. That's never going to change. We can't move on from that."

"Don't hate me for saying this, but I don't believe that. I don't believe that he doesn't trust you with his kid. He was just upset. You know the thing with his father hurt him. And then he was faced with losing Ruby again. You know that had to kill him. He was probably just in a bad place when he said those things."

"Is he going to say them every time we get into an argument? He's supposed to love me. He was way too quick to turn on me when things got a little tough."

Carmina and Ellis exchanged looks.

"What?"

"Nothing." Her mother stood up and kissed her forehead. "Call me tomorrow. Okay?"

"Yeah, me too." Ellis rose as well. "And no work tomorrow, either. You've still got that wicked bruise from the accident. I think I'm more pissed with him about that. You were hit by that truck, too, and he didn't even seem to care. You could have died that day, too."

"But I didn't. I'm okay. I'll be okay."

They both looked at her disbelievingly. She didn't blame them. She didn't believe her words herself.

"Cherri will be over tomorrow," Ellis said as she and Carmina walked out the door. "She found that southern pecan gelato you like. You two are going to commence the pig-out stage of the breakup. I wish I could be there for that, but the baby gets mad when I eat stuff I'm not supposed to."

"We'll pig out on shoes. Let's go shopping next week."

"Sounds like a plan. Good night, honey." Ellis kissed her cheek.

"Yes, my Pudge. Have a good night," Carmina said. "And call me if you need me."

"I will. Good night."

She closed the door behind them and went back to her couch, easing back down on her sofa carefully to avoid her still-aching side. She needed to snap out of this funk, this depression. She needed to get out of her house, she needed to come out of hiding, come out of this zombie state she was currently in, but she was afraid to. She was afraid to go out because she might run into him. He was the last person she wanted to see right now, even though she missed him. She was mad as hell at him but she missed him. She missed going to bed with him at night and waking up to him running his fingers through her hair. She missed how they would just sit in bed at night and talk. She missed showing up at his office with lunch sometimes. She missed his smell and the feel of his skin and the taste of his lips and she knew if she saw him again that missing would multiply tenfold. She refused to go back to him after a couple of *I'm sorrys*. She refused to be spoken to like that, to be treated without thought. She had put so much time into him, but it never seemed to work out. She could never seem to make it work with the man she loved.

There was a light knock at her door and she glanced at her clock. It was just past nine PM. Her mother and Ellis had barely been gone fifteen minutes. She thought about ignoring the knock, pretending she hadn't heard it, but she didn't. What was the point? All she was doing was sitting there with her painful thoughts.

She forced herself off her couch and answered her door. It wasn't Ellis or her mother.

It was Ruby.

And she was alone.

"Hi," she said softly. She had her backpack on her back and a pillow in her arms. "I came to live with you."

"What?" She scooped Ruby up and smashed her against her, squeezing her tighter than she should have, but she couldn't stop herself. She had missed her too much. "I'm so happy to see you, baby doll, but what are you talking about?"

"I'm very sad. I want to live here with you."

"How did you get here?"

"I walked."

"You walked here at night?" She pulled away from the child slightly. "Are you insane? Do you know what could have happened to you?"

"I'm sorry, Belinda. I was a bad girl last week in the park. I didn't listen to you and Daddy got mad and you went away." The tears streamed down her cheeks. "I miss you. I want to live with you now."

"You're not a bad girl. You're not. This is not your fault. Your father and I had a fight, but it's not your fault. I never want you to think that."

"Then why won't you come home?"

CHAPTER 26

Alone again . . . naturally.

Carter got out of the shower that night feeling no cleaner than he went in. He had stayed in for a long time, too long, letting the hot water rain over him, hoping it would make a small change in his mood. Maybe feeling cleaner wasn't what he was looking for. He wanted to feel lighter, but he felt heavier than ever before.

This was worse than the first time Belinda had left. Much worse. The last time he had Bethany there to distract him, Bethany there to focus his anger on. He had Ruby there to wonder over. He had a major life change thrown at him, but now he just had his thoughts and time to think about how stupid he was. And all the wrong things he'd said and how his actions had ruined the best thing he had ever had. There was Ruby, too, who was so mad at him that she was barely speaking to him. Ruby who cried before bed and at random times of the day.

He had taken away her mother, she told him just that

night as he put her to bed. She was so very mad at him. He went to her bedroom to check on her, thinking about how different the house felt since Belinda had gone, how quiet it was, how empty it felt. He had taken for granted sharing a meal with her. He had taken for granted being the first person to see her when she got up in the morning and the last person to see her before she went to bed at night. He missed their quiet times. He missed their lazy Sundays when they just lay in bed and watched TV all day with Ruby. He missed the smell of her on his sheets and the way she loved his kid. He missed her. He missed every part of her.

He needed her back.

He opened Ruby's bedroom door—which was odd, because she never kept it closed while she slept. He walked inside and turned on the light, but she wasn't there. Her bed was empty and unmade. There were no signs of her.

He backed out of the room and looked in the bathroom. Empty. The living room. Empty. The kitchen. Empty. She wasn't there. She wasn't there and he felt paralyzed. He reached for the phone, ready to call the police, when it rang in his shaking hands.

Belinda. The caller ID said BELINDA. "Hello?"

"I have her, Carter. She came here."

He ran out the door and sped to Belinda's house, his heart pounding out of his chest. Ruby had left him. She had walked out on him at night. All the crazy possibilities had run through his head, all the things that could have happened to her on her short three-block trip to Belinda's house, and he knew he couldn't blame anybody else for any of them. This was his fault. He made his little girl run away.

The door opened as soon as he pulled into her driveway. He jumped out of the car and ran up to Belinda. For a moment he just stared. Her skin was pale, her eyes were red. Her face was splotchy. He had done this to her. He had hurt her.

"She's on the couch."

She stepped aside, letting him in to see that his daughter was okay. She was sound asleep. Curled up in a little ball, her hand tucked beneath her chin. His heart almost exploded in that moment.

He had to touch her, to make sure she was real, and there, and okay. She didn't stir. She had to be exhausted. She looked as weary as he felt.

"She looks so peaceful. I don't want to move her."

"Can I keep her tonight, Carter? Please. It's been a week. I miss her. I need to see her."

"Yes," he said without hesitation. He looked up at her and saw the tears swimming in her eyes. "Of course you can keep her."

He dropped to his knees before her, wrapped his arms around her waist, and buried his face in her stomach.

"We have to do something about this, Carter. This is serious. She ran away. She could have been hurt. Anything could have happened to her."

"I know. It's my fault. I'm sorry, Bell. I'm sorry. I know you love her. I know you wouldn't do anything to hurt her. I was an asshole. Come home. Please come home."

She was silent for a long time. He looked up at her ready to repeat his plea, but she opened her mouth. "I can't. I'll come and get her in the afternoons. You can pick her up at my store."

"Okay," he agreed even though he didn't want to. But if he wanted her back he was just going to have to give her some space.

A month had gone by. Summer arrived and with it school came to an end. Carter had kept his promise to Belinda. He had let her take Ruby in the afternoons, and now that school was over she spent three days a week at camp and the other two with Belinda.

"I'm going to go to a sleepover this weekend." Ruby told her. They were snuggled together on the couch in her office at Size Me Up. Business had slowed down at the store a bit and she was able to spend a lot of time with Ruby during the days she had her.

She would help her hang up clothes and put out shoes and even though most of the time she wasn't very helpful, Belinda enjoyed having her in the store. Truthfully, sitting with her and doing nothing was her favorite way to spend their time together.

"A sleepover? How exciting! Are you going to gab about boys and eat popcorn and slow dance with each other?"

"What? No. We are going to play Just Dance on the Wii and listen to Justin Bieber songs."

Belinda sighed. "Oh, Bieber. How have you brainwashed this generation with your crappy pop songs. Now, the Backstreet Boys . . . They were a great boy band. I still have their first album."

Ruby frowned at her. "I don't know what you are talking about, Belinda."

"I know, baby. You're five."

"Hey, Ruby." Ellis walked into her office. "Your daddy is here."

"Oh." The disappointment was clear in her face. It mirrored Belinda's own.

"Good-bye, baby doll." She lifted herself off the couch, Ruby still in her arms, and squeezed the girl tightly. "I'll see you the day after tomorrow."

"You don't have to wait to see me. You could come home with me and Daddy tonight. We could have dinner and watch TV like we used to."

The invitation as sweet as it was also was like a hot knife in her gut. It was hard to let Ruby go over and over again. It couldn't go on like this forever. It wasn't fair to Ruby.

"I'm sorry, kid, but I can't come over for dinner."

"Maybe another time?"

She couldn't tell her that that wasn't going to happen. She didn't want to crush her hope. "Maybe another time."

"Okay. I'm sorry, Belinda."

"For what?"

"For running into the parking lot. For Daddy being mean to you and sending you away."

"You didn't do anything wrong, Ruby. You have to stop thinking that. You have to stop apologizing. You didn't do anything wrong. You didn't make him send me away."

"I'm still sorry." She kissed Belinda's cheek and wiggled out of her arms. Then she was gone, off to spend the rest of the night with her father.

"Belinda," Ellis said softly. She had just witnessed the whole thing, but without speaking. Belinda didn't think she could take it if she had. She came and wrapped her arms around her, and that's all it took for the tears to come.

"Bell . . ." She didn't know when Carter walked in, but his arms replaced Ellis's and soon she was crying into his chest. She didn't miss him any less as time went by. She missed him more. She hurt more. "I love you. I'm sorry, you know I am. Just come back."

She looked up at him, unable to speak, just shaking her head because words were too hard.

"I know I was wrong. I know I was an asshole. I know you should be mad at me." She saw anger flash in his eyes. "But you are taking this too far. I was in a bad place. You have to understand that. But you won't even let me make it up to you, because it's always easier for you to just run. I love you. I want you in my life and in my home. I want you to be the mother of my child, my children.

And I'm sorry I hurt you. All I can promise you is that I'll try to be a better man. I'll try to be a man who deserves you, but you've got to meet me halfway." He took a step away from her.

"I'm not sure I can."

"Well, I'm not sure I can do this anymore. I'm not going to let Ruby keep getting hurt by us. I'm not going to watch her heart get broken every other day just because you can't forgive me. I'm going to have to walk away this time. For good. I can't keep on seeing my kid so hurt."

"Hey, Lancaster!" he heard behind him. "Hey, dumb-ass!" Ellis caught up to him, grabbing his arm and forcing him around. "What the hell is your problem? You go and break her heart, not once but twice, and you give her an ultimatum? Are you insane?"

"It wasn't an ultimatum. I can't live like this anymore. It's bad enough that I can barely function when she's gone, but Ruby is a wreck. You'll know when your kid is born. You'll see how hard it is to watch them in pain and be powerless to fix it."

"Do you want Belinda back because you love her or because she makes life easier for your kid?"

"I'm in love with her! I moved all the way across the damn country to be with her. I married her after knowing her a month. I fell in love with her at first sight. She's my best friend, and if she doesn't take me back I can't stay here. I can't be in this town and walk through the streets and see her and not hurt. And neither can my kid."

"Okay," Ellis said. "Then you've really got to go for it with her."

"What do you mean?"

"You've got to romance her. Wine and dine her. Get her a ring so big she can barely hold up her hand. Words are cheap, my friend. This time you've got to pay in actions."

* * *

"Hey, Junior." Her father showed up at her store the next weekend while she was working in the front.

"Hey, Papa Bear." She leaned in and hugged him. He wrapped his arms around her and kissed her forehead. This display of affection was off for them. She couldn't remember the last time he had done more than ruffle her hair, but she was grateful for it. She needed this hug very much. "What are you doing here? I hope it's to tell me that you're going to take me out for double bacon cheese-burgers."

"I will if you want. I'll even spring for dessert. But I'm here to tell you that I think it's time you go back to your husband."

"What? I thought you would be on my side. I thought you wanted to break his legs."

"He hurt you, Belinda. I know that, but he's a good man. He loves you and he loves his kid and he'll make you a good husband. I think it's time you go back because you're miserable without him and because you love him. People search their whole lives to find a love like the one you have with him. I know you were hurt, but it's time to let that go. It's time you really let yourself be loved again."

"You called me Belinda."

"I did. You're a woman now. Maybe I should start call-ing you by your real name."

"Please don't." She hugged him again. "Nobody else calls me Junior."

"So are you going to think about it? Are you going to think about going back to Carter?"

"No," she said, closing her eyes.

"No?" Disappointment crossed his face.

"No, I already thought about. I'm going back. I was going to tell him tonight."

"Why wait? Go now. Your mother and I . . . The only

thing we ever really wanted for you is for you to be happy. Please be happy, Belinda. You don't know what kind of guilt there is being a parent. When you're miserable we feel like it's our fault even when we weren't the cause of it. I wish this kind of torture on you one day."

"I think I already know. I feel that way about Ruby. I never knew love could hurt so much."

"Go get them back, Junior. Go get your family."

She took her father's advice, going straight to Carter's office—but when she walked in it was empty. Like really empty. His desk was too neat. Not a coffee cup in sight, not a plan out. Not even Ruby's things were around. She stood in the empty room for a moment, her brain unable to come to terms with what she was seeing.

"He left for the airport a few minutes ago. He came to bring Ruby to tell me good-bye."

She turned around to face Steven. "Good-bye? They're leaving?"

"They left, Belinda. You might be able to catch them. I don't think the flight leaves for another hour or so."

She pushed past Steven and out of the building. He'd said he was going to leave but she didn't think he would. She didn't think he would actually go, that he would take Ruby, take her kid, take her heart with him.

She could kill him for this. She would kill him for this. As soon as she saw him again. If she saw him again.

The speed limit ceased to exist for her as she drove to Stewart Airport. She didn't know if that's where he was going. He could have gone to Albany. He could have taken a flight out of the city, but for some reason the small airport seemed like the place he would go.

It was nearly empty when she pulled up, only a few summer travelers entering through the doors, and that's when she spotted him. Ruby held his hand, rolling a tiny pink suitcase with her. Her heart did a somersault. That was her girl and he was her husband and he was walking away from her, without a last good-bye, without a final warning.

She threw her car into park and ran up the sidewalk after them. There was karma in this or irony or something otherworldly. She had done the same thing to him. She had left without warning, without a last good-bye. And because of that they had stayed apart for four years. She couldn't do it again. She couldn't miss out on more years of Ruby's life. She couldn't put her future on hold anymore.

Carter was who she wanted. It was time she stopped running from him and from love. It was time she stopped being afraid of being hurt and let him love her. He was right when he accused her of holding back before, of protecting her heart. It got her nowhere in the end. If she didn't go for this, if she didn't get them back . . .

"Carter! Ruby!"

She didn't want to think of what a lifetime without them would be like.

Ruby looked back first. Carter didn't seem to hear her. "Ruby! Ruby! Wait!"

She broke away from her father, running toward Belinda, slamming into her so hard that she lost her balance and her breath and fell to her knees with the child.

"Belinda, did you come to say good-bye to me?"

"No." She felt the tears slide down her cheeks. "I came to get you back."

"Belinda?" Carter approached them, surprise etched on his face. "What are you doing here?"

"How dare you, you bastard. How could you just take her away from me like that, without a word, without a good-bye? She's my kid. She may not have born of my body but she's my kid and I love her and you have no right to do this to me. You have no right to move her across the country without a word to me."

"Move?" He frowned at her.

"I love you, damn it. I always have. I was coming to tell you. I was coming back to you because I want my family. I want to spend the rest of my life with you and have a wedding and build a home and do all those things we missed out on the first time. I just needed some time, Carter. I was coming back. I just needed some time."

"I'm not moving away, Belinda."

"Excuse me." A police officer came up to them. "Is there a problem here?"

"Hush!" Belinda ordered him. "What did you say, Ruby?"

"I'm not moving away. I'm going to spend some time with Grandma while Daddy asks you to marry him. She's got a beach house in Florida."

"What?"

"Daddy was going to kidnap you and take you away till you agreed to marry him. He showed me the place he was going to take you. It's in the woods."

"Excuse me, folks." The cop stepped forward. "Somebody want to tell me what's going on here?"

"I'm sorry, Officer. My daughter is a little confused. This crying woman is my wife. We had an argument. I'm sending my daughter to stay with my mother in Florida for a couple of weeks while I take my wife away for a little while. I'm not moving my daughter across the country. I'm not really kidnapping anyone. In fact, I'm giving my daughter to her." He pulled a folded set of papers out of his suit jacket. "I just came from my lawyer's office. I had adoption papers drawn up."

The officer didn't move, just looked from Belinda to Ruby and then back at Carter. "Is any of that true, ma'am?"

She ignored the curious cop. "You're going to give her to me?"

"There's nothing to give. She's already yours. I'm just making it legal. I'm making us a family."

"Daddy said I could call you mommy if it's okay with you."

"It's okay! I promise." She stood up and spun Ruby around. "I would love to be your mommy." She put Ruby down and focused her attention on Carter. "As for you . . ." She jumped into his arms. "I love you, you idiot. I love you. I love you. I love you. And I want to marry you again. And I want a big wedding and I want to build a house with you and I want to build a life with you. I'm ready and I'm not going to take no for an answer."

"Okay. I surrender." He smiled as he kissed her. "You got me. You caught me four years ago and you haven't let go."